Rulesien Crossroads

Shawn Sodman

Copyright © 2015 Shawn Sodman

All rights reserved.

ISBN:069253167X
ISBN-13:978-0692531679

Dedicated to David Sheathelm.
Thank you for sparking my imagination.

CONTENTS

	Acknowledgments	i
1	The Lady of the Red Dawn	1
2	Just to be Clear	8
3	Lunch With the Captain	13
4	Visit From the Past	18
5	Letters From the Heart	27
6	The Scouting Party	32
7	Storm on the Horizon	39
8	Eye of the Storm	44
9	Lost Innocence	52
10	Years Lost and Gained	58
11	The Common Foe	64
12	Backfire	71
13	Morning 'till Dusk	80
14	Watchful Eyes	84
15	The Eighth Sister	92
16	First Blood	97
17	Revealed	103
18	Restless Night	111
19	Stirring Passions	118
20	Intermission	124
21	Cold Sunrise	127

22	Treasure Hunt	129
23	To the Mountains and Over	135
24	Frostbite	141
25	Good Morning	148
26	Over the Edge	150
27	Burning Bridges	158
28	Heart to Heart	165
29	Ithil Pandrel	169
30	Sanctuary	179
31	Off Limits	186
32	Eternal Night	190
33	Not a Little Girl	196
34	A Matter of Trust	200
35	Encampment	202
36	Downpour	210
37	Warmth of the Light	215
38	The Wait	218
39	Coldrock	221
40	Littlest of Giants	228
41	Return to Bastion	232
42	A Little Pick Me Up	240
43	Midnight Run	242
44	Reputation	246

45	Who's Following Who	252
46	Crossroads	257
47	Rain of Fire	260
48	The Mysterious One	266
	About the Author	276

ACKNOWLEDGMENTS

I would like to give special thanks to Ami and Kristen. They read all of my material as I wrote it and kept me going as they waited for more. I can honestly say the book very well may not have been completed if not for them.

I would also like to thank Leonardo Borazio for the incredible artwork that he created for the cover of this book. He was able to take my limited description and transform it into a wonderful piece of art that perfectly captured my vision of the characters. More of his work can be found on deviantart.com if you search for Runfell or dleoblack.

Chapter 1
Day 1
The Lady of the *Red Dawn*

    Cloaked in the darkness of night, the ship known as the *Red Dawn* waits just off shore of the eastern capital city of Sheathelm. Though not much larger than a small galleon, the *Red Dawn* is still one of the most feared ships in all of Runefell. The ship's deck and hull are built with finest totara wood. It is stained so deeply that under the night sky the *Red Dawn* appears as black as coal. Only in the light of day is the red blood-like tint, hidden within the wood's grain, revealed. This coloration is one of the inspirations behind the ship's name.

    Like other ships of this world the *Red Dawn* is without cannons, as they have not yet found their way to these lands. Instead, magical spells and flaming arrows are the weapons of choice on the high seas of Runefell.

    Thunder is heard off in the distance from an approaching storm as the crew of the *Red Dawn* wait patiently in the unusually calm waters for a few of her crew to return from Sheathelm. Two dozen of her forty man crew look out over the dark waters.

    High up among the ropes and the sails, near the top of the center mast, a man in the crow's nest calls down: "They're coming! I see them! Directly off the port bow." Several men scramble to the side and lower ropes in preparation to haul in the approaching row boat.

    The first mate, an old gray haired dwarf named Torgus, looks out over the water. His long hair is pulled back into a tail, and his thick beard is tied into two braids and hang down to his waist. A flash of lightning from the approaching storm allows him to see the boat. He calls out to a young man, "Allen! Go fetch the Captain, tell her they have returned."

    "Aye, Sir!" Allen answers. The clean shaven man with a boyish good look about him, almost seems out of place with the seasoned veterans of the sea. He rushes to the Captain's quarters and stops at the door preparing to knock, but hesitates. Then he takes a deep breath before knocking and says, "Captain, the crew has returned." He then quickly steps back away from the door. A few moments later the door opens and the beautiful Captain, Ariella Stormrage, steps out.

    She wears a white ruffled blouse with long sleeves. A long leather vest is kept tightly around her waist by a brown silk sash. The tops of her tall leather boots meet with her pleated trousers just below her knees. From underneath her black tricorne hat with a single white feather, her long crimson hair flows as she walks past Allen. She makes her way through the officer's quarters and out onto the deck. Compared to her crewmen, she looks diminutive as she storms across the deck through the sea of men who scramble to get out of her way.

    She walks over to the edge of the ship and looks down over the railing to see four of her men in the small boat. They have with them another man. He wears a long dark blue coat over his white shirt. His hands are bound behind his back and there is a bag over his head. With a dwarven accent, almost indistinguishable from an Irish one, she yells out, "What the hell took you so long? You should have been back an hour ago. There is a storm on its way." The crew works to raise the small boat up. The four men, along with their prisoner, board the ship. Ariella says to one of them, "Drake, you were sent to get a map. Who the hell is this?"

The tall muscular man named Drake towers over the Captain. He has a scar on the bridge of his crooked nose. Somehow this menacing looking man is humbled by the much smaller Captain. "I'm terribly sorry Capt'n. We did as you instructed and went to the Silver Gauntlet Tavern. We saw the goblin with the red hat who you said would have the map, but when we asked about it he told us that he had already given it to this man." Drake points to the well-dressed prisoner.

"So he has the map then?" Ariella asks.

Drake looks at the other three men who went to shore with him. They look down, and Drake then turns back to the Captain and says, "No, Capt'n, he—"

"—He what?" Ariella snaps as she takes a step firmly towards him.

Drake flinches as he looks down and explains, "He ran from us, Capt'n, and by the time we caught up with him he no longer had the map."

"Perhaps, my lady, I may explain what happened," the bound man says with a smooth Spanish accent. This grabs everyone's attention including the Captain's.

A flash of lighting from the approaching storm illuminates the ship as Ariella walks over to him and pulls the sack off his head revealing a handsome dark haired man with a thin mustache and goatee. If she is impressed by his appearance, she does not show it. Ariella stares up at the man and asks, "And just who might you be?"

A smile crosses the face of the handsome captive and he says calmly, "Buenas noches, Captain, I am Fernando Greythorn Hernandez, and it is an honor to be in your presence."

"Well, Mr. Greythorn," she says sounding a bit intrigued, "my name is—"

"—Ariella Stormrage," Fernando says, interrupting the Captain's sentence. "You are the daughter of renowned dwarven privateer, Red Beard Stormrage. You are the Lady of the *Red Dawn*, are you not?"

"Yes," she answers, sounding surprised, "but no one uses my first name. Understand?"

"Lo siento, Captain, I am sorry," he replies. "You know, the rumors of your beauty is a thing of legend. I see now with my own eyes that these legends are true." He grins as he continues to look Ariella in her eyes.

A hint of a smile begins to appear on her face. The crew seems unsure what to make of this when finally Torgus says, "Captain, the map?"

Then as if from out of a trance her smile disappears. She walks up to Fernando and says, "You have something that belongs to me. Where is it?"

Fernando, with an innocent smile, replies, "I am afraid, my dear, I have no idea what you are talking about. I believe that your men have simply confused me for someone else.

Crossroads

Ariella looks at the man holding Fernando and asks, "Leon, are you certain this is the man the goblin told you he gave our map to?"

The man named Leon, whose height rivals that of Drake's, answers, "Yes, Captain. There is no mistake. He either still has the map or knows where it is."

Fernando, seemingly not intimidated by his situation, calmly replies, "Well, it certainly is not on me, but by all means feel free to search for yourself, por favor."

The crew begin whisper among themselves. Ariella looks around at the men and they quickly silence themselves as they look down or away nervously. The winds now start to pick up as Ariella stares at Fernando for a moment without saying a word. She steps next to him and begins to pat him down. When she reaches his groin she does not hesitate. She firmly checks the area causing a bit of discomfort to him. Many of the men on deck watching this wince a little as well.

She completes her search and stares at Fernando frustrated. He smiles and asks, "Did you find anything interesting?" A few of the crew cannot contain their laughter.

This outburst is quickly subdued as Ariella glares at them. She looks back at Fernando and replies, "No, Mr. Greythorn, I found nothing interesting." Then with a grin she adds, "As a matter of fact, I found nothing at all."

Now the crew laughs freely at their captive. More lightning flashes as the Captain turns to leave. Fernando asks, "My lady, if the rumors of your beauty are true, as they clearly are, may I ask if another rumor of you is true?"

A silence falls once again over the crew. Made curious by the question, Ariella slowly turns and walks back. "And what rumor might that be?" she asks.

"Well, it's kind of personal," he answers. "Come closer and I'll ask you."

She hesitantly moves closer as he leans down and whispers something in her ear. A look of pure hatred overtakes her as she takes a step back before backhanding him across the face. Storming off she yells out, "Drake, Leon! Take him below and make sure he cannot escape!" She then turns back to her men then adds, "Do NOT harm him in any way! I want the pleasure of breaking him personally. I'll send for him when I am ready. Everyone else prepare to weigh anchor!" The crew springs into action as they scramble to the three masts and prepare to get the ship underway. Ariella walks up the stairs to the quarterdeck. She then says to her first mate, "Torgus, get us out of here now. That storm will be here soon."

"Aye, Captain," Torgus responds as the sound of thunder can now be felt reverberating along the ships planks.

Ariella walks back down the stairs and returns to her quarters. She enters her room slamming the door behind her. Leaning back against the door she takes a deep breath to calm herself. She stares ahead and quietly says to herself, "I don't know who you are, Fernando Greythorn, but I promise I am going to find out what you have done with my father's map."

*****

"When you said you were going to tell them a story," Danielle says to her cousin, "I didn't think you were going to tell them about Ariella Stormrage."

High up in a modern luxury apartment, a small group of people are gathered in the dark with only the light of a few candles to see by. A storm rages outside the large windows and there is no power.

"I'm sorry," Kyle replies. The man with medium curly blonde hair then adds, "Ariella Stormrage is important to the story, and I figured they were old enough."

"Come on, Aunt Danielle, we aren't little kids anymore," pleads Haley who is not quite a teenager.

"I know," Danielle replies. Then looking down she adds, "I just don't know if your parents would have approved."

Josh, who is only a little older than his sister Haley, replies, "It's just another story like the ones you told us when we were younger."

"It's alright guys," Kyle says, "Danielle is your legal guardian now, and if she says that you are too young then perhaps I should tell you a different story."

Laura, the older sister of Josh and Haley, has been quietly lying on the couch reading texts. She looks up from her phone and asks "Wait, is it really that bad? What kind of story is this?"

Kyle smiles and answers, "Just a tale of adventure, treasure, battles, and some romance as well. Have you been listening so far?"

Laura, in her later teens, smiles and replies, "Yes, Uncle Kyle, I have been. I like the Captain already."

Danielle rolls her eyes and says, "You would like her."

"No offense, Aunt Danielle," Laura replies, "but the stories I remember from Runefell were from when I was ten years old. They were good and all, but they were more for kids."

Danielle laughs and replies, "Fine, Kyle can tell what ever story he wants, but that could be a very long story. Are you sure you have time?"

"Of course," Kyle replies looking out the window. "Look outside, where else am I going to go?"

"Oh, that reminds me," Danielle says, "I am sure you didn't come here just to tell stories while the power is out did you?"

"No," Kyle says with a laugh. "There's something I need to talk with you about, but it can wait until later." Then he looks at the kids and asks, "For now though, would you like to hear more about the *Red Dawn*?"

"I do," Laura answers as she puts down her phone. "I want to know what Ariella does to get her map back."

"Keep it clean," Danielle warns, "and be aware that some of your listeners are still a bit young."

Kyle grins and says, "Okay, I'll make sure that I'll keep it PG 13. Now then where were we?" Kyle continues to tell the story in an appropriate way for the age of his audience while the original story went a little more like this...

*****

Crossroads

The *Red Dawn* begins to sail away to avoid the oncoming storm while below deck, Fernando is thrown into a cell by Drake and Leon. It's a small room with two cage cells made up of iron bars. There is a desk and two chairs. Along the walls of the room there are iron shackles. John and Jacob are the two men left to guard him. The two men, in their forties, have brown beards with patches of gray.

After Drake and Leon leave the room the man named John asks Fernando, "Hey you, can I ask you something?"

Fernando sits down on a bench in his cell and asks, "Of course, what is it?"

John looks to make sure the door is closed and asks, "What did you say to the Captain right before she hit you?"

Fernando lightly laughs to himself and replies, "If I tell you, can you keep it a secret?"

"Yeah, sure I can," he answers. "Tell me."

"John," Jacob says interrupting the conversation, "Don't talk to him. The Capt'n wouldn't like it."

"I can't help it," John replies. "I just want to know what set her off like that."

"It was nothing really," Fernando says to them.

"It really pissed her off, whatever it was," John says. "I haven't seen her that mad in a long time."

"Really?" Fernando asks. "John, is it? What do you think she will do with me?"

Jacob interjects, "You will be lucky to be alive if you don't give her what she is looking for." "I see," Fernando says, sounding a bit concerned. "And your name, sir?"

"The name's Jacob," he answers.

"Well, Jacob," Fernando says, "what will your Captain do if I do not have what she is looking for?"

"Then you better know where it is. You see, my friend," Jacob explains. "The Captain, she is fair and treats us all well when we do as we are told, but," Jacob pauses for a bit, "she does not tolerate disobedience. If she believes you have something of hers, you can bet your life she will do everything in her power to get you to turn it over, and if you don't have it, you better be able to get it or I fear for your safety, Mr. Greythorn."

"So, I just have to know. What did you say to her?" John asks again.

Jacob also looks at Fernando and says, "Have to admit, I am a bit curious myself."

Fernando looks around to make sure they are alone, and says with a smile, "Well, my friends, you know the Captain first hand. I have only heard of her though stories and rumors. So I asked her if the rumors were true that her sexual appetite was as great as her beauty."

"You didn't!" John says astonished.

Jacob adds, "You are lucky she wants that map so bad or you might be dead already."

They laugh and Fernando asks them, "So, are the rumors true?"

Their laughter is cut off with the question, and Jacob says, "What kind of question is that? How would I know?"

"Well, I can't say for sure," John says, "but she does fancy the company of men when we are at port," John smiles and adds, "and sometimes women."

"Don't tell him that!" Jacob yells at John. "Why would you say that?"

"Well, it's true," John whines.

"Yeah, but you don't need to tell him that," Jacob says.

"So does she mix business with pleasure here on the ship?" Fernando asks.

"No! Never!" Jacob snaps.

"Not with the crew," John adds. "Never."

"Well, except maybe..." Jacob says before pausing and looking at John.

"Right," John says. "Except for him."

"Who is 'him'?" Fernando asks trying to get as much information from these two as he can.

"None of your business," John answers. "We have said too much already."

"Come now," Fernando says with a smile to assure them. "Surely, what we discuss will remain between us. I am only interested to know who my competition is."

"Well, I don't know about competition," Jacob says to him. "It's not like she is in a relationship with him or anything."

"So she is just using this man for pleasure then," Fernando concludes.

"No," John replies. "I didn't say that!"

"I am sorry," Fernando replies. "I did not mean to put words in your mouth. Please explain what you meant so I do not have to ask the Captain myself."

John sighs then walks over to the door and opens it to check to see if anyone is outside. He closes the door and walks back over to the iron bars of the cell. "Alright, I'll tell you," he says quietly, "but you did not hear this from me. You see, some believe that something is going on with her and her cabin boy, Allen."

"The cabin boy?" Fernando asks.

"I guess he is a bit old to really be a cabin boy—he's twenty I think—but most everyone on board calls him that," John explains. "Every once in a while she will call him into her quarters. Sometimes she says it's because he missed a spot while swabbing the deck. Other times she don't say why. Either way she calls him in to her quarters and punishes him. The thing is though, Allen listens well. I ain't ever heard him talk back to the Captain or ever treat her with any disrespect."

"But she still punishes him?" Fernando asks.

"Yes," John answers.

"Does she treat others the same way?" Fernando asks.

"Not like that, no," Jacob answers. He looks down and takes a deep breath before continuing. "First you have to understand something. We are all loyal to the Captain, Mr. Greythorn. As I said before, she is fair to us. Almost everyone on this ship served her father. We respect her, but if we are ever out of line, she makes sure to set a good example to the rest." Jacob lifts his shirt reveling his chest.

Fernando looks at Jacob's chest and sees a scar in the perfect shape of a small hand. "Fernando asks, "The Captain did this to you?"

"Yes," Jacob explains, "I once got really drunk on shore and lost my temper with a bar maid, and while I am not proud of it, I slapped her. Well, anyways, the Captain saw it all, and right there on the spot she made an example out of me."

"How did she leave such a mark?" Fernando asks.

"Magic," Jacob says as he puts his shirt back down. "She made her hand as hot as an ember."

"So the rumors of her magic are also true," Fernando says.

"Aye, that they are," Jacob says. "As for young Allen, I wouldn't worry too much about him. Like I was saying, there are a few of us who thinks that she gives him more than just punishment."

"I am not so sure," John interrupts. "If you listen close you can hear her using the cat-o-nine on him."

"'Tis true," Jacob says. "But that only lasts about five minutes or so, and he is in there for much longer than that."

"Personally," John says, "I think he just passes out from the pain."

"Either way," Jacob continues, "none of us knows for sure. You can ask him but he doesn't say much. I have seen him leave her quarters though with more than just welts on his back. Sometimes you can see him smiling."

"I see," Fernando says. "Thank you, gentlemen, this conversation has been most enlightening."

Just then Drake and Leon enter the room. Unlike the bald head of Drake, Leon has long brown hair to his shoulders with some gray. The two of them walking side by side is enough to intimidate almost anyone. They approach the cage.

Jacob says to Fernando, "I think you are being summoned."

They open the cage and Leon says to Fernando, "You are to come with us."

"And if I decline?" Fernando asks.

Leon backhands Fernando knocking him down. Drake steps in between them and says, "Remember what the Capt'n said. No one is to hurt him except her."

Leon gives a grunt and grabs Fernando off the ground. Blood runs down Fernando's lip as they drag him up the stairs and take him to the Captain.

"Do you think he will be alright?" John asks Jacob

"Only if he has the map," Jacob answers. "And only if he is smart enough to give it up."

Chapter 2
Just to be Clear

    Fernando is brought up onto of the quarterdeck of the ship by Ariella's two enforcers. From there they enter what was once designated as the navigation room. It now doubles as a personal dining space for Ariella and her officers, and is referred to as the Captain's lounge. The men bring him in as he sees a small round table in the center of the room. Places to eat have been set for two. The room is well lit with small enchanted stones. Each shining with the brightness of a small torch. On the port side is a portrait of a dwarf with a thick red bead. Next to the portrait is a desk with a map laid out and a compass. Above the desk is shelving stuffed with scrolls and parchments—presumably maps. Along the back of the room are beautiful and intricate stained glass windows with a doorway in the middle. To the starboard side is a doorway that leads to a small private galley.

    "So, Mr...Greythorn is it?" Ariella says as she approaches them.

    "Yes, ma'am, but you can call me Fernando," he replies with a confident smile.

    She gets closer and stops when she sees the blood coming from Fernando's lip. She turns her attention to her men. "Which one of you is responsible for this?" she asks as she grabs Fernando's face and turns his head to them.

    Leon stands there cold faced as if at attention and explains, "I am sorry, Captain, but he would not come willingly."

    "I see," she says calmly. She removes her left glove and says, "Are you saying the two of you couldn't handle him without hitting him? After all, you both seem to be fine to me. He must not have been too much trouble."

    "My lady, I am fine," Fernando says as he takes a couple steps away from them. "I assure you, your boys did not harm me. I did not even notice that I was bleeding."

    Leon, infuriated by the slight, takes a step towards Fernando, but the Captain gets in his way. She holds her left hand in front of his face as sparks of electricity crackle between her fingers. Leon stops immediately. "Please, Captain," he says sounding a bit nervous. "I am sorry, but he mocks me."

    With her right hand she slaps him with the glove and says. "Control yourself or so help me the next time I will not hit you with my glove."

    Leon stands back at attention and says, "Yes, Captain, I understand."

    "Good," she says as she dissipates the energy in her hand. "Now leave us."

    "Ma'am?" Drake asks sounding confused. "Are you sure?"

    "Yes," she says confidently, "I can handle myself, but just so we are all clear here," she grabs Fernando's chin and continues, "If Mr. Greythorn here tries to harm me or escape, then Leon, you may do with him as you wish." Leon smiles as she turns to Fernando and asks, "Are we clear?"

    "Crystal," Fernando answers.

    She turns to the two hulking men and motions them to leave and as they do, Leon stares at Fernando, who calmly smiles back at him.

The door closes behind them as Ariella says, "Sit, Mr. Greythorn, let us discuss business."

"Of course, my lady," he says taking a seat. "What business shall we be discussing?"

"Do not play coy with me, Mr. Greythorn," she says as she walks to the other end of the table. "You have something that belongs to me."

"Oh, and what would that be?" Fernando says sounding not at all convincing.

"Mr. Greythorn, do not mistake my kindness for weakness," she warns. "I will get what I want. One way or another. Now, how I obtain it is up to you. We will try to do this the easy way first. If that does not work then," Ariella pauses and takes a drink from a mug, "well, we can come back to that later. I hope you like seafood, Mr. Greythorn." Ariella rings a small bell.

A cute young woman wearing a black corset with white lace trim comes out of the small galley. Her white ruffled skirt covers her legs down to her knees. She is carrying a silver platter. She sets it down on the table before removing the lid. There are two large fillets of fish on the platter and she proceeds to serve them. She glances at Fernando who smiles at her. She brushes back her long black hair and smiles before shyly turning away. Then to Ariella she asks meekly, "Will that be all, my lady?"

"Marie," Ariella says introducing the two of them, "I would like you to meet Mr. Fernando Greythorn. Mr. Greythorn, this is my personal assistant, Marie."

Fernando stands and walks up to Marie. She curtsies and says nervously, "A pleasure, sir."

"The pleasure is all mine," Fernando says as he takes her hand and kisses it. She smiles and looks nervously at Ariella.

"Thank you, Marie," Ariella says. "That will be all."

"Yes, ma'am," Marie replies. Fernando watches her as she exits to the galley and closes the door behind her.

Ariella stands up and says, "Mr. Greythorn, it is not polite to undress the help with your eyes in front of your host."

"I assure you, Ariella," Fernando says, taking her hand and kissing it, "that you are the only one my eyes are undressing."

"My, you are a silver tongued one, aren't you?" Ariella says with a smile, then she slaps Fernando across the face. "Rule number one, Mr. Greythorn, and I already warned you once, nobody calls me by my first name. You will address me as ma'am, or Captain, do you understand?"

Fernando nods and answers, "Yes, ma'am."

Ariella continues, "Good. Rule number two, when you are with me, your eyes will remain on me. Marie is a pretty young thing, but Mr. Greythorn, she is a bit young for you."

"Forgive me," Fernando replies. "I meant no disrespect."

"That is good," Ariella says as she walks behind him and runs her hand across his chest. "Because if you ever disrespect me...I will make you regret it."

Smiling, Fernando responds, "Of that I am sure."

She walks back around in front of him and as she slowly runs her fingers across his chest she says, "Don't think for a moment that I am just some simple bar wench that you can have your way with before leaving the next morning. I require a bit more attention and I demand respect. If you treat me well I will return the favor."

Fernando smiles as he places his hands on her hips and pulls her close. "My lady, I will treat you like a queen, and you shall want for nothing," he says softly as he leans in for a kiss.

Just before their lips meet however, Ariella turns and walks away. While he is left standing there, she sits back down in her chair. Fernando grins as he ponders what has just happened. He slowly walks back to his chair and sits.

"No more games, Mr. Greythorn," she says as she begins to cut her food. "Where is my map? I know you have it somewhere. So what did you do with it?"

"Very well," Fernando says as he cuts the fish on his plate. "What if I told you that I destroyed the map?" he asks as he takes a bite of his food.

"And why in the world would you so something as stupid as that?" Ariella says angrily.

"Well, allow me tell you what happened in Sheathelm," Fernando explains. "I had heard rumors of a map that belonged to Red Beard would be exchanged at the Silver Gauntlet. I watched for weeks for someone who I thought may have it. Finally, a goblin appeared who I figured might be the one with the map, so I simply pretended to be a member of your crew. I gave him a small sack of coins and bought myself a map. Then as I was leaving, your men arrived. They gave chase to me, but I lost them without much problem. I then studied the map and memorized the location of the treasure and then I burned it. I went down to the docks to find a ship who was willing to take me when your men found me and took me captive."

"I see," Ariella says as she stands up and wipes her face with a napkin. "So now I have no map, but something even better." She walks over to Fernando as he finishes eating. "I have a guide. You, Mr. Greythorn, are going to lead me to my father's treasure."

"And if I refuse?" he asks with a grin.

Ariella walks behind him and as he sits in his chair she begins to rub his shoulders. She asks, "Tell me, have you ever heard a man cry out in such pain and agony that he begs to die? Or on the other hand, cry out a woman's name while he is in pure ecstasy? Mr. Greythorn, I assure you that I can make you cry out either way. Now, how you will cry shall be entirely up to you."

"Well then," Fernando says, "since you put it that way. I am certainly up for some pleasure."

"I thought you might be," Ariella says. "If you take me to my father's treasure I will give you all kinds of pleasure."

"That certainly sounds more appealing than the alternative," Fernando says. "Captain, you may have your men fooled but I can see the kind of woman you really are. I can tell by the look in your eyes you have no desire to hurt me."

"Of course I don't *want* to harm you," she says as she removes her glove. "But as I have said before, do not mistake my kindness for weakness." Instead of electricity arcing through her fingers, this time her hand glows with a gray mystical energy. Fernando is unaware of what is happening behind him. She places her hand on Fernando's shoulder and her touch makes him fall asleep.

When he awakes moments later his ankles are bound together and his wrists are tied behind his back. When he realizes his situation he says to her, "My lady, if you wanted to have your way with me, all you needed to do was ask."

Ariella laughs and says, "I know that, my darling, however I think I need to make it clear to you that no matter how charming you are, I will do whatever is necessary to make sure that I have your cooperation."

"I see," Fernando says calmly, trying not to show his fear. "So you plan to burn me with your magic? Perhaps leave a scar on me like Jacob?"

"So," she replies, "you are getting to know my men. What else did they tell you?"

"They only warned me that if I did not cooperate that I may suffer," he answers.

"Make no mistake that I can and will leave a mark if I have no other choice, but I have a way to cause pain without actually harming you. Unless of course you have a weak heart. In that case it probably wouldn't have worked out between us anyway." She then stands behind him and says, "You will have to forgive me, Mr. Greythorn, but I have a reputation to uphold here." With that, she casts another spell, and her hand takes on a dark and ominous aura. She then places her hand on Fernando's chest.

Fernando feels pain like he has never felt before. He collapses to the floor and lets out a loud agonizing yell that can be heard throughout the entire ship.

Below deck, Jacob looks at John and says, "That poor Mr. Greythorn."

Elsewhere, the big enforcer Leon sits sharpening his knife. He smiles when he hears Fernando's suffering.

In his hammock below deck, lies Allen. He lies awake staring at the overhead, and when he and the others hear Fernando's pain, one of the others jokingly says, "Hey, Allen, maybe the Captain will stay off your back for a while." The others laugh as Allen gives him half a smile but as he looks back at the overhead above him it quickly fades.

Back in the Captain's lounge Fernando is on the floor writhing in pain. Marie opens the door just enough to peer into the room. When Ariella sees the concerned look on her face she ends the spell. "It's all right, Marie," she says to her. "He will be fine."

Fernando's cries of pain stop as the spell ends. While catching his breath, Fernando is left on the floor. Ariella says to Marie reassuringly, "See, the spell is only for pain. He is not harmed in any way." She then kneels down and says to Fernando, "Mr. Greythorn, consider that your only warning. You will lead me to my father's treasure, then I will make sure that the only screams from you will be that of pleasure."

"Yes, Captain," Fernando says as he regains his composer. He gets to his knees and continues, "You do not need to demonstrate your resolve to me any further. I will do as you ask."

"I am glad we have an understanding," she says with a sly smile. "Now let me untie you." Ariella begins to untie the thick rope that binds Fernando. When she is done she says to him, "It is late, Mr. Greythorn. We shall begin our search in the morning. For now, though as much as I want to take you to my bed, I need to make sure you don't try to sneak away in the middle of the night." She then walks to the door and opens it. Standing outside the door is Drake. "Take Mr. Greythorn to back to his cell," she orders him.

"Yes, Capt'n," Drake answers as he waits for Fernando.

Fernando walks slowly to the door and takes Ariella's hand. He slowly raises it to his lips and kisses it. He then says, "Until the morning then, my lady."

She closes the door behind him as he leaves. She then lets out a deep sigh.

"He seems nice, ma'am," Marie says to her.

"Yes, he does," Ariella says. "A bit too nice. I'll have to keep my eye on him. Come, Marie, let's go to bed."

Chapter 3
Day 2
Lunch with the Captain

The next morning as the sun rises over the bow of the *Red Dawn*, Fernando is brought up to the quarterdeck to where the navigator and the Captain are waiting.

"Good morning, Mr. Greythorn," Ariella greets Fernando.

"Buenos Dias, Captain, and a fine morning it is," Fernando says returning her pleasantries. "The way the morning's new light shines in your eyes. They shimmer like a thousand emeralds and sapphires."

She smiles a bit then says, "Save your flattery, Mr. Greythorn. I need you to tell my navigator, Chris, the proper heading."

"My pleasure," Fernando says. Behind the ship's wheel, against the exterior wall of the captain's lounge, is a table. Chris unrolls a map onto the table as he and Fernando begin to study it.

The ship is quiet, save for the few who work the early morning hours. Many still sleep down below. Allen is up however, and is polishing the brass. As he does so, he watches Fernando closely. He is so distracted by him that he neglects to watch where he is going and bumps into the captain.

"Sorry," Allen mutters as he looks up. Realizing who he had just collided with he says more urgently, "I-I mean...sorry, Captain!" looking down he continues to plead, "Please, forgive me."

"It's all right Allen. I am fine," she says to him. "Don't forget to wipe down Mr. Torgus's orbs." She says as she points to a fist sized blue orb mounted in the mast. Fernando looks up to see what it is she is referring to.

"Of course, Captain," Allen replies. He glances at Fernando for a moment before returning to his work.

Chris orders the helmsman to bring the ship around. Fernando says to Ariella, "Well, it appears that my work here is done. It will take us full day to reach our current destination."

Ariella looks at the map and asks, "Where exactly might that be?"

Fernando points to the map and answers, "Right there."

"And that is where we will find my father's treasure?" Ariella asks.

"There? No, that is just going to bring us to the next part of the journey," Fernando explains, "We are about three days from our final destination."

"I see, and why not just show us on the map where that final destination is?" Ariella asks.

"My lady," he explains with a smile, "if I simply did that you would have no further use of me, and as long as I am the only one who knows where we are going, that assures me a bit of safety."

Ariella grins and says, "Very well, Mr. Greythorn, we will do things your way for now."

"Thank you, Captain," Fernando says. "Now if that is all, Captain, I would like to look around the ship, if I may? With your permission, of course."

She sighs and calls out, "Allen! Would you please show Mr. Greythorn around the *Red Dawn*?"

"Me, Captain?" Allen questions as he looks up from his work. "Wouldn't Drake or Leon be—"

"—Are you questioning my orders, Mr. Allen?" she snaps.

The few crew that are around stop what they are doing and look at Allen as he answers, "No, ma'am, Captain."

"Then show Mr. Greythorn around the ship," she repeats in a more serious tone. "When you have completed the tour you will bring him to me. Do you understand?"

"Yes, Captain," he answers looking down. "Follow me, Mr. Greythorn," he says with a bit of disdain as he walks past them and down the stairs.

While Allen leads Fernando to the bow of the ship, Ariella watches them, a bit puzzled. She turns to Chris and says, "Have you noticed Mr. Allen behaving a bit strange lately?"

"He does seem a little distracted, Captain," Chris answers.

"Thank you, Chris," she says as she heads to the lounge.

At the bow of the ship, Allen is showing Fernando around when Fernando spots an orb just like the one Allen was cleaning earlier. Fernando says, "Allen, I have a question."

"Yes," Allen says with a heavy sigh.

"What are those orbs for?"

"I am not really sure if it is my place to tell you, Mr. Greythorn."

"I understand," Fernando says, as they continue walking. "So how long have you been a member of the ship's crew?" he asks as they start to head below deck.

"About a full season," he answers. "Myself and a few others were the first recruits after the attempted mutiny that killed the Captain's father."

"Ah, yes, Red Beard," Fernando says. "Word of the mutiny spread rather quickly, I must say. They also say it was the shortest mutiny ever."

"Well, I wasn't there of course," Allen continues, "but my understanding is that the Captain's, or I should say, *former* Captain's best friend, Corthag, betrayed him after almost forty years of serving together."

"So what happened?" Fernando asks.

Allen stops and says, "Look, I don't know much more about it. Perhaps you should ask someone else these questions."

"You don't like me much do you?"

"Mr. Greythorn, my opinion of you doesn't matter. The only opinion that matters on this ship is the Captain's."

Fernando smiles at Allen and asks, "You have feelings for her don't you?"

"I don't know what you are talking about," Allen says calmly.

"Oh, I think you do," Fernando replies, "She is a beautiful woman. What man would not admire her?"

"Whether or not I find the Captain attractive is not relevant," Allen says. "The only thing you need to know about me is this: Ariella Stormrage is my Captain, and I will do anything for her, Mr. Greythorn, including giving my life."

Back in the Captain's lounge Ariella and Marie are talking.

"Are you worried that Fernando will try to leave?" Marie asks.

"Well, if he does, Torgus can find him," Ariella answers. "Besides, we are a half days travel from the nearest shore, and I doubt he has any magical spells up his sleeve otherwise he would have been gone by now."

"I suppose you are right," Marie replies. "So where is he now?"

"Allen is giving him a tour around the *Red Dawn*," Ariella says. "They will be joining us for lunch."

"He and Allen are coming here for lunch?" Marie asks. She turns to the mirror and begins to fix her hair.

Ariella laughs and says, "Yes, they are. Don't worry about your hair, you look beautiful."

"Really?" Marie asks, as if she does not believe her.

"Yes, darling you look wonderful," Ariella says. "Marie, I want you to be careful. I don't quite trust Fernando Greythorn and I don't want you to get hurt by him. Do you understand?"

"Yes, ma'am," Marie replies distractedly, still looking in the mirror. "We don't trust Fernando. Don't worry, Captain, it isn't Mr. Greythorn that I—" Marie stops and looks nervously at Ariella. "Never mind," she adds.

The realization of what Marie has just said sinks into Ariella, and a smile appears across her face and she says, "Marie? Are you saying that Allen...?"

"I am sorry, ma'am," Marie says sounding concerned. "Please don't be mad. Nothing has ever happened between us," Marie explains desperately.

"Marie," Ariella says soothingly, "I am not mad at all. I think it is wonderful, Allen is a sweet young man. I think the two of you would be good for each other."

"Thank you," Marie replies sounding a bit confused, "but I thought that you and he—"

"Shh," she says putting her finger over Marie's lips. "What I do with Allen is," Ariella searches for the right words, "well, it's complicated. It's more about power and pleasure than anything else. I will end all that if you have feelings for him, and you will have my support."

"Oh, thank you Captain," Marie replies with a sad smile, "but I don't think Allen even notices me."

"Nonsense," she says as she picks up a brush and begins to brush Marie's hair. "Allen would have to be blind not to notice you. Now all you need to do is show him how you feel."

"How do I do that?"

Just then there is a knock at the door. Ariella walks to the door and says, "Just relax, my dear, and watch me." She opens the door and Allen and Fernando are standing there. "Come in, gentlemen. You are just in time."

Fernando and Allen enter the cabin and Marie is standing at the table. Fernando says, "Ah, Marie, you look lovely today. It's a pleasure to see you again."

Marie smiles and says, "Thank you." Then she quickly turns to Allen and says, "Hello, Allen."

Allen, shyly looking down, replies, "Good afternoon, Miss Marie."

"Well," Ariella says, "Fernando, please have a seat over here. Allen, if you would please join us for lunch, we have a place for you over there next to Marie."

"Yes, Captain, thank you," Allen replies still looking down. He walks over and sits next to Marie.

As they sit down for lunch Ariella asks, "So, Mr. Greythorn, did you have any questions about the ship?"

"Well, I did have a question about those orbs I see around," Fernando answers. "I asked Allen but he didn't think he should tell me."

"Torgus's orbs, yes," Ariella replies. "You see, there are a few members of this crew who have been around as long as my father. Torgus is one of them. His quarters are down below. He is a powerful wizard and uses the orbs to watch over the ship. He keeps to himself mostly. So if you are thinking of trying anything just remember Torgus could be watching you."

"I see," Fernando says.

The four of them begin to eat in silence. Finally Ariella says, "Marie, you look beautiful with those earrings on. Wouldn't you agree, Allen?"

Allen, caught off guard, looks up and says, "I am sorry, Captain, what was that?"

"I was saying how beautiful Marie looked today," Ariella says to him more directly. "Wouldn't you agree, Allen?"

"Yes, Captain," Allen says as he glances at Marie. "She looks nice."

Fernando cringes at the shyness of Allen's answer.

Ariella sighs and says, "Don't tell *me*, Allen. Tell *her*."

"Oh," Allen says, realizing his mistake, "Of course, I am sorry." He does his best to look at Marie and says, "Marie, you look very beautiful today. N-not that you don't look beautiful every day," he adds nervously, "*because you do.*" Allen's face begins to turn red. "I-I mean, I just mean to say that..." then turning to Ariella he says, "I am sorry, Captain, may I please be excused?"

Ariella answers, "No, Allen, you may not." She looks at Fernando as they smile at each other with amusement at Allen's attempt to complement Marie.

Marie asks Allen, "Thank you, Allen, do you really mean it?"

Allen begins to cough. "Of course I do." He reaches for his glass of water, but accidentally knocks it over spilling it onto Marie's plate and lap.

Marie stands up, and Allen quickly says, "I am sorry, Marie, I didn't mean to—"

"It's alright, Allen, I know," Marie quickly replies.

"I am sorry, I have to go now," Allen says as he starts to head for the door.

Ariella says, "Allen, you are NOT excused. Now sit down, and that's an order!"

"I am sorry, Captain," Allen snaps. "Discipline me if you must, but I have humiliated myself enough for one afternoon." Allen turns and walks out.

Ariella is stunned by Allen's display. She stands up and as she begins to go after him Fernando says, "I'll go and talk with him, Captain."

"Thank you," Ariella replies. Fernando leaves as Ariella walks over to Marie who looks upset. She puts her arm around her and says, "Don't worry Marie, everything will be alright."

Meanwhile on deck Allen is at the railing overlooking the horizon. Fernando walks up and stands next to him. After a few moments Fernando finally says. "It could have been worse. It could have been hot tea."

Allen cannot help but to laugh and says, "Thanks."

"Don't mention it," Fernando says. "It was an accident and Marie knows that. Besides, I think she likes you."

"What makes you think that?" Allen asks.

"If there is one thing I know, Allen, it is women," Fernando says. "At least as much as any man can know about them. There are some things I don't think we will ever understand about them though." They look at each other and laugh a bit.

"I just don't understand," Allen says. "I have always liked Marie, but I never thought she noticed me. I also never thought the Captain would approve."

"Oh, and why is that?" Fernando asks.

"Never mind, it's nothing," Allen answers.

"Well, according to some of the crew," Fernando says, "they think you and the Captain are involved somehow. That you and her...you know."

"*What?*" Allen asks sounding shocked. "No. No, it's not like that really. Well kind of but," Allen sighs. "Alright, fine. I'll tell you, but you have to promise not to tell anyone. Promise?"

"Of course," Fernando replies, "it is just between you and me."

Allen looks around to make sure that no one is nearby. Then he turns to Fernando and says quietly, "Alright, the Captain punishes me when I mess up. Everyone knows that, but when she is done," he pauses and takes a deep breath. He looks around again and continues, "When she is done with that, she makes me do things for her."

"What kind of things?" Fernando asks.

"Sometimes it's rubbing her feet," Allen explains. "Other times I have to rub her back with oils. Then sometimes she has me..." he stops, unable to finish.

"I understand," Fernando says. "Say no more."

"So, I don't know what to think," Allen says.

Fernando ponders for a moment. He leans back against the railing and says, "You live to please the Captain. So now maybe the Captain just wants you to be happy, and maybe she feels Marie can do that."

"I don't know," Allen says. "Maybe."

Just then Ariella calls down to them. "Gentlemen, lunch is getting cold."

"Yes, ma'am," Fernando answers, "we will be right up." Then he asks Allen, "Are you ready?"

"I guess so," Allen answers. Then as they start to go up the stairs he adds, "And Fernando, thank you."

Fernando smiles and pats him on the shoulder as they rejoin Ariella and Marie to finish lunch.

Chapter 4
Visit From the Past

The sun hangs high in the sky just past mid-day as the *Red Dawn* continues toward its destination. The lookout in the crow's nest calls down, "Captain! I think we are being watched!" He points up to the sky where high above a giant eagle is circling. He then adds, "I don't think it's a regular eagle, Captain. Take a look."

Ariella takes out her looking glass and peers through it. She spies the very large white headed eagle. Other than its head and tail the rest of its feathers are dark brown. In its claw it carries a white banner with a blue shield on it. She says quietly to herself, "No, it can't be."

"What do you make of it, Captain?" Torgus asks.

She hands the looking glass to Torgus and asks, "Torgus, how many great eagles do you think would carry the banner of Sheathelm?"

He looks up at the sky at the eagle and answers, "I can only think of one."

"That's what I thought," Ariella replies. Then calling out to the crew she says, "Run up the white flag and stand down!"

"Captain? The white flag?" John questions.

"You heard me," she says giving him a glare, "raise it now, unless you want to swim back to land."

"Yes, ma'am," he replies as he quickly digs around in a chest. Soon he pulls out a white flag, and shakes the dust off it. He begins to lower their flag that has the colors of a morning sunrise.

"What is it, Captain?" Fernando asks looking up in the sky.

"Unless I am mistaken, Mr. Greythorn," Ariella explains, "we are about to have a very distinguished guest."

The crew looks up in the sky while the white flag is raised and the great eagle starts to descend. It gets closer and closer and many who have not seen a great eagle are amazed at its size. It finally lands on deck, and the crew watches it nervously. Other than its enormous size it appears to be a normal white capped eagle. When Ariella looks closer she can see one other unusual feature. The eyes of this eagle are blue.

Before their very eyes the man sized eagle begins to transform. Its feathers disappear and its wings become arms. It becomes taller as it takes on a humanoid shape. Soon the transformation is complete, and an elf now stands on their deck. His fine dark armor with gold trim tells the men that he is not a mere messenger. His red cloak flows in the wind along with his long blonde hair. He looks around at the almost two dozen men around him. Unsure if he is welcome, his hands are ready to draw the two swords at his sides.

Ariella looks upon the elven visitor, and thoughts of her past begin to fill her head. This is not the first time she has met this man. When his eyes, as blue as the sky, meets hers he says, "Ariella? Is that you?"

As if a dam holding back her past had burst, the memories of her first encounter with this elf come flooding back.

Crossroads

She is fifteen years old, and is walking along the deck of the *Red Dawn* when she comes across a young blonde elf sitting and watching the sun set. She sits down next to him and says, "Hello. What is your name?"

He smiles and replies, "My name is Chance Na'Moon. What is yours?"

"My name is Ariella," She answers.

"That is a beautiful name," Chance replies. "It is a pleasure to meet you."

The young Ariella smiles brightly at him.

Now Ariella's memories flash forward to another moment in time. She is a few years older now and she sits on the deck at night with Chance. He is showing her how to shape fire. She is attempting to concentrate as he instructs her.

"Now picture the shape of a flower in your head," Chance says as he holds a small ball of fire in the palm of his hand.

Ariella stares at the fire and it begins to move and take the form of a flower. Then as Ariella starts to loose concentration the shape of the flower is lost and the fire reverts back to a ball of flame.

"I can't do it," Ariella says sounding frustrated.

"Yes, you can," Chances says reassuringly, "I believe in you. Just think of the flower in your mind. Like this." As Chance concentrates the fire takes the shape of an intricate rose.

"That's so beautiful," the young Ariella says in amazement.

"I know something even more beautiful," Chance says. He looks back at the fire and as he moves his fingers around, the flames seem to dance as they take shape of Ariella's face and hair.

"Oh, Chance," she says blushing.

Chance concentrates again and soon the flames take the form of an eagle and it flies off as the spell dissipates. Chance says, "Someday, I will learn how to transform into an eagle. Then I will be able to fly were ever I want to go."

Ariella says, "Well, I hope that you will still come see me even when you don't need to use my father's ship anymore."

"Of course I will," Chance says as he puts his arm around her. "I will use your father's ship whenever I can. Besides, my friends won't be able to fly," he laughs. Then looking her in the eyes he says, "Once I can fly, I will soar in the sky. No ocean nor sea, shall keep you from me."

"Oh, Chance," Ariella gasps. "Do you mean that?"

"I promise," Chance replies, "I will come for you." Then as he takes her hand in his, they are caught in each other's gaze. Chance whispers, "I love you, Ariella."

"Chance," Ariella says trying to catch her breath, "I love you too."

They embrace tightly for moment then looking each other in the eyes they lean in to kiss. They are interrupted when a red bearded dwarf in the background says. "Ariella, it is time for bed." They jump as they are both startled. Red Beard gives Chance a stern look.

"Alright, father," Ariella says. The dwarf walks off as Ariella turns quickly and gives Chance a kiss on the cheek and asks, "I'll see you in the morning?"

"Of course," Chance replies with a smile.

Ariella's memories fade and she now finds herself looking into the same blue eyes she remembered from her youth. Though he is a bit older, he still looks remarkably young, as elves always do.

The crew looks at their captain who seems to be at a loss for words. She walks slowly down the stairs and doesn't say a word. She walks up to him and for a moment they just stare at each other. "After all this time," she starts to say. She pauses and then after taking a deep breath she tries again. "After all this time, why are you here now?"

Chance is also at a loss of words. After a moment he finally asks her, "May I have a moment with you, please?"

"What is it?" Ariella asks.

Chance looks around at the crew and feeling a bit uncomfortable he asks again, "Please, can I speak with you alone?"

Ariella, who is still in a bit of shock, replies coldly, "Whatever it is you have to say to me you can say right here."

"Very well," Chance says with a sigh. "I am here to warn you that several vessels have gone missing over the last few days."

Ariella, with her mind once again clear, says sardonically, "So King Arioch has sent you out like a messenger bird to warn us? How sweet."

Chance looks down at the deck in silence.

Ariella looks at him and asks, "There is more, isn't there?"

"No," Chance answers as he drops his eyes.

"You liar," Ariella says. "You never could tell a lie. Let me guess, King Arioch thinks we have something to do with the missing ships, doesn't he?"

Chance sighs deeply and says, "Some on the counsel have questioned that since the *Red Dawn* has not been seen in this area for years, for you to suddenly show up just as ships have gone mis—"

Before he can finish the sentence Ariella slaps Chance across the face. "Twenty years!" she yells. "Twenty years and this is how you greet me?" She slaps Chance again. "How dare you!"

"Please, Ariella—"

Ariella strikes Chance a third time and snaps, "You have some nerve coming here after all this time just to accuse me of piracy." She turns and starts walking up the stairs and to the lounge.

Chance follows and calls to her, "Please, I am sorry. My words were ill chosen. Would you just talk to me?"

They reach the lounge door and she turns and says, "Oh, you have said quite enough."

"I am not talking about the ships," Chance explains. Then quietly he adds, "I want to talk about what happened between us."

With a look of both sadness and anger, Ariella says, "What could you possibly say to me now that you couldn't say twenty years ago? Did it take you this long to learn how to fly? I wrote you so many times, Chance Na'Moon, that I lost count, and you never had the decency to write me back even once!" Ariella turns and walks into the lounge.

"But I did write," Chance says as she slams the door in his face.

The crew now stirs at the mention of his name. While most of the men have heard of Chance, with the exception of Ariella and Torgus, no one else on board has ever seen him in person.

Allen says to John, "That's Chance Na'Moon? I always thought he would be, I don't know, taller."

"Excuse me," Torgus says to John as he makes his way through the crew that has now crowded the deck. He enters the officers' quarters and climbs down the stairs to the lower deck.

Chance looks around at the crew staring at him. They try to look busy doing their work, but Chance knows all their eyes are on him. Chance looks back at the door as the memories of his past come back to him.

It is years ago and he is on the deck of the *Red Dawn*. It is the morning after Chance and Ariella had said good night and they are docked at Sheathelm. Captain Red Beard greats Chance and his companions, "Gentlemen, I am sorry but we have to be going now."

Chance says, "But sir, I was hoping to say goodbye to Ariella."

Red Beards says to Chance, "Sorry, lad, but we have no time for that. A storm is coming in and we have to go now. Prince Arioch, thank you for sailing with us again."

Chance's companion, a human prince named Arioch Ravenguard, says, "Come on, Chance, let's go. You will see her again soon enough." Arioch and his other companions lead him away as Chance stops at the edge of the ship. A less grayed Torgus is there.

Chance says to him, "Thank you, Torgus, for showing me those new spells."

Torgus says to him, "My pleasure, Chance."

Then Chance hands him a letter and quietly says to him, "My friend, can you see that Ariella gets this, please?"

Torgus says to Chance, "I'll see what I can do," as he takes the letter.

Chance's memories fade away while on the other side of the door Ariella is sitting at the table holding back tears. Marie is there and she asks, "I am sorry, ma'am, are you alright?"

Ariella sniffles and says, "Oh, Marie, I am fine."

Marie looks out the porthole and sees Chance. She asks, "Who is that, ma'am?"

Ariella sighs and says, "That my dear Marie, was my first love."

"He is so handsome," Marie says. Then after thinking for a moment she turns to her and asks, "What's his name and why is he here?"

Ariella explains, "His name is Chance Na'Moon and he is here because some of King Arioch's ships have gone missing and he wants to know if we knew anything about it."

"He thinks we had something to do with it?" She asks.

"He didn't directly say, but yes," Ariella answers.

"Why does that name sound familiar?" Marie asks as she looks out the porthole at Chance who is now talking with Fernando and Allen.

"Well, you weren't born yet," Ariella explains, "but he and King Arioch of Sheathelm stopped the dragon slayers many years ago in what is now called the Dragon Wars."

"Oh, I think I remember hearing about it in some bards' tales," Marie says.

"Yes, there are a few," Ariella says. "Then about five years after that, Chance would lead the armies of Sheathelm and The Amazons of the Silver Moon across the north destroying all the orcneas in the land."

"That's where I have heard his name," Marie says. "Isn't he called the 'Orcnea Slayer'?"

"Yes," Ariella replies. "They say he burned entire orcnea villages to the ground."

"By the gods," Marie gasps. "That's horrible."

*****

Back in the modern day apartment Haley raises her hand. Kyle asks her, "What is it?"

Haley asks, "What is an orcnea?"

Josh says, "They are the green creatures I fight against in my video game online. You know, the ones with the big teeth on the bottom."

Laura says, "I have never heard them called orcneas before."

"They have been called many things," Kyle explains. "Orcneas and humans first met thousands of years earlier. Through magic portholes humans had already traveled to other realms where they were greeted by the elves, dwarves, and other races. Humans had only heard of the orcneas through stories told by the others. These stories differed depending on who was telling it. In some stories the orcneas went by different names. The size and intelligence of orcneas were also inconsistent. Even the color of their rough skin varied from story to story. An individual orcnea could have almost any color and shade of skin, depending on where it was from. In all of the tales, however, orcneas seemed to be more like monsters and demons than a humanoid race."

"What color are the orcneas of Runefell?" Josh asks.

Danielle answers, "They have reddish-orange skin."

"Cool," Josh replies.

Kyle continues to explain, "When a scouting party of humans came across the first orcneas they had ever seen, the results were tragic. Fighting ensued and the two scouting parties almost perished before both retreated. After that day stories have been told by both humans and orcneas that the other race was not to be trusted. Throughout many realms, humans and orcneas have gone to war countless times over the many years since. The world of Runefell was no different. Now back to the story..."

*****

Marie says to Ariella, "I don't understand how someone could burn an entire village. Even if it was an orcnea one."

Crossroads

"The Chance that I knew and loved was from before that time," she explains. "We were young and innocent, but now so many years have passed," she pauses and then adds, "for both of us. He has changed, but then again, so did I after I saw him take his vows."

"Vows? What do you mean?" Marie asks curiously.

"One day he just left without saying goodbye," Ariella pauses reflecting on her thoughts. "After years of getting close he was just gone. I wrote him all the time and he never returned my letters. Then a few years passed and we were docked at Sheathelm. I ran as fast as I could to the palace to see him, only to find..." Ariella stops to take a breath as a tear roles down her cheek.

"What, ma'am?" Marie asks as she takes the Captain's hand.

Ariella gains her composer and continues, "I found Chance in the courtyard of the palace taking vows with an elven woman."

"Oh no," Marie replies.

"Yes," Ariella continues. "She was an Amazon of the Silver Moon. I guess they had met during the Dragon Wars. Over the years, they ended up having three children together before she was killed in an orcnea raid in the northern territory of Sheathelm."

"Oh, that's terrible," Marie says as she looks outside once again.

"Yes," Ariella explains, "that is why he was so relentless in the Orcnea War. It was the raid that killed his wife that started it all."

At that very moment outside on the quarterdeck, Chance, who has been talking with Fernando, Allen, and a few others, continues telling his story, "So you see, I wrote her every time her ship would pass, but she never wrote back. I knew that her father didn't approve, but I didn't think it would stop her from writing."

Allen asks, "Pardon me for asking, sir, but are you sure that she actually received your letters? I mean, if her father never liked you and found out about them..."

Chance ponders for a moment. He then says, "I suppose it's possible. Could it really be as simple as that?" He looks again at the lounge door.

Still inside Marie asks, "Captain, are you sure, he ever got your letters?"

"I never really thought about it," she answers. "I had always just gave my letters to Torgus. He said he would take care of it. I never had any reason to doubt him." Ariella thinks for a moment and then says, "Just as I slammed the door I thought I heard him say that he did write me."

"Well, he is here now," Marie says, "perhaps you could ask him."

"You're right, Marie, thank you," Ariella says as she stands and walks towards the door.

On the other side Chance is standing there at the door. Just as he is about to knock the door opens. Face to face, Chance and Ariella stand there for a moment startled. Then simultaneously Chance and Ariella ask each other the same question, "What did you mean when you said you wrote to me?"

Then as the entire ship's crew stares at the two of them, there is a long silence that is broken by Torgus's voice. "Perhaps I can be offer an explanation," he says. Torgus walks towards them while carrying a small sack in each hand.

Ariella turns to Torgus and asks, "What do you mean? Torgus, what are those?"

Chance then adds, "Torgus? Don't tell me you never gave her my letters."

Torgus bows his head and says to Ariella, "My dear, I am sorry. Your father knew about the letters you had written." Then looking at Chance he adds, "That both of you had written."

Ariella and Chance look at each other with eyes full of sadness and yet still, within their gaze, there is a spark of happiness and a clear feeling of relief. After years of not knowing the truth they were now both learning that the other had written back after all. Torgus continues to explain, "He ordered me not to deliver or send your letters to each other. I received all of them over the years. He wanted me to destroy them, however I knew that someday Chance would find you again. I couldn't bring myself to do it." He looks down at the two sacks then hands each of them one.

"I don't know what to say," Ariella says looking inside the small bag revealing the letters inside. "There are so many," she says as she fights back the tears swelling in her eyes.

"It is my fault," Chance says to her, "I should have known. Your father hated me. Even though I did search for you the very same day I learned to fly, I should not have given up so soon. By then the Dragon Wars had started, and then..." Chance drops his eyes unable to finish his thoughts.

"Then you took your vows," Ariella says finishing.

They stand there for a moment again in silence. Ariella looks up at her men who are still watching them. "Alright, get back to work!" she snaps. The crew quickly jumps back to their jobs. She then turns to Chance and says, "You can tell Arioch that we have nothing to do with the missing ships."

"For the record," Chance says, "I knew that you didn't."

"Care to join me for dinner?" Ariella asks with a smile.

Chance smiles back but before he can accept her invitation, the watchman from the crow's nest calls down, "Debris dead ahead!"

The crew scramble to their posts, and Chance rushes to the bow of the ship and watches as they approach a small debris field of a floating shipwreck.

"There is not much left of whatever ship it once was," Fernando states.

Small pieces of wood are everywhere. Jacob notes, "Whatever it was, it was completely destroyed."

Ariella orders, "Haul in what you can! I want to know what ship it is from!"

The crew brings aboard pieces of wood and a small crate as Chance and Ariella gather around. They spot the markings that say GTC.

"What is it, Captain," Allen asks.

"The Goblin Trade Company," Fernando says.

Chance sighs heavily and says, "This is worse than I thought." He pulls Ariella aside and says, "I have to report this to Arioch. I don't suppose I could convince you to return to Sheathelm instead of continuing south?"

Ariella replies, "I am sorry, but I *have* to go south. I am looking for a treasure of my fathers. Do you really have to go now?"

"I do," Chance says. "This has just become a lot more urgent. I am sorry, but I will return I promise." Then taking her hand he kisses it and says, "Be careful."

"I will," Ariella replies. "Chance," she says grabbing his hand, "I..." as she looks into his eyes she is unable to find the strength to say what is in her heart.

"I know," Chance says as he kisses her forehead. "Me too." He secures the bag of letters that Torgus had given him to his belt. He steps back from her and closes his eyes. Ariella watches him take the form of a giant eagle. With his claw he grabs the banner of Sheathelm and takes flight.

Fernando says to Allen, "Well, he certainly knows how to make a dramatic exit."

Allen laughs a bit.

"Alright everyone!" Ariella yells out. "Stay alert! We don't know what we are up against, but neither do they! If it's a fight they want we will be sure to give them a proper one!"

The ship cheers loudly with enthusiasm. Ariella, clinching her bag of letters, heads towards her cabin. She passes Chris and says, "Let me know the first sign of anything out of the ordinary."

"Aye, Captain," Chris responds.

The ship is loud with excitement and anticipation. Ariella walks down the stairs from the quarterdeck and walks through the officers' quarters before entering her cabin. She closes the door behind her. Then in the muffled silence of her room, she sits down and places the bag of letters on the table in front of her.

Marie who has been cleaning the captain's quarters says, "I'll leave you alone, ma'am."

"Thank you, Marie," Ariella replies. She then reaches into the bag and pulls out one of the many letters. Then after staring for a long while she takes a deep breath. She opens it and as she begins to read Chance's words written years ago, it is too much for her. She lays her head on the table and closes her eyes.

A few hours pass and back in Sheathelm Chance is informing his good friend, and now King, Arioch of his findings. The King, in his forties, is a bit shorter than Chance. With no audience or dignitaries around, Arioch sits on the throne while wearing scale-mail armor. His crown, which he rarely puts on his shaven head, sits beside him next to the throne on a small pedestal.

"So whatever is destroying the ships out there must be a serious threat," concludes Chance.

"Attacking the Goblin Trade Company makes no sense," Arioch says. "They have always remained neutral and are willing to sell to anyone."

"Perhaps they were less interested in buying as they were taking," Chance says.

"Hopefully whatever cargo the goblins had on that ship went down with it as well. You know very well the Goblin Trade Company doesn't usually transport anything unless it is either very powerful, valuable, or both. I hate to

Runefell

think what weapons they may have had on board that these raiders would find it worth attacking them for," Arioch says.

"Well, if I am not mistaken," Chance says, "I'd be willing to bet the Goblin Trade Company was able to abandon their ship with most all of their valuable cargo. Goblins usually have good escape plans."

"Well, if there were any survivors we should be hearing from them soon when they ask for more protection along the water ways," Arioch says. "Perhaps, if any goblins did escape, they can tell us who attacked them. I'll send for a representative at once. In the meantime, Chance, you should take some time off. You have been working far too much."

"I would, but I have to get back to the *Red Dawn*," Chance replies, "I am worried."

Arioch laughs and says, "No doubt about the daughter of Red Beard?"

"I couldn't believe it was her, Arioch, after all these years," Chance says. "She is as beautiful as ever, and even more so."

"I remember how much you two cared for each other," Arioch says with a grin. "I also remember her father not being happy with it at all."

"Yes, well, I am planning to leave in the morning and try to reach them before they run into any trouble," Chance says.

"I am sure she will be fine," Arioch says. "You remember how tough their crew was."

"Yes, and Torgus is still with her," he says, looking down at the bag full of letters.

"Well, then whoever is attacking those ships will not be able to take them without a fight," Arioch says. "Torgus was a wizard, wasn't he? A powerful one if I remember correctly."

"Yes, he gave me a lot of good advice on magic," Chance answers. "Well, I am going to turn in for the night."

"Goodnight, my friend," Arioch says.

"May your dreams safely guide you to the new day," Chance replies. He then turns and heads towards his room down the white marble halls carrying with him the letters from Ariella.

Chapter 5
Letters From the Heart

The storm still rages outside the windows of the modern day apartment. Laura asks, "So what did the letters say?"

"Do you want to hear more about the letters?" Kyle asks Haley.

"Yeah," Haley replies.

"It's a love triangle," Laura says. "What does Fernando do about it?"

"Who cares about some stupid love letters," Josh says. "I want to know what happens to Chance's clothes when he transforms."

"It's magic," Kyle answers. "As long as he isn't carrying too much it transforms with him."

"Oh," Josh replies. "What is so special about the Goblin Trade Company?"

Kyle explains, "Well you see, in Runefell almost all the goblins work for the Goblin Trade Company. They are like a big multinational corporation. They don't get involved in wars unless it is to sell weapons."

"Kind of like an arms dealer?" Laura asks.

"Yes," Kyle answers, "and they have many weapons. They mostly like to deal with magical items. They trade with almost every faction in Runefell and even to other realms. This gives them great access to rare items. While it may be temping for a pirate to attack a Goblin Trade Company ship, most wouldn't dare. That is because the Goblin Trade Company has so much wealth and power in the land, and if a pirate were to attack a goblin ship they would find themselves being hunted down by every bounty hunter in the realm."

"So what did the letters say," Laura asks again, "and who does Ariella end up with?"

"Well, we are getting ahead of ourselves. Let's just start with the letters," Kyle replies. "OK, so that night on the *Red Dawn*..."

*****

Fernando is being escorted once again to his cell by Drake and Leon. Leon says, "I still can't believe that the Captain and Chance Na'Moon have a history together."

"Me neither," Drake replies. "I guess that means that Mr. Greythorn here doesn't have a," Drake smiles before finishing, "*Chance*."

Drake and Leon both laugh as they open the cell door and Fernando walks inside.

"Apparently not," Fernando says. "Thank you, gentlemen, for escorting me to my illustrious accommodations."

Leon locks the cell door and says, "You're welcome. Remember if you need anything, don't bother me with it." Drake and Leon both laugh as they walk off.

John and Jacob walk into the room as the big guys leave. "Quite a day, eh?" John asks

Jacob says, "I'll say, a visit from the legendary Orcnea Slayer here on this very ship."

Fernando says, "Yes, I have stayed in Sheathelm many times and I have never met Mr. Na'Moon before today. Some say that he had gone mad after the orcneas killed his wife."

"He seemed nice enough to me," John says.

"I can't believe that he and the Captain have a past," Jacob says.

"Yes," Fernando says as he ponders. "That is most interesting."

Upstairs in her quarters Ariella is sitting at her desk reading her letters from Chance. The room is roughly the same size as the lounge located above. The desk is located in the aft corner on the port side. In the opposite corner of the room is Ariella's bed with a small table next to it. Separating the desk and bed is a round table for private dining. It is smaller than the one in the lounge and only has two chairs. Unlike the dark stained deck of the ship the wooden planking within this room is lightly colored cedar.

There are two entrances. The first is the main entry that leads out to the main deck through the officers' quarters. The second is along the side of the room at the foot of Ariella's bed. This door accesses a small hallway that leads to the Marie's room and has a steep stairway to the galley above. It is this door that Ariella hears a knock.

"Enter," Ariella says as sets down the letter she is reading.

Marie enters and says, "If you won't be needing me for anything more tonight, ma'am, I think I will go to bed now?"

"Thank you Marie," Ariella says as she holds a letter in her hand. "I have a few more letters to read from Chance and then I will be turning in myself. Goodnight, Marie."

"Goodnight, ma'am," Marie says closing the door. Ariella opens one of the few remaining letters and begins to read it:

My Darling Ariella,

Every day without you is like a week. Every week that passes is like a year. It has been several months now since I last saw you, and while it now feels like a lifetime ago, I can still feel your kiss on my cheek. Please, my love, tell me if I have offended you. I have written you many times and yet I still have heard no word from you.

If only I could fly. I would come out to see you instead of watching the Red Dawn sit in the bay of Sheathelm as your father sends Torgus to get supplies. It is agony to see you so close and yet not be able to reach you. Torgus tells me that he is delivering my letters to you every time, but says that you have not written back.

My friends and I have to travel soon. We have heard rumors of a powerful ice staff in the far north. My close friend, Kyle Drakesbane, is very interested in it. I just want you to know that no matter where I go, no matter how far the distance, my heart will always be with you. I hope that I am close to your heart as well. Please write back soon. I miss you deeply.

Crossroads

I hope to be able to fly soon. I have been practicing the transformation spell. As soon as I learn it, I will come for you. My only hope is that by then you will not have forgotten me.

Love,
Chance

Ariella folds the parchment and places it on a pile of opened letters. From a smaller pile Ariella picks up another sealed letter. After opening it she reads:

My Sweet Ariella,

Words cannot express how much you are missed by me. My eyes long to see you. My ears listen for the sound of your voice. My arms ache to hold you close. My lips craving to kiss you. This deep void in my heart can only be filled by being with you once more.
I will once again place this letter in the care of the supplies that your ship will need sometime next week. I only pray that you are receiving these letters and that I will hear from you soon. I am leaving tomorrow for the Mana Forest. My friends and are visiting the Elven capital of Elonfar. I am not sure when I will be back to Sheathelm. I hope however that when I return there will be a letter for me waiting.
I love you, Ariella.

Love,
Chance

Back in the palace of Sheathelm, Chance also sits at a desk reading letters as well. One letter reads:

My Dearest Chance,

I pray that I will hear from you soon. Torgus tells me that he delivers my letters to the palace, so I know you must be getting these. However every time he returns, he tells me that there is no letter from you.
I forgive you for leaving that morning without saying goodbye. I am sure my father had something to do with that, though he won't admit it. I beg him to let me go ashore with Torgus to fetch the supplies but he will not let me. So I stand on the deck looking over the bay hoping to catch even a glimpse of you.
Now every day I look to the sky. When I see an eagle I pray to the gods that it is you coming for me. You said that no ocean or sea would ever keep you from me. Please come for me soon. At the very least would you write back and have your letter sent with Torgus the next time we anchor. I miss you so much.

Always and forever,
Ariella

Chance opens another letter and it reads:

Dear Chance,

I have heard stories from the crew that you and your friends are at war with the Dragon Slayers. I worry so much about you. Please be careful. Torgus has been teaching me more spells. Soon I will be as good a mage as you.
The last time we visited I did not receive a letter from you, again. Have I done something wrong? I worry that you are angry with me and I do not know why. I hope that Torgus will return with a letter from you this time however. If he does not, I am not sure if my heart can bare it. Every time we anchor here and I get nothing from you I die a little more inside. I beg of you, please write back. Tell me what is bothering you and I will make it right. We have spent so much time together over the years that I feel you at least owe me that.
I never knew how much being apart from you would hurt.

Always and Forever,
Ariella

Chance opens one final letter and it reads:

Chance,

I cannot believe that you would do this to me. We finally dock at Sheathelm and I come to see you and what do I find? You taking vows with another woman! I thought you loved me. Even though you never wrote back I still hoped that maybe there was a reason. Now I see that there was a reason. Just not one that I hoped for.
If you didn't love me all you needed to do was tell me. Maybe you were too much of a coward to tell me how you really felt. Well, I am not afraid. I loved you, Chance. I loved you more than you will ever know, but now the very thought of you makes me ill. If I never lay eyes on you again it will be too soon.
You have broken my heart but I swear from this day forward no man will ever hurt me again.

Goodbye
Ariella

A tear falls onto the parchment as Chance wipes his cheek. He folds the letter then places it in a drawer before closing it. "How?" he asks himself. "How could I have been so foolish?"

Back on the *Red Dawn*, Ariella is still reading letters. With tears flowing freely down her face she opens the last one.

Crossroads

My Beautiful Ariella,

This is the hardest letter I have ever had to write you. It has been years since I have seen you last. I will place this letter like all the others with the supplies for the Red Dawn. By now I have no idea what possible reason there could be for you to not write me back. I have seen Torgus himself and he assures me that he gives you the letters personally and that you simply have never given him anything to deliver to me.

So it is with a heavy heart that I can longer continue the pursuit of your love. I would never wish the pain that I have felt while longing for you on anyone. I certainly hope that you never have to have your heart broken the way that mine is right now.

Tomorrow I am leaving for what may be my final battle. We have discovered what the Dragon Slayers are planning to do for the final step of their plan. We are going to try to stop them. If I do not survive I want you to know that I love you. I have loved you since the first day I saw you. I told you once in another letter that no matter where I go, my heart will always be with you. That is still true today. I will always love you, until the day I draw my final breath.

I wish you well, my love. If I am not the one who can make you happy, I do hope that you find that special someone someday. You deserve that. I only wish it could have been me.

Love,
Chance

Ariella places the final letter on top of the pile. She slowly makes her way to her bed, then as she lies down she grasps her pillow. With tears streaming down her face, she eventually finds peace in her sleep.

Chapter 6
Day 3
The Scouting Party

It is morning in Sheathelm, and Chance is in the courtyard preparing to leave. He hears King Arioch call to him, "Chance! Wait!" Chance turns to see Arioch approaching with a goblin following behind him.

Goblins are about half the size of humans. They have sizable pointed ears and rough green skin. Their noses are long and also pointed. Their teeth are sharp as well as their long claw-like fingernails.

"What is it?" Chance asks. "Is there news on the attacks?"

"I am afraid there is, my friend," Arioch says with a concerned look, "and you are not going to like it."

"Well then, what is it?" he asks, "Who has been behind the attacks?"

"This is Resheck, from the Goblin Trade Company," Arioch says introducing the goblin. "I will let him tell you what he knows."

The goblin approaches Chance and looks up at him. With a raspy voice, typical for a goblin, he says, "Mr. Na'Moon, it is a true pleasure to meet you."

"Thank you, Resheck," Chance replies. "Please, you have some information about these attacks? I was just about to leave to help the *Red Dawn*."

"If anyone can help them it would be you, Mr. Na'Moon," Resheck says, "You see, as I am sure you are already aware that one of our ships was attacked. Fortunately most of those aboard were able to escape. When we asked them what had happened, many of them told us about a great storm that came out of almost nowhere. The next thing they knew they are under attack by a ship in the middle of the storm."

"Yes," Chance says, "it is not uncommon for a ship to use weather spells when attacking. Did any of your men see who they were?"

Resheck sighs and looks at Arioch. Arioch says, "Chance, Resheck has said the survivors saw orcneas."

Chance says under his breath, "Ariella." Then he says to Resheck, "Thank you for this information." Then to Arioch he says, "Your Majesty, I will deal with these orcneas."

"My friend, there is more," Arioch says with a somber voice. He turns to Resheck and says, "Tell him the rest of what you told me."

"For years now we goblins have stayed to ourselves," Resheck explains. "As you already know, we don't get involved in the affairs of other races. In exchange, we have always been allowed to open our trade shops almost everywhere. The orcneas were no different. You may have wiped them off this land but across the sea there are many more in the Red-Rock Plains. A few years ago the orcneas started to buy up magic books containing lightning spells. We gladly sold them as many as they could afford."

"Orcneas don't usually spend a lot of time studying magic," Arioch says.

"Yes," Chance replies, "and with lightening spells they are also likely to know other storm spells."

"Well, that explains the storms surrounding their ships," Arioch says.

"Exactly," Resheck says. "We thought it was unusual for them to request so many. Well, as it turns out they had opened a training camp for their shamans. For years now they have been training hundreds of shamans."

"By the gods," Chance says. "They have created an army."

Resheck says, "And a very powerful ocean force as well. They have been building ships at all of their cities along the coast. Now normally, Mr. Na'Moon, we would never share such information as it is none of our concern. We are not in the business of being spies. But now they have attacked one of our ships. They have crossed the line, so we have pulled all of our shops out their cities."

"I must go now. The *Red Dawn* may be in trouble," Chance says.

"I understand," says Arioch. "It appears that we may once again be at war. I have sent a small scouting party to the north. They will check out the old orcnea lands to see if they have returned. I have also sent word to the Amazons of the Silver Moon. If the orcneas are back, we will need them once again. Oh, and Chance," Arioch puts his hand on Chance's shoulder, "be careful, my friend."

"I will," Chance replies.

Chance turns and transforms into his great eagle form and takes flight. As he flies off, Resheck says to Arioch, "Don't you think you should have told him who you sent in the scouting party?"

Arioch replies, "You want me to tell him that I am sending his oldest daughter? The same daughter who witnessed her mother die at the hands of orcneas when she was five year old? No, I think not."

"He'll be upset when he finds out," Resheck says.

"Yes, he will," Arioch replies, "but do not forget my daughter is also in that scouting party."

"Why would you send them on such a dangerous mission?" Resheck asks.

"You have never met our daughters," Arioch says as he watches the great eagle fly off out of sight. "When they found out about the orcneas, I couldn't stop them from going."

*****

Back in the apartment Josh asks, "So the King sent Chance's daughter and the Princess on a scouting mission? How old were they?"

"Well," Kyles answers, "at the time they were eighteen."

"What!" Haley says in disbelief. "Eighteen?"

"Back then you could have been married off at age fourteen," Laura laughs.

"Your sister is right," Kyle explains. "However, eighteen was still a little young even then, but you have to understand that King Arioch rose to power from a common soldier. He never forgot his roots, and made sure that Princess Kianna was trained and skilled as both a royal princess and a worthy fighter.

Her best friend, Ya'leigh Na'Moon, was of course trained in combat as well. Their friend Gena Lotusblossom, was a halfling who was very good at magic."

"What is a halfling?" Haley asks.

Kyle smiles and answers, "A halfling is kind of like a dwarf, but without all the facial hair. They are less stocky as well. They are often mistaken as children when they are among humans. Gena met Ya'leigh and Princess Kianna at the magic school of Dicean. Gena knew many spells that were useful for adventurers."

"So, did the king just send girls?" Josh asks.

"No," Kyle replies. "No matter how talented Kianna and her friends were, Arioch would never send them without two of his most trusted warriors. One of them was Garrin Silvertin. He was a hardened warrior from the Second orcnea War. He was also a skilled blacksmith, and was trained by both dwarves and elves in armor and weapon making. Then finally there was Isen. Picked more for his brawn than his brains, he was the personal body guard of the Princess. He was taller and stronger than most men, and was always ready to put himself in harm's way for the others when trouble started. Many times it was trouble that had been started by him. This was the group that Arioch sent to scout the northern territory. Now, before I get further side tracked..."

*****

Along the road heading north, Princess Kianna is leading her group. Her long black hair covers her pointed half elven ears. Her well-crafted armor is polished and looks new. She has a sword at her side and a shield on her back. She looks more like a soldier than royalty. She is driving a wagon full of supplies for the town of Troven. The supplies are covered by a large canvas. Riding alongside her in the wagon is Ya'leigh. Much like her father, Chance, she has long blonde hair. Without a shield, she prefers to use two curved swords similar to small katanas."

*****

"Katanas?" Josh asks, interrupting the story.

"Yes," Kyle explains, "after the different worlds were mixed up during the Great Collapse there were many cultures in Runefell, including Asian cultures."

"And the elves use katanas?" Josh asks.

"Sort of, yes," Kyle replies. "They respected the craftsmanship of the Japanese sword and some elven blacksmiths worked with the Japanese sword-smiths to learn their crafting technique."

"That's cool," Josh says. "They are like, Elven Samurais."

Kyle laughs and replies, "Yes, something like that."

"Okay, Josh," Laura says impatiently, "let Uncle Kyle continue with the story now."

"Sorry," Josh says.

Kyle smiles and continues.

Crossroads

*****

Aside from her two swords, Ya'leigh has a finely crafted elven bow on her back. Riding next to the wagon on horseback is the tall body guard Isen along with Garrin, both heavily armored. In contrast is their friend Gena who has no armor. Aside from her regular clothing she only has a robe and a staff.

"I wish Aria was here," Ya'leigh says.

"Me too," Kianna adds. "We could use her if we get into trouble."

The hard of hearing Garrin asks, "Why are we in trouble?"

"We said we could use Aria if we got into trouble!" Gena says loudly so he can understand.

"Oh, right," Garrin replies.

Up ahead they can see a family of four with a pack mule. They have stopped for a rest along the side of the road. The young father and mother look exhausted. Their two children, a boy and a girl no older than ten, are eating some rations as they sit on the ground. There cloths are tattered and their faces are dirty.

"I'll go and make sure they aren't a danger," Isen says.

Kianna looks at Ya'leigh and laughs. She then says to her over protective body guard, "Isen, I don't think those kids are much of a threat."

"You never know, Your Highness," Isen replies. Then with a grin he adds, "They could be orcneas in disguise." He then rides his horse up ahead of the group towards the family.

"Did he say orcneas are wise?" Garrin asks.

"No," Gena answers with a sigh.

The princess continues to approach the family on the wagon while Isen reaches them first. "Good morning," Isen says with a friendly smile.

"Good morning," the father says as he gets to his feet.

"My name is Isen," he says as he dismounts his horse.

"I am Marcus," the man replies as he looks over the massive dark haired warrior before him. "This is my wife, Ellen, and our children Orin and Cassie."

Isen nods at Ellen and the two curly haired children. "Which way are you heading?" Isen asks.

"We are heading to Sheathelm," Marcus answers. "We are from the north along the base of the Northwind Range."

"We are heading to the north," Isen explains. "Have you seen any orcneas lately?"

"Seen any? No," Marcus replies, "but we have heard that there have been sightings to the north western side of the range."

"Near Sapphire Lake?" Isen asks as Kianna and the others reach them.

"Yes," Marcus answers. "I heard there was a small raid on the monastery there."

Kianna looks at Ya'leigh and says, "That's where the Iron Fist Monks are."

"Skunks?" Garrin asks. "Where?"

"I said that is where the Iron Fist Monks are!" Kianna repeats.

"Ah, yes," Garrin says. "I believe the Iron Fist Monks are near Sapphire Lake."

Shaking her head Ya'leigh says to the scruffy looking Garrin, "We know."

"Your Highness," Isen says, "we should be able to go there straight from Troven."

"I am sorry, but did he say *Your Highness*?" Marcus asks.

Ya'leigh shakes her head and says to Isen, "Isen, you're an idiot."

Isen cringes and replies, "I am sorry, I forgot. I don't think they are much of a threat though."

"That's what I said earlier," Kianna says with a laugh.

"Oh," Marcus say nervously. "I assure you we mean you no harm. We are just heading to Sheathelm in case there are more orcneas coming."

Isen replies. "Well, this is Princess Kianna, of Sheathelm."

The man bows his head and says, "It is an honor, Your Royal Highness."

Ellen quickly stands and curtseys. "Your Highness, my apologies."

Kianna, feeling a bit awkward, smiles and says, "There is no need for apologies. I hardly look the role of a princess right now."

Marcus says, "Your Highness, I should warn you that if the rumors of the orcnea raids are true, then might I suggest that you return to Sheathelm."

"We have some supplies that we are taking to Troven," Kianna answers.

"Forgive me for saying so," Ellen says, "but that could be dangerous."

Kianna looks at her group and answers, "Yes, it could be, but I have a good group of companions, if we come across any orcneas."

The young boy Orin says, "Mother, I am still hungry."

"We are almost to Sheathelm," she quietly answers. "We will have some money for food soon."

Isen opens a bag that hangs from the side of his horse and takes out two large apples. He walks over to the two small children and holds out the fruit and says, "Here you go. That should last you until you reach the city."

The soft voice of Cassie replies, "Thank you." Her hands are so small that she must use both of them to hold the large apple from Isen.

Kianna asks, "What do you plan to do when you reach Sheathelm?"

"We plan to sell the mule and what belongings we have," Marcus answers. "It isn't much but it should be enough to get us buy until I can find work."

Kianna looks at the poorly dressed family. She watches as the two children eat the apples as if they haven't eaten in days. She pulls out a small pouch from her belt and climbs down from the wagon. She walks up to the father and says, "Here, take this." She hands him the pouch.

Marcus takes the small purse from her he can hear the sound of coins from inside. He says, "Your Highness, you are too generous."

Kianna smiles and says, "That should be enough to get you started on your new life."

Marcus looks at his wife who rushes over and grabs his hand. "Thank you, Your Highness," Ellen says, trying to hold back tears.

Kianna replies, "My father once told me that we are leaders only because the hard work of the good people allows us to be. If our own people cannot feed their families, then we have failed them as leaders."

"Long live King Arioch," Marcus says proudly.

"When was the last time you two have eaten a full meal?" Kianna asks.

Marcus looks down at the ground and answers, "Our rations ran low two days ago, and we have been saving them for our children."

"Well, I can do something about that," Gena says. She pulls a silver serving platter from her backpack. She sets it down on the ground in front of her. She takes a deep breath and as she slowly moves her hand over the platter food begins to appear. The family watches in amazement as bread, cheese, and grapes appear from thin air. A few moments later and the patter is full of food.

"Look!" Orin yells.

"Is that a magic platter?" Marcus asks in amazement.

"No," Gena answers, sounding a bit out of breath. "It is just a platter, but I happen to know a few spells."

"Is the food real?" Cassie asks.

Gena laughs and answers, "Yes, the food is real. Please help yourselves."

Orin and Cassie start picking at the grapes. "We cannot thank you enough," Ellen says as she takes some bread from the large platter.

Isen takes some bread and cheese from the platter and walks over and sets it down on the back of the wagon. He then walks to his horse to get some water from his wineskin, and as he does a small hand reaches out from underneath the canvas covering the wagon and takes his food.

When Isen returns he notices that it is gone. He looks around a bit and then looks up in the sky to see if a bird had come and taken the food. He then walks back over to the platter that is now empty. He sighs and asks Gena, "Can you make some more food, something happened to mine."

"Yeah," Ya'leigh replies with a laugh, "you ate it."

"No," Isen explains, "I didn't. I set it down over there and some animal must have taken it."

"Alright," Gena says with a disgruntled tone, "I'll make more, but you have to wait a minute. I still have to rest from the last spell."

"Thanks," Isen replies as he looks around again for his missing food.

Later, as the two groups finish eating, Orin slowly walks up to Ya'leigh and asks, "Is that a magic bow?"

"Yes, it is," Ya'leigh replies with a smile.

Orin asks, "What does it do?"

Ya'leigh stands up and takes the bow from her back. The beautiful long bow, with red stained wood, looks graceful in her hands. She says, "You don't need arrows for this bow." As she draws back the bowstring, an arrow magically appears already drawn. Flames emit from the summoned arrow. "The bow's name is *Incendia*," she says as she slowly relaxes the bowstring. As the tension on the bowstring is released the flaming arrow disappears.

"That is quite a weapon," Marcus says.

"Yes, it was my mother's," Ya'leigh says sadly as she slings the bow back over her shoulder. Without saying another word Ya'leigh walks back to the wagon.

Marcus looks to Garrin and asks, "I am sorry, did I say something wrong?"

Garrin answers, "Her mother died in an orcnea raid years ago."

"Oh," Marcus replies. "I didn't mean to upset her."

"It's alright," Garrin says. "She just doesn't like to talk about it much. My wife and her mother were part of a caravan. They were following along the base of the Northwind Range when they were attacked by the orcneas. Ya'leigh and my daughter, Aria, were with them, and were the only survivors."

"Oh," Ellen replies, "I am so sorry."

"Thank you," Garrin says as he reflects on the past. "It was the raid that started the Second Orcnea War. One of the wagons overturned and Ya'leigh and my daughter were caught underneath it. They were only five years old. If not for being hidden under the wagon, we may have lost them as well."

"I can understand why she doesn't want to talk about it," Marcus says. "I am sorry for your loss."

"Thank you," Garrin replies. "I just hope that the rumors of the orcnea's return aren't true."

"We should be going," Isen says.

The groups start to get up and gather their things. Marcus says to them, "I hope that the orcneas have not returned, but if they have I wish you the best of luck."

"Thank you," Kianna says as she gets back on the wagon where Ya'leigh is waiting patiently. "Good luck to you as well."

"Thank you again, Your Highness," Ellen says as Kianna's group starts to move out.

"You're welcome," Kianna answers back to the family. Then turning to Ya'leigh she asks, "Are you alright?"

Ya'leigh looks at her friend and replies, "I will be. Just as soon as I get to kill some orcneas."

Chapter 7
Storm on the Horizon

It is late morning on the *Red Dawn*. Fernando is still sound asleep, albeit, uncomfortably in his cell. Ariella enters the small room with Drake and Leon. She has John open the cell door. As he does Fernando wakes up and says, "I couldn't think of a better way to begin my day then with the sight of you."

Ariella sighs and says, "Mr. Greythorn, we have arrived at the coordinates that you gave my navigator yesterday. It's time for you to enlighten us all with the next leg of our journey."

Fernando smiles and says, "My pleasure, Captain." He slowly stands up and stretches his back and neck. Fernando then turns and almost runs right into Leon. He stops and as he looks up at the much taller man he smiles and says, "Pardon me." Then he steps to the side and walks past the big man.

Leon just shakes his head and follows the group up the stairs.

When Fernando reaches the top of the stairs he takes a deep breath. "What a beautiful morning," he says. He walks up to Chris, and looks at the map. He points to a spot on the map to the south of where they are and says, "Right there, Mister...uhh," Fernando struggles to remember his name.

"It's just Chris, Mr. Greythorn," Chris says with disdain. Then he says to the helmsman, "Jackson, come about thirty degrees to port."

"Aye, sir," Jackson replies. "Coming about."

Fernando walks back down from the quarterdeck to Ariella and says, "Well, Captain, it looks like we are set for another day. Perhaps now would be a good time to discuss my compensation."

The crew looks nervously at each other in an uncomfortable silence. Allen stops swabbing the deck as he now waits for the Captain's response.

"Compensation, Mr. Greythorn?" Ariella asks while giving him a stare. "The only reason I have not tortured the location from you is because your screams were upsetting Marie. As I told you before, do not mistake my kindness for weakness. If you try to escape us your freedom will be short lived. Torgus can and will track you down, and then, Mr. Greythorn, if you think I made you feel pain before..."

The crew quietly laughs a bit. Leon in particular has a big smile.

Fernando's smile quickly fades, but he continues to plead his case, "I understand, Captain, but please, I beg of you to reconsider. I have a personal reason for finding this treasure. Captain, do you even know what this treasure is?"

"No, Mr. Greythorn," Ariella answers, now sounding a bit annoyed, "but I suppose you do?"

"I have heard a few things, Captain," Fernando replies, "and if what I have heard is true, then I am only asking for you to allow me to claim something that rightfully belongs to me."

"We will discuss your request over lunch later this afternoon," Ariella says, "but for now, Mr. Greythorn, I ask that you earn your passage on this ship." She grabs a mop and hands it to him. The crew starts to laugh. It is Allen now, who has a big smile on his face. Ariella then says. "I assume you know how to swab a deck, Mr. Greythorn. If you do not, ask Mr. Allen." she turns and walks off leaving Fernando holding the mop as the crew still laughs.

    Later that afternoon, Fernando is still swabbing the deck. The crew watches him somewhat amused. Allen looks at him with and says. "You missed a spot." They both laugh a bit.

    Fernando asks Allen, "So, Allen, what made you decide to join this ship's crew?"

    Allen ponders the question for a moment then answers, "Well, my village was attacked by the orcneas right before the second Orcnea War began. My parents were both killed. I was only seven and I was sent to stay with my uncle in South Haven. I remained there until last year when the *Red Dawn* stopped for supplies. I asked one of them if they were looking for any new crew members. The Captain heard me ask and said she could use me. My uncle wasn't going to let me go but, the Captain..." Allen pauses and thinks back to Ariella with her glowing hand around his uncle's neck. "Let's just say she persuaded him. Anyway, that was when I joined her crew."

    Ariella comes down the stairs and approaches them. "Mr. Greythorn, would you please join me for lunch?"

    "Of course, Captain," Fernando says. "It would be my pleasure."

    Ariella looks around at the freshly swabbed deck and says, "Looks like you did a fine job on the deck, Mr. Greythorn."

    "Thank you, Captain," Fernando says as he places the mop in the bucket.

    Then she looks at Allen's side with disapproval. She walks up to Allen and says quietly to him, "If I didn't know better, Mr. Allen, I would say that you didn't even try. That is not like you, Allen. Are you feeling well?"

    "Yes, Captain," Allen says, looking down. "I will do better, Captain."

    "See that you do, Allen," Ariella replies. She turns and says to Fernando, "Come, Mr. Greythorn, we have matters to discuss."

    Ariella and Fernando walk away as Allen puts his mop in his bucket. Frustrated, he kicks the bucket, knocking it over.

    "Easy there," Drake says. "Allen, are you alright?"

    "Yes," Allen answers as he closes his eyes.

    "Are you sure?" Drake asks, looking at the deck. "If you ask me I'd say you were upset with something or someone."

    Allen picks up the mop and as he begins to clean up the water he just dumped he says to Drake, "I am not mad at anyone in particular, Drake. I am just..." he stops himself unsure how to explain. "I don't know," he says as he cleans up his mess.

    "Are you jealous of Greythorn?" Drake asks.

    "No!" Allen protests. Then looking down he says, "Well, maybe kind of. I don't know. He is a really nice guy."

    "Yes, he is," Drake says. "Almost too nice."

    "I can't explain it. Ever since he has been aboard, the Captain has been..."

"A lot nicer," Drake finishes.

They both laugh a little and Allen says, "I don't know. I guess it shouldn't bother me."

"I think I know what you mean," Drake says. He looks around to see if anyone is nearby. Then he says quietly to Allen, "You know, the new word is that you and Miss Marie may have something going on."

Allen smiles and says, "How do you know about that?"

Drake says, "You know how fast news spreads on the *Red Dawn*."

"I guess," Allen replies as he finishes cleaning his mess.

"So maybe you should be happy Greythorn is on board," Drake says. "Otherwise the Capt'n may not let you play with her."

"I don't know what you are talking about," Allen says as he empties the bucket of dirty water over the rail.

"I don't mean to embarrass you," Drake says. "We all know how the Capt'n treats you, and we all know that you like it."

"I am done with this conversation," Allen says as he goes below deck.

Drake follows him to the stairs. "Hey, Allen! Should we get Marie a whip too?" He yells down and laughs.

Allen closes his eyes and clinches his fist. After taking a moment to calm himself Allen walks off.

Fernando and Ariella are having lunch in her personal quarters. She says to Fernando, "So, Mr. Greythorn, what exactly do you mean when you say that a part of this treasure belongs to you?"

Fernando looks up from his plate. He looks at Ariella and asks, "Captain, what do you know about this treasure besides that it is your fathers?"

"I know that it is from a time before I was born," Ariella replies. "My father split up the treasure after they rescued me from a ship that was attacked by orcneas. He then hid his portion of the treasure. He put the map in care of the Goblin Trade Company. After my father was killed, the instructions that he left them were clear. They contacted me to inform me that they had the map and all I needed to do was come and retrieve it. This all went according to plan until you, Mr. Greythorn, stole my father's map that was intended for me. So now tell me, what is your stake in this?"

"I will, but first you said that your father rescued you from orcneas? Was that ship named the *White Feather*?"

"Yes, Mr. Greythorn, I assume you already know that my father, Red Beard, is not my father by blood."

"Since you are not a dwarf, I assumed it was either that or you were half dwarf."

"Well let me enlighten you," Ariella explains, "Red Beard is not my real father. He did, however, save me when my mother's ship was attacked by orcneas. You see, my father, Red Beard, came across the *White Feather* in distress after an orcnea attack. When the crew of the *Red Dawn* arrived they killed the orcneas and searched the ship for survivors. My mother was alive but badly wounded. My father healed her as much as he could, but as you may be aware, Mr. Greythorn, healing spells become less and less effective when cast more than once on the same wounds."

"Yes," Fernando replies. "I am aware of that."

Ariella continues her story, "He was able to heal my mother, but not completely. She was pregnant with me at the time, and she was still weak from her injuries when she began to give birth. My mother lost even more blood and though my father tried everything he could think of, he could not save her. She died giving birth to me, Mr. Greythorn."

"I am so sorry," Fernando says sadly.

"The dwarf you call Red Beard, delivered me and raised me as his own. I became the only survivor of the *White Feather*," she explains. "The ship eventually sank as it was too badly damaged." Ariella walks over and opens a small jewelry box on her desk and pulls out a locket. "This, Mr. Greythorn, is all I have from my mother. Red Beard tried to find my real father but had no luck."

"I am very sorry for your loss," Fernando says. "I, too, lost someone on the *White Feather*. My father was on that ship when it was attacked. He had a sword that was bound to him by magic. While the sword is very powerful it will only serve someone of Greythorn blood. It is my hope that somewhere in your father's treasure is my family's sword."

"I am beginning to understand you, Mr. Greythorn. If your family's sword is a part of my father's treasure, you may have it."

"Thank you, Ariella," Fernando says seductively.

Ariella looks at him sternly and says, "Mr. Greythorn, while I admire your persistence, you will still address me as either Captain or ma'am. Do you understand me?"

Fernando smiles and says, "Yes, ma'am. You can't blame a man for trying though."

Ariella smiles and says, "I suppose not."

"I do have another question however. If I may ask."

"What is it, Mr. Greythorn?"

"Well, I was wondering, after you took over the *Red Dawn* a year ago, why did you never dock at Sheathelm and search for Chance?"

Ariella is thrown off by the question. She takes a drink from her mug and explains, "Mr. Greythorn, you have to understand that I have spent half my life making sure that no man would ever steal my heart again. Until yesterday I never knew the truth about why I never heard from Chance. There was I moment that I almost set sail for Sheathelm, but when you spend half your years living a lie it is hard to let go."

"I understand," Fernando says as he takes a drink. He then asks, "So your feelings for him...?"

"Are none of your concern," Ariella says coldly.

Up in the crow's nest of the *Red Dawn* the lookout spies a dark thundercloud ahead. Bolts of lightning are flashing in the concentrated cloud. He calls down, "Storm ahead!" He rings the bell to alert the crew.

The crew runs to the railings and look off into the distance. Most of the men are nervous, while a few, like Drake and Leon, remain calm.

Torgus, who is sitting down below in his quarters, is in a meditative state. With incense burning around him he suddenly opens his eyes and says, "Orcneas."

Fernando and Ariella look at each other when the bell sounds. They immediately stand up and head for the door. Marie enters the room from the stairway and nervously asks. "What is it, Captain?"

Ariella opens her door and looks though the officer's quarters. Outside she can see the dark clouds. She turns and says to Marie, "It looks like a strong storm. Stay inside—do you understand me?"

Marie nods her head then returns to the other room closing the door behind her.

Ariella and Fernando leave the cabin and walk out onto the deck to see the dark storm approaching from the horizon, unaware of the true danger inside.

Chapter 8
Eye of the Storm

The waves of the oncoming storm crash against the *Red Dawn*. The crew is getting soaked with the raging sea. Rain now starts to pour down and visibility is almost completely gone.

Ariella and the crew stare off into the dark storm. Torgus comes up from below deck and makes haste to the Captain's side. He yells over the roar of the storm, "Captain! This is no ordinary storm. I think these are orcneas we are dealing with."

"Are you sure?" She asks, yelling over the wind.

"Yes, captain, I sense them close by."

Ariella calls down to Drake, "Prepare everyone for battle. Now!"

Drake nods and starts to make his way around the ship warning everyone.

Leon looks at Allen and says, "Where's your weapon, boy?"

Allen looks up at Leon then turns and makes his way down below. Squeezing through the men as they make their way through the narrow passage, Allen finally makes it to his hammock. Underneath there is a chest. Allen opens it and pulls out a short sword. He nervously looks at it before closing the chest and returning topside.

"Can you see them through the storm?" Ariella asks Torgus.

"Yes, I can," Torgus answers, "but I'll have to cast the spell to do it!" Torgus closes his eyes for a moment. When he opens them once more they are glowing with blue light. He looks out into the tempest and says, "Captain, they are right there." He points off the port bow.

Just then a large bolt of lightning hits the ship. This bolt does not come from above. Instead it comes from the direction from which Torgus had pointed. Splinters of wood explode from where the bolt strikes. Two men are thrown from the explosion and land unconscious on the deck.

The rest of the crew scatters as lighting from the storm lights the sky. For the first time the crew can see the silhouette of the larger orcnea ship. It slowly comes into view as grappling hooks fly in and attach to the railing of the *Red Dawn*. Now tied together, the ships are brought closer by the grappling lines.

"Here they come!" Ariella calls out to the crew.

The two ships collide and the jolt sends some of the crew to their knees. Torgus, who can see clearly through the rain, studies the enemy ship. The large ship with three masts is bigger in size than the *Red Dawn*. As typical of orcnea ships the rough design may not make it the fastest or most maneuverable, but it is tough. Torgus holds out his hands before him and magically forms a large stone that when released will become a deadly projectile.

Drake wipes rain from his bald head then stands defiantly in the storm griping his sword tightly. Allen with his short sword looks on nervously. Then suddenly an area over the front port side of the ship starts to crackle with sparks of lightning. Torgus yells to the crew standing in the area, "Spark storm! Get out of there!" A few of the crew leap out of the affected area to safety. Leon is not as fortunate and is shocked several times. He turns to flee as an orcnea throws a spear striking him in his right shoulder. This causes Leon to fall to his knees. The spark storm continues to shock those who are caught within its range. Several others collapse and fall, but Leon continues to try to crawl to safety.

Allen watches for a moment, then sheaths his sword and runs into the electrical field. Ariella yells, "Allen! Don't!" but her warning is too late. Allen runs in and tries to help Leon up. Every moment in this zone seems to hurt the men, but Allen continues to push himself past the pain. The weight of Leon becomes too much for Allen to bear and they both start to falter.

Ariella casts a spell and a blue glow passes over her body. She runs into the crackling air and assists Allen in carrying Leon to safety. The Captain, now immune to the effects of the lightning, returns to the spell zone and begins to drag others to safety. She then stops and stares over at the other ship. She spots two orcnea shamans with their hands out in front of them. The palms of their hands are glowing with magical energy. Figuring that they are the ones behind the spark storm, she yells out, "Torgus! Take out those shamans." With that, she concentrates on a spell of her own. She creates a large fireball in her hands and takes aim at one of the orcneas.

The orcnea shaman responsible for the spark storm pauses in his ritual casting and looks with great fear as Ariella releases the fire ball right at him. He ducks for cover and the fireball misses, but the spark storm quickly disappears.

Torgus releases his spell at the other shaman. A scull size rock is hurled towards the orcnea. Even though this shaman also ducks for safety, it does him little good as Torgus was aiming at the ship's deck where the orcnea stood. The wood of the orcnea ship splinters and explodes as the speeding rock slams into it. The force of the impact sends the enemy flying.

Two more orcnea shamans charge electrical bolts, and throw them at the *Red Dawn*. The ship is now getting bombarded by the spells. Through it all the crew of the *Red Dawn* stands ready for combat, however no orcneas ever attempt to board the ship.

Ariella yells to Torgus, "Catch those bolts, Torgus. They are tearing our ship apart!"

Torgus waits for the next bolt of lightning to come his way. It does not take long before an orcnea casts another spell at the deck of the *Red Dawn*. The spell is intended to hit right next to Torgus. He quickly moves his hands and pulls the lighting to him. Though it is a dangerous spell to attempt, Torgus has successfully caught the orcnea's lightning bolt in his hands and holds it as he prepares to fire it back. The shaman that cast it yells out something in orcneish. Torgus then aims the spell at the attacking ship and launches it. The impact damages the orcnea ship, and the shamans stop casting their spells.

For a few moments only the sound of the raging storm fills the air. Allen escorts Leon to the far side of the ship. When they reach the stairs to the quarter deck Leon sits down on the stairs. Allen checks on the spear stuck in Leon's shoulder.

"How bad is it?" Leon asks.

"I don't know," Allen replies. "Torgus will have to look at it."

Waiting in the middle of the deck Fernando holds a sword in each hand and watches the edge of the ship for any signs of movement. Suddenly the brief reprieve is broken with the sound of the loud war-cry of orcneas as they charge over the railings onto the deck of the *Red Dawn*.

High in the storm above, Chance flies in eagle form as fast as he can through the vortex of clouds. Diving strait down to gain more speed, he finds he is unable to see very far ahead. He slows his descent to match his speed to that of the falling rain around him. With the rain no longer getting in his eyes he can see much more clearly.

Looking down he sees the two ships locked in combat. Orcneas are charging across to the deck of the *Red Dawn* as the melee is just getting underway. He descends as he watches Drake waste no time in spilling the orcneas' blood. Using all his strength Drake uses his sword to carve into one orcnea after another. A short distance away Fernando and Ariella are side by side. As orcneas try to approach them they easily parry the attacks and strike back at them. Chance then looks at the orcnea ship. He watches as the shamans begin to shoot their bolts of lightning at the *Red Dawn* again. He dives right for one of them and pulls up at the last moment while he transforms back into his elven form. The shaman turns quickly to face him, but he is not fast enough to dodge the two large jets of flame that shoot out of Chance's hands. Before the orcnea has time to react, Chance engulfs him in fire. The orcnea howls in pain and falls back over the railing and down onto the lower deck where he crashes through a table. Two orcneas near the table look up, and when they spot Chance, they start to head his way.

On the *Red Dawn* Ariella is locked in combat. Through the chaos she is able to see an orcnea heading into the officers' quarters and towards her cabin. Looking around she finds only Allen nearby. "Allen!" she calls. Allen looks up from assisting Leon and sees the captain pointing to the now open cabin door. "Help Marie!"

"Go," Leon says. "Protect the girl."

Allen nods to Leon then rushes through the officers' quarters as he draws his sword. He enters the Captain's quarters at the stern of the ship. The loud storm outside is replaced with the sound of Marie's scream. At the far end of the room the orcnea has Marie by the wrist and is laughing at her.

"Hey!" Allen yells at the orcnea, "Why don't you fight someone who can fight back?"

The orcnea releases Marie's wrist and says something in orcneish that Allen cannot understand. The orcnea then laughs, and with his sword also drawn, he starts to come at Allen. The large reddish skinned creature is crudely dressed. He has worn leather on his chest and groin. His bare arms and legs offer little protection for his limbs but allows him to move quickly. Long pointed ears to stick out the sides of his leather cap. His feet are bare. Allen is only as tall as this orcnea's chest.

Marie runs through the door and into the hallway she was hiding in earlier. She hides behind the door but continues to peek out. The orcnea goes straight for Allen, grabbing and throwing chairs out of his way as he moves. Allen waits nervously assessing the situation. Then as the orcnea gets close he swings his sword at Allen. With very little room to maneuver, Allen dives under the small dining table in the center of the room. The orcnea flips over the table and as it flies back against the wall, Allen stands up and slashes his sword across the orcnea's chest. The tattered leather absorbs most of the strike but the orcnea is now bleeding.

The orcnea lets out a menacing yell as he swings at Allen again. This time Allen simply backs up out of reach. The orcnea wildly swings again as Allen's back hits the wall behind him. Allen is careful not to fall or trip over the debris all over the floor. The orcnea, however, stumbles over a chair and Allen sees an opening and makes his move. He steps forward and thrusts his sword in to the orcnea's gut. The orcnea stops and drops his sword. Letting out a painful grunt he grabs Allen's face with both hands. Allen grips his sword tightly and as he looks the creature in the eyes he twists his blade. The orcnea's yellow eyes almost seem to glow as he pushes Allen away. Allen manages to hang on to his sword, pulling the now bloody weapon from the orcnea who holds his hands over the wound. Allen hesitates, not sure what to do next.

The orcnea turns his head to find his sword on the ground next to him. He makes his move for it, and grabbing it off the ground he turns to attack Allen. To his surprise, however, the orcnea finds himself once again impaled on Allen's sword. The orcnea lets out his last breath as he drops to his knees. Then as Allen pulls back his blood soaked sword, the orcnea falls face down to the floor.

Allen turns to Marie and asks, "Are you alright?"

She doesn't say anything. She just stands there behind the door in shock for a moment. Then looking past Allen she sees another orcnea enter the room behind him. "Allen, look out!" She warns.

This orcnea has a short whip much like the cat of nine tales, but heavier, and with metal barbs tied into the knots. Before Allen is able to turn around, the orcnea whips Allen's back. Allen turns to face the orcnea just as he tries to whip Allen for a second time. Allen puts his arm up and the whip wraps around Allen's wrist. Allen looks at the orcnea and says, "I know a woman who whips harder than that." Allen then yanks the whip from the orcnea's hand, then charges at the red creature.

Outside on the deck, Fernando and Ariella are having little problem with the invaders. Fernando easily parries one orcnea's attack, and then with both swords he spins around and thrusts them both deep into the orcnea's chest. Then as he ducks another attack he slashes the attacking orcnea across the neck, and before the orcnea even hits the deck he is dead.

Ariella's approach is a little different. In one hand she has a short sword she uses to parry oncoming attacks with. For offense, however, she is wielding an electrical whip formed from magic. It is has a short reach, but it is very powerful. With the Captain's graceful movements it almost looks like a dance as she keeps the attacking orcneas at bay. When an orcnea steps within her reach she makes him pay.

On the other ship Chance continues to burn any orcnea that tries to challenge him. With flames jetting from both hands he makes his way across the deck to the shamans on the other side. After dealing with them Chance hurls a fireball at the main mast. This ignites the tree-like mast and captures everyone's attention. Ariella turns to see the fire on the orcnea ship but does not see Chance.

This distraction, however, allows an orcnea to take Ariella by surprise. One of the last remaining orcneas on the deck of the *Red Dawn* charges the Captain and knocks her down. The lightning whip disappears and she is left stunned and looking up as the orcnea begins to swing his sword at her. Just as the sword is about to strike, Fernando intercepts the blade with his own sword. He looks at the orcnea and says, "That is no way to treat a lady." Then with a quick twist of his sword he throws the orcnea off balance and impales his blade into the orcnea. The life fades from the orcnea's eyes as he collapses.

Fernando holds out his hand to Ariella. She takes it and he swiftly pulls her up and into his arms. Fernando takes the opportunity to kiss the Captain who is completely caught off guard. She resists the kiss at first but is soon gives in to passion.

Fernando, still holding Ariella, asks, "Are you alright?" Ariella is lost in his gaze.

"Look! It's Chance!" Jacob yells out.

"The Orcnea Slayer has returned," calls out another voice.

Ariella glances over to the other ship and can see Chance looking back at her. She realizes that he had seen it all. Chance turns around and returns his attention to the orcneas. He unleashes a raging fire that surrounds him and engulfs the entire deck of the orcnea ship. Within the flames, Chance stands completely unharmed. In disbelief Ariella says to herself, "He came back." She watches the towering flames begin to devour the orcnea ship. Chance is unable to see Ariella break free from Fernando and slap him across the face.

With no orcnea threat left on the deck of the *Red Dawn*, the crew watches in silence as Chance makes his way through the flames and down a stairway into the lower deck of the orcnea ship. Ariella and the others watch as orcnea after orcnea emerge from the lower level completely in flames. Some manage to throw themselves into the sea, others are unable to make it as they burn to death on deck.

Ariella watches the carnage looking a bit unnerved. "By the Gods," she says.

Drake, watching on, says, "Burn them all, Orcnea Slayer."

Ariella calls out, "Cut those grapple lines now!"

The men run to the edge of the ship and begin cutting the lines that bind the two ships together. The storm now begins to clear up rapidly and soon the sun begins to break through the clouds. The *Red Dawn* begins to drift away from the ship that now burns like an inferno.

Ariella then remembers Allen and calls out, "Marie!" She immediately runs to her quarters and Fernando follows. As they enter the cabin they see Allen covered with blood standing over four dead orcneas.

Fernando surveys the damage and says, "Impressive."

"Marie?" Ariella asks, "Are you two alright?"

Allen looks at Marie to see how she is doing. Marie smiles and says, "Yes, ma'am, thanks to Allen."

"Good work, Allen," Ariella says.

"I only did what I had to, Captain," Allen answers with blank look. He then walks right past Ariella and Fernando and out the door.

On the deck, Torgus is with Leon who is still sitting with the spear in his shoulder. Drake walks up to them and says to Leon, "Looks like I got the most kills this time."

They laugh as Torgus says to Leon, "Now hold still, lad. This is going to hurt." Torgus pulls the spear from his back as Leon closes his eyes and winces in pain. "Alright, now that it's out I will try to heal the wounds." Torgus holds up his hand and as it begins to glow with a white energy, he touches Leon's shoulder and the wound begins to heal. "That's all I can do, my friend. The rest of it will have to heal on its own."

Leon stands up and shrugs his shoulder. He winces in pain and says, "Thanks."

Allen walks out on deck and past them as if he doesn't notice them. He is pale in the face, and Drake asks him, "Allen? Are you alright?"

Allen looks up at Drake as if he didn't hear him then after pausing for a moment he runs to the rail of the ship and violently vomits over the edge.

Drake then walks over and places his hand on Allen's shoulder. He asks again, "Are you alright?"

Allen, catching his breath looks at Leon and says, "I am fine. Thanks."

"Is Marie alright?" Leon asks sounding fearful of the answer.

"Yes," Allen says, "She is fine."

"Don't worry, Allen, we understand. Your first kill can be..." Drake stops and looks at Leon who nods.

"Horrible," Allen finishes his thought. "I was so afraid, at first then," he pauses, "and then I wasn't. When the second orcnea attacked I became filled with rage. I easily killed him. Then the third one came in and—"

"Wait a second," Drake interrupts. "Third? You killed three orcneas?"

"Four, actually," Allen answers, staring off at the horizon.

Leon says, "So, let me get this straight, you risk yourself to pull my ass to safety, then go and protect that pretty young girl from not just one, but four orcneas? Damn, I think I am getting too old for this crap." He looks at Drake as they all laugh.

Ariella emerges from the officers' quarters and says, "Find me one of these orcneas that is still alive!"

"Aye, Capt'n," John says, as he begins to search the orcneas.

As if from out of nowhere Chance's voice says, "This may be useful information." Chance is standing there, without a mark on him. He reaches under his breastplate and pulls out handful of scorched scrolls. "A few of them are damaged," he says, "but we should be able to read them still. I only got a glimpse of them, but they appeared to be battle plans. Is everyone alright here?"

Ariella looks at Torgus and asks, "How many did we lose?"

Torgus looks down and sighs heavily and answers, "We lost Mr. Richards and Mr. Berry."

"Then we were very fortunate indeed to have only lost two," Ariella replies. She tries to make eye contact with Chance but he avoids it as he looks around the ship. She continues, "Chance, if you hadn't come back it would have been much worse. Thank you."

"You don't have to thank me," Chance says as he now makes eye contact with her. The look in his eyes is cold and distant. "I will help heal the remainder of the wounded."

"Chance," Ariella begins to say.

"I will start by healing those who are hurt the worst," Chance says not letting her finish. "Then, when we get underway, we can look at these plans together."

As Chance walks past Ariella, Leon whispers to Drake, "What is going on? They are acting like they don't know each other."

"I am not sure," Drake says under his breath, "but something ain't right."

John calls out, "Capt'n! I found an orcnea that is still alive!"

Ariella looks over at John and says, "Good. Now take him down below and lock him up."

"Yes, ma'am," John answers. Drake and Leon help John take the orcnea below.

Ariella looks around and finds Chance tending to a few of the injured men. She walks over to him and watches as he places his white glowing hands on one of them. As he does the man's injuries are mostly healed.

"Thank you, Mr. Na'Moon," the crewman says to him.

"You're welcome," Chance says.

The man walks away as Ariella asks, "Chance, can we please talk?"

Chance almost ignoring her says, "I think everyone is healed. I will not be much help with repairs, but I'll do what I can."

"Chance, please!" Ariella yells as she grabs his arm.

Chance stands there looking down, once again not able to look her in the eyes. He doesn't say a word as Ariella continues to hold his arm. "Look at me," Ariella says quietly, almost begging, "Please."

Chance looks up, and now Ariella can see the pain in his eyes. "What is it?" he asks softly.

"What you saw earlier," Ariella begins to explain, "It's not what you think."

"It doesn't matter if it is," Chance replies, "I have no claim to you. I expected you to find someone else by now."

"Fernando Greythorn is not my lover!" Ariella shouts. Ariella then looks around at the crew realizing how loud she had just said it. Some of the crew who have stopped working to listen jump back to their tasks as the Captain looks in their direction. She then quietly continues, "I have only known him for two days."

"Two days?" Chance asks sounding disappointed.

Crossroads

Ariella sighs knowing how bad that sounded. She takes a moment to calm herself, and then keeping her voice down she explains, "Fernando Greythorn knows where to find my father's treasure. Once he leads me to it, he will be gone. He means nothing to me."

"What about all the others?" Chance asks as he now looks at her.

Ariella looks at him but drops her eyes. She has a sinking feeling throughout. Knowing the answer she still asks, "What others?"

Chance says, "You know full well what I am talking about. You do have a certain reputation..."

The sinking feeling is now quickly replaced with anger as Ariella strikes him across the face. "How dare you!" Ariella snaps. "Those *others* would never have happened if you had come for me like you promised." Chance now is the one who looks down as she continues, "When you took those vows with that Amazon, I swore that day that no man would EVER hurt me again, and you know what? Till this day, no man has."

Ariella storms off and leaves Chance standing there alone. He looks up at the sky, and the clouds now are completely gone as the bright sun shines down on the damaged, blood stained deck of the *Red Dawn*.

Chapter 9
Lost Innocence

An hour passes as the crew finishes repairing what they can. "Well, that should just about do it." John says to Ariella as he stands up from a patched hole in the deck.

"Good work, John." Ariella says as she looks around the ship. The damage is still evident almost everywhere. She walks up the stairs to the quarterdeck and asks Chris, "How far to the nearest port that can handle repairs?"

Looking at the map Chris says, "Depending on the wind it's about a half days travel back to South Haven. Or we are about three days from East and West Artos."

"Mr. Greythorn," Ariella calls out. "Your assistance, if you would please."

"Of course, Captain," Fernando says as he ascends the stairs. "How may I help you?"

"We need repairs, Mr. Greythorn. The question is do we head back to South Haven, or continue around the southern edge. Considering you are the only one who knows where our final destination is, what do you think?"

"East Artos, Captain. We can retrieve the treasure from there while the repairs are being done."

"Very well. We shall make way for East Artos."

"Aye, captain." Chris says.

"I have some business to attend to now, gentlemen," Ariella says to them. "If you will excuse me." She turns and enters the Captain's lounge. Inside Chance is looking at maps that are spread out over the table. He is reading them with Torgus. Marie is sweeping the floor of the mess caused by the orcneas.

"It is just as I feared," Chance says to Torgus, "According to these orcnea battle plans, there are several dozen of these ships, and it looks as though they plan to keep the entire east coast blockaded."

Torgus looks up and says, "I think I found the next step in their plans." He hands Chance a parchment.

Chance takes the scroll and says, "It's been a while since I read orcneish, but unless I am reading this incorrectly it says that at the first moon the first group of ground troops will land and take back the north. These are orders to protect the supply and transport ships at all costs." Chance looks up at Ariella and says, "That's in three days!"

Torgus says, "Looks like there is more," He hands Chance another scroll.

Chance reads it aloud, "On the second moon the rest of the troops will arrive and they will begin the invasion starting with the city of Northwind."

"Looks like we are at war after all," Torgus says.

"I have to go back and warn Arioch," Chance says as he begins to gather up the plans.

"Torgus, would you give us a moment, please?" Ariella asks.

"Of course, Captain," Torgus says. He gets to the door, but before he leaves he turns and says, "I must apologize again to the two of you." He looks down at the floor then continues, "I am very sorry for my part in deceiving you both. I hope that you understand that it was not my wish to keep those letters from you."

"Thank you, Torgus," Ariella says.

Chance nods to Torgus and says, "It is not your fault, my friend."

"Thank you," Torgus replies as he leaves closing the door behind him.

Marie sets down her broom and says, "I am going to go get some fresh air." She then leaves quickly behind Torgus.

Now only Ariella and Chance remain. Chance finishes putting the last of the parchments in a small bag. Ariella walks slowly up to him, unsure what to say. She reaches for him and takes his hand. He stops what he is doing and they stand there in silence. He is unable to look at her as she stands before him staring up and waiting for him to say or do anything.

Chance says to her, "I am sorry about what I said earlier."

"I don't want to talk about that anymore," Ariella says. Chance looks at her with teary eyes. She places her hand on his cheek and says, "What is wrong?"

"It has been twenty years, Ariella, and even now as we stand here, I cannot have you," Chance says. He then takes her hand from his cheek and kisses it.

"Why?" Ariella asks. "We are together again. My father can no longer keep us apart."

"I know, but there are so many things happening right now," Chance says, unable to keep the kiss he saw earlier between Ariella and Fernando out of his mind.

"So go back and tell king Arioch of the orcneas," Ariella says, "Then come back." Ariella then puts her arms around Chance. "Please come back. I don't want to lose you again."

Chance embracing her tightly says, "If only it were that simple."

"Why isn't it?" Ariella asks sounding frustrated. "What ever happened to 'No ocean or sea can keep you from me'?"

Chance kisses her on the forehead. "This time it isn't either of those things that are the problem," he pauses and then says, "Unless you are willing to give up all this and come stay with me in Sheathelm?"

"What?" Ariella questions. "Leave my ship and crew? Chance, this is my whole life. I can't just walk away from it just like that."

"I know," Chance says.

"But you could come and be with me," Ariella says.

"I still have my children," Chance explains. "I can't ask them to leave everything behind to live on a ship."

"Don't you send them to Dicean for magic training?" Ariella asks.

Chance asks, "How did you know that?"

"You live in the Palace with Arioch," Ariella answers. "Why wouldn't you send them to the best magic school in all of Runefell?"

Chance sighs and replies, "I suppose."

"Then come be with me when they are away," she says.

"You know that wouldn't be the same," Chance answers.

Ariella looks down and sadly says, "It would be better than nothing."

Chance now lifts her chin and looks her in the eyes and says, "As long as the orcneas are a threat I cannot allow myself to..." he drops his eyes looking down for a moment. He looks back up at her and says, "I have already lost someone I loved to them. I can't lose you too."

"Then come back and be with me," she says grasping his hands. "Then you know I'll be safe."

Chance thinks for a moment before saying, "You just continue west to Artos for now. According to the plans and maps it doesn't look like the orcneas are going there. I have to go back to Sheathelm. If the orcneas are planning an attack then I have to be there."

Ariella realizes that she cannot stop him from leaving again. She lowers her head and says, "I understand." She then smiles and says, "Can you at least stay the night? I promise I'll make it worth it."

Chance smiles and says, "As much as I would love to..." he stops, and again the thought of Ariella kissing Fernando flashes in his head. "I just cannot." He then lifts her chin and says, "Look at me." He tries to look her in the eyes but she continues to look down. "Ariella, look at me, please." She looks up with watery eyes and doesn't say a word. He then asks, "As you look into my eyes, can you honestly tell me that I am the same person you fell in love with years ago?"

A tear rolls down her cheek as Chance wipes it away. With a sad smile she says, "On the surface no, but I can see deep down you are still the same."

Chance then says, "As I look into your eyes I too can still see the girl I once knew." He wipes away more tears from her face and says, "I also see a whole new woman that I have never met. We have spent half our lives apart since we last saw each other. Yes, there is still a part of me that hasn't changed, but we both have been through so much."

Ariella now thinks back to Chance on the orcnea ship earlier. With the fire all around him he burned the orcneas without remorse. She finally says to Chance, "I know. I guess after reading your letters last night I just felt like..."

"I know," Chance says. "When I read your letters it was like I was eighteen again."

"So now what?" Ariella asks.

"For us? I don't know," Chance answers, "but I do know that I have to return to Sheathelm and help defend the kingdom from the orcneas. After that I just don't know. I promise I will come see you when I can."

"You have made that promise before," Ariella snaps.

"I will," Chance tells her reassuringly. He puts his arms around her and holds her close.

She sighs and holds Chance tightly and says, "Can you at least stay and hold me for a while?"

Chance closes his eyes and says, "Of course." Then in silence they hold onto each other tight.

On deck, many of the crew are distracted by the sight of the young and beautiful Marie as she walks with purpose across the deck to Drake and Leon, "Have you seen Allen?"

Leon laughs and says, "Aye, you mean the new Orcnea Slayer?"

Drake points down the stairs and says, "I think I saw him down below."

"Thank you," Marie says as she turns and head towards the stairs.

Drake and Leon watch her walk away as Drake turns to Leon and asks, "What do you think she wants with Allen?"

Leon laughs a bit and answers, "What do you think?" They both chuckle.

Marie cautiously walks down the steps below deck looking for Allen. She makes her way through the lower deck stepping around all the clutter as she finally comes across Allen sleeping in his hammock. She watches him for a while, then as she starts to lean in for a kiss, Allen opens his eyes. Surprised, he jumps and tries to sit up. In the struggle he only manages to fall out of the hammock and onto the floor.

"Ow!" he yells as he quickly stands up getting tangled in the hammock. "What are you doing here?" he asks.

"I just wanted to thank you," Marie says shyly looking down.

"For what?" Allen asks as he untangles himself and pushes the hammock netting off his head.

"For saving me," Marie says looking still at the floor.

"Oh," Allen replies. He smiles then takes her hand and says, "Your wel—"

Before Allen can even finish the words, Marie grabs his shirt, pulls him close and kisses him. Allen, caught off guard at first, resists but as the kiss goes on he closes his eyes and gives in.

When they break Allen says, "Well that was awkward."

"What do you mean?" Marie asks.

"I mean...I suppose it wasn't that good was it?" Allen asks unsure of himself.

"Oh," Marie gasps. "I see." Devastated by his words, Marie's eyes begin to water. "I am sorry," she says as she turns to leave.

"No, wait," Allen says as he reaches for her arm. She turns around and looks down as the tears fall to the floor. "That is not what I meant," Allen says as he gently lifts her chin to look at her.

"Then what did you mean?" she asks.

"I was nervous," Allen explains, "I don't have much experience with girls and..." Allen desperately searches for the words that will not make matters worse. "I just meant that I probably wasn't that good, and that I am sorry if I...if I didn't do it right. I didn't mean to say that I didn't enjoy it." He leans in closer and says, "Or, that I didn't want to do it again."

He softly kisses her as she puts her arms around his neck. The kiss becomes a passionate one and by the time it is over both Allen and Marie stare at each other out of breath.

"You were right, Allen," Marie says with a smile, "that was much better."

Allen smiles and without another word Marie turns and walks away. Allen stands there for a moment with a smile on his face before sitting back down on his hammock. Then while lost in his thoughts of Marie, he lies back down and loses his balance falling onto the floor yet again.

Up on deck, Fernando watches out over the horizon, as Ariella and Chance emerge from the Captain's lounge. He turns his attention to them as he tries not to be too obvious that he is listening in.

"Are you sure you won't reconsider?" Ariella asks. "You could leave in the morning."

"I am sorry," Chance says, "We are heading in opposite directions. I must not delay any longer. If I leave now I can be there by morning."

Ariella quietly says to Chance, "Chance, I am not waiting for you this time. I just can't. Not again."

Chance replies, "I understand. I wouldn't expect you to." Then he glances over at Fernando.

Ariella sees his look and says with a sigh, "I don't mean him. I am just saying that I will not wait for you or your letters this time." Then with a smile she laughs and adds, "Who knows, maybe by the time you see me next, I will be the one who is married."

Chance laughs and says, "Well, whoever has what it takes to make you settle down will be a lucky man." He looks at Fernando who quickly looks away, as if he wasn't listening.

"No man will ever make me settle down," She replies. "I am going to make my man do as I wish. He will follow me wherever I go and do as I please."

He smiles at her for a moment then finally says, "Goodbye, Ariella."

Ariella's smile fades as she replies, "Goodbye, Chance."

Chance walks to the side of the ship next to Fernando, who is alone. He puts out his hand and says, "Mr. Greythorn, it was a pleasure seeing you again."

Fernando shakes his hand and says, "The pleasure was all mine, Mr. Na'Moon."

Chance shakes his hand and says quietly to him, "Take good care of her."

"Of course," Fernando replies quietly. "I understand."

As Fernando tries to release the handshake Chance does not let go. He instead pulls Fernando close to him and says in a soft but intense voice, "I don't think you do, so let me make myself clear. I know of your reputation, Mr. Greythorn. You have a way with the ladies. If I find out that you are using her, or hurt her in anyway, I will find you." Chance finally releases his grip.

"Of that, my friend, I have no doubt," Fernando replies, as he looks around and smiles as if to show the crew that everything is fine.

John and Jacob are down on the lower deck watching. John asks Jacob, "What do you think that was about?"

"Not sure," Jacob answers, "But I certainly don't think it was a simple goodbye."

Chance walks over to the edge of the ship and transforms once again into a giant eagle and grabs the small bag containing the orcnea plans in his talons as he takes flight. Marie, who is still smiling from her kiss with Allen walks up and stands next to Ariella. They watch as Chance flies away. The Captain looks at her and asks in a teasing way, "So how is Mr. Allen? I assume that is why you have such a big smile on your face."

Marie smiles and looks up at the sky. "He is wonderful," she says.

Ariella replies, "Good for you, Marie. I am very happy for you."

John approaches Ariella and says, "Captain, the orcnea that we captured is awake now."

"Oh, yes, I almost forgot him," she replies. Then she calls out to her two big enforcers, "Drake, would you and Leon please help prepare the orcnea for an interrogation. I will be down in a few moments."

"Aye, Capt'n." Drake answers.

Leon and Drake go below to the brig. Torgus asks, "What are you going to do with him, Captain?"

"I am just going to ask him a few questions," Ariella answers. "He just better hope that he knows the answers."

Chapter 10
Years Lost and Gained

A short time later Ariella is alone in the Captain's lounge. She walks over to the desk and opens a drawer. She lifts the bottom up revealing a hidden compartment inside. She pulls out a dark leather tomb before closing the drawer again.

Down below in the brig, Drake and Leon secure the orcnea to chains that are mounted on the wall. The orcnea struggles but they are able to handle him without any problem.

Ariella walks in holding the dark book. Leon says to her, "All set, Captain. Just let me know if you want me to kill it when you are done."

"Thank you, gentlemen," Ariella says, "that will be all."

"Aye, Capt'n," Drake says as they leave.

Torgus looks at the book Ariella is carrying and asks, "What is that?"

"It's just a little something that our old friend, Corthag, left behind," Ariella answers with a smile.

"Corthag's dark book?" Torgus questions. "Ariella, you should not use those spells."

"Your concern is noted, my friend, Ariella says as she sets the book on the table. "Let's just see if our friend here will cooperate without it."

"I wish we had done this earlier while Chance was still here," Torgus says.

"It won't make much difference," Ariella says, "I doubt this grunt soldier knows anything that we don't already know from the plans."

"You are probably right," Torgus says, "but just in case he does say something important, I would feel better if Chance was here to hear it."

"I understand," Ariella says as she walks up to the orcnea. "To be perfectly honest though, I don't really feel comfortable with Chance watching me do this. I don't think he would approve of my methods."

"Ariella, you saw what Chance did today on that ship," Torgus says to her. "He has no sympathy for orcneas."

"I know that," Ariella says. "I am not worried about him feeling sorry for the orcnea. I just don't want him to see *me* causing the suffering."

Torgus replies, "Judging from his actions today, I'd wager that it may not bother him as much as you fear."

"You may be right, Torgus," she says sadly. "We have both been through a lot in our lives, but I still prefer that he does not see my darker side. Now then, cast a spell that will allow this...*thing*...to talk to us."

"Yes, Captain," Torgus says as he concentrates and waves his hand over the orcneas face. Then looking at the orcnea he asks, "Can you understand me?"

The orcnea looks at him surprised and answers with a low rough voice, "Yes, dwarf, I can."

"Good," Ariella says, "I have to ask you a few questions."

The orcnea laughs, "I know nothing, and even if I did I wouldn't tell you."

Torgus walks back and sits down in a chair. The orcnea looks at the

Captain and laughs as he says, "I do not fear you, female."

"That's alright," Ariella says, "soon you will understand why I am the one in charge here." She removes her glove and a dark glow emanates from her hand as she places it on the orcneas head.

The agonizing screams of the orcnea can be heard through the cabin walls. Drake says to Leon, "Sounds like the Capt'n isn't going to leave you with anything left to fight."

"Well, that's too bad," Leon says. "I didn't get to see any action today."

Drake says, "Allen did more fighting today than you."

They laugh a bit and Leon says, "The boy did good though didn't he?"

"Aye, that he did," Drake answers.

At the front of the ship Marie sits with the wind blowing through her hair. She is looking out over the blue sea watching the waves. Fernando and Allen are talking when Fernando notices her. He nudges Allen and says, "Now, Mr. Allen, is your chance. With the fresh air, the beautiful clear sky, it is the perfect opportunity to get close to her."

"Thanks, Fernando," Allen says. "For the record, though, we have already gotten pretty close." Fernando gives him a smile as Allen turns back and heads towards Marie. When he finally reaches her he says, "Quite a view, isn't it?"

Marie, who did not see him approach, jumps a bit as she turns and says, "Oh, Allen. I didn't hear you coming."

"Sorry," Allen replies, "I didn't mean to startle you."

Marie smiles and pulls her hair back from her face and says, "That's alright, Allen. And yes, it is a beautiful view."

Staring at Marie, Allen says under his breath, "*I'll say.*"

"What was that?" Marie asks.

Allen nervously says, "I said, yes it is a beautiful view."

"Hard to believe that only a few hours ago we were fighting an orcnea ship in the middle of a storm," Marie says.

"I know," Allen replies, "It was pretty intense there for a while."

John, Jacob, and Fernando watch Allen and Marie. John says, "Ah, young love?"

"Yes, indeed," Fernando says. "I remember my first love."

"Oh, who was she?" Jacob asks.

"Her name was Elizabeth," Fernando says as he thinks back. "I was just barely a man and she was," he stops and smiles, "well, twice my age."

"Really?" John asks, "How did you know her?"

"She was a bar maid in East Artos," Fernando says.

"So what happened?" Jacob asks.

"Her husband came back after being away at sea," Fernando answers with a laugh.

The men laugh as they continue to talk.

In the brig, the orcnea stops screaming as Ariella stops the spell.

Torgus says, "I don't think he knows anything, Captain, perhaps we should just kill him now."

"They may pay good money for him in Bastion," Ariella says. "They are always looking for entertainment in the arenas there."

"You would sell him as a slave, Captain?" Torgus asks.

"I don't like the idea much either," Ariella says as she walks over and picks up the book from the table, "but I don't like executions either. I do have one more thing that I need from him though." She flips through the pages and stops when she finds what she is looking for. She says with a smile, "Ah, yes, this is the one."

Torgus looks at her with concern and says, "Ariella, are you sure you want to do this? Once you start messing with the dark magics it is very hard to turn back. Corthag was the perfect example of that."

"Corthag was always evil, Torgus!" Ariella snaps at him. "You know how twisted he was. You, he, and my father had known each other your entire lives, and he betrayed you both. I am not like him, Torgus."

"I know you're not," Torgus says as he takes the book from her. Then looking at the page he reads aloud, "Steal Youth? Ariella, these are dark spells you are dealing with indeed."

"That is easy for you to say," Ariella replies as she snatches the book back. "You dwarves live a lot longer than humans, and elves, well they..." She stands there staring at the pages.

"So this is about Chance then?" Torgus asks.

"Torgus, look at me," Ariella says. "I am not as young as I once was, but Chance—" She slams the book down onto the table. "It's not fair!"

"Listen to me, Ariella," Torgus says softly, "Chance may not age like you and I, but there are other ways to stay young. Stealing the youth from another individual is risky and cruel."

"I know," Ariella says, "and if it were any other being than an orcnea, I wouldn't do it, but how long do you think this orcnea will last at the arenas in Bastion? Is that not cruel? They will just slaughter him for entertainment, at least I can make better use of his life."

"In the arenas, Ariella," Torgus says, "he will at least have a chance. Look, I am not going to stop you. This is your decision. I have done some things in my life that I am most certainly not proud of. Not the least of which was helping your father keep Chance's letters from you. I have robbed you of years with someone you love. Robbing this creature of his years will not make up for it, but you need to make that decision for yourself. I will not be a part of it however. Now, if you will excuse me, I am going to go down to my quarters and meditate."

Torgus passes the orcnea as it spits on the ground and says, "You dwarves will all die just like your allies, the filthy humans." The orcnea then laughs at Torgus.

Torgus stops at the door and opens it. He turns to Ariella and says, "You know, Ariella, on second thought, I don't think this orcnea will miss a few years." Torgus then walks out and says to Drake and Leon who are waiting on either side of the door, "The Captain is almost done with him."

Ariella closes the door behind Torgus. She picks up the book, and finds the spell. She says to the orcnea, "You know, in a dark sort of way I should thank you. It was the orcnea attacks on the ships that brought Chance back into my life. On the other hand, however, it is your impending attack in the north that has taken him from me again." She looks back down at the book and begins to read it out loud. It is an ancient language that is mixed with Latin, Elven, Dwarven, and even some Dragon. Holding the book with her left hand Ariella continues to read the passage as she begins to gesture with her right hand.

A darkness comes over her hand as she moves it over the orcneas chest. The orcnea screams in pain as its chest begins to glow with green light. The light is absorbed into the dark aura surrounding Ariella's hand. As this happens, hairs on the orcnea turn gray and some wrinkles form on his face. Conversely, Ariella appears to get younger. The small bits of gray in her hair turn to their original vibrant red. The small wrinkles around her eyes fade away.

After a few minutes of this the orcnea passes out and she stops. Walking over and looking in the mirror, she smiles and adjusts herself in her dress. She even checks the firmness of her breasts, and grins. Ariella walks to the door. She opens it and says to Leon and Drake, "You boys can put him back in his cell now."

"Aye, Captain," Leon answers as he stares at the Captain for a moment.

"Is something wrong?" Ariella asks.

Leon coughs and answers, "No, Captain." He and Drake then enter the room as Ariella leaves.

They unchain the orcnea and Leon asks Drake, "Did you notice something different about the Captain?"

Drake shrugs his shoulders and says, "Kind of. Not sure what it was though."

The sun begins to set in front of the ship. Ariella asks Fernando, "Well, Mr. Greythorn, I don't suppose you would like to join me this evening for dinner?"

"Captain, I would love to," Fernando answers. Then as he notices her younger appearance he adds, "Captain, have you done something with your hair?"

"Yes," Ariella says with a laugh, "something like that."

Just then a voice calls down from the crow's nest. "Captain!" the lookout calls. "More storms dead astern!"

The Captain and Fernando rush up the stairs to the quarterdeck, then up another stairway to the very top of the poop deck. With her looking glass Ariella can see far off in the distance a line of dark clouds. She then hands the looking glass to Fernando and says, "Looks like we will have company soon."

Fernando looks at the dark ominous clouds and says, "At least it will be dark soon. Perhaps if we can out run them in the night they will give up by morning."

"We can only hope, Mr. Greythorn," Ariella says to him.

Torgus walks up from the quarter deck below. He walks to the back of the ship and says, "I knew I sensed trouble. At least they are behind us, Captain. It will take them a while to catch up, but we are going to have to create a little extra wind of our own."

"I'll grab the wind stones," Ariella says as she leaves to her cabin.

"Wind stones?" questions Fernando.

Torgus laughs and explains, "I assume you know what a power stone is, Mr. Greythorn?"

"Of course," Fernando says. "Most everyone knows what they are. I just have never heard one referred to as a wind stone before."

"That was Ariella's doing," Torgus said with a laugh. "When she was very young I was teaching her about the air spells, we would use these power stones during her lessens. She called them wind stones. Her father and I felt no need to call them anything different."

"I see," Fernando says.

*****

"So what is a power stone?" Haley asks.

"Well," Kyle explains, "think of it as a rechargeable battery for magic, but instead of electricity, it holds mana, the energy for casting spells."

"Do magic users have to use one?" Josh asks.

"No," Danielle answers. "A mage, wizard, or sorcerer has a natural ability to cast spells, but it can be tiring. A power stone helps to cast bigger spells or to maintain a spell longer."

"Some power stones can only be used to cast certain kinds of spells," Kyle explains. "The ones that Ariella is getting can only be used for spells from the storm school."

"School?" Haley asks, sounding confused.

Kyle laughs and says, "Just think of school as a type of spell. So if someone says they studied the fire school, then it means they know some fire spells."

"Did Chance use a power stone on the ship?" Josh asks.

"Yes," Kyle replies. "Chance has something more than just a power stone. He has a talisman that was given to him, by a dragon."

"That is so epic," Josh says.

"So why didn't Chance just go around a burn all the orcnea ships?" Laura asks.

"Well," Kyle answers, "all power stones need time to recharge, even Chance's dragon talisman. While it didn't need as much time as a regular power stone, Chance used a lot of mana to destroy the orcnea ship. It would take several days to regain it all. So do you all understand what a power stone is now?"

The three kids nod their heads. "Good," Kyle says. "Now back to the story."

*****

Ariella returns holding two amulets with sapphires in the center. She hands an amulet to Torgus and puts one on herself. She says to Fernando, "I am sorry but I am going to have to cancel our dinner plans tonight."

"I understand," Fernando replies, "Perhaps tomorrow night then?" He takes her hand and kisses it.

"If we are still alive then," Ariella answers, "then yes, tomorrow will do nicely." Then turning to Torgus she asks, "Shall we get started then?"

"Yes," Torgus replies, "Let's make ourselves comfortable. We may be up for a while."

Torgus and Ariella sit down as Fernando climbs back down the stairs to the quarter deck. The *Red Dawn* sails towards the clear western sky as the sun sets before them, while behind them the faint sound of thunder can be heard from the dark storms that follow.

Chapter 11
Day 4
The Common Foe

The new morning's sun shines upon the stone walls of Sheathelm. Chance has been flying all night, and as Sheathelm comes into his view, he spots a large airship flying above the city. It has an enormous canvas balloon on the top shaped like a giant egg. Below the balloon hangs a galleon style ship. Thick ropes hang down from the balloon binding it to the ship. To maneuver, it has sails almost like gills on the sides of the balloon portion. Chance studies it and notices the very common GTC symbol on the side, the insignia of the Goblin Trade Company.

The castle of Sheathelm sits near the water's edge. It is only separated from the sea by the fortified outer wall that encompasses the entire city and the docks just beyond the wall. The castle itself is a four sided rectangular structure with high walls and a tower at each corner. A large atrium sits high above the walls and overlooks the ocean. The atrium is circular and has high vaulted archways all the way around. While it would be easier for Chance to enter the castle this way, he does not wish to alarm the guards that stand on watch—one for each archway. Instead, Chance eyes the courtyard located on the opposite side of the castle, facing the city.

Chance lands in the courtyard and transformations back to his regular elven body. A guard approaches him and says, "Master Na'Moon, welcome back, sir. The King has asked me to send for you as soon as you arrived."

"Thank you," Chance says as he walks pass him toward the main entrance.

"You're welcome, sir," the guard replies.

Chance enters the main hall and is greeted by a large crowd. When people notice him they move out of his way. Among all the noises of the crowd Chance picks up on what some of the people of Sheathelm are saying.

"Chance will help," a woman's voice says.

"There he is," says a man

"Where has he been?" says another voice.

One person even says, "That's Chance Na'Moon? I always thought he would be taller."

As he makes his way to the front of the crowd he can see that the king is talking with several men, the goblin Resheck, and a dwarf.

Standing out among the representatives with the king are three beautiful elven women. They are Amazons of the Silver Moon, and Chance has met them before. The long dark haired leader, A'ranah Ree stands in the middle. She is slightly taller than Chance, and the Amazon to her left, Serena La'harn, is even taller. With their fitted chain-mail armor that has a bright white, silvery sheen, it is clear they are ready for battle. A'ranah has tribal markings on her face and arm of stars and a crescent moon, while Serena's markings are made up of dark curves and sharp points. These intricate patterns are stained upon the amazons' faces using henna and other plant extracts.

Crossroads

Chance glances at them for a moment before turning his attention the third member. On the other side of A'ranah is Finna Dri'el. She is the smallest of the three and is fair complected with light blonde hair. Instead of chain mail her armor is made up of heavy cloth and is covered by a long dark green robe. Her face is stained with green vines and eloquent white flowers. This organic display is common for those from the house of Dri'el. Finna looks over her shoulder and sees Chance coming to the front of the crowd. She smiles at him.

Chance smiles back as he breaks through to the front. King Arioch now sees him as well and yells, "Chance!" The others take notice and look at him. "Chance, please join us. We were about to move to the planning room."

"Good," Chance says as he holds the bag with the plans from the orcnea ship, "I have some very important information."

The crowd becomes unsettled and the people begin to shout questions.

"Are the orcneas back?" a man in tattered clothing asks as he grabs Chances arm. The guards quickly step between Chance and the man separating them.

Chance does not know how to respond and he quickly looks up at the King.

Arioch stands up to gain control of the crowd and yells, "People of Sheathelm. Please, you have nothing to fear. We must now discuss these matters in peace. Now please return to your homes and allow us to confer." The crowd of people groan with disappointment as Arioch motions to the guards and they start to clear the hall. Then Arioch turns to the small gathering near him and says, "If the representatives would please follow me, we can discuss this elsewhere." Arioch turns and begins to walk down the grand hall as the small group follows him.

"Chance," Finna calls as she stays back from the group.

Chance walks over to her and says, "Finna, it is good to see you."

"It is good to see you too, brother," Finna says as she hugs him. They begin to follow the King and the others down the tall marble hallway. She quietly asks, "So, can you tell me what you found?"

Chance answers, "The orcneas are back, but I believe with these plans that I found we should have time to ready ourselves for them."

"Oh good," she says with a sigh of relief. "I have not seen you in some time. How are the children?"

"They are well," Chance replies. "Ya'leigh is home for the summer, but Ambra and Kelik have decided to take a few summer classes in Dicean."

"I would like very much to see Ya'leigh if she is around," Finna says as they enter a room with a large table in the middle.

"We will go and find her after this then," he says as he takes his place by Arioch's side. Finna continues around the table and stands next to A'ranah.

Arioch says to the group, "Gentleman," then looking at three elven women he adds, "and ladies. You all got to know one another earlier, and most of you already know Chance. Chance, I would like to introduce you to Bortak. He has come from the Northwind Range," Arioch says as he motions to the dwarf.

Bortak's long brown beard is scruffy and unkempt. His clothing is more for mining than diplomacy. He gives a nod to Chance who nods back.

Arioch continues, "This is Michael of East Artos." Though his clothing is a bit worn, Michael is far more appropriately dressed than Bortak. He also nods to Chance before Arioch moves on to the last man to be introduced. "This is Romnelius, of West Artos," Arioch says as he motions to a tall thin man. Romnelius is finely dressed with white sleeves and a bold yellow vest with ruffles. His pleated trousers match the yellow of his vest. The brightness of his clothing makes the pale man look sickly.

Arioch says, "We all know why we are here. An unusual amount of ships have gone missing the last several weeks. Then a few days ago a ship owned by the Goblin Trade Company was attacked. Survivors of this ship were able to tell us that the attacking ship was of orcnea origin." He then turns to Chance and says, "Chance has just returned from warning a ship of the dangers. Now, Mr. Na'Moon, you said you have some important information?"

Chance pulls out the small bag and as he takes out the papers he obtained from the orcnea ship he explains, "Yes, Your Highness, I have discovered something of great importance." He unrolls one of the scrolls and continues, "It appears that the orcneas have plans to land their forces in the north territory beyond the Northwind Range and re-claim their old lands. From what I can gather from these plans the orcneas should be arriving in two days."

"Those lands have been vacant for years," Arioch says, "but Bortak tells me that there has been some orcnea activity in the Northwind Range recently. We have sent a small group to scout it out, but that was just yesterday morning. They will not arrive for a few more days."

"The orcneas will have already made landfall by then," A'ranah says. "We too have sent a scouting party, however ours should be reaching the mountains as we speak. A week ago we heard about a raid on the monastery on Sapphire Lake. We sent a few of our younger sisters to look into it. It is supposed to be part of their Rite of Passage. Of course, we had no idea at the time the seriousness of the situation."

"Wait," interrupts Chance, "A'ranah, you said that there was a raid a week ago?"

"Yes, the monastery on Sapphire Lake," A'ranah says. "At the western base of the Northwind Range."

Chance turns to Bortak and asks, "You say that there has already been activity to the north, correct?"

Bortak nods and says, "Yes, there have been a few small attacks on a mining village just north of the city of Northwind. I think the first one was just over a week ago."

Chance looks down at the maps and says, "These first set of plans do not make sense then. It says on the first moon they will land with their forces."

Romnelius, with an arrogant tone, suggests, "Perhaps they are merely a scouting party sent to the area before they land their forces."

"May I see that map?" Bortak asks. Chance hands the map over to him. Bortak studies the map and says, "I think you have the plans right, but I don't think there is any way to tell what moon they were considering to be their First

Moon. Maybe it was last month."

"He is right," Resheck says. "The orcneas celebrated their new year just a month ago. I'd be willing to bet that last month was the First Moon."

"So they may have already retaken the territory north of the mountains without any resistance," A'ranah says.

Chance then takes out a second scroll and says, "If that is the case, then I am afraid that what I am about to show you is even worse."

As Chance lays down a second parchment, Bortak steps up and looks at it closely. After a bit he looks up and say, "By the gods, if this is correct and we are right about the moons, they are not going to land in two days—they are *attacking* in two days."

Arioch looks at the maps and says, "I can't read the orcneish language, but it is clear from this that they plan to attack the city of Northwind first."

Chance looks at Arioch and says, "They are defenseless."

"I know," Arioch replies. "We are currently gathering troops, but it will be days before we can reach Northwind."

Romnelius comes around the table and looks at the map for a moment and says, "Gentlemen," then looking at the amazons he adds, "and ladies, I will leave you to your planning. It is clear that you have a lot to deal with." He then starts to leave.

"Where are you going?" Michael asks.

"It is obvious that this conflict does not involve us," Romnelius says. "We are here because some of our ships have been attacked along the east. Now that we know where the orcneas plan to be we will simply not send any more ships to Sheathelm, and we shall be left alone."

"Then what will you do if the orcneas overtake Sheathelm?" Arioch asks. "Do you really think they will stop then?"

Michael says, "He is right, Romnelius. We have to help in any way we can, or East and West Artos could be next."

"What would you have us do?" Romnelius asks. "If we send our armies we will be vulnerable to an attack from Bastion. You know full well they are barbaric and ruthless. If they knew we were weak they would attack."

"That is not true and you know it," Michael says. "Yes, they are ruthless and barbaric, but they have no interest in leaving the southern jungle. Besides, I am not saying we should send all of our troops."

Romnelius says, "If East Artos wishes to send their armies, so be it, but I will not be sending the armies of West Artos. Good luck, gentlemen." He turns and leaves the room.

"Well, Arioch," Michael says, "You can count on having my support and the support of East Artos. The matter will have to go before the council, of course, but I am confident they will understand the urgency of this matter. I will go immediately."

Arioch says to him, "Thank you and good luck."

Michael also leaves the room and Bortak says, "Two days! I better get going too. I have to warn the mines. I just hope I can get there in time." Bortak rushes out the door.

Arioch says to Chance, "My friend, I have to tell you something else important. It is about the scouting party."

"What is it?" Chance asks.

"I'll leave you alone to talk about this," Resheck says, he quickly leaves the room before they can continue their conversation.

"Ya'leigh and Kianna are in that scouting party," Arioch says.

"Arioch!" A'ranah exclaims. "How could you? Ya'leigh is my granddaughter, and Kianna is our..."

"I know," Arioch says as he takes her hand. "I am sorry. I had no idea at the time what we were up against."

"All is not lost," Chance says, "Arioch, do you know which way they were going?"

"They are delivering a wagon full of medicines to Troven," Arioch answers. "After that, I believe they were going to go north along the river to Sapphire Lake to the Monastery, and try to find a way over the mountains that way."

"It sounds like they are taking the same path that our young ones are taking," A'ranah says.

"Very well," Chance says. "They couldn't have gotten to the river by now. I will head them off and tell them to return. After that I shall head to the city of Northwind and find out if the orcneas really are going to attack there."

"Very good," Arioch replies. "If you do find an orcnea army, evacuate Northwind. Send them south and tell Lord Damion that as soon as we can muster enough troops we will send reinforcements to meet with them and we shall make our stand then."

"Yes, Your Highness," Chance says to Arioch. "I will leave at once."

"Chance," Arioch says. "You haven't gotten any sleep since yesterday."

"I'll be alright," Chance says. "I doubt I could sleep right now anyway."

"Wait!" A'ranah calls to Chance, "After you scout the army, would it be possible for you to check on our sisters?"

"Of course," Chance says. "I'll check on them after I scout the orcneas and warn them of the danger."

"No," Serena interrupts.

"What do you mean, no?" Finna asks.

"Please, I am sorry, sisters," Serena replies, "but this is their Rite of Passage. We cannot have him interfering with them. They must prove themselves worthy on their own."

"Serena," A'ranah interjects, "that was before we knew we were at war. They could be facing an entire army of orcneas. That is not an appropriate challenge for them."

Serena explains, "But if the plans Chance brought back are accurate, then the real army will march along the eastern coast and strike Northwind. Our sisters will be coming in from the west and may only have to deal with a few scouting parties. If that is all they have to face then it is the ideal challenge for the Rite of Passage."

They look at each other and finally A'ranah says, "Chance, please look over them. If you find that the orcnea armies are too great of a threat, then inform them what is happening, and have them fall back and find us. If, however, they are only facing scouting and raid parties then perhaps you could make yourself unknown to them."

"I understand," Chance says. "I'll make sure they are alright and only interfere if they are in danger. However, I must inform the Monastery of the threat as well as any nearby settlements. If they happen to be there when I arrive, then my information would only be a coincidence."

"Is this acceptable, Serena?" A'ranah asks.

"Yes," Serena answers, "I am sorry. Please understand, I do not want any harm to come to them either."

"I understand," Chance says, "You would rather they succeed on their own."

"Yes," Serena replies, "and if they knew that we sent Chance Na'Moon to watch over them..."

"Say no more," Chance says, "I will not draw their attention. Well, I better leave now if I am to reach Northwind before nightfall."

Arioch asks, "Chance, I almost forgot to ask—where did these plans come from?"

"We fought an orcnea ship," Chance says. He points to the map and says, "We fought them right there. We destroyed them but it took all my mana reserves from my talisman to do it. The *Red Dawn* is damaged now, but they are on their way to Artos as we speak. Hopefully they will not run in to any more trouble."

Finna looks at the map and says, "The elven ship, *Silver Tide*, is on its way from Artos right now. They should encounter each other soon. You said you were aboard the *Red Dawn*?"

"Yes," Chance answers, now sounding worried. "Do you think that the *Silver Tide* will attack the *Red Dawn*?"

"Well," Finna says sounding concerned as well, "while The *Red Dawn* has not been considered a threat in quite some time, I do not know for sure what they will do considering the circumstances."

A'ranah asks, "Finna, isn't your sister on board the *Silver Tide*?"

"Yes, Eveoh is aboard," Finna answers.

"Can you communicate with her so that she can warn the captain?" A'ranah asks.

"I will of course try, but it may take some time," Finna answers.

"Chance," A'ranah says, "we will do our best to contact the captain of the *Silver Tide*. We will ask them to assist The *Red Dawn*. You should go now, and don't worry, even if the orcneas take Northwind, we will fight at your side."

"I know," Chance replies, "Thank you."

"Not only was Sha'al your wife, she was my daughter," A'ranah says. "Now go and warn Ya'leigh and Kianna before it's too late. I do not wish to lose my daughter and granddaughter to these beasts."

"They will have to kill me first," Chance says.

Chance begins to leave the room as Finna calls to him, "Chance." She runs up to her brother and hugs him again and says, "Please be careful, brother."

"I will," Chance says with a smile. "I won't let anything happen to them."

"I know you won't," Finna replies. She walks back to the others and sits down and begins to meditate as Chance walks outside and transforms once again before taking flight.

Chapter 12
Backfire

On the ocean to the south the new mornings light lifts the darkness from the *Red Dawn* just as storm's edge begins to overshadow them. Throughout the night Ariella and Torgus have taken turns channeling their spells, and creating winds to help keep the orcnea ship from overtaking them.

Fernando comes up from below and immediately goes above to the poop deck. It is Torgus's turn to create the winds, and as he concentrates Fernando looks up at the sky above them. The enormous storm front is almost directly overhead. "Where is the Captain?" he asks, Torgus.

"She is getting some rest," Torgus answers.

"How much longer can you keep this up?" Fernando asks.

"We have already exhausted the gems," Torgus says, "They are getting very close."

Fernando looks around at the still damaged ship and says, "Then I fear we are lost."

Ariella emerges from her cabin and walks out onto the deck as the clouds become darker and the waves get rougher. Suddenly the lookout calls down, "Ship dead ahead!"

Ariella looks through her looking glass and she can see a small caravel off in the distance. It is coming straight for them. Ariella says under her breath, "Damned elves."

Torgus asks, "What is it, Captain?"

"A small elven scout ship," Ariella answers.

"Elves, eh," Torgus says. "I hope they know we are the least of their problems."

Ariella calls out, "Raise the white flag."

"Aye, Captain," John replies.

At the same time, on the deck of the elven ship, the *Silver Tide*, Captain Resif is peering through his looking glass. The elf at the helm asks. "Who are they, Captain?"

"If my eyes do not deceive me," Resif says, "we are looking at the *Red Dawn*."

"The *Red Dawn*?" another crewman asks. "I thought Red Beard was dead."

"Red Beard *is* dead," Resif replies, "His daughter, however, is another matter."

On the top deck another elf who is also looking out at the *Red Dawn* says, "Captain, it looks like she is damaged."

"It would appear so," Resif says. "Everyone be alert! The daughter of Red Beard should never be taken lightly."

The helmsman asks, "Captain, what about the storm?"

"The storm is what we were sent to investigate," Resif replies. "There are rumors of orcnea ships hiding inside. If it is true, I just need to know what side Captain Stormrage is on. It's not likely the daughter of Red Beard would fight on the side of orcneas, but we must be ready for anything."

Just then, Eveoh runs up from below deck. With her light blonde hair just like her sister, Finna, she runs straight to the captain and says, "Captain Resif, Captain, wait."

"What is it, Eveoh?" Resif asks.

"Is that the *Red Dawn*?" she asks.

"Yes, it is. How did you know?" he asks

"I just received a message from my sister, Finna," Eveoh explains. "She is in Sheathelm; and she tells me that The *Red Dawn* has been fighting the orcneas and may be in need of our assistance."

Just then the lookout calls down, "Captain, look! They have raised the white flag."

"So they have," Resif says. "Come about and match their heading. We will allow them catch up."

The helmsman spins the wheel and *Silver Tide* turns about.

On the *Red Dawn*, Ariella says, "Looks like they are going to let us close in. I hope that means they want to talk."

Soon the ships are alongside each other. Resif says to his first mate, "I'll be right back." He walks over to the edge of the ship while two crewmen lay down a long plank creating a pathway to the *Red Dawn*. John and Jacob hold it down on the other side as Resif quickly runs across.

When he steps foot on the *Red Dawn*, Ariella greats him. "Welcome aboard the *Red Dawn*, I am Captain Stormrage."

"Thank you, Captain," Resif says, "I am Resif, captain of the *Silver Tide*. I understand, Captain, that you have been in contact with orcneas?"

"You could call it contact, I guess," Ariella says. "We had a battle with one of their ships yesterday, and now another is looking to finish us off."

Resif nods and says, "Captain, I have to be completely honest with you. While I have no personal grudge against you, I do have my concerns. Even though your father redeemed himself during the Second Orcnea War, the *Red Dawn* has always remained a name that most captains are still leery of. However on this day we have a common foe once again."

"Agreed," Ariella says.

"Furthermore, we have gotten word from Sheathelm that King Arioch wishes us to aid you." Resif says, "While we have no duty to the human king, we respect King Arioch and will honor his request. So I assume you can no longer out run the orcneas?"

"That would be correct," Ariella says.

"How many aboard your ship can catch and return spells?" Resif asks.

"Only Torgus," Ariella answers.

"I see," Resif says, "I will send over someone to assist you. We have more than enough spell casters who can defend us from those incoming spells."

"Thank you," Ariella replies.

"Now, what do you say we turn around and face the orcneas head on?" Resif asks, "We will stand with you, daughter of Red Beard, and send these beasts to the bottom of the sea."

"Nothing would make me happier," Ariella says, "Shall we then?"

"I shall take the *Silver Tide* to the north and try to come in and flank them," Resif says. "We should be fast enough to reach them by the time you do."

"Very well," Ariella replies.

Resif nods to Ariella and then looking to Torgus he nods to him as well. Torgus grunts a little to himself and reluctantly nods back. Resif makes his way back to the edge of the ship. He quickly runs across the plank back to the *Silver Tide*. Fernando watches as Resif walks over to Eveoh and says something to her. She nods, and then in a blink of an eye, she disappears from the deck of the ship and immediately appears on deck of the *Red Dawn*.

Eveoh walks up to Ariella and says, "Captain, my name is Eveoh, I am here to assist you. Where would you like me to deflect the orcneas incoming spells from?"

Ariella looks at Torgus for a moment and then says, "Torgus, you take the bow of the ship and, Eveoh, you take the stern."

"Aye, Captain," Torgus says.

"As you wish, Captain," Eveoh answers.

Ariella looks at the crew and yells, "Bring us about and let's go kill us some orcneas."

The crew cheers loudly as the ship turns into the storm.

Meanwhile in the eye of the storm, on the orcnea ship, one of the crew members enters a room with the captain. The ship is crude and built with large split logs. Even the rooms have a rugged look. The grunt walks up to the captain and says, "Captain, the *Red Dawn* is finally turning to fight. There was another smaller ship with them, but they seem to be leaving the *Red Dawn* behind."

The captain stands up from his chair and says, "Good. Now prepare the weapons that we got from the goblin ship."

"Yes, sir," the grunt says. He then leaves the room as the captain sits back down in his chair and begins to laugh.

On deck of the *Red Dawn*, the storm is raging and the rain is making it hard to see. Ariella is next to Chris at the wheel. She yells out, "Can anyone see them yet?"

Eveoh yells back over the storm, "I can see them, Captain, they are approaching just off the port bow."

"How the hell can you see them through the storm?" Ariella asks over the sound of the howling wind.

"Elves have keener senses, Captain," Eveoh answers, "and I have a spell that helps me see through the rain."

Ariella looks ahead and sees only the raging storm. She then mutters to herself in a mocking tone. "*Elves have keener senses, Captain.*" Still under her breath she adds, "I have that same spell, you damned elf."

"What did you say, Captain?" Chris asks.

"I said, I am glad we have the help of that elf," Ariella answers.

Runefell

Torgus is at the bow of the ship. Fernando is there behind him along with Drake and Leon. Fernando asks, "Any sign of them?"

"As a matter of fact," Torgus answers, "Yes, here they come." He points out and through the dark storm, the orcnea ship appears. Off the port bow the two ships come along side of one another. Torgus summons a large stone and magically hurls it at the orcnea ship. It impacts, and pieces of the ship splinter into the air. The orcneas scatter in fear.

From the orcnea ship, lightning is thrown from the shamans. Torgus manages to catch one bolt and sends it back. Three more bolts fly past him. One hits the mast with a thunderous impact. Shards of wood explode from it. Though it is heavily damaged, the mast remains standing.

The second bolt almost hits the captain as she dives for cover. It hits the cabin wall behind her and causes an explosion, leaving a hole in the wall large enough to put a man's head through. Ariella quickly gets back to her feet.

The final bolt comes towards Eveoh and she catches it like Torgus. She takes a moment to aim carefully at the shaman who fired it, and launches it back at the attacker. With a simple wave of his hand the shaman magically deflects the bolt harmlessly away. Eveoh clinches her fist in frustration.

The orcnea ship is now alongside the *Red Dawn*. Expecting orcneas to board them, Fernando draws his sword. Drake and Leon also stand ready, eager for battle. Allen stands further back and while he has his sword drawn he looks very nervous. The rest of the crew also stands ready, waiting for hand to hand combat. Unlike the day before, this time the orcneas do not board.

Instead of boarding, five long rounded chambers made of iron are pushed up along the orcnea ship's port side. The crew of the *Red Dawn* look on, confused.

"What the hell are those?" Drake asks Leon.

"I have no idea," Leon answers, "Some kind of mini catapult maybe."

Then they all watch as an orcnea gives a command to the others. Five orcneas hold torches to the back of the long iron tubes. Only a second later there is a deafening boom that surprises everyone, including the orcneas.

*****

"Cannons," Josh says, interrupting the story. "They were cannons."

Kyle looks at him with a smile and replies, "Very good. You are correct."

"Wait," Laura interjects. "They didn't know what a cannon was?"

"Up until this point," Kyle explains, "The *Red Dawn* had never faced the power of a cannon. It was a new weapon to Runefell, brought to the world by the goblins. The goblins found that they were too dangerous and did not want to sell them to the other races."

"So that was what they got from the goblin ship," Josh concludes.

"Yes," Kyle answers. "When the orcneas heard about this new weapon they decided that they had to have them and when the goblins refused to sell them the orcneas simply took them.""

"So what did they do?" Haley asks, sounding worried.

Crossroads

"It's okay, Haley," Laura says, as she puts her arm around her sister trying to calm her. "I am sure they'll be fine."

Kyle says, "Okay, so the orcneas just fired the cannons..."

*****

The incoming shots tear into the *Red Dawn*'s deck. Men go flying and there is panic everywhere as the men begin to scatter.

One of the iron balls flies over Torgus as he ducks. "What the hell was that?" he yells.

Fernando answers, "I have seen them on a goblin ship before, however I have never seen them used."

"Well, they are damn powerful, whatever they are!" Torgus yells. "I couldn't catch it." Torgus looks back at Eveoh who looks confused as well.

The orcnea ship now passes them by, and the orcneas begin to reload the cannons.

Ariella yells, "Where the hell are the elves?"

No sooner than the question is asked, the *Silver Tide* comes into view. They are right behind the orcnea ship and begin to fire several spells at the orcneas. The smaller and faster elven ship starts to pull up alongside the orcnea ship.

"They are going to get torn apart by those weapons," Ariella says. "Bring us about! We have to stay in this fight."

Chris spins the wheel as everyone watches the orcnea ship and the *Silver Tide* continue to close in on each other. The elves continue to attack the much larger vessel with their spells. By the time they are next to the orcneas, the orcneas have prepared the cannons for another round. They open fire with a volley that shreds the main deck of the *Silver Tide*. The main mast falls and the elven ship is heavily damaged.

On the *Silver Tide*, elves are assisting the wounded and look bewildered. Resif is pinned down under some debris. He frees himself and quickly stands up. Angrily he casts a fireball then throws it recklessly at the orcnea ship. The orcneas scatter and dodge the incoming ball of fire. It then strikes a barrel full of black powder behind them and it catches fire.

Before the orcneas have a chance to react, the barrel explodes violently. Everyone on the *Silver Tide* and the *Red Dawn* are startled at the sudden giant fireball that almost rips the orcnea ship in half.

Captain Resif then yells out, "All those who can cast fire, take aim at those barrels!" Several elves who are high enough on the smaller ship to see over the rails of the much larger orcnea ship, now throw fireballs at the barrels.

As the captain of the orcnea ship realizes what is happening he orders, "Shamans, protect those barrels!" Several shamans try to reach the barrels, but before they can arrive, the elven fireballs hit three more barrels that are unprotected. The orcneas turn and run as the barrels are engulfed in flames. The barrels explode, destroying the orcnea ship completely.

The crews of the *Red Dawn* and *Silver Tide* watch as what is left of the orcnea ship burns. On the *Red Dawn*, Drake says to Leon, "Well, it looks like you still don't get to fight any orcneas."

Leon sheaths his sword and says, "Only because they were too cowardly to come over and fight. If they had I would have shown them."

Fernando looks back at Allen who looks relieved to be putting his sword away. He walks up to Allen and pulls him aside and asks, "Are you alright?"

Allen looks at him and says, "Yes, I am fine." It is clear that he is unsettled.

"You know, it's alright to be nervous," Fernando says, "I have often found that those who crave battle the most are the ones who usually find death sooner."

"I guess," Allen says looking down. "I just don't know if I am cut out for this."

"My friend," Fernando says as they walk across the deck, "Even I get nervous in battle. The important thing is doing what must be done when it is necessary. I have watched you put yourself in harm's way to save Leon. Then charge into the Captain's quarters to save Marie from danger."

Allen smiles and says, "I guess so. So, you still get nervous?"

"Of course," Fernando says with a smile. "Let me tell you about the time I was in the Rusty Dagger in East Artos."

Fernando and Allen walk off as Ariella surveys the damage. Then looking at Chris and Torgus she says, "We need repairs soon."

Meanwhile, north of Sheathelm, Chance glides high above on the wind currents. He is looking for his daughter and the princess. Finally he spots the small group of people on horseback pulling a wagon. He makes his descent and lands ahead of them and transforms.

Ya'leigh looks at him and says, "Father? What are you doing here?"

"I am here to tell you to go back to Sheathelm," Chance says. "The orcneas are back and are planning an attack on Northwind in two days."

"Two days!" Kianna says. "Is my father sending troops then?"

"We are, Princess," Chance says, "but they will not get there in time. I am going to go and start an evacuation. I want you all to return to Sheathelm where it is safe."

"Can we at least finish delivering the supplies in the wagon to Troven, and then return?" Kianna asks. "They are much needed medicines."

"Very well," Chance says. "You do have a gate stone to the palace do you not?"

"Yes," Kianna answers holding out an amulet made of sandstone, "we do."

"Good," Chance answers, "If we are correct, the orcneas are not going to be in the west, but just in case we are wrong don't hesitate to use it. I wish I could stay longer but I must get to Northwind as soon as I can."

"Wait!" Ya'leigh says, "If the orcneas are attacking Northwind then I want to go with you."

"Absolutely not," Chances replies, "I am only going there to scout the orcneas and if necessary, start an evacuation. We do not plan to fight them there. We are not prepared. Arioch is gathering troops and we plan to regroup and to

Crossroads

take our stand south of Northwind River." Chance walks up to the wagon and hugs Ya'leigh tightly. "Be careful, and I will see you soon. I love you."

"I love you too, father," Ya'leigh replies. As Chance transforms and flies off, Ya'leigh asks Kianna, "Are we really going back after we deliver the supplies?"

"Well," Kianna says, "he did not say that my father *ordered* us to return. Besides, if the orcneas are going to attack Northwind that means they are coming from the east. So then our plan to enter the old orcnea lands from the west should still be relatively safe."

"I am not sure about this," Garrin says. "There may be too many of them for us to handle."

"I understand," Kianna answers, "but with the orcneas coming down from the east, they may leave themselves open. We may be able to get behind the enemy lines and cause them a lot of damage. Believe me, tactically this is our best option. Besides, Ya'leigh and I wouldn't be allowed in the fight if we go back. This way we at least can do something."

Ya'leigh adds, "If we run into any real trouble we can still use the gate stone."

"It sounds like a crazy plan," Isen says, "so you know I am up for it."

"So then," Kianna asks, "is it agreed?"

They all nod and say, "Agreed."

Later that day, on the deck of the *Red Dawn*, the crew is finishing the cleanup from the attack. They are tethered to the *Silver Tide*. Ariella is talking with Captain Resif.

"Well, Captain," Ariella says to him, "thank you for your assistance."

"You are welcome," Resif replies. "Are you going to be able to make it to your destination?"

"Yes," Ariella says. "How about you?"

"Well," Resif answers, "we have taken a lot of damage, but I think we will make it. So until next time, Captain." Resif nods to Ariella then makes his way back to his ship. When he boards he signals the elves manning the ropes. They untie the ships from each other and soon they are separated.

Fernando approaches Ariella and says, "Well, this made for an exciting day."

"Indeed, Mr. Greythorn," Ariella replies.

Fernando then says softly to Ariella, "Perhaps, Captain, you would like to make an interesting evening as well."

Ariella smirks and says, "Why, Mr. Greythorn, what exactly do you have in mind?"

"Well, Captain," he says as he moves close and puts his arm around her, "why don't we have dinner tonight. Just the two of us and I'll show you."

Ariella takes a step back and puts her arm out to keep Fernando back and says, "Perhaps tomorrow night, Mr. Greythorn. I am just looking forward to getting some rest tonight without a storm chasing us."

"As you wish, my lady," Fernando says as he kisses her hand. He then bows and walks off.

Ariella turns and yells up to Chris, "Set our heading for East Artos, and then let the night crew take over so you can get some sleep too."

"Aye, Captain," Chris says.

As night sets in over the land, far to the north Chance has had a very long day. Having flown all night and throughout the day, he lands just outside a large keep within the city of Northwind. After he transforms back into his natural elven form he calls up to the two watchmen at the guard tower window, "Good sir, I am Chance Na'Moon of Sheathelm I am here on very important business. Please, allow me to enter and speak with the lord."

One of the guards checks with the other, "Did he say, Na'Moon?"

"Yes, he did?" The second guard answers. "I'll go get the captain." He hurries off as the first guard watches over Chance.

A few moments later the guard returns with their captain. The dark haired captain looks down and says, "Chance, it's been a long time. How are your two sons?"

Chance smiles and replies, "Levin, my two daughters are very well. Along with my only son."

Levin laughs and says to one the guards, "That's him. Open the gate." He turns to the other and says, "Go make sure Lord Damion has not turned in for the evening. Tell him Chance Na'Moon is here."

"Yes, sir," the guard replies.

Soon the gate raises and Levin greets him at the entrance.

"I assume you are here to talk to Damion about the orcneas," Levin says as they begin to walk across the courtyard to the main hall entrance.

"Yes," Chance replies, "you are all in great danger."

Levin leads Chance into the hall where a dark haired man wrapped in a long blue silk robe sits in a large chair behind a table.

"Greetings, Lord Damion," Chance says.

"Chance," Damion says, "What brings you here? I was just getting ready to turn in for the night." Damion stands to greet Chance. He is much taller than Chance and Levin.

"I wish it were good news," Chance replies, "however, I must inform you that we believe that in two days orcneas will be invading from the north."

Levin says, "So it's true, they are back."

"Yes, they are," Chance replies, "Arioch is sending what forces he can but they will not arrive in time. I will know in the morning if the orcneas are indeed on their way. If they are, the plan is for an evacuation. You will head south until you meet with the forces of Sheathelm. Any able body men are to then join Arioch and his men. You will then turn back, and with your combined efforts take the fight to the orcneas."

"Can't we just stay and fight them now?" Damion asks. "Just like old times."

"I am afraid we would not last long," Chance answers. "Remember, we were not alone then. Drakesbane is now on the other side of Bruen, teaching at

Dicean. Arioch will be here soon, but not soon enough, and I have not heard from Thordir in years. The walls of Northwind are strong, but I am afraid with all the shamans they have trained they are more powerful than ever. They will most likely attack from the sky as well, and you have no defenses if they do."

"I understand," Damion says. "Are you sure about the attack?"

"We are certain they will attack," Chance says. "It is just a matter of when. In the morning I will head north and see for myself before heading west."

"What is in the west?" Damion asks.

"I have to look after a few of my sisters who were sent to scout the orcnea lands," Chance replies.

"Sisters?" Damian asks with a laugh, "How old are they?"

"Just coming of age," Chance says glaring at him, "and too young for you my friend."

"I had to ask," Damion says with a smile. "You must be tired, I'll make sure a room is prepared for you."

"Thank you," Chance says, "but first, if I may bother you for something to eat. I am starving."

"Of course," Damian says, "Follow me. I was just about to get something to eat before I went to bed. So tell me, how have things been?"

Damian, Levin, and Chance walk off down the corridor as Chance begins to tell him about the last few days.

Chapter 13
Day 5
Morning till Dusk

It is morning aboard the *Red Dawn,* and Fernando walks across the still damaged deck. The skies are clear and the sun is at their backs. "A beautiful morning isn't it, Mr. Greythorn," Ariella calls down to him from the helm.

"Yes, Captain," Fernando replies, "but not nearly as beautiful as yourself."

Chris, who is behind Ariella, shakes his head.

Ariella smiles and asks, "You never quit do you?"

Fernando replies with a grin, "Quitting is not in the Greythorn's blood." Fernando walks up the stairs to the top of the quarterdeck and asks, "So, are you feeling up to having dinner with me tonight? Just the two of us?"

Ariella steps back and thinks for a moment before answering, "Very well. If we have an uneventful day, and I do not have to turn in early, then yes. I would have you join me tonight."

"Thank you, Captain," Fernando says as he takes the Captains hand and kisses it. "Let us hope that today is a quiet one then." He then turns and walks away with a smile.

Behind Ariella and Chris, Marie is watching them through the porthole of the Captains lounge. She turns and says to herself, "Ariella was right. You are a bit *too* nice, Mr. Greythorn. I'll be keeping my eye on you."

In the city of Northwind it is also morning, and Chance is preparing to leave. Damian is with him and says, "So, I will continue with the evacuation unless you return and tell me differently."

"Yes, my friend, I will travel along the coast. It is the path they are supposed to take," Chance explains. "If I find nothing, I will return, and we can call it off. If I do not return, however, assume the threat is real and continue the evacuations. I'll be making sure my sisters are not getting in over their heads to the west."

"Well then, I hope to see you soon," Damian replies.

"Me too," Chance says, he then turns and changes into his eagle from and takes flight.

Chance flies north along the eastern coast. After about an hour of travel he comes upon a large orcnea camp. Thousands of troops stretch across the land. Chance veers to his left and begins to fly inland across the mountains.

As midday approaches, far to the west, Princess Kianna, Ya'leigh, and the rest of the caravan arrive at the small town of Troven. Three men approach them. One of them steps forward. He bows and says, "Welcome, Princess Kianna. It is good to see you again."

"Steven, it is good to see you two," Kianna replies. "How is your father?"

"He is well," Steven replies. "He will be glad to hear the medicines have arrived. Thank you for coming all this way to bring them."

Crossroads

"You are most welcome," Kianna replies as she climbs off the wagon.

"My lady," says Steven, "is it true that the orcneas have returned?"

Kianna answers, "The latest information is they are marching toward Northwind now. There is no word on any other plans at this point. My father is rallying troops for a counter attack. If you have any extra men, it would be wise to send them."

"Of course, my lady," Steven answers. "I tell my father at once."

Isen removes the cover of the wagon and discovers two extra passengers. One is a young elven female in her early teens. She has strait blonde hair and a very thin build. The other, is a young elven boy. He looks to be a couple years younger than the female. He is also thin with blonde hair, however his hair is full of curls.

Isen says, "Ambra, Kelik, what are you two doing here?"

Ambra ignores the question and says, "Hello, Isen."

Isen calls to the others, "Ya'leigh! You may want to see this."

Ya'leigh walks over to the wagon and she finds two familiar faces. It is her brother and sister and as they climb out of the wagon she yells, "Kelik, Ambra, what are you doing here?"

"Isen already asked that," Ambra replies with a grin.

Isen says, "Your father will not be happy with you two when he finds out."

Ambra looks up at him and says, "I know. Just don't tell him."

Ya'leigh angrily asks, "Why did you come with us! Aren't you supposed to be taking the summer courses at Dicean?"

"Well, we were supposed to go," explains Kelik, "but we wrote them a letter telling them that we would not be able to attend."

"So," Ambra says, "everyone at Sheathelm thinks we are at Dicean and everyone at Dicean just thinks we are at Sheathelm."

Kianna walks over and asks Ya'leigh, "So, what do you want to do?"

Ya'leigh, still glaring at her siblings, says, "Well, I don't want to go back now, but it is too dangerous to bring them."

"No, it's not," Ambra insists.

"Yes," Kelik adds, "I can shoot a crossbow."

Kianna and Ya'leigh look at each other and shake their heads.

"We could use the gate stone to send them back," Isen says.

"Yes, but that would leave us with no way back of our own," Ya'leigh replies. "Remember? It's one use only."

Gena says, "I have an idea. We will give them the gate stone and make sure they stay next to one of us. If we get into trouble they can be the ones in charge activating it."

"I still don't like it," Ya'leigh says. "It's too dangerous."

"And how old were you when you first went with father on a journey?" Ambra asks.

"I was Kelik's age," Ya'leigh answers, "but Father is not here to protect you."

"It's not like we are going to fight the war," Kelik says.

Ambra adds, "You are only supposed to scout the north, not fight the north."

Garrin asks, "Did they say we are going forth?"

"No!" Gena yells at Garrin.

"They do have a point, Ya'leigh," Isen says. "Besides, I am here to protect them. What could possibly happen?"

"Don't challenge the gods, Isen," Kianna says with heavy sigh. She turns to Ya'leigh and says, "They are your brother and sister. I'll leave the decision up to you."

Ya'leigh looks at Kelik and Ambra who smile as brightly as they can. "If we run in to trouble do you promise to let us handle it and stay close to one of us?" She asks.

"Yes," Kelik answers.

"I'll just stay behind Isen," Ambra says as she peers out from behind the big man.

Ya'leigh looks at Kianna and says, "Alright, we continue on."

"Yes!" Kelik exclaims.

Kianna says, "I'll get them a horse that they can share, and then we will head out. We can still get a good half days travel before we have to set up camp."

Later that day, Chance continues to fly over the mountains to the west. It is a long, and thankfully, uneventful journey. The sun begins to set before him just as Sapphire Lake comes into view. The clear blue glacial waters stretch across the horizon. Even from his soaring heights Chance cannot see the other side of this massive body of water. It is a beautiful sight as the sky looks as though it has been painted with reds and oranges from the sunset. Those colors are reflected in the waters directly ahead of Chance. In contrast, to either side of the setting sun, the lake still holds a deep blue sheen.

Chance looks down and spots, tucked away among the tall coniferous trees, a large stone monastery facing the lake. Behind it is a sprawling garden full of shrubs, plants, and trees containing an assortment of flowers, fruits and vegetables. Tall stone walls encompass the gardens and connect at either side of monastery. Chance begins to descend quickly as he looks for guards on the walls. He is surprised not to find any.

Chance lands on the lake shore before transforming. Protected only by its size and the high placement of its windows, the front of the monastery does not have walls surrounding it. He follows the narrow pathway up a steep incline to a set of colossal wooden doors.

Just as Chance is about to knock, the doors are opened by a young bald man in a robe. "Good evening, Mr. Na'Moon," he says as he steps back from the door and bows his head. "Please come in. Brother Edward is expecting you."

"Thank you," Chance replies confused.

"My name is Joseph," he says as Chance enters the large doorway. "I shall fetch Brother Edward for you."

Chance nods his head as the monk begins to walk down a corridor. Chance looks around at the huge mural tapestries on the wall. There is one particular tapestry that catches his eye. The first image is of a dragon bound in chains. A man is standing over the dragon with a staff that has a large crystal affixed at the top of it. The next image is of a floating city with several dragons flying around it. Next to that is a depiction of the same city in ruins, and on the ground. Five men are standing on top of the rubble. As Chance looks close at it he can see one of the men is a blonde elf. Looking even closer he can see a large red dragon handing the elf a talisman.

"Do you like our tribute to the Dragon War, Mr. Na'Moon?" a voice says from behind him. Chance turns to see another bald man in a robe. Before Chance can answer the man says, "It is good to see you again."

"Brother Edward," Chance replies. "It is good to see you as well. How did you know I was coming?"

"Since the orcnea raid a few weeks ago we have been on high guard. Those of us who are able to do so, meditate and watch over the monastery with our spells," Edward explains. "I sensed your presence and had informed Joseph to let you in. So, I assume you are here to investigate the orcnea problem?"

"Yes," Chance replies, "they are back to wage war yet again."

"I see," Edward replies. "Are we in immediate danger?"

Chance says, "Fortunately the plans that we have recovered do not show that they will attack here to the west. Though I am afraid that by tomorrow the city of Northwind will be lost."

"Oh my," Edward replies.

"I intend to make sure that there is no imminent threat to the west side of the mountains," Chance explains. "If there is, I will be sure to return and warn you."

"Thank you," Edward says.

"I am also looking for a group of Silver Moon Sisters," Chance says. "They may have come through here recently. Have you seen them?"

"Indeed," Edward answers. "There were seven of them and they headed out this morning up the mountain to a small mining town named Copper Pass. They should be there by now."

"How would I find this town?" Chance asks.

"It should be easy for you to find," Edward explains. "The main path from our back exit goes straight there. You could reach it in an hour if you fly."

"Thank you, Brother Edward," Chance says. "I must go now then, I do not wish leave my sisters in an unfamiliar town by themselves."

"I think they are capable of handling themselves," Edward says.

"It isn't them that I am worried about," Chance says with a smile. He pulls out a hooded cloak from a small bag and puts it on. He opens the door and steps outside. "Thank you again, Brother Edward."

"Good journey to you, my friend," Edward says as Chance turns back into the eagle and flies off.

Chapter 14
Watchful Eyes

At this time, far to the south, Ariella and Fernando are laughing over dinner on the *Red Dawn*. They are in the Captain's lounge and they have already eaten. The Captain takes a drink from her large mug before slamming it onto the table. Fernando pours her more wine from the pitcher.

"Oh no," Ariella says, clearly tipsy from the alcohol, "I shouldn't."

"Don't worry," Fernando says, "I will not take advantage of you."

"You?" Ariella questions, "You couldn't take advantage of me anyway. *I* am the one who would take advantage of *you*."

"Oh, really?" Fernando says with a laugh, "and just how would you do that?"

Ariella takes another drink and stands up. She takes a wobbly step over to Fernando who is sitting next to her in his chair. As she lifts her leg up and steps over him and sits down on his lap facing him she says, "I would start like this." She leans in and kisses his neck. Fernando smiles and puts his arms around her. He runs his fingers through her hair.

Fernando says, "Well that is a nice start, my darling, shall we continue this elsewhere?"

Ariella gets up and takes Fernando's hand and leads him into the adjacent galley and down the stairway leading to the Captain's quarters. As they enter Ariella's room she leads him over to her bed and pushes him back onto it. She climbs into bed with Fernando and straddles him. She then leans down and slowly drags her hair across his face. He reaches up and tries to put his arms around her but she grabs his wrists and pins them down over his head. She then says, "Oh no you don't. I am the one in charge here."

"Yes, ma'am," Fernando says with a smile. "I see that you are."

She then reaches up and takes a small bottle of oil that is on the small table next to the bed, and says, "Now, you can start by rubbing my shoulders." She then hands him the bottle of oil before unbuttoning her ruffled shirt. Then as Fernando sits up, Ariella lays face down and pulls her shirt up over her head then throws it on the floor next to the bed.

Fernando replies, "Of course, my lady." He takes the oil and pours a little in his hands and begins to rub her shoulders.

Ariella lets out a deep sigh and says, "Oh that feels so good."

Fernando leans down and whispers in her ear, "Anything for you, darling. Now close your eyes and relax. Let me take care of all your needs." He continues to rub her shoulders as she closes her eyes.

As Ariella begins to fall asleep she says softly, "Thank you, Chance." Before she realizes her mistake she is completely out.

"Captain?" Fernando whispers. He gently shakes her shoulder and says a little louder, "Ariella, are you awake?" When she does not respond Fernando leans down and kisses her cheek. He whispers, "Ariella, you truly are an amazing woman. Chance is a lucky man to have your love." He runs his fingers through her hair. He then takes a blanket from the base of her bed and covers her up. He sits beside her for a while then looks around the room. Fernando slowly makes his way over to Ariella's desk and opens the jewelry box. He pulls out Ariella's locket, and looks closely at it.

"Mr. Greythorn?" Marie's voice breaks the silence surprising him. "What are you doing?"

Fernando places the locket back in the jewelry box and closes the lid. He turns nervously and replies, "Marie, hello. I was just looking at the Captain's portraits of her father."

Marie looks at the desk and sees the portraits of Red Beard. She thinks for a moment then smiles and says, "Oh, I see. Please, forgive me, I didn't not mean to imply—"

"Oh, no," Fernando cuts her off. "I am the one who should be apologizing. I should not still be here. I will return below and turn in for the night." Fernando walks to the door.

"Fernando," Marie hesitantly calls him.

"Yes?" Fernando asks.

Marie says, "The Captain seems to care about you."

Fernando smiles and replies, "And I care for her."

"Good," Marie says, "I just don't want to see her get hurt."

"I assure you," Fernando states, "the last thing I wish to do, is hurt her. Now if you will excuse me, it is late and I must get some sleep. Goodnight, Marie."

"Goodnight, Mr. Greythorn." Marie says. Fernando closes the door behind him, and Marie walks over to the desk. She looks at the jewelry box for a moment before opening it. She takes out the locket and looks at it puzzled. She places it back in the box before closing the lid and returning to her room.

While Fernando heads back below deck, it is now very dark and cold in the Northwind Mountains where Chance flies into the small town of Copper Pass. Not having seen orcnea activity in over ten years, the walls that surround Copper Pass are more for wildlife than an attack. At the northern entrance there is a newly constructed guard tower. Chance lands unnoticed in an alley. He changes back into his natural form. He walks out of the alley as he pulls the cloak tight over his head. It is very cold here, and the wind makes it almost unbearable. The few buildings that are in this small outpost of a town, are covered with snow. Only the largest seems to have any activity in it. On the sign out front it reads The Pick Ax.

Chance enters the inn and the small crowd inside stops what they are doing. They stare at him for a moment before resuming their activities. The warmth of the place is welcoming, even if it does smell strongly of ale. Instead of going to the innkeeper and making an announcement of the orcneas return, Chance decides to wait and see if the Amazons are already there, and if so he figures he can wait one more day to warn the town after the sisters have moved on. Chance looks to his right and in the corner, next to a large fireplace, he sees an empty table. He makes his way over to it and sits down. Looking up from under his cloak he begins to look around the tavern. Across the room he sees the innkeeper, a dark haired dwarf. His beard is twisted into thick braids down to his round belly. Sitting at the counter a few unassuming men are conversing and drinking.

A small goblin wearing furs is sitting at the counter as well. He is having a conversation with an elven female. She has markings of a yellow star over the top of a blue crescent moon stained on her right cheek. Chance figures she must be one of the young amazons A'ranah wanted Chance to look after. Chance looks beyond her and in the far corner of the room, under the balcony of the upstairs, there are six more amazons sitting at a table.

They are drinking and laughing, except for one, who is reading a book. Chance notices that on her right cheek a depiction of a leaf is prominently displayed as well as three small stars below it. All of the young women have some form of henna tattoo on their face to indicate which of the three houses they are from.

One of them accidentally spills her mug and laughs. The dark haired amazon can be heard over the rest of the crowd as she seems to be having the most fun. Chance can tell from the black jagged markings on the side of her face that she is from the house of La'harn. She takes a drink from the mug of her sister sitting next to her.

Even before her drink was stolen this sister didn't seem to smile as much as the others. With her less than welcoming demeanor though, she is still stunningly beautiful. Her straight blonde hair is down to her elbows. She stands up and Chance can see that she is as tall as most of the men in the room.

After concluding her talk with the goblin, the first amazon joins her sisters at the table. She says something to the others. The others look at each other and shake their heads no. Whatever they are discussing they seem to be in agreement. Chance tries to tell what they are saying but they are too far away.

Chance continues to observe them as best he can without being noticed, when one of them looks up in his direction. Her eyes—the bluest that Chance has ever seen—captures his attention. For a brief moment he is caught in her stare. As he realizes what is happening he looks away, but it is too late. She says something to others and before Chance is able to stand up and leave his table, the seven sisters walk over to him.

The one who was talking with the goblin earlier says, "Excuse me, my name is Evelena Ree. My sisters and I are looking for a guide to help us cross the Northwind Range. Might you be able to help us?"

Looking down at the table, Chance replies, "I am sorry, but I am not familiar with the mountains."

"Oh?" Evelena's questions. Now curious, she asks, "So you aren't from around here?"

"No," Chance answers, trying to keep his answers short.

"So, where are you from?" coldly asks the stern looking blonde.

"Rehma, don't be rude," says the one who stole her drink. She sits down next to Chance and says, "I am sorry, my sister can sometimes be a little," she pauses before saying, "too straight forward." Rehma gives her a glare as she continues. "My name is Gelana La'harn. This is my sister, Rehma," she says as she looks back at the tall blonde amazon. "She is also from the house of La'harn."

Chance looks up at the woman named Rehma for a moment. He looks at the black curved markings on her face that begin at the top of her forehead and continue down the side of her face. The markings disappear below the neckline of her chain-mail armor.

Gelana continues with the introductions, "You already met Evelena. Next to her is Kel'ana and Yentroc. They are from the house of Ree." Chance studies the faces of the women. Kel'ana has a bright yellow star painted on her face around her right eye. Her golden blonde hair hangs down in tight spirals. By contrast, Yentroc has long dark hair. She has three small blue stars painted on her right cheek. It was her eyes that caught Chance's attention earlier.

Gelana introduces the last of the other women, "Over here you have Ja'noa, and Lyra. They are from the house of Dri'el." Both Ja'noa and Lyra are smaller than the other five amazons. Ja'noa has dark wavy hair and her face is adorned with the markings of thorny vines. These stained tattoos arc down her right cheek and wraps around her neck.

Lyra, the one who was reading at the table earlier, is the smallest of all. Though she is roughly the same age as the others, you would not know it from her youthful appearance. She looks at Chance and says, "I am also part Ree." She points to the stars painted on her face, and adds, "From my father's side."

Gelana turns to Chance and asks, "So, now that you know our names, may we have yours?"

An awkward silence follows for a moment as Chance thinks. "Kyle," he finally answers with the first name that comes to mind.

"Kyle?" Gelana repeats sounding doubtful. "So, Kyle, are you sure you can't help us cross the mountains?" She asks seductively, as she brushes back her raven dark hair. "Please?"

"Are you going to seduce every guy we come across?" Evelena asks.

"You don't even know what he looks like," the blue eyed Yentroc adds, referring to the cloak that still covers Chance's head. Under the hood they can only see Chance's chin and the tip of his nose.

"I am sorry we bothered you," Evelena says to Chance. "It is clear you wish to be alone. Come on everyone, let's go back to our table. Maybe we will go with the goblin after all."

"Not until I can see what is under that cloak," Gelana says.

"Gelana!" Rehma says, "Now who is being rude?" The normally serious face of Rehma cracks a small grin.

"That's alright," Chance says. Then looking at Gelana he asks, "If I remove my hood, will you leave me alone?"

"Maybe," Gelana answers.

"Very well," Chance says hoping that since he doesn't recognize them or anyone else in the inn, that no one will be able to identify him.

The others now gather closely and watch as Chance pulls back the hood of his cloak. His ears protrude through his hair. The young women seem to be taken a bit by surprise.

"An elf!" Gelana exclaims. "Well now, isn't that a surprise."

"I claim him," Yentroc states boldly.

"I beg your pardon," Gelana says to Yentroc, "but he is mine." Gelana gets up out of the chair and stands face to face with Yentroc.

"I claimed him first," Yentroc replies.

"Ladies, this isn't necessary," Chance says as he tries to stand up.

Gelana, ignoring him, pushes Chance back into his chair and says to Yentroc, "I challenge your claim." Gelana unties the leather string of a beaded necklace she is wearing and removes a small white bead from it. She places the bead on the table in front of them.

"Please," Chance protests. He again tries to stand up, but this time Yentroc pushes him back.

"Very well," Yentroc says to Gelana. She pulls her long dark hair to the side so that she can take off a similar necklace. After untying it, she slides off one of the white beads and says, "I cannot believe you would challenge my first claim, but if you insist." She then places it on the table next to Gelana's bead and says, "There, now that we both have our honor on the line, I hope you are happy."

"Are you two serious?" Ja'noa asks. Even with a disgruntled tone Ja'noa's voice comes across as pleasant and cheerful. "There are other elves out there you know."

"But we are traveling north," Kel'ana replies. "We aren't likely to find any up there. It could be a long time before we find any men."

"Are you challenging Yentroc too?" Ja'noa asks.

"No," Kel'ana answers, "I just want to see them fight."

"Don't encourage them," Evelena says.

Chance tries again to reason with them. This time he does not try to stand as he says, "Ladies, there is no need to fight."

Gelana looks at Chance for a moment. With a grin she looks at Yentroc and says, "He is right, there is no code that says we can't *both* have him."

Yentroc smiles back and says, "Well, we wouldn't earn any claim honor, but I am alright with that."

Chance, now blushing, says, "That is not what I meant."

Lyra, interrupting the conversation, asks, "Aren't you two are forgetting something?"

Yentroc and Gelana look at each other, puzzled. They turn to Lyra who points to her right ear and asks, "Are there any markings?"

"Oh, right," Yentroc says, "I forgot."

"I'll check," says Gelana. She grabs Chance by the hair and turns his head.

"Hey!" Chance yells. "Careful." He turns his head allowing Gelana to check the back of his right ear.

"There is a mark of Dri'el, and," Gelana pauses, "I don't believe it," she says releasing Chance's hair.

"What is it?" Yentroc asks.

"The first male elf I come across on our Rite of Passage, and I am related to him," Gelana says sounding frustrated. She grabs her bead from the table.

Kel'ana laughs and says, "Gelana, you just tried to sleep with your brother."

"He is not my brother," Gelana snaps. "At least, I don't *think* he is."

"He is La'harn?" Rehma asks. "I don't believe it." She walks over and grabs Chance's hair. She turns his head again to look for herself.

"Ow!" Chance yells out. "Really, ladies, you could just ask."

Evelena, with her hand over her face, shakes her head in disbelief.

Rehma looks at the back of his right ear and says, "Dri'el and La'harn. He is both." She releases Chance, who is now looking annoyed.

"I am so sorry about this, "Evelena says. "We don't travel much."

"I can tell," Chances replies.

Lyra says, "Two houses? That is rare. I don't get to meet many others from two houses."

"Well, there are no marks of Ree on him, so I guess he is all mine," Yentroc says with a smile at Gelana who still looks angry.

"Look," Chance says, trying one final time to be heard, "I am sorry, but I am not here for—"

Before he can finish, Yentroc announces, "I claim this male as mine! Evelena, Kel'ana, only the two of you can challenge my claim."

Evelena sighs and says, "I have no interest in challenging your claim." She looks at Chance who seems to have given up in trying to speak.

Yentroc looks at Kel'ana and asks, "You weren't interested right?"

"Let me think about it for a moment," Kel'ana says with a smile. She brushes aside a long blonde curl from her face to get a better look at Chance. Chance, notices that the color of her eyes are as blue as his own, though neither of their eyes are as blue as Yentroc's. Kel'ana strokes the beads on her necklace for a moment making Yentroc wait. Then she finally says, "No, you can have him."

Yentroc smiles and sighs with relief. "Good," she says as she turns to Chance and reaches for his hand.

"I deny your claim," Chance says as he stands up.

Yentroc looks stunned as she says, "What?"

Chance, no longer finding this situation amusing, says to Yentroc, "I am very sorry, I know that this will cause you to receive dishonor, but I must decline." Chance looks at Evelena and says, "I wish you all the best of luck. I am sure you will have no problem finding a guide."

Gelana laughs and says to Yentroc, "You just got rejected." She opens a small pouch from around her waist and pulls out a black bead.

"Wait," Yentroc says, "does that really count?"

"Yes, it does," Lyra answers.

Yentroc angrily snatches the black bead from Gelana. She picks up her white bead from the table and begins to thread the beads onto her necklace.

"I am sorry," Chance repeats, "I tried to tell you."

"Wait a second," Evelena says. Walking up to Chance she asks him, "How did you know that would cause her to earn dishonor?"

"That is common knowledge," Chance replies.

"No, it isn't," Evelena replies sounding suspicious. "People do know about our honor necklaces. In fact we are quite proud of them, but you are not likely to know something that specific unless you have spent some time with Amazons. Since Kyle isn't a common name for an elf, I have to ask, who are you really?"

Fortunately for Chance, at that very moment the small crowd of the inn cheers as tall ruggedly handsome man enters the Pick Ax. He stands taller then everyone in the inn, and is covered from head to toe in thick furs. He has a short reddish blonde beard. His hair is the same color and hangs down to his broad shoulders. Chance recognizes him and quickly looks away as he pulls his cloak back over his head. This goes unnoticed by everyone except Evelena.

With a heavy Slavic accent the man announces loudly to everyone, "Sven has returned. Everyone gets round of drinks on Sven!"

*****

"What is a Slavic accent?" Haley asks.

"It's what a Russian accent sounds like," Kyle explains.

"Sven isn't a Russian name," says Laura.

Kyle nods his head and says, "You're right, it isn't, and Russians do not refer to themselves in a third person narrative. You have to remember that the cultures in Runefell are mixed. We well learn more about Sven later, but first..."

*****

The crowd cheers for Sven as Yentroc and Gelana look at each other with a grin. They shrug their shoulders, and start to make their way to the big northerner.

While everyone's attention is on Sven, Chance takes the opportunity to get away. As he passes Evelena he leans over to her and whispers, "This man can help you. Just don't say that I sent you."

Before Evelena can respond, Chance slips through the crowd and finds his way to the innkeeper. "Here," Chance says, handing a gold coin to the dwarf behind the counter. "I want a private room."

"Sure thing," he says handing him a key. "Straight up the stairs the first door on the left."

"Thank you," Chance says. He then moves through the crowd and then up the stairs to his room. He turns and looks down from the balcony watching as Evelena introduces herself to Sven.

Chance enters his room as Sven says to Evelena, "So, what can Sven do for you lovely ladies?"

Of the seven sisters, Yentroc and Rehma are the tallest. Yet as tall as they are, they still only comes up to this man's shoulders. Yentroc looks at Gelana and the two of them giggle as Evelena says, "My sisters and I are looking for a way to get across the mountains into the old orcnea territories. Would you be able to guide us?"

Sven laughs and says, "Now why would such beautiful women want to go to such an ugly place?"

"We have our reasons," Evelena answers. "One of which is to see if the orcneas have truly returned."

"Orcneas, yes," Sven says with a sigh. "There have been a few small raids lately, but nothing too big."

"So would you like to show us the way?" Gelana asks with a smile.

"Sven cannot say no to so many beautiful women," he says with a grin. "Let us sit down and discuss what we will need to bring."

Chapter 15
The Eighth Sister

In his room Chance is preparing to go to sleep. He walks over to the bed and takes off his cloak. He unbuckles his breast plate and places it on a chair next to his bed. Just as he is about to take off his talisman there is a knock at his door. He tucks the powerful relic back in his shirt and cautiously walks to the door. Chance asks, "Can I help you?" He then listens for any sign of who may be on the other side.

Another knock at the door startles him. He unlocks the door and opens it only to find no one there. He looks around and then steps out into the hall. The hall is empty so Chance returns to his room and once again locks the door. Then he stops suddenly realizing that he is not alone.

He creates a small fireball in his hand then clinches his first extinguishing the flame. He then swipes his hand in front of him leaving a heavy trail of smoke. He takes a step back and watches as the smoke continues to dissipate before him. Then suddenly, as the smoke advances away from him, a shape begins to from. It is the shape of a person. In an instant Chance has his sword at the smoky figure's neck.

"Reveal yourself," Chance commands.

"Very cleaver," a female voice answers. Then an elven female appears as she pulls back a cloak from her head. She is as tall as Chance and has long red hair. On her right cheek are the markings of a fiery comet. On her left temple, arcing around her eye, is a silver crescent moon. She, much like all the other Amazons of the Silver Moon, is beautiful.

"Who are you and why are you in my room?" Chance asks as he lowers his sword.

The Amazon ignores Chances question and asks, "Why are you following my sisters?"

"I am not following anyone," Chance tries to explain. "I am merely—"

"Do not lie to me," she interrupts. "You may have them fooled, but I don't believe you, Kyle, if that is even your real name."

Chance smiles and says, "So, you were down stairs watching. Why don't you tell me your name? I can already tell you are from the house of Ree."

"You seem to know a lot about us," she replies, "and you do look familiar. Have we met before?"

Chance tries to remember if he has ever seen this woman before. "What is your name?" He asks.

"My name is Kristieana," she answers.

Chance cannot remember anyone named Kristieana. "I am sorry I don't believe we have met."

"Very well," Kristieana replies. "I am looking after my sisters and making sure they are safe. I have had my eye on you since you arrived here."

"Oh," Chance replies. "Well, I am no threat to them, and as I already told your sisters, I am not interested in being anyone's claim." Chance then opens the door and says, "Now unless there is anything else..."

She storms over to the door and slams it shut. "That is not what I am here for!" She says angrily. Then she looks at Chance with a grin and adds, "But for the record, if I chose to claim you for my own, I doubt you would deny me."

Chance calmly looks her in the eyes and says, "Well, if you are not here for pleasure then what?"

She quickly grabs Chance by his shirt and pins him against the wall. She then warns, "If you are lying to me, Kyle, I will make you regret it."

"Bold words for someone who just had a sword at her neck," Chance replies.

She then reaches up with her left hand and turns Chance's head to the side and looks at the markings on the back of his ear. Chance sighs and does not resist. "So you *are* La'harn and Dri'el," She says. "Impressive."

Chance grabs her hand and pulls it free from his head. Then with his other hand he takes Kristieana by her hair. He turns them around, and now he is the one pressing her against the wall.

"So, there is fight in you after all," Kristieana says with a smile.

"Do they know you are following them?" Chance asks as he continues to hold her against the wall.

"No," she replies, "and if you tell them—"

"Again with the threats," Chance says with a small grin. "You are hardly in the position for that right now."

"So, what are you going to do with me?" She asks softly with a grin of her own.

Chances doesn't say a word. He only holds her there against the wall in silence. He looks her in the eyes for only a moment before looking down. He releases his grip on her and as he turns and walks away from her she asks, "Where are you going?" When Chance does not answer her she continues, "You don't start something like that with me and just walk away."

Chance stops and replies, "I don't know what you're talking about."

"Is that so?" she asks as she walks up behind him. She reaches out and turns him to face her.

The two of them stand there looking each other over for a moment. "Why are you still here?" Chance asks.

"It's been a long time for me," she answers. "I am deciding if I want to take you for the night or not."

Chance moves in closer to her. Now with their faces only inches apart he says, "I thought you said you weren't here for that."

"Who says I can't reconsider?" she answers. "I would have to break one of my own rules though, and I am trying to figure out if you are worth it or not."

"And what rule is that?" Chance asks.

"I usually require a man tall enough that I have to look up," Kristieana says with a smile.

"I think it is time for you to leave," Chance replies as he turns and walks back over to his bed.

Kristieana follows him and continues to stay close as she softy asks, "What is wrong? Did I hurt your feelings?"

Chance turns back to face her once more and replies, "I assure you that my feelings are fine."

"Do you not like women?" she asks.

Chance can't help but laugh a bit at the question before answering her, "Of course I do."

"Alright," she says thinking for a bit. Then she asks, "Are you capable of being with a woman?"

"Trust me that is not a problem," Chance answers, somewhat annoyed by the question.

"You do not have a ring on your finger," She says as she now slowly walks around him, "Do you belong to someone else?"

Chance gives the question some thought. It has been over a decade since his wife had passed, though he still feels for her he has been ready to move on for some time. Then he thinks of Ariella, though he once loved her as much as anyone, so many years have passed. Then, of course, there is the kiss between Ariella and Fernando that he can't get out of his mind. All these thoughts go through his head.

"There is someone else," Kristieana says, "isn't there?"

Chance caught up in his own thoughts almost doesn't hear her. He finally looks up and answers, "No. There is no one else."

Kristieana abruptly stops circling Chance. Then with a look of confusion and frustration she asks, "So, what is it then? Is it just me?"

"No," Chance says trying to explain, "that is not it at all."

By this time Kristieana is visibly angry. She snaps at Chance, "I don't know what your problem is and I don't care." She pushes Chance out of the way and starts to head for the door. "I seriously doubt you could have handled me anyway."

Suddenly she is stopped as Chance grabs her arm and pulls her back to him. He holds her tightly pinning her arms at her sides. They are face to face again and she struggles a bit to free herself, but he does not let go. She stops and says, "Let go of me."

"I don't think so," Chance replies. "Not just yet."

"Hmm. So you do want me to stay?" Kristieana asks with a smile.

"Who says *I* can't reconsider?" he asks mimicking her earlier statement. With his heart beating loud and fast, Chance cannot remember the last time he felt such exhilaration.

"You are a clever one?" Kristieana replies. She demands again, "Let me go!" as she tries once again to break free.

"Say please," Chance says.

Kristieana laughs and says, "I will do NO such thing."

"Well then," Chance says still with a grin on his face, "I guess if you like it here so much in my arms you can stay."

Kristieana stops struggling. "I have been in worse places," she says drawing her face in a little closer to Chance.

Chance also moves closer, and says, "I am sure you have."

Then as their lips are just about to touch he stops. Moments go by that feel much longer. Chance loosens his hold a bit and brings his right hand up to her face. He lightly brushes her cheek and then runs his fingers through her hair. She closes her eyes and tries to move in the last bit to kiss him, but when his hand reaches the back of her head he grabs her long hair tightly and pulls her head back exposing her neck.

Kristieana gasps and asks, "Why are you teasing me?" Chance does not answer her. Instead he inhales deeply taking in the scent of the Midnight Tear blossom, commonly applied by elven women to their necks due to its sweet aroma. She can feel his warm breath on her neck. She then says, "It's been a long time since a man really knew how to handle me. What other surprises do you have?"

With one hand still holding her head back by her hair, he uses his other hand to pull her necklace out from underneath her robe. He looks at all the different colored beads around her neck. While most of the beads are white, he notices a dozen silver beads.

"Silver beads?" questions Chance as he releases her hair. "So, you are a healer then."

"It is my specialty," she replies. Chance spots three blue beads and smiles. "What are you smiling about?" she asks.

"Three blue beads?" Chance asks as he lets go of the necklace.

"Yes, three," Kristieana replies, with a confused tone. "What is wrong with that?" She adds sounding a bit offended.

"Nothing, I just figured..." Chance doesn't finish realizing that what he was about to say could be considered highly offensive.

"You figured what?" Kristieana asks angrily, "That I would have claimed more men? Is that what you thought?" Kristieana breaks free from Chance's embrace. She steps back and glares at him awaiting an explanation.

Chance searches carefully for the right words. "You are clearly beautiful," he says, "and you most certainly are not timid. I doubt many men would deny a claim by you. I mean no offense, but yes, I am a little surprised that you only have three."

"If you must know," Kristieana replies, "Most men are not worth claiming." She then smiles and teases, "Just like you, I have no intention of adding you to my claims."

"I see," Chance says with a grin. "So you just intend to lay with me without any claim."

Kristieana, now smiles, and asks, "There is no code against that is there?"

"No, there isn't," Chance replies. Then thinking a bit Chance realizes that he has to tell her who he really is. "There is something I have to tell you." He finally says.

"Oh, and what it that?" She asks as she lightly runs her fingers through his hair.

"I have to tell you who I really am," he replies.

She smiles and grabs his shirt. She turns him around and pushes him on to the bed and says, "Don't *tell* me who you are. *Show* me."

Runefell

The words of Kristieana seem to take Chance off guard as he asks, "What did you say?" Kristieana stops and looks at him. It is clear to her that something is wrong. Chance stands up and slowly walks to the window.

"Did I say something wrong?" She asks, sounding concerned.

Chance doesn't immediately answer her. He stands there for a moment as if his mind is far away. "It's nothing," he finally manages to say. He turns back to the beautiful red haired woman and continues, "It just that I have heard that said before...long ago."

"Oh," Kristieana replies, "I am sorry." She walks over to him and takes his hand and asks, "Then tell me, Kyle, what is your real name?"

But before Chance can speak, they are interrupted with the sound of a loud bell from outside. Chance quickly opens the window. He hears the sound of a watchman calling out "Orcneas! Orcneas are attacking!"

Chance turns to warn Kristieana, who is already pulling her cloak over her head before disappearing. He hears her voice say, "Come on! We have to help."

"Go!" Chance says, as he looks out the window, "I will go this way." Chance leaps down onto a roof only a few feet from the window. He changes into the eagle and begins to fly. He looks down and can see two guards holding the rear gate to the town closed. On the other side of the giant swinging gate are a few dozen orcneas. Chance lands next to a small building on the edge of town near the gate. The house sits on a small hill and Chance is able to see the gate clearly. He changes back into his elven form as he tries to stay hidden in the darkness along the building's side.

Chapter 16
First Blood

    From out of the Inn the seven sisters appear with others from inside. Sven of the North is with them. He draws out his massive great sword. They make their way to the gate and position themselves around the gate entrance. The half circle formation is made up of townsfolk with various weapons including picks and hammers. Only a few have swords. Mixed in among them are the amazons. Their fine weapons and armor make them stand out from the rest.
    Evelena yells to the others, "Here they come. Everyone get ready! Lyra, take point and get ready to blind them with the flash spell, then fall back immediately. Everyone else, be ready to cover your eyes or look away when I give the signal!" The townsfolk listen and nod at Evelena's orders.
    "Just tell me when," Lyra says as she starts to walk toward the gate. After two steps she disappears, becoming invisible.
    Gelana, with her dark hair pulled back from her face, stands ready with her spear in one hand and her shield in the other. Rehma eagerly awaits with a sword in each hand. Yentroc concentrates and a dark mist begins to take form in her right hand. It takes the form of a sphere and gives off a faint dark glow. Kel'ana has her bow drawn and has her eyes closed tight awaiting Lyra's flash spell. Ja'noa prepares a very large ball of lightning that requires both hands to hold. Evelena stands right in the middle, she summons a large stone sphere in her hands and waits.
    The two guards can no longer hold back the enemy from the other side. They run back and take formation with the others as the gate bursts open.
    "Now, Lyra!" Evelena yells.
    Lyra yells, "Cover!" A split second later a bright flash comes from the center of the half circle formation. Most cover their eyes as they were told. Only a few townsfolk are caught off guard. The entire front line of orcneas stop dead in their tracks and are blinded by the incredibly bright flash of light. Lyra runs back to the line and as she passes Evelena she says, "I am clear."
    "Good work," Evelena tells her. Evelena then yells, "Fire!" Evelena releases her stone sphere hitting an orcnea square in the chest. The impact is as if he had been hit by a small catapult. Not only does it kill the orcnea, it knocks it back into two others, knocking them to the ground.
    Gelana throws her spear and it finds its mark straight into the heart of the nearest orcnea. She then quickly draws her sword and awaits the final order to move in.
    The orcneas that were behind the front lines try to push through the blinded orcneas in the front. One breaks though and is struck down by Ja'noa's lightning bolt. Across her chest, Ja'noa wears a leather sash holding six throwing daggers. In an instant she quick-draws one of the daggers and throws it, wounding an orcnea.
    The orcnea grabs the dagger, and as he pulls it out he is finished off by an arrow fired from Kel'ana's bow. Yentroc fires her spell at an orcnea that has

pushed its way through. The orcnea sees it coming and drops to the ground. While the orcnea escapes the effects of the spell, the blinded orcnea behind him does not as the spell strikes him. The orcnea clutches his chest as the dark bolt takes his life.

Other orcneas begin to push through and they begin to advance into the middle of the semi-circle defense. Rehma is very anxious and says under her breath, "Come on. Give the order."

Evelena yells out the command that Rehma has been waiting for. "Attack!"

Rehma charges quickly and engages the first orcnea she can. The orcnea is caught off guard by her aggressiveness. Rehma spins around and ducks down low. This maneuver confuses the orcnea who was prepared to block with his shield at chest level. Rehma is able to easily thrust both of her swords up and into the orcnea's gut. She stands up and pulls her swords from the orcnea. He falls to his knees and Rehma makes sure he is dead as she slashes the orcnea across his reddish-orange neck. Blood spatters onto Rehma from her first kill.

Chance anxiously watches in the distance as the battle unfolds. Suddenly he hears a voice behind him. "Aren't you going to help them?" Kristieana asks.

Chance quickly turns to see her standing there. "I didn't hear you there," he says as he turns back to watch the battle.

"You *can* fight can't you? Or is all that fancy armor just for show?" She asks.

Chance sighs, knowing that he is going to have to explain who he really is. "I have been known to slay a few orcneas," he finally answers.

"Still, you could help," she says.

Chance puts out his hand and closes his eyes. He opens them again and when he raises his hand a fire comes up from the ground beneath an orcnea.

"Did you do that?" Kristieana asks.

"No," Chance lies. With another movement of his hand the fire begins to move and follow the orcnea as it tries to flee. Even though the flame is not as powerful as a fireball, the orcnea soon falls and Chance moves the fire to another target.

"You *are* doing that," she says, "but we are thirty or forty paces away. How is that possible?"

"I have been told that I am not too bad with fire spells," Chance answers as he continues to help from a distance. "They are doing quite well," he says. "I am impressed. They seem to be very organized"

"Well," Kristieana says, "I did help train them."

They watch together as Evelena blocks an orcnea's attack with her shield. She then lifts the shield quickly pushing the orcnea off balance as she slashes the orcnea with her sword. Gelana also uses her shield to her advantage bashing it against an orcnea's head.

Just behind the front lines of the melee, Ja'noa throws her last dagger, killing a charging orcnea. She reaches for another not realizing she is out. An orcnea charges her with a large two handed mace. She rolls to the side dodging

Crossroads

the orcnea's wild swing. Drawing two short swords from her back she stands up as the orcnea comes at her again. She dodges again barely avoiding the hit. She then tries to parry the next attack but her sword is knocked from her hand by the large mace. The orcnea begins to swing again, and Ja'noa ducks and rolls toward it. When she comes out of her roll she finds herself right next to the red creature. She tries to swing her sword but she is too close. The orcnea grabs her wrist and tries to throw her to the ground, but Ja'noa rolls and ends up on her feet. The orcnea readies for another swing with his mace but before he can swing his weapon Ja'noa's eyes glow blue, and lightening shoots forth from them. The orcnea is shocked to his knees before falling face down in the snow. Holding her injured hand from the attempted parry, she falls back to catch her breath.

Also behind the front lines Kel'ana shoots arrow after arrow into the orcneas. While she is not as powerful as Rehma or Gelana, her speed is uncanny and her aim is steady. Shot after shot she wounds each of her targets only to quickly notch another arrow to finish it off. One orcnea closes in on her unnoticed. She only manages to see it out of the corner of her eye as the orcnea swings a two handed ax at her. Kel'ana barely manages to get out of the way. With her bow still in her left hand, she casts a spell with her right. Her hand begins to glow with a light blue aura. When the orcnea swings again she is waiting. She leaps out of the way and grabs the orcnea's arm. The touch of her hand freezes the orcnea's arm, and as the orcnea stumbles back in pain she then casts another ice spell. This spell creates a large, sharp icicle. She releases it and it hits the orcnea with the same precision as her arrows. The orcnea is killed as Kel'ana takes a few steps back and readies her bow again to resume her attacks.

In the heat of the battle and on the front line, Rehma swings her swords at an orcnea. The orcnea blocks the attack with his shield. Rehma continues to advance as the orcnea retreats. Rehma soon finds herself surrounded by orcneas. She quickly turns her swords in her hands to a reverse grip. Then as she takes a step backwards, she thrusts her swords behind her striking the orcnea that has flanked her. An orcnea to her left swings and misses as she dodges. The orcnea to her right seizes the opportunity to strike her with his mace. It hits her right shoulder and forces her to drop the sword in her right hand. She quickly turns to face him. Swinging her left sword she catches the orcnea right across the throat. With two more orcneas close by, Rehma is still in danger.

Gelana, seeing that her sister is in trouble, steps forward with her shield and blocks an incoming attack that is intended for Rehma. Chance's flames engulf the other orcnea and it flees.

"Careful with those flames, Kel'ana!" Gelana yells.

"It's not me," Kel'ana says.

Rehma backs up as Gelana places herself in between the orcneas and her injured sister. Yentroc runs over to Rehma and says, "Hold still, I'll heal you." Yentroc hands glow white and she places them on Rehma's shoulder.

Rehma looks to Yentroc and says, "Thank you." She then draws her larger two handed sword from her back and grips it tightly. She rejoins the front line and stands next to Gelana as they continue the fight.

While all of this is happening, the town folk are doing the best they can against the raiders. One man is stabbed in his right thigh and falls to the ground. The orcnea that stabbed him tries to finish him off but before he can, Sven grabs the orcnea by the neck and pulls him back, throwing him into the fire that Chance is still moving around the battlefield.

Off in the distance Chance and Kristieana sill watch as Chance moves the fire once again to help the inn keeper who has become surrounded but three orcneas. The dwarven inn keeper swings his ax at one of the orcneas just as the fire from Chance chases another away. Sven steps in and almost cleaves the third orcnea in two with his sword.

"I can only count six of the girls," Chance says sounding concerned.

"Lyra is probably still invisible," Kristieana replies.

Kristieana's theory is correct. Lyra has managed to sneak around the orcnea lines while staying invisible. The orcneas that were blinded earlier are now starting to see clearly. Lyra is making sure that one by one she is disabling them as she hits them on the backs of their heads with her staff. During this a bigger threat comes out of the darkness.

Chance and Kristieana watch as a huge ogre standing as tall as a single level building emerges from the cold dark night. "By the gods!" Kristieana gasps.

Lyra becomes aware of the threat when she hears the giant beast taking a deep breath of air behind her. She slowly turns around to see the ogre, as big around as a five hundred year old oak, sniffing the air for Lyra's scent. The ogre cannot see her but it can smell her. Lyra freezes fear. The ogre takes one final deep breath before it lets out a loud roar and swings his massive fist sweeping the entire area in front of him.

Lyra is sent flying, and as she hits the ground she almost loses consciousness. Her spell is broken now and she is visible again. Even though the last of the orcneas are slain, this massive beast stands before them and Lyra is directly in its path.

"Lyra!" Evelena calls to her.

Lyra can barely move. To her the world is spinning. She can barely make out the giant ogre as it takes a step towards her. Yentroc launches another Dark Bolt at it but it doesn't have any affect. Kel'ana shoots it with three arrows that only harmlessly stick into it. Ja'noa shoots a lightning bolt at it. This does make the beast flinch, but it still closes in on Lyra.

Sven, yells to the ogre, "Here! You ugly beast," but the ogre ignores Sven and puts its two fists together and prepares to crush Lyra with a powerful blow.

Suddenly a huge ball of fire strikes the ogre. The brute survives the massive blast but is hurt badly and is stunned. Evelena looks behind her to see who cast the spell. She sees Chance pulling his cloak back over his head. He steps back into the shadows where Kristieana is hiding.

Rehma and Gelana close in on the ogre and begin to stab fiercely into the giant threat. Kel'ana now releases a large ice sphere at its head. The scorched beast falls to the ground. Sven finally reaches the ogre and makes sure it is no longer a threat by taking his sword and removing its head.

Kristieana stares at Chance in amazement. "Who are you?" She asks.

The question goes unanswered as Chance turns and walks along the far side of the building out of site from the others.

Though the battle is done, the scene is a chaotic one. Many of the town's people are injured, but surprisingly none have died. Because of this the mood seems to be a positive one as the town has successfully defended itself from the orcnea attack.

Yentroc quickly runs over to Lyra and casts the healing spell on her. "Lyra, can you hear me?" she asks.

Lyra groans as she brushes her brown hair from her face and opens her eyes. She asks Yentroc, "What...happened?"

Yentroc sighs with relief. She then smiles and jokingly says to Lyra, "Well, there was this festival..."

Gelana then continues to have fun with her and says, "And you had way too much to drink."

"Ugh," Lyra says, "I hope I at least had fun."

Everyone laughs as Evelena looks over to where Chance had been. When she doesn't see him she looks carefully around at the crowds of people.

Kel'ana walks up to Rehma and says, "Hey, Rehma?"

"What?" Rehma asks.

"You dropped something," Kel'ana says as she hands Rehma her sword that she dropped earlier in the battle.

"Thanks," Rehma says with a smile.

Kel'ana then walks over to Ja'noa and says, "Ja'noa?"

"I know," Ja'noa answers putting her hand out.

"You dropped something," Kel'ana says anyway handing her the short sword that was knocked from her hand.

Now they all laugh even louder, as Ja'noa says, "Kel'ana, you always say, 'you dropped something.'"

"Well," Kel'ana explains with a smile, "it's always true."

"So, Evelena," Rehma says with a smile. "When do we get our honor beads?"

"Is that all you are worried about?" Evelena asks with a sigh.

Sven asks, "What are you talking about?"

Lyra holds out her necklace to him and says, "See this? Each bead is a token of honor. The different color beads stand for different achievements. Red ones, are for kills in combat. Evelena is in charge of awarding those."

"What are white ones for?" Sven asks looking at Lyra's necklace.

"They are the tokens for common honor given to us by the elders for doing certain tasks," Lyra explains. "They are also the ones we use to challenge each other with."

"How do you mean, 'challenge'?" Sven asks.

"Think of it like betting your honor," Gelana explains. "Each amazon puts one of her beads on the line. The winner keeps them. You can challenge someone to almost anything really. As long as they both agree to put their honor on the line."

"Sven understands," Sven says sounding intrigued, "and what about black ones?"

"Oh, these?" Lyra replies uncomfortably. She tucks her necklace back under her shirt.

"Those are dishonor," Gelana says giving Lyra a grin. "You get those for disobeying," She looks at Yentroc and adds, "and for getting denied a claim."

Yentroc glares at Gelana and says, "Oh, be quiet."

"For disobeying?" Sven asks.

Gelana laughs and says, "Lyra is always causing trouble and is a bad influence on us all."

They all laugh except for Lyra who seems to be embarrassed. Sven looks a Lyra and smiles. "Sven, somehow doubts that this little one would be big problem," he says.

"Alright, everyone, enough talk," Evelena says interrupting the conversation. "Let's help these people first then we can worry about honor."

The Amazons begin to help the injured the best they can. Yentroc is the only one with any healing spells. She tends to those with the worst injuries as the others help move the injured inside.

The innkeeper approaches Evelena and says, "Thank you so much for helping us. I don't think we could have done it without you."

"You are welcome," Evelena replies.

"They will sing songs of this battle someday," Sven says. "The day that Amazons, and Sven of the North saved Copper Pass."

This was the first of what would someday be many battles. This was the first blood for these seven Sisters of the Silver Moon.

Chapter 17
Revealed

A short time later as the girls gather themselves together, Evelena spots Chance with the hood of his cloak over his head. She watches him as he tends to one of the injured. He heals the man then moves quickly from one injured person to the next.

While healing one of the men Chance hears Kristieana as she whispers in his ear, "It looks like you have everything under control. I'll be waiting for you back in the room. I have some questions for you."

Chance continues to heal the people while a few men finish patching the gate. Soon everyone is heading back into the inn. Chance decides that he has done as much as he can, and decides to go back to his room. He heads back to the inn as Evelena follows him closely. She now has some questions for Chance and she is determined to get straight answers.

The rest of the seven sisters are already inside the Pick Ax. They are at a table with Sven, and are listening to Lyra tell her story about what happened to her.

"The next thing I remember," Lyra says to them, "you were telling me I was at a festival."

They laugh as Chance enters the room. With the hood of his cloak over his head he starts to make his way pass the table and avoids eye contact. Evelena is still right behind him. As Chance passes right in front of the table, Yentroc asks, "So who cast that big fireball?"

"He did," Evelena answers as she pulls the cloak from Chance's head. "Alright, Kyle," she demands, "Who are you really?"

Chance looks away from the table and ducks his head. Evelena grabs his arm and turns him to face her. "Answer me!" Evelena demands again.

"Chance?" The loud voice of Sven calls out. "Chance Na'Moon! How are you, my old friend? Why did you not tell Sven you were here?"

Now everyone in the inn is watching and Chance knows that his cover is blown. He forces a smile and looks up to Sven and says, "I am well, my friend."

"Did he say Chance Na'Moon?" Rehma asks Gelana. Rehma stands up and starts to walk over to Chance.

"Rehma, wait," Gelana says as she also stands up.

Sven yells out to everyone in the tavern, "Everyone! The Orcnea Slayer, Chance Na'Moon, is here!"

The crowd lets out a cheer. Kristieana comes out from Chance's room to see what all the noise is about. She has her cloak over her head, but has not activated the invisibility spell.

Chance forces another smile as Sven announces, "Everyone gets round of drinks of Sven in honor of guest Chance!" The crowd cheers again.

Ja'noa whispers to Kel'ana, "That's Chance Na'Moon? I always thought he would be taller."

Evelena looks at Chance. "Why?" she asks. "Why didn't you tell us?"

Chance stands there looking at her, unsure what to say. Just then Rehma reaches him and asks, "So you are Chance Na'Moon?"

"Yes," Chance answers.

Gelana, who is trying to get to her sister, is caught up in the crowd. She calls out, "Rehma, stop!"

Yentroc looks at Gelana puzzled for a moment. Realizing that Gelana is trying to stop Rehma, she quickly stands up and also tries to make her way through the crowd.

Rehma smiles brightly and says, "I have always wanted to meet you." She extends her hand to Chance.

Chance doesn't quite know what to make of this as he takes her hand and shakes it, "The pleasure is mine," he says politely.

"Oh no," Rehma replies, "the pleasure is definitely all mine." She firmly clutches Chance's hand and pulls him towards her as she punches Chance in the face. The onlookers of the inn are stunned. Caught completely off guard, Chance falls to his knees and is now an easy target. Rehma, still grasping his right hand, lifts Chance's arm and kicks him in his side. Her foot catches him just behind his breastplate. Dazed and cringing in pain, Chance looks up at Rehma, who now sees blood dripping down from his nose and lip. Still refusing to release her grip, Rehma says, "I have waited a long time for this." She pulls Chance towards her again. This time she drives her forearm and elbow across his face. Barely conscious, Chance is knocked onto his back.

"Rehma, what are you doing?" Evelena yells as she grabs her arm.

"Stop it, Rehma!" Gelana yells as she and Yentroc close in.

Rehma pays no attention to her sisters as she pulls free from Evelena. She kneels down on top of Chance, pinning him to the ground. She finally lets go of his hand only to grab a fist full of his hair. Still stunned from the first three hits, Chance is unable to defend himself as Rehma begins to land one fist after another into his now bloodied face. Blood splatters on her armor and now covers her right hand as she relentlessly continues to strike him.

Gelana and Yentroc finally reach Rehma and each grab one of her arms. They pull Rehma to her feet as she stomps on Chance's chest. She kicks him again in the side before they are able to get her away.

"No!" Rehma screams. "Let go of me. He's mine!"

Chance, lying in a small pool of his own blood, roles over to his hands and knees. His ears are ringing and his vision is hazy. He cannot remember the last time he was knocked down like that. He tries to stand but falls back to his hands and knees. He takes a deep breath as more blood falls to the floor. He looks up at Rehma who is kicking and screaming at her sisters.

"He killed my mother!" she screams. "He's the reason she's dead."

Gelana and Yentroc hold their sister back, as Chance tires to clear his head. Anger gives way to grief and soon Rehma stops fighting and falls into Gelana's arms as she tries to comfort her.

"I am so sorry," Evelena says as she checks on Chance, "are you alright?"

Chance looks at her and tries to focus. "I think so," he answers.

"I am really sorry, sir," Evelena says nervously. "Please, I am sure she doesn't mean it."

Evelena helps Chance slowly get to his feet when he suddenly remembers. "Teresa?" Chance says softly to himself.

Rehma glares at Chance and again her face fills with rage. "Don't you dare say her name!" She screams as she tries to come at Chance once more. "I will kill you!" She yells as Gelana and Yentroc struggle to hold her back.

"Rehma," Evelena yells, "that's enough!"

"What is going on?" Sven quietly asks Lyra.

Lyra answers, "Rehma's mother died in the Second Orcnea War while protecting Chance."

"Oh," Sven says. Then, as what he just heard sinks in, he repeats, "Oh!"

"It's his fault my mother is dead!" Rehma yells again.

The crowd that has been in total silence to witness these events now start to talk among themselves once more. Many go back their chairs while a few stay and continue to watch.

Yentroc has made her way back over to Chance she says, "Let me heal you."

"Don't you dare heal him," Rehma warns.

Yentroc looks at her and says, "Rehma, you can't be serious. He losing a lot of blood."

Rehma looks coldly at Chance and replies, "Let him bleed."

"It's alright," Chance says to Yentroc. "Thank you."

"I am so sorry about this," Evelena says again.

"It's not your fault," Chance replies. He looks around at the crowd who nervously look away. He glances up to the balcony and can see Kristieana looking down at him. She turns away and walks back into their room. Still feeling a little shaky, Chance slowly turns to Rehma who is still glaring at him. He slowly walks over to her as he wipes more blood from his face. Yentroc and Gelana hold Rehma a little tighter as Chance approaches. He stops and tries to look Rehma in the eyes, but can't. "Rehma," Chance says looking down, "I am sorry for the loss of your mother." He looks up at her and can see tears streaming down her face. "If I could have traded places with her..." Chance drops his eyes again. The silence feels like an eternity to Chance. He takes a deep breath and looks up again and says, "I am sorry."

Rehma doesn't respond. She instead rests her head on her Gelana's shoulder as Yentroc puts her arm around her as well.

Chance turns to Sven and says, "My friend, I am sorry we could not meet again under better circumstances."

"Sven is sorry too," he replies. "Are you going to be alright?"

"I have felt better," Chance says, "but I will be fine."

Putting his hand on Chance's shoulder, Sven says, "Sven will be guiding girls tomorrow over mountains. It will take couple days, but if you wish to join us..."

"No," Rehma interrupts. "If he goes, I will not."

Chance, holding his right side, smiles at his friend and says, "Thanks, my friend, but I have other matters to address."

With blood still covering his face Chance begins to speak loudly to the people in the inn. "Good people of Copper Pass. I come to you from Sheathelm to investigate the orcnea threat to this town."

Despite his appearance, Chance's words seem to put the crowd more at ease. "The Orcnea Slayer will protect us." Yells out one. The crowd responds with loud cheers.

"I have some bad news, however," Chance continues, as a serving wench hands him a towel. The crowd quiets down as Chance says, "To the east the orcneas are on the move." Now the crowd mumbles with concern.

"By tomorrow," Chance says as he wipes blood from his face with the towel, "the city of Northwind will have fallen."

The crowd erupts with loud conversation and Chance then tries to yell over them, "Tomorrow I am going over the mountains!" The crowd is too loud however and they do not hear him.

"People!" the loud voice of Sven booms over the inn.

The crowd quickly quiets. Chance glances over to his friend Sven who gives him a nod of support. Chance then turns back and continues, "Tomorrow I am going to fly over the mountains to find out if the west is in similar danger of invasion. If I find a serious threat from the orcneas, I'll be back to warn you. If I do not find orcneas in threatening numbers, I must return to the south where King Arioch is rallying the troops for war. Thank you."

The crowd now seems more positive as they begin to talk amongst themselves again.

"Sven," Chance says to his friend, "may I speak with you a moment please?"

"Of course," Sven replies. They walk over to the bottom of the stairs as Chance receives a few pats on the back from the crowd while others thank him for being there.

Yentroc and Gelana finally release Rehma, and as they watch Chance talking with Sven, they see Sven looking over at them and nod his head. "What do you think they are talking about?" Yentroc asks Gelana.

"I don't know," Gelana answers. "He is probably explaining why Rehma attacked him." They continue to watch Sven and Chance talk, and soon Sven pats him on the shoulder and then walks back over as Chance heads up the stairs.

When Sven gets back to the group Gelana asks, "So what was that about?"

Sven answers, "Uh...it was nothing. Just two friends catching up."

Chance finally reaches the top of the stairs and enters his room. Kristieana is already inside. "I knew I recognized you from somewhere," Kristieana says.

Chance looks at her for a moment. He shakes his head and says, "I am sorry, I still don't remember you."

"You wouldn't," Kristieana replies, as Chance closes the door. "I was only a young girl at the time. You and King Arioch came to our village. I remember it because it was the first time I ever saw a male in our village. I hid behind a tree and watched as you told A'ranah that Sha'al was killed."

"The start of the orcnea war," Chance says looking down. "I remember that day."

"Me too," Kristieana says as she walks up to Chance and lifts his chin. "I remember thinking how handsome you were, but I also remember the sadness in your eyes. A sadness that I still see now."

"Since the return of the orcneas," Chance says as he walks over to the window and looks out at the gate, "I have been facing many memories."

"So," Kristieana says as she walks over to Chance, "What was it you said? You have been known to slay a few orcneas? I would call that an understatement."

"That is why I stayed out of sight," Chance explains. "I know these girls are trying to prove themselves and I doubt they would want any help from me. Especially Rehma."

"You are probably right about that," Kristieana replies. "I must say though that I can't help but find a little humor in the fact that the great Chance Na'Moon got beaten by a young Amazon on her Rite of Passage."

Chance looks to her with a bloody smile and says, "It should be noted that she did so while my guard was down and she shook my hand."

"Sounds like an excuse to me," Kristieana says as she laughs. She then looks closely at Chances face that is now swelling and showing bruises. "She really hit you hard, didn't she?" she says, as she takes the towel from Chance's hand and wipes away some more blood.

"I don't remember the last time anyone hit me that hard," Chances says. "Or for that matter, so many times."

"I lost count of how many times she hit you, "Kristieana says. "Does it hurt?"

"Yes," Chance answers, still holding his ribs. "It hurts to breathe."

"It looks painful," Kristieana continues to tease.

"Alright," Chance says sounding a little more serious. "If you are going to just mock me—"

"Oh, listen to you," Kristieana says still having fun, "All tough now are we? You might want to watch that tone or instead of healing you I may just hit you myself."

Chance cannot help but laugh, and as he does more pain shoots through his side. "Alright, I am sorry. Now are you going to heal me, or are all those silver beads just for show?"

"Say please," she teases.

"Please," he says knowing that he is at her mercy.

"Since you asked nicely," Kristieana says. "You said it hurt to breathe, right?"

"Yes," Chance answers. "It's like a dagger is in my side."

"She probably broke a rib then," Kristieana says as she gently lifts his right arm. She places her hand on his side and closes her eyes. The soft white glow of her hand soothes the pain as it heals Chance.

"Oh," Chance says taking a deep breath. "Thank you."

"Now hold still," she says as she places her hands on Chances face. She straightens his nose with her thumbs. Chance winces a bit, and she says, "You know I have heard more than one telling of the story about how Rehma's mother died."

"Please," Chance interrupts. "I really would prefer not to discuss it."

"If you wish," Kristieana replies, "but just so you know, I don't believe it was your fault."

"Thank you," Chance says, "but I am not so certain."

"Alright, I am almost done," she says. Her hands glow white again for a moment, and when she removes them Chance's face is no longer swollen and the bleeding has stopped.

"Thank you," Chance says.

"Feel better now?" Kristieana asks, as she takes the towel and wipes away the remaining blood.

"Yes," Chance replies. "Much better."

"Good," Kristieana says with a smile. Then without warning she slaps Chance across the face. "Ow! What was that for?" Chance yells.

"That was for lying to me about who you were," Kristieana snaps. Then leaning in she quickly kisses the cheek she had just slapped and adds, "and that is for saving Lyra." She steps back and says, "Goodbye, Chance Na'Moon."

"Wait," Chance asks, "where are you going?"

"I know that there is no code that prevents me from being with you," Kristieana says, "but you did take vows with someone from the house of Ree. Sha'al Ree was my great, great, aunt, and while I know that doesn't make us related, I still am not sure how I feel about that."

"I understand," Chance says. "You don't have to go though. I'll sleep over there," he says as he points to a chair on the other side of the room.

Kristieana smiles and says, "My, you are a chivalrous one, aren't you?" She then looks at the bed and says, "No, you can sleep in the bed."

"Then where will you sleep?" Chance asks.

"In the bed too," Kristieana answers. "I am certainly not sleeping in a chair."

"Oh," Chance replies confused. "I see."

"And don't even think about trying anything," Kristieana warns as she removes her cloak, "because if you do I'll punch you in the face myself."

Chance smiles and laughs and says, "I understand, but how do you expect me to lay in the same bed as you and actually fall asleep?"

"Well, that's your problem and not mine," she replies with a smile.

Downstairs Sven and the other seven amazons are still sitting at the table.

Sven asks Rehma, "Sven knows this may not be something you want to talk about, but how is Chance responsible for your mother's death?"

Rehma stands up ignoring Sven's inquiry and says, "I am going to go clean up now and go to bed." There is still blood on her hands and arms from Chance. No one says a word to her as she leaves, and as she walks to the stairs, the people in the inn avoid getting in her way.

Evelena says to the group, "I am going up to our room, too. May your dreams guide you all safely tonight."

As Evelena gets up to leave, Yentroc and Gelana walk over to Sven. Yentroc asks, "So, Sven, do you have your own room here?"

"Of course," Sven answers. "Best room in all of Copper Pass."

Yentroc and Gelana look at each other and smile. Gelana leans against him and seductively asks, "We were wondering if maybe you would like to show us your room."

Sven nervously replies, "I...um...would like to but..."

"What's the matter?" Yentroc says as she leans against him. "Don't tell me that a big strong man like you is afraid of us."

Sven laughs and says, "Oh no, it is not *you* that Sven is afraid of."

Now Yentroc and Gelana look at each confused. Gelana asks, "Then what is it?"

Sven says, "The two of you are very beautiful. All of you are, of course, but Chance has already told Sven how young you are."

"What!" Gelana yells. "That is ridiculous. We are not children."

"The whole point of our journey," Yentroc explains, "is to experience the outside world."

"Believe me," Sven replies, "Sven would like nothing more than to give you both experience you would never forget, however Chance told Sven to take good care of you, and warned Sven not to touch any of you. He said that you were his sisters, and Sven respects that."

Yentroc looks at Gelana and says, "The next time Rehma gets her hands on Chance, let's just watch."

"I agree," Gelana says. "Come on, let's go to bed."

Gelana and Yentroc head to their room as Yentroc asks, "Sven didn't count as a denied claim, right?"

"No," Gelana replies, "we never officially stated we were claiming him."

"Good," Yentroc says as they walk up the stairs. "It would be humiliating to be refused twice in one night."

Sven says, "Sven is going to turn in now. Goodnight everyone. We will be leaving first thing in morning."

Lyra, who has been reading a book the whole time, looks up and says, "May your dreams guide you safely, Sven." Then to the others she says, "I am going to our room and read some more of this. I am curious about something." Lyra leaves the table and heads up the stairs to their room.

Ja'noa and Kel'ana are now left alone at the table. Kel'ana asks her, "Well, I am ready to go to bed, how about you?"

"Yes," Ja'noa replies. They get up to leave as two men at a table watch them closely. One of the men says something to the other and they laugh. Ja'noa and Kel'ana make their way pass them to the stairs when one of the men asks, "Hey ladies, where are you off to?"

Ja'noa smiles, and with a sweet voice she responds, "We are going to bed now."

"Well then," the man says, "you are going the wrong way. My room is down the hall."

Some of the men at the inn laugh. The innkeeper says, "Alright lads, leave the ladies alone."

"I am just having fun," says the man. Then he turns to Ja'noa and asks, "You like to have fun, don't you?"

Ja'noa smiles and cheerfully replies, "Oh, I like to have fun. Would you like to play a favorite game of mine?"

"Sure, sweet heart," the man says with a laugh. "What game might that be?"

Ja'noa walks over to nearest wall and takes out a dagger and sticks it into a wood beam. She then walks back and says, "Whoever can hit closest to the target is the winner. Do you have a knife or a dagger, or do you need to borrow one?" She displays her sash of daggers.

The man looks to be taken off guard by the question then finally says, "I have one," as he pulls out a large knife.

"Good," Ja'noa says, "you go first."

"Alright," the man says as he stands up and looks closely at the dagger in the wall.

"You can do it," says his friend.

He throws his knife and it sticks into the wall below the target dagger. It is about the length of the knife away from the target.

"Good throw," says his friend.

Ja'noa looks at the wall and says, "Oh, you are good. I don't know how I am going to beat that." She then pulls out two daggers, one in each hand, and throws them both simultaneously. Both daggers stick into the wall—one on each side of the target. They are less than half the distance away from the target as the man's throw.

The men cheer and laugh at the man who has just been bested at the hands of Ja'noa. As Ja'noa walks over and retrieves her daggers, Kel'ana follows her. The man grabs Kel'ana's wrist and says, "How about you, darling?"

Kel'ana doesn't say anything. She nervously looks at Ja'noa who says, "Let go of my friend or we can play a different game."

The man smiles and says, "And what is that?"

Ja'noa, in the blink of an eye, has her sword drawn and at the man's throat. She says sweetly, "It's called, let's see how much blood one man can bleed before passing out."

The man quickly releases Kel'ana's wrist and nervously says, "There is no need for that, ma'am. I was only kidding."

As Kel'ana moves over to the stairs Ja'noa puts her sword away and smiles. Then as they walk up the stairs Ja'noa turns back and says, "Thank you so much for playing, I had fun. May your dream guide you safely."

The girls enter their room at the end of the hall upstairs. The innkeeper says to the men, "Now you see why I wanted you lads to leave them alone?"

Chapter 18
Restless Night

Less than a half day from East Artos, the *Red Dawn* sails through the night. In her cabin, Ariella suddenly wakes up from a bad dream. She sits up startled and looks around for a bit. When she realizes where she is she takes a deep breath to calm herself. "Fernando," she quietly calls out as she gets up out of her bed. After looking around again she decides to go out on deck to search for him. She throws on a robe and exits her quarters.

The night helmsman greets her, "Good evening Captain. Can I help you?"

"Good evening, Jim," Ariella replies, "have you seen Mr. Greythorn?"

"Yes, ma'am," he replies, "I saw him head below deck just a little while ago."

"Thank you," Ariella replies. She makes her way below deck and finds Fernando sleeping in his cell. The cell door is open and she walks in and sits next to him on the floor. She watches Fernando as he sleeps and says softly to herself, "Fernando Greythorn, I do believe I was wrong about you." She puts her arm around him as she lays next to him. While curled up alongside him she soon falls asleep.

In Copper Pass there are a few others who are having a hard time sleeping. After some tossing and turning in the night, Kristieana says, "Chance, when I told you if you tried anything I would punch you in the face, you knew I was joking right?" When there is no response from Chance she rolls over only to find she is alone in the bed. "Chance?" she says as she looks around the room. Finding no one in the room she gets out of bed and puts her cloak on and wraps it tight around her. She then goes to the door and exits out onto the landing. As she looks down over the railing to the now empty inn, she can see Chance sitting alone at a table. In his hand he is holding a fire ball. He closes his eyes for a moment and soon the fire takes the shape of Ariella.

Just then Kristieana hears a door open down the hall. She quickly pulls the hood over her head and becomes invisible. She looks down the hall and can see that it is Evelena. Kristieana moves out of Evelena's way as she walks down the hall and across the landing. Evelena stops at the top of the stairs and also looks down at Chance, who has not noticed her.

Both Evelena and Kristieana stand there and watch as Chance stares deep into the fire in his hand. The fire changes shape from Ariella to his former wife, Sha'al Ree. Chance continues to sit there unaware that he is being watched. Then he changes the shape of the fire once again. This time it takes the form of Kristieana. Surprised by this, Kristieana gasps loudly.

Chance looks up to see who is there only to find Evelena. "Oh, hello," Chance says to her. "I didn't know you were there."

Evelena, also looking for who made the gasp, shifts her attention back to Chance. "Good evening, Mr. Na'Moon," she says nervously as she walks down the stairs. "I am sorry, I didn't mean intrude."

"You are not intruding," Chances says as he dissipates the fire in his hand, "and please, call me Chance."

Evelena says, "Yes, sir. I mean, Chance." She walks over to the table where Chance is sitting and asks, "May I sit here?"

Chance stands up and replies, "Yes, of course. Please do."

Kristieana slowly makes her way down the stairs so that she can hear what they are saying.

"I am very sorry about what Rehma did to you earlier," Evelena says.

"Thank you but, you have nothing to apologize for," he replies. "You are Evelena, am I right?"

"Yes," Evelena answers sounding nervous.

"Are you alright?" Chances asks.

"I am fine," Evelena replies, "Thank you." Then after pausing for a bit she says, "I am just a little nervous."

Chance smiles and laughs then says, "It's alright. There is no need to be nervous."

Evelena relaxing a bit says, "It's just that we have all heard stories about you. I never thought I would actually meet you."

Kristieana now carefully sits in a chair nearby and listens.

Evelena says, "The woman you created in your hand out of the flames, I know her."

"Oh?"

"Yes, I definitely know her," Evelena says. "That was Kristieana."

"Yes," Chance replies, "it is."

"How do you know her?" Evelena asks.

Chance, not wanting to give away that Kristieana is here, lies the best he can, "I met her...a while ago."

"Ah," Evelena says, unsure of his answer.

After a brief silence Chance tries to change the subject, and asks, "You couldn't fall asleep?"

"No." Evelena answers.

"Was that your first battle?" Chance asks.

Evelena nods and answers, "Against a real enemy, yes."

"You ladies did very well out there," Chance says.

"Thank you," Evelena replies. "But if it weren't for you Lyra may have..."

"I am just sorry I didn't help more," Chance says.

Just then Kel'ana walks down the stairs and says, "I guess I am not the only one who couldn't sleep."

Chance stands up and says, "Please join us."

"Yes, sir, thank you," Kel'ana says also sounding nervous as she sits.

"Not you too," he says with a laugh, "please, you can just call me Chance."

Kel'ana nods her head and says, "Alright."

Chance then asks, "Kel'ana, is anyone else still awake?"

"No," Kel'ana replies, "everyone else is asleep."

"Good," Chance says with a smile. "I think I have seen enough of Rehma for one night."

Crossroads

They laugh, and then Kel'ana reluctantly asks, "Forgive me for asking Mr. —I mean Chance, but what happened with you and Rehma's mother? All I have ever heard was that she died protecting you."

"You don't have to tell us if you don't want to," Evelena says.

"It happened in the Second Orcnea War," Chance begins. "We had been fighting for days slowly pushing our way across the north. The battles were intense. Teresa La'harn and I were fighting one day close to each other. She was seriously injured and I was able to pull her back from the front lines to heal her. Well, as I was doing so, a large ogre happened to rush the front line and push its way through. I had my back to it and didn't see it coming. Teresa, however did, and as it was about to run a giant spear through me," Chance stops. He takes a slow breath before continuing, "She pushed me out of the way..." Chance struggles to continue as his voice begins to waiver. "The ogre hit her instead. We tried to heal her afterward, but she was already gone. It was my fault."

"You can't blame yourself," Evelena says to him.

"I was careless," Chance says as he gathers himself. "I had my back turned to the front line and that cost Teresa La'harn her life."

"Did they try to resurrect her?" Kel'ana asks.

"Yes," Chance answers, "but it was not successful. After that day I left the front line. I flew beyond the orcnea army and began to hit them deep into their territory by myself. I would burn their crops, supplies, and even villages."

"I remember the stories," Evelena says. "That was the breaking point for the orcneas. That's how you got the name—" She stops suddenly unsure if she should say it.

"Orcnea Slayer," Chance finishes sounding somber. "After that we easily pushed them from the lands. They left the continent of Bruen and returned across the sea to the Red Rock Plains."

"Yes," Evelena says. Then she asks, "Chance, why didn't you tell us who you were?"

"There are two reasons," Chance explains. "The first is that when you were sent to scout out the north, no one had any idea what to expect. When we discovered two days ago just how serious a threat the orcneas are, A'ranah asked if I would make sure you were safe."

"So, A'ranah asked you to check on us?" Evelena asks.

"Don't let Rehma find out," Kel'ana says.

"Exactly my point," Chances replies. "Serena knew that any intervention would appear as if we were interfering with your Rite of Passage. She asked me not to reveal myself and only help if it were necessary. That is why I kept out of sight during the fight earlier."

"Well, I am certainly glad you helped when you did," Evelena says.

"You said there were two reasons you didn't tell us who you were. What was the second?" Kel'ana asks.

"The second reason," Chance pauses as he looks into the fire in the fireplace. "The second reason is because everywhere I go when people find out who I am they treat me differently. Many are nervous around me, like the two of you," he says with a laugh. "I am always called a hero, or worse, the Orcnea Slayer."

"You don't like being called that do you?" Evelena asks.

Chance shakes his head and says, "No, I do not. I had to do things in the war that I did not enjoy in the least. Every farm and village that I burned is still in my mind. It is one thing to fight an armed warrior who is trying to kill you, but when you are setting entire villages on fire... Watching as the female and young orcneas fleeing in terror, I felt like a monster."

A silence sets in and it is finally broken when Evelena says, "I don't know if I am ready for this."

"Me neither," Kel'ana says.

"You did well out there tonight at the gate," Chance says, "you will do fine."

"What about the orcnea children?" Evelena says. "I can't kill them."

"You don't," Chance says. "You burn the houses, you burn the crops, but you let the women and children go. That is ultimately what I did."

"Then they grow up to hate us," Evelena says sadly.

"Yes," Chance replies, "and when they do grow up..."

"They attack us in a whole new war," Kel'ana finishes.

"Yes," Chance replies, "It seems to be a never ending cycle of hatred. One that I am very much guilty of being a part of. No doubt many of these orcnea warriors can tell stories of how the dreaded Orcnea Slayer burned their village to the ground when they were young."

"That is ridiculous," Evelena says, "what were you supposed to do, kill them?"

"I don't know," Chance says. "It is possible that they wouldn't be attacking right now had I done that."

"Do you regret not killing them?" Kel'ana asks.

"No," Chance says firmly. "If I had to do it all again I still could not bring myself to slaughter children, whether they were orcneas or not."

After a few moments without a word Chance creates a fireball in each hand. He looks at Evelena and Kel'ana for a moment then stares at the fireballs. He moves his fingers as the fires appear to dance, and soon take shape into the form of Evelena's and Kel'ana's faces.

"That looks just like us," Kel'ana says.

"You are really good with that," Evelena says. "That reminds me, earlier when you were shaping the fire, before Kristieana's image there was another Amazon, but I didn't recognize her."

"Wait!" Kel'ana interrupts, "Kristieana? Do you know her?"

"Yes," Chance answers.

"How?" Kel'ana asks. "When did you meet her?"

"Not too long ago," Chance replies.

"Where?" Kel'ana asks.

Chance, thrown off by the direct question, is not sure what to say. Thinking of an answer he hears Kristieana's voice whisper in his ear, "Tell them we met a year ago at Elonfar."

Chance grins and says, "I met her at Elonfar about a year ago."

"Oh yes," Evelena says, "I remember wanting to go with them to Elonfar, but they wouldn't let me."

"She must have been memorable," Kel'ana says with a smile, "since you are still creating her image in flames."

"Kel'ana!" Evelena says with a sigh.

"It's alright," Chance says with a smile. "Actually she was quite memorable."

"So who was the other Amazon?" Evelena asks. "If you don't mind my asking of course."

"Not at all," Chance replies. He extinguishes the fire in his right hand. "First, this is Ariella," he says as Ariella's image once again is formed in his left hand. "She was my first love."

"Aw," Kel'ana says. "What happened?"

Chance explains, "We were young and in love, but her father didn't approve. We wrote to each other but her father made sure we never got each other's letters."

"That's terrible," Evelena says.

"That is so sad," Kel'ana says.

Chance continues, "It would be three years before I finally gave up. That was when the Dragon Wars ended." Chance waves his right hand over the fire and it changes to look like Sha'al. "That is when I met her."

"Ah," Evelena says, "That must be Sha'al Ree then."

"Yes," Chance answers.

"Oh," Kel'ana says, "tell us how you met."

"Well," Chance begins to explain, "when the armies of Sheathelm and the Amazons of the Silver Moon celebrated our victory over the Dragon Slayers, I saw Sha'al for the first time. There she was, with long blonde hair in a thick braid. She was looking around as if she was trying to find someone. When our eyes met she smiled and walked straight over to me. She told me to stand up, and when I did she looked me over and checked my marks. She said 'Dri'el and La'harn, excellent. You will do nicely.'"

"Really?" Kel'ana asks.

Chance smiles as he reflects fondly on his first meeting with Sha'al. "She then announced to everyone around that unless I refused her, I would be hers. She then said that if anyone wished to challenge her claim, they should step forward and face her wrath."

"Did anyone challenge her?" asks Kel'ana.

"No," Chance answers. "She then grabbed my arm and pulled me away from the crowd. She took me to a place near the floating city that we had just brought down. She found a quiet spot and threw me up against a wall. She said 'I am Sha'al from the house of Ree and together our blood shall unite the three houses.' I tried to tell her my name, but before I could she just backhanded me across my face and said, 'don't *tell* me who you are, *show* me'."

Kel'ana laughs and says, "I have heard about others saying that to men. I always wondered if it was true or if it worked."

Chance smiles and says, "Well, it worked on me."

"When did she leave the sisterhood and take her vows?" Evelena asks.

"To be honest," Chance replies, "after that night I never thought I would see her again. After all, that is usually how it happens. I thought about her all the time. It was seven months later when a small group of Amazons came to visit Sheathelm. A'ranah was there to visit Arioch, and Sha'al was with her. She told me that she was bearing our child. We spent a lot time together during the week-long visit. Before they left I begged her not to leave. It took some convincing to receive A'ranah's blessing, but soon we ended up taking our vows."

"That is so sweet," Kel'ana says.

"It was also during that visit that A'ranah would conceive King Arioch's child. Nine months later," Chance continues, "A'ranah would give birth to Princess Kianna, and because no half elf would be allowed in the sisterhood, A'ranah came and left the infant in the care of Arioch. Sha'al would help care for her baby half-sister. Now my daughter, Ya'leigh, and Princesses Kianna are very close." Chance ends the fire spell in his hand and says, "I am sorry, I must be boring you with these stories."

"No," Kel'ana says, "you are not. In fact I always wondered about the relationship between A'ranah and King Arioch."

"They see each other from time to time," Chance explains, "but I never really discussed it with him."

Evelena asks, "So why can't you sleep?"

"Well, first," Chance begins to explain, "there was some movement in my room, and I thought it might be a rat."

"Oh my!" Kel'ana exclaims.

Suddenly Chance feels a sharp pain as Kristieana kicks his leg. Then she whispers in his ear, "If you are talking about me..."

Chance smiles and says, "Then, there was just this awful smell too."

"You better ask for your money back," Evelena says as she stands up. She says to Kel'ana, "Well, I think I am ready to go to sleep now."

"Yeah me too," Kel'ana says as she yawns.

"Thank you for everything," Evelena says.

"Thank you for the company," Chance replies.

Chance stands up, and Kristieana whispers in his ear again, "You are going to pay for those remarks." She punches him in the back. The thump is loud enough that it is heard by Evelena who stops and looks at Chance who tries to hide the pain he is in.

"Are you alright?" Evelena asks.

"Yes," Chances says, through gritted teeth. "I tripped on the chair. May your dreams guide the two of you safely to a new day, and good luck."

"Thank you," Evelena says as she climbs the stairs and heads down the hall to her room.

Chance looks around for Kristieana when he hears a door opening upstairs. He looks up at the door to his room and can see Kristieana as she removes the hood of her cloak. She gives Chance a grin and softly says, "If you don't like the room, Chance, then you can sleep out here."

Chance hurries up the stairs as she closes the door. He reaches his room and can hear the door latch. He checks his pocket for the key but it is gone. He tries to open the door, and just as he feared, it is locked. He knocks quietly, and so that he doesn't disturb anyone else, he softly says, "Come on Kristieana, open the door."

Then from the other side, Kristieana answers, "Say please."

Chance smiles and with a sigh says, "Please." Then he waits and listens for a response.

After a moment Kristieana says, "I think you can do better than that."

Chance swallows his pride and says, "Kristieana, would you please open the door for me? I am very sorry." Chance listens and soon he hears the door unlock and the door opens. "Thank you," he says to her as he enters. Chance closes the door and locks it and as he turns around he is met with another slap across the face from Kristieana. "What was that for?" He asks.

Kristieana just smiles and says, "For calling me a rat, saying that I smelled, and because I liked the way it felt when I slapped you earlier."

"So you like to be rough?" Chance asks with a grin.

"I think you already know the answer to that one," She replies. "Chance," she says softly, "I had no idea that Sha'al had said those same words to you."

"You couldn't have known," Chance replies as walks over to the bed and lays down. "I lied about who I was, remember?"

"Well," Kristieana continues as she sits at the foot of the bed, "I am sorry if I brought back any painful memories."

"The only memories you brought back were good ones," Chance smiles. "The bad ones took place much later."

"I must say," Kristieana says as she crawls over to her side of the bed, "I never knew how fast you and Sha'al fell in love. You only knew her for a week's time."

"Well," Chance looks at Kristieana and says, "I guess I just know when I find someone worth fighting for."

Kristieana's face begins to blush as she smiles and looks away. "Chance..." she begins to say.

"Don't worry," Chance says, "I'll stay on my side of the bed." He turns to the candles on the table and with a wave of his hand they go out.

In the darkened room Kristieana is facing Chance's back as he lies on his side. She reaches for him but hesitates just before placing her hand on his shoulder. Instead, she roles over on her back and replies, "May your dreams guide you safely, Chance."

Chapter 19
Day 6
Stirring Passions

The sun begins to shine through the window in Chance's room at the Pick Ax as Kristieana rolls over to find that she is once again alone. She gets up and begins to get dressed. She is about to grab her cloak when she finds a letter addressed to her. She opens it and begins to read:

Dear Kristieana,

I am sorry for leaving you without saying goodbye, but as I sit here writing this, I simply cannot bring myself to wake you. You are so beautiful as you sleep and you look to be at such peace. I do not wish to disturb whatever dream you may be having.

No matter how much I have tried I have not been able to fall asleep tonight. I do not know if it is because of the orcneas or if I simply cannot fall asleep next to you. Whatever the reason, I am going leave now and follow the northeast pass. It should be the same path that Sven will take the others across. I plan to scout all the way across the range and make sure that it is safe for them. If there is no army waiting on the other side, I will head southeast to Northwind and join King Arioch.

Even though we have only just met, I feel as if I have known you for much longer. When I look into your eyes I can see the fire and passion that burns inside you. For many years I have lived without the desire to be with someone, but from the moment we first touched, I could feel something stirring inside me that I have not felt in a very long time.

If circumstances were not as they are, and if you feel for me even a fraction of what feel for you, last night may have been much different. In another life I would have fought for you, however, I know that in this life, because of who I am, you cannot be with me.

I do not know if we will ever see each other again. If we do not, I want you to know I will always remember our brief encounter. In the short time that our paths have met at the crossroads of life, you have left an everlasting mark on my soul.

I wish you well in watching over our sisters on their journey. Good luck.
Forever grateful,
Chance

As Kristieana finishes reading the letter she says to herself, "Oh no, Chance Na'Moon." She puts the letter in her small backpack and puts on her cloak. She opens the window and as she climbs up on the window sill she says to herself, "It does not end like this." Then, just like Chance, she transforms into a giant eagle and flies out the window.

Crossroads

Later that morning out in front of the Pick Ax, the seven sisters are just getting underway with their guide Sven. They are all dressed for cold weather and are wearing furs, with the exception of Kel'ana who is dressed lightly. Sven asks, "Are you sure you don't want to wear something a little warmer?"

"No, I am fine," Kel'ana answers. "I have a spell that keeps me warm. If I wear too much I will not be accurate with my bow."

"Oh," Sven replies. "Very well then, if everyone is ready now you can all follow Sven."

As they exit the town gate, Lyra, who even reads as she walks, calls out, "Hey everyone, you are not going to believe this."

The group stops for a moment as Lyra explains her findings in her book. "We all know that Chance Na'Moon's mother was Shar'on, a second generation Dri'el. She was killed in the first orcnea war."

"Yes," Evelena says. "What else did you find?"

"Well, according to the records," Lyra continues, "Chance's father was a thirty year old male from the La'harn bloodline."

"Did you find him?" Gelana asks. "How closely am I related? He is not by brother is he?"

"Will you let her finish?" Yentroc says.

"Well, Gelana you are not his sister. In fact you are a distant relative to Chance," Lyra says. "Rehma, however..."

Rehma looks at Lyra and asks, "What is it?"

Lyra hesitantly says, "According to this there was only one male La'harn that matched that age at the time. Knowing that it was easy to find which La'harn gave birth to Chance's father."

"And?" Rehma impatiently asks.

Everyone looks at each other waiting for the answer. Lyra smiles nervously and says, "Chance's father was your mother's twin brother."

"I don't believe you!" Rehma says.

"It's true," Lyra says, "Chance is your cousin. In fact, other than your younger brother and sister, Chance is the closest relation you have."

"It doesn't change anything," Rehma says as she starts walking away. "The next time I see him I am still going to break his nose again."

Gelana turns to Yentroc and says, "See, I told you he wasn't my brother."

They laugh as the group resumes their journey.

Meanwhile, on the other side of the Northwind Range, Chance is crouched on top of a very large rock and is looking down on a small orcnea encampment. The orcneas are around a fire trying to stay warm in the cold mountain air. There are five orcneas and one ogre. They are cooking something on the fire for breakfast. There are two very crude shelters made from some type of hide. Chance cannot tell if there are more orcneas inside or not.

Chance decides not to wait any longer. He slowly stands on the rock and begins to cast a fire ball. He channels more magic into it and it grows larger and larger as he uses both hands to control it. Soon, he aims it at the very center of the campfire the orcneas are gathered around. He releases it and as the spell hits the ground it explodes violently. The shock of the explosion kills the orcneas immediately, but the ogre, though badly hurt, is still alive. Chance casts another fireball and hits the confused ogre. The colossal beast is slain and falls to the ground. Soon after, two more orcneas run out from one of the fur tents. Chance easily picks them off one by one as his fire spells rain down upon them. Then he throws two final fireballs at the tents catching them on fire.

He watches for a little while making sure there are no more orcneas are inside before he comes down from the rock. He takes out his sword and makes sure the orcneas are dead by piercing their hearts. As he finishes the last one, he hears Kristieana's voice say, "You are leaving quite a path of destruction. Rehma is going to be very upset."

Chance turns to see Kristieana standing several paces behind him. "You really know how to sneak up on me," he says, as he leaves the carnage behind and approaches her. "What are you doing here?"

"You have some nerve, Chance Na'Moon," she says holding his letter. "This is how you say goodbye? You write me a letter and then just leave?" She walks up to Chance with the letter holding it up in his face.

"I thought it was a great letter," Chance says, "Do you know how many times I re-wrote that to make it right?"

"I am not mad about the letter," Kristieana replies.

"Then what?" Chance asks. "What do you want me to say?"

"I don't know," Kristieana answers as she puts the letter away and starts to rub her arms trying to get warm.

"Are you cold?" Chance asks.

"Of course I am cold," she snaps at him. "Aren't you cold?"

"No," Chance calmly explains, "I have a spell that keeps me completely comfortable in cold weather. Would you like me to warm you up?"

"Yes," Kristieana says sounding angry. "Please."

"Alright then, since you asked so nicely, come here," Chance says as he puts his arms around her. "There, is that better?" He asks.

"A little," she replies. Then after thinking a bit she asks, "Is holding me part of the spell?"

"Spell?" Chance questions. Then with a smile he adds, "Oh, you wanted me to cast the warmth spell on you."

"I see," Kristieana says smiling back, "you just wanted an excuse to hold me again."

"Well," Chance replies, "you are the one who just flew across an entire mountain range to yell at me about writing you a letter. If I didn't know any better, I would say you are just using it as an excuse to see me again."

"Don't flatter yourself," Kristieana says, "I am just scouting ahead like you."

As he stands there with his arms still around her, he looks in her eyes. Then he leans in close and softly asks, "So, are telling me that you didn't feel anything special last night?"

"Nothing at all," she says staring back at him.

"Then why are you still shaking?"

Crossroads

"Because I am cold," she answers.

"No, you aren't," Chance says with a smile. Then he leans in even closer and whispers in her ear, "I have already cast the warmth spell on you. The air should feel the same to you as a spring day."

"Oh," She says as Chance rubs his cheek against hers, "so you have." Then they slowly turn their heads to face each other. With their foreheads press against each other, they both stare into the others eyes. Kristieana finally asks, "So, why are you still holding me?"

"Oh, I am sorry," Chance says teasingly. "Would you like me to let you go?"

"I didn't say that," she whispers, as she brings her hands up to Chance's face. Then with both hands she gently takes the back of his head and holds him close.

"You are so difficult to understand," Chance says, as he now brings his hands up and runs them through her hair. "First you want me to stop teasing you. Then when you find out who I am, you say that you cannot be with me. Now here you are once again in my arms. Please, Kristieana, if this is some sort of test or game..."

"I am not testing you or playing any games," she says as she continues to look into his blue eyes. "I admit when I first found out who you were I was upset. I was angry that you didn't tell me yourself, but since then I have come to terms with who you are."

Both of them are breathing a little harder and their hearts are beating fast. Chance asks, "Now what?"

"What do you mean now what?" Kristieana says intensely. "What the hell are you waiting for? Just kiss me and—" Pulling her towards him, Chance leans in as their lips finally meet. No longer fighting their attraction to one another, they break only for a second, gasping for air before they become lost once again in each other's kiss. Kristieana starts to push Chance back against a large boulder. As she traps him against it he quickly reverses their positions and as they continue to kiss fervently, he presses her back against the stone. She reaches down and unbuckles his breastplate. He quickly pulls it over his head and tosses it aside into the snow. She grabs him again by the shirt underneath and begins to pull it up as well.

Chance abruptly pulls back. "Wait," he gasps.

Kristieana sternly replies, "I'll give you two seconds to catch your breath. Now come here."

She pulls at his hand trying to draw him closer, but Chance doesn't move. "That's not it," Chance says regaining his composure.

"That is twice now that you have started something with me, Chance Na'Moon," Kristieana says angrily. "You better finish this, or you may not get a third chance."

"I am sorry," Chance replies. "It's just that..."

"I don't believe this," Kristieana says frustratedly. "Now who is difficult to understand?"

Chance looks back at the slain orcneas and says, "I feel like we are wasting time here."

"What!" Kristieana yells. "So now I am a waste of time!"

She starts to walk away, but Chance grabs her arm and pulls her back. As he does Kristieana tries to slap him but this time Chance is ready and grabs her wrist. With his other hand he takes her by the chin and says, "Look at me!" She looks into his eyes and is taken by the intensity of his gaze. "Now listen to me very carefully when I tell you, that you are not a waste of my time." He takes her hand and places it over his heart. "This," he says as he stares at her, "this is what you do to me."

"Really?" she questions as she feels his heart beating hard and fast. "Then why?"

"Because," Chance answers. "Right now at this very moment there is a war going on. I don't know how far they have advanced. I don't know what kind of army Arioch has gathered together. I don't even know if my children are safe."

"I am sure they are safe," Kristieana replies as she brushes back Chance's hair. "The orcneas are a long way from Sheathelm, and even still, Sheathelm would not easily fall. Besides, you will be there soon enough to help them." She pulls Chance closer and softly kisses him then asks, "Can't you just relax for even one moment?"

"And then what?" Chance asks, as he releases her hand and takes a step back. "I go back and fight in another war, never to see you again?"

"What are you talking about?" Kristieana asks.

Chance explains, "You are an Amazon of the Silver Moon. When this is all over I know how this will end."

Kristieana places her hands on his cheeks. "Chance, you are spending too much time worrying about what may or may not happen. If all you ever think about is what *might be*, then you will miss out on what *already is*. Right here, right now, I am with you."

Chance asks sadly, "What if I want more than just right now? What if I want more then you can give?"

"How do you know what I can or cannot give?" she asks, "How will you ever know if you are not willing to try?"

Chance sighs deeply knowing she has a point. "Are you always this difficult?"

Kristieana laughs and says, "Only most of the time."

Chance smiles and says, "Good." Looking down again he says, "Kristieana, while men leave their families behind to fight in this war, I simply cannot do this. I must go now and help the King. When it is done—"

"Chance," Kristieana interrupts sadly, "The war could take years. I cannot make any promises that I will be here for you when it is over."

"I understand," Chance says, "but as someone recently told me, I will never know if I am not willing to try." He smiles and steps up to her again and takes her hand. He places it again on his chest. "I don't care how long the war takes, as long as my heart beats like this for you, I will fight for you," he lifts her hand and kisses it, "and then you will belong to me."

Crossroads

Kristieana laughs and says, "I am an Amazon of the Silver Moon. I will not so easily be taken."

"Not only do I know that," Chance says with a smile, "I am counting on it."

Chance puts his breast plate back on. Kristieana puts her arms around him and pulls him in for one last kiss. Then she smiles and whispers, "How do you know that I will not be the one who makes *you* belong to *me*?"

Chance laughs, as he steps back. He looks at Kristieana again and asks, "So are you saying that you are going to claim me in front of the others?"

"I might," Kristieana replies. "Then again, I might not." She grins and asks, "If I did, would you deny me?"

Chance smiles and says, "I guess you are just going to have to claim me in front of your sisters and find out." Before Kristieana can say another word Chance changes into an eagle and takes to the sky.

As Chance flies over the mountain ridge, Kristieana takes out the letter once again. She smiles as she smells Chance's scent on it. Then, as she finds a small rock to sit on, she reads it again before returning to her sisters.

Chapter 20
The Intermission

Back in the luxury apartment, the power returns and the lights come back on. Laura, Josh and Haley cheer.

"Just in time," Kyle says. "So, that is how the famous hero of Runefell, Chance Na'Moon, first met the Seven Sisters of the Silver Moon."

"Some hero," Laura laughs. "He got his butt kicked by Rehma."

"Well," Kyle replies. "I wouldn't say that."

"I would," Danielle says with a smile.

"You know," Kyle says, "there is this thing called chivalry. A real man would never hit a woman."

"Even if she was pounding the hell out of his face?" Laura asks with a laugh. "How tall was Rehma anyway?"

"She is about six foot," Kyle answers as he holds his hand up at about his chin.

"So she was taller than Chance?" she asks.

"Actually, they were pretty much the same height," he answers

"I thought Chance was short," Josh says.

"For an elf," Kyle explains, "being six feet tall is just a bit under average for a male. People who never met him, but heard his stories, always thought he would be taller."

"That makes sense," Laura says. "You build up an image of some grand hero and he turns out to just be average."

"Exactly," Kyle replies.

"I want to know what Rehma did when she found out Chance killed all the orcneas in their path, Laura says, "I'll bet she was pissed off."

"Wait a minute!" Josh exclaims. "What ever happened to Fernando and Ariella? Did they find Red Beard's treasure?"

"We never finished that part did we," Kyle asks. "What part of the story do you like, Haley?

"I like the princess!" Haley says with an excited smile.

"But she didn't do anything in the story," Josh says.

"So?" Haley replies, "I just like princesses."

"Can you stay and tell us more, Uncle Kyle?" Josh asks.

Kyle looks at his watch and then looks at Danielle and says, "Well, I don't really have any place to be right now. If you really want to hear more, maybe we should make sure it is alright with Danielle."

"That's fine by me," Danielle says, "The kids don't have school tomorrow. As long as you don't mind staying."

"No," Kyle says. "I don't mind at all."

"Wait a minute," Laura says. "First I have to go to the bathroom."

"Me too," Haley says. Laura and Haley run off down the hall.

Josh asks, "Danielle, can we have some popcorn?"

"Sure, I will go make some," she replies. "Kyle, can you give me a hand in the kitchen?"

"Of course," Kyle replies. Kyle and Danielle enter the kitchen as Josh walks over to the window to see the lights that have just come back on in the city below.

Danielle laughs to herself, as she gets out some microwave popcorn from a shelf in the kitchen.

Kyle asks her, "What is so funny?"

"Nothing," Danielle says with a big grin. "I am just thinking about Rehma punching the "Hero of Runefell" to a bloody pulp."

Kyle replies, "She totally caught him off guard."

"If you say so," Danielle says with a smile. "Right up in the cupboard next to you is a big bowl. Can you grab it for me?"

"Sure," Kyle says as he reaches up and starts to pull out a large plastic bowl. As he pulls it out a plastic cup falls onto the counter.

"Hey, Kyle," Danielle says, "you dropped something."

Kyle laughs as he brings the bowl to Danielle. He looks out in the living room at Josh who is still looking out the window. He says, "You know, Kel'ana, after five hundred years that is still funny."

"Shh," Kel'ana says quietly. "Don't call me that. Josh may hear you."

"Relax," Kyle replies, "he is far enough away."

Kel'ana puts a pouch of the popcorn in the microwave and starts it. She says, "You know, Kelik, its strange hearing you talk about how we met your father for the first time."

"Yeah, well it is kind of strange talking about him like that," Kelik says.

"I had forgotten that he called himself Kyle at Copper Pass," Kel'ana says as she looks around the corner of the door to check on Josh.

"That is one of the reasons I picked that name," Kelik replies.

Kel'ana watches the popcorn in the microwave. "I miss him."

"Me too," Kelik says.

The microwave beeps and Kel'ana empties the bag of popcorn into the bowl.

"Hey! We are ready," calls Josh from the living room.

Kel'ana takes the bowl of popcorn as they return to the living room to resume the story.

"Okay," Kelik says, "where were we?"

Josh replies, "You were going to tell us about Ariella and her father's treasure."

"No way," Laura says, "I want to hear about Rehma and the other amazons killing some orcneas."

"Uncle Kyle?" Haley asks.

"What is it?" Kelik asks.

"I want to hear a story about the princess," Haley says.

"Alright," Kelik says. "We have a lot of ground to cover. First you have Chance, who is now on his way to join King Arioch on the front lines of battle. Then you have Princess Kianna who is traveling with a small group of people including Chance's son and two daughters. Up in the mountains you have the

Seven Sisters of the Silver Moon trying to cross over to the orcnea lands on the other side. Finally you have Captain Ariella and Fernando who are looking for her father's treasure, but before we get back to them there is one more part of the story I have to add..."

Chapter 21
Cold Sunrise

At the northern walls of Northwind, the orcneas march on the abandoned city. Thousands of orcneas wait outside as a few hundred storm the deserted interior. Leading the orcnea army are three generals. One of them is a huge ogre who goes by the name of Cron. Wearing a fur vest and a loin cloth, the mammoth general has little to protect him in battle with the exception of an iron helmet with three horns. He laughs and says, "The cowards ran."

Another general, an orcnea shaman named Vork Carr, adds, "They didn't even burn the place down. They are either confident they will win it back or don't have stomach to do it." He sticks the base of his staff in the ground and looks up at the third general, Lortec Ka, and asks, "Why do you look so displeased?"

Lortec Ka stands and watches as the orcnea troops run through the streets of Northwind unopposed. With a deep and commanding voice, the tall brutish orcnea general finally answers, "I was hoping for a challenge. This hardly feels like a real victory."

Vork laughs and replies, "The orcneas have not held this piece of land since before the First Human War. Whether it feels like it or not, this *is* a victory."

The three generals start to enter the city as Lortec says, "I know how important this day is. I have been looking forward to it my whole life. The humans were right to abandon this place. Even though it means they knew we were coming, it also means they couldn't do anything about it."

Cron adds, "The humans have grown weak."

"Perhaps," Lortec replies, "or maybe we just caught them off guard and they are preparing for a counter attack."

"It will make little difference," Vork says with a laugh. "We are prepared for them. This city will not be returned to them."

As they reach the town square they stop and look around. "I hope you're right," Lortec says. "I still feel that the attack on the goblin ship was a mistake."

"Yes," Vork replies, "but if our reports are accurate, Chance Na'Moon is out at sea. At least we have that to our advantage."

Lortec grits his teeth and says, "That's too bad. I would have rather faced the Orcnea Slayer myself."

"I know you would," Vork replies, "It is all you ever talk about. If I didn't know better, I would say that you are more interested in that one single elf then you are in the entire war."

Lortec doesn't reply. He just continues to look around at the new orcnea stronghold. Just then an orcnea soldier runs up to the generals and says, "My lords, the bridge across the Northwind River has been destroyed."

"So," Vork says with sigh, "the humans weren't entirely foolish about their retreat." Then he looks at the enormous Cron and says, "Gather some of your men and begin to gather wood from the forest. We will need to rebuild that bridge as soon as we can."

"Of course," Cron replies. As he walks off Lortec and Vork enter the gates to the keep.

"So far our plans have worked perfectly," Vork says to Lortec.

"So it would seem," Lortec replies.

"You are still worried though, why?" Vork asks at they reach the center of the main chamber.

"I have learned one thing about humans and elves," Lortec answers, "Never underestimate them."

"Don't worry," Vork replies, "We will be ready to take our losses as well as the victories. Humans seem to take their losses harder than most. This city is the perfect example. They simply let us take it rather than burn it to the ground."

"Yes," Lortec says, "but what you see as a weakness, I see as their strength. It is the very same attachment to others that makes them both weak *and* strong when they are threatened. They will be back for this city. The only difference is...we will not run."

Chapter 22
Treasure hunt.

Midday arrives on the *Red Dawn*. Ariella approaches Fernando as Drake and Leon follow behind her. "Well, Mr. Greythorn," she says, "it seems we are about to dock at East Artos. You will forgive me for being cautious, but," she motions Leon and Drake who step forward with iron cuffs and chains.

"Of course, Captain," Fernando says. "I understand."

Leon and Drake lock the cuffs on his ankles and wrists. Soon the *Red Dawn* docks and the men scramble to secure it. They throw down ropes and tie them to the moorings below. It doesn't take long and soon they are secured.

"John," Ariella calls out.

"Yes, Captain?" John replies as he runs over to her.

Ariella orders, "I want you and Jacob to find out how much and how long it will take to make full repairs."

"Aye, Captain," John replies. He walks off to find Jacob.

"Torgus," Ariella says, "You will join Drake, Leon, Mr. Greythorn and myself on a little walk." She then turns to Fernando and asks, "You did tell me that we could find it from here, did you not?"

"Yes, Captain," Fernando answers. "It is not far at all in fact."

"Good," Ariella says. Then she says to Leon, "Make sure you and Drake keep an eye on him."

"My pleasure, Captain," Leon says with a smile.

"Allen!" Ariella calls out.

Allen runs over and replies, "Yes, Captain?"

Ariella smiles and says, "Until we return, I want you to keep an eye on the ship."

Allen looks shocked as he asks, "Me, Captain? Are you sure?"

"Yes, Allen," Ariella says as she pats him on the shoulder. "Just make sure no one enters my cabin or the lounge, except for Marie of course."

"Yes, ma'am," Allen says enthusiastically. "You can count on me."

"As for everyone else!" Ariella announces to the crew. "Make sure you do not tarnish the name of this ship with foul behavior. Otherwise, have fun and make sure you are back on board by morning's light!"

The ship's crew cheers loudly as they begin to disembark. Ariella asks Fernando, "So, Mr. Greythorn, if you would please lead the way?"

"Yes, Captain," Fernando says, "just follow me." As he starts down the plank to exit the ship, Leon and Drake follow him close behind. Torgus and Ariella also follow as they begin to head through town.

On the ship, Allen looks around with a smile. Marie walks over to him and says, "So you're in charge. How does it feel?"

Allen looks at her and replies, "I can't believe it. She actually left me in charge. Sure, we are not out at sea and no one is really left on board, but still."

"The Captain has a lot of faith in you," Marie says. Then as she put her arms around him she adds, "and so do I."

On the edge of town Fernando leads Ariella along the river bank that divides East and West Artos. There are steep rock walls that have been carved away over many years by the river. Fernando looks around at the canyon walls and says, "If I remember correctly it should be around here somewhere."

"What exactly are we looking for?" Ariella asks.

"That," Fernando says, pointing to a rock formation. The very tall and narrow standing tower of rock splits the path in two. To the left the river continues on. To the right is a small narrow passage within the rock. As they enter one at a time they make their way through the tight divide. When they come out the other side they find themselves standing in what appears to be large pit carved into the earth. "This should be the place, Captain," he says as he walks slowly around the edge feeling the cliff walls.

The four others watch Fernando as he continues to make his way around the crater-like hole. Finally Fernando stops and says, "I think this is it." He starts to push on what looks like a large boulder.

"Go help him," Ariella says to Drake and Leon.

The two stronger men join Fernando as they try to push the large rock. At first it doesn't give, then suddenly the rock seems to move on its own. They stand back and stare as a cave entrance is reviled. Fernando immediately disappears into the darkness inside.

"Fernando!" Ariella yells. "Come back out here!"

"Of course, Captain," Fernando says as he reemerges. "I think we are going to need some light anyway."

"Torgus," Ariella says, "You go first and light our way."

"Of course," Torgus replies. He then picks up a rock and casts a spell making it glow brightly. As he walks in the entrance of the cave the light fades and disappears. Torgus turns and says, "Ariella, there is no mana in the cave."

"A perfect place to hide a treasure," Ariella says as she looks around. She picks up a large stick and casts a spell catching the end on fire. "This won't be very bright," she says, "but the flame should continue without magic."

Ariella makes her way into the cave. She notices on the inside the entrance there is an iron gate that has already been opened.

"Looks like someone has already been here," Fernando says.

"For your sake," Ariella replies, "you better hope not."

She continues inside with the make shift torch as Torgus walks next to her. Leon looks at Fernando and says, "After you."

Fernando smiles and says, "Thank you." He walks into the darkness of the cave as Leon and Drake follow. It takes a while for everyone's eyes to adjust. Fernando stops and watches as Ariella and Torgus reach a wood door. It is locked but it doesn't look to be very solid.

"Drake!" Ariella says. "If you would please."

Drake and Leon walk over to the door and Drake says, "Yes ma'am." He drops his shoulder and easily smashes the door down. Suddenly they hear the clank of the iron gate closing. Ariella turns to see Fernando on the other side of the gate. Having picked the locks on his wrists he is now removing the shackles on his ankles.

Crossroads

"I am terribly sorry about this, Captain," Fernando says he steps back from the gate.

Leon runs up to the gate and tries to open it but it doesn't budge. "Captain, it's locked. I am going to kill you, Greythorn!" Leon yells furiously.

"I am sure you would if ever given the chance." Fernando replies. "Ariella, I only hope that someday I will be able to make this up to you."

"Why?" Ariella asks, unable to hide her disappointment as she looks through the bars of the gate. Drake and Leon grab some large rocks and bring them over to the entrance.

"Someday," Fernando answers, "I hope you will understand, but for now I do not have the time to explain as I am sure that gate will not hold you long. I truly am sorry." He opens his fist and there is a small gold medallion in his hand. He puts it around his neck before running off down the narrow passage they entered through. Leon and Drake start smashing the large rocks against the gate as Ariella slowly backs away with no trace of emotion on her face.

"We'll get him, Captain," Torgus says.

"Why, Torgus," she asks. "Why did he do this to me?"

"I don't know, my dear," Torgus replies, trying to comfort her, "but we will find him and he will answer for what he has done."

Ariella's expressionless face is overtaken with furor. "Fernando Greythorn *will* pay for this," she says with a scowl. "Someday, somehow, I will make him suffer."

Back on the *Red Dawn*, Allen and Marie are sitting on the edge of the ship looking out to sea. Marie asks, "So what do you want to do when you are done serving the captain?"

"I haven't put that much thought into it," Allen responds. "I guess I just always thought I would buy a house back in South Haven. I already know how to grow my own food. Maybe find the right woman," he adds as he looks at Marie with a smile, "and have children."

Marie smiles and says softly, "That sounds wonderful." She moves a little closer as Allen puts his arm round her.

Allen asks her, "So what are your plans for the future?"

"I don't know," Marie answers with a grin, "I guess I always thought I would find some nice man with a home in South Haven. Someone who knew how to grow his own food. We would have children and I would give him my love and make him as happy as he does me."

"That sounds wonderful," he says with a smile. They face each other as Allen leans in and they kiss ever so softly.

Marie whispers to Allen, "I would do anything to make you happy."

"You already do," Allen replies. They kiss again as Allen's fingers run through her hair. She holds him tight as they become lost in the moment.

They barely hear the footsteps behind them. They turn to see Fernando coming out of the officers' quarters. Allen quickly gets to his feet and asks, "Mr. Greythorn, why are you back? Where is the captain?"

Fernando says with great enthusiasm, "The captain is still loading up all the treasure. There will be a great celebration tonight! She just asked me to come back and grab something for her. We will be back shortly." Before Allen has a chance to question him any further, Fernando quickly makes his way down the plank and runs back into town.

Allen and Marie look at each other with concern. "I don't like this," Allen says, as they head to the captain's quarters. They look inside and Allen says, "What do you think he took?"

Marie looks at the desk and spies Ariella's jewelry chest open. "Oh no!" she cries as she runs over to it. She picks up a note laying on top of the jewelry box and says, "It looks like he left this, but I think her locket is gone"

Allen closes his eyes and sighs. "The captain is going to kill me," he says.

"It is my fault," Marie says as she takes Allen's hand. "I should not have been distracting you. Let me talk with her."

"No," Allen says looking down. "This was my responsibility, I will tell her."

"Tell me what?" Ariella says from behind them.

Marie and Allen turn and see Torgus and Ariella, who looks furious. Marie walks over to Ariella and begs, "Please ma'am, it's not his fault! I was—"

"Silence!" Ariella snaps at Marie. Then turning back to Allen she asks coldly, "Tell me *what*, Allen?"

"It's Mr. Greythorn, ma'am," Allen starts to explain. "He was just here, and—"

"Drake, Leon!" Ariella yells out the door to her men. They run to the door and she says, "Fernando, was just here. Find him!"

"Aye, Captain!" they shout as the turn and leave the ship.

Ariella turns back to a frightened Allen. "Tell me, what was he doing here?"

No matter how much the young man's confidence has grown over the last week, in the face of Ariella's ire, Allen is once again reduced to feeling like a timid boy. "Well, ma'am," Allen nervously explains, "H—he was here a—and we think...um."

"You think what!" she demands.

Allen clears his throat and says, "We think that he may have taken your locket."

Ariella walks over to her jewelry box and looks inside. Marie holds out the letter and adds, "I believe he left this, ma'am."

Ariella, who is visibly furious grabs the letter from Marie's hands and looks at it. It is addressed to her. She does not open it, and instead turns once again to Allen and asks, "I only have one question for you, Mr. Allen. How did he get in here?"

Allen looks down and says, "It was my fault, Captain, I was not paying attention to my duties."

"No!" Marie interjects. "Please, Captain, it was my fault. I was talking with Allen. I didn't mean to distract him."

"Enough!" Ariella yells. She clinches her fists and takes a deep breath. "Get out," she says while trying to calm herself.

Crossroads

Allen says, "Captain, I am—"

"Get out!" Ariella screams. "I will deal with you later, Allen."

"Yes, ma'am," Allen says as he leaves.

Marie, trying to calm Ariella, says, "I am so sorry, Captain."

"Out!" Ariella yells at her.

Marie rushes out of the room in tears.

"Torgus?" Ariella tries to say calmly.

"Yes, Captain," Torgus replies.

Ariella says, "You said that you couldn't sense Mr. Greythorn when we left the cave."

"Correct, Captain," Torgus explains. "That medallion that he was putting on outside the cave must be shrouding him from my search spell."

"Can you search for my locket?" Ariella asks.

"Of course, Captain," Torgus replies. He closes his eyes for a moment and concentrates. Then he opens them and says, "It's not far away. Hurry, Captain, follow me."

Ariella stuffs the letter into her coat pocket and they quickly leave the ship and head back into town.

A short time later they arrive at a small magic shop. Torgus closes his eyes and concentrates again and says, "Captain, I am afraid I no longer can sense your locket, however this was where I last felt it."

"Thank you, Torgus," Ariella says. She then enters the shop.

Inside the shop an old gray haired man greets them, "Hello, how can I help you today?"

Ariella steps up to the counter and asks, "We are looking for someone, perhaps you have seen him. He would have been here only a few minutes ago. Tall, dark hair, and a mustache?"

"Yes," he answers, "he was just here."

"Torgus, go outside and see if you can find him," Ariella says.

"Yes, Captain," he replies as he exits the shop.

"May I ask what it was he bought?" Ariella asks.

"Yes," the old man says politely. "He bought a small bottomless bag."

"A bottomless bag," she says quietly to herself.

"Yes, ma'am," the man says. "You know, a bag that is magically larger on the inside."

"Yes, I am aware," Ariella replies, "I was just thinking about something. Did you happen to see which way he went?"

"I believe he went south, ma'am," the old man answers.

"Thank you," Ariella says. Then she exits the shop and walks up to Torgus and says "He bought a small bottomless bag. If he put my locket inside you wouldn't be able to track it, would you?"

"No, Captain," Torgus replies. "Until he takes it back out again, I will have no luck finding it."

Ariella sighs and says to Torgus, "Come on, let's get back to the ship."

Later as they board the *Red Dawn*, Ariella heads straight for her quarters.

Torgus says, "Ariella, do not worry. I will continue to search for Fernando and your locket each day. Sooner or later Fernando Greythorn will make a mistake, and when he does..."

"When he does, Torgus," Ariella interrupts, "he will pay." She turns and enters her quarters, closing the door behind her. She then sits at her desk and pulls out the letter that Marie had found. She opens it and it reads;

To my dearest, sweet Ariella,

I know you will find this hard to believe, but I cannot tell you how much I regret what I have to do. I wish there was some other way. To make matters worse, I cannot tell you why I had to take your locket. I can only say that someday I hope to return it to you. My darling, I never thought that I would grow to care for you as much as I have. I did not expect such a complication in my plans. You surely are everything the legends said you to be.

When we meet again I hope you will find it in your heart to forgive me. I will gladly throw myself at your feet and beg for your mercy. Then I hope to be able to answer all your questions. Until then my dear—

Fernando

Ariella folds the letter and places it in the drawer of the desk. She looks into the jewelry box and says to herself, "Fernando Greythorn, when next we meet, you better believe that you will beg for mercy. And I swear to the gods that if you don't have everything that rightfully belongs to me, it won't be me who you will have to beg. Only the gods will be able to save you."

Chapter 23
To the Mountains and Over

It is later in the afternoon, and Princess Kianna and her small group are about three days from the Monastery on Sapphire Lake.

"Is anyone else hungry?" asks Isen.

"Well, I know I am," replies Garrin.

"We can stop and rest then," Kianna says.

As the group stops and dismounts from their horses, Ambra and Kelik walk over to a shrub and begin to pick some bright red berries.

"Oh!" Isen says as he picks some from the bush. "Are these safe to eat?"

"Yes," Ambra answers, "they are safe but—"

"Good," Isen says before Ambra can finish. He puts a small handful of them in his mouth.

Kelik and Ambra look at each other with a knowing smile. They watch Isen as he begins to chew the berries. Then in an instant he spits them out and starts to cough. "Those are terrible!" he says. "I thought you said they were good."

"No," Ambra says while laughing.

"You asked if they were *safe* to eat," Kelik says. "She didn't say they were *good* to eat."

Isen continues to spit out the fruit and rinses his mouth out with water from his wineskin. "Why are you picking them then?" he asks.

"I like to boil them in water," Ambra explains. "They are way too bitter to eat plain, but they make a good drink."

Isen's face is still cringing from the bitter taste. He asks, "Are you sure I am going to be alright?"

Kelik and Ambra laugh, and Ambra says, "You will be fine."

Isen walks back over to the others who are sitting down on a few small boulders as Kelik and Ambra pick a few more berries. Garrin is eating some rations while Gena takes out an empty bowl from her backpack. She closes her eyes and passes her right hand over the bowl as bread and cheese magically appear inside. Gena passes the bowl to Kianna.

"Thank you," says Kianna.

"You're welcome," Gena replies. "Who else needs some?"

"I do," Isen answers. "I ran out of my rations this morning."

"We just left Troven yesterday," Ya'leigh says.

"I forgot to get more," Isen explains. "Then I was really hungry this morning."

Gena hands him another bowl and says, "Here you go."

"Thank you," Isen says with a big smile trying to look innocent.

"How long do you think it will take to get to the monastery?" Ya'leigh asks.

"We should be able to make it there in two days," Garrin answers.

"This river should take us all the way to Sapphire Lake," Kianna explains.

"Then what is the plan?" Isen asks.

"Well, if I remember the maps correctly," Kianna explains, "there is a small mining town in the mountains near the monastery."

"Copper Pass," Garrin says, "I've been there a few times."

"Well," Kianna continues, "according to my studies the mine there is connected to the old dwarven city of Coldrock. It fell in the first orcnea war."

"Wait," Ya'leigh asks. "Are we planning on going through the mountains rather than over them?"

"Sounds dark and dangerous to me," Isen says, "let's do it."

Ambra and Kelik walk back now and sit down. As they do Kelik finds an open area and creates a fire using magic while Ambra pours some water in a small pot and then places the berries in it. Ya'leigh looks at her brother and sister and says, "Danger is something we should avoid if we can. Are you sure we will be able to go all the way through?"

"That part," Kianna says, "I don't know. I hope that maybe some of the miners may be able to help us. I think if it goes all the way through it would be faster, and we wouldn't have to deal with the outside cold and wind."

"It will still be cold," Garrin says, "but it would be much better than being outside."

Gena adds, "We should have no problem with light, but we might be limited on the fires we can build to stay warm."

Isen says, "I can carry some wood. Just load up my backpack."

"We may have to," Kianna says.

Ya'leigh says, "If we can't make it all the way through, I suppose we could use the gate stone."

"Let's just hope we don't have to use it," Garrin says. "Those things are not cheap."

"Fortunately that is not too big of a problem for my father," Kianna says.

Isen says, "I just hope that both of your fathers don't get too mad at us for not coming back."

"I agree," Garrin adds, "I don't think they'll be too happy when they find out."

Ya'leigh replies, "I know my father wouldn't worry as much about me, but with Ambra and Kelik here he definitely will not be happy."

Ambra says, "Father wasn't much older than me when he went out on his own."

"That's true," Ya'leigh replies, "I guess we are just like him."

Kianna asks, "Are we almost ready to go?"

"Yes," Ambra answers. "The juice is done."

"We have a long road ahead," Kianna says as she stands up.

The group gathers their things and Ambra carefully pours her berry juice in her wineskin. Kelik puts out the small fire, and they mount back up on their horses and continue on their way.

Further to the north, the Seven Sisters are making their way across the rocky terrain with their new found guide, Sven. They reach a small encampment that has been attacked. There are five dead orcneas and a burnt tent.

"I am going to kill him!" Rehma yells. "This is the third orcnea camp that that we have come across, and they are all wiped out."

"Relax," Sven says. "It may not have been Chance."

"Do you really expect me to believe that?" Rehma asks. "Kel'ana, can you tell us what happened here?"

Kel'ana looks around for a moment. "Judging from the burns on the orcneas," she says as she studies the ground, "and that the orcnea tracks seem to be running away from the fire, I would say they were attacked from..." she pauses and turns. She gazes upon an elevated rock behind her. She walks around and climbs on top of the rock and continues, "Right here."

"Are you sure?" Evelena asks.

"There are giant eagle tracks right here," Kel'ana explains as she points down to the snow on top of the rock. Then she adds, "Right next to them are boot tracks. There are no other tracks coming and going from this spot, so I would think it is safe to say that it was Chance."

"Chance is just trying to help," Sven says, trying to keep Rehma from getting angrier.

"We do not *need* his help," Rehma snaps.

"I have to agree," Yentroc says. "It is not that I really want to kill, but these are small encampments and are hardly a real threat."

Ja'noa takes dagger from the sash and throws it at a log. The dagger sticks into the log and Ja'noa says, "Kel'ana and I could have taken them by ourselves."

"On the bright side," Lyra says, "At least he is saving us time."

Gelana is searching the bodies and says, "There is nothing of value on them."

"Of course not," Sven says. "They're orcneas. Come, we go now."

"Sven!" Yentroc calls out from up ahead.

When the others reach her they come across a deep ravine. A rope bridge spans to the other side about fifty paces across.

"Is this the way we are supposed to go?" Lyra asks.

"Yes," Sven replies. "This is Windy Pass."

"I can see why," Yentroc says as she holds the hood of her coat tight to keep the wind from blowing it off. The sisters approach the edge as they look to the left and to the right of the ravine. It stretches as far as they can see. With the blowing snow limiting their vision they cannot see the bottom. Lyra stays far back from the edge.

Sven says, "Sven will go first. If bridge holds Sven, then it is safe for all of you."

Lyra quietly says to Gelana, "I can't do this."

"Yes, you can," Gelana says. "Just look straight forward."

Sven slowly puts his weight on the bridge. The ropes creak a bit but hold him. He heads across, and though the wind is blowing hard, he eventually makes it to the other side. He waves back and Ja'noa goes next. With very little effort she quickly manages to get across, making it look easy. After Ja'noa is clear, Kel'ana begins to cross. She reaches the middle of the bridge as a stiff gust of wind knocks her down. The others gasp and Lyra looks away closing her eyes. Kel'ana manages to hold onto the hand ropes and as the wind lets up she makes it back to her feet. Kel'ana makes it the rest of the way without any further trouble.

"I can't do this," Lyra says hysterically, "I can't, I can't. The wind is going to blow me off!"

Evelena, holding Lyra's arms, tries to calm her. "Look at me," she says. "Take a deep breath and focus on something else. You can do this. I am going next, just watch me."

As Evelena starts to cross, Gelana and Rehma continue to try to help Lyra calm down. Gelana says, "It's no different than the rope bridges in the Mana Forest."

"There is no wind in the forest trying to knock me off!" Lyra yells.

"You will be fine," Rehma says, "just hold on tight to the ropes. If a gust of wind comes just wait it out."

They watch as Evelena finishes crossing and Yentroc starts to cross. When Yentroc reaches the other side, Sven asks her, "Is the little one going to be alright?"

"She is really scared," Yentroc answers. "She is worried about the wind."

"Yes, wind is very strong today," Sven says. "She is so small she will have to be careful, but Sven has idea." Sven opens his bag as Rehma finishes crossing. He pulls out a long rope and says, "If someone can take one end of rope across to Lyra, we can tie it around her and Sven can hold rope over here."

"I will do it," Ja'noa replies. She takes the rope and ties it around her waist and then makes her way back across to Lyra and Gelana. When she reaches the other side she unties the rope and hands it to Lyra and says, "Sven says to tie this around your waist."

"There you go," Gelana says as she begins to help tie the rope around Lyra. "Extra protection just in case."

Soon Lyra is ready to go as she steps to the edge very slowly. She looks down and then clutches the hand ropes of the bridge.

"Don't look down," Ja'noa tells her.

Lyra closes her eyes and takes a deep breath. She opens them again and looks straight ahead. She takes a step on the center rope of the bridge as everyone watches closely. On the other side, Sven is holding onto the other end of the rope that is tied around her. With every step she takes he lightly pulls in the extra rope. Step after step she crosses. Every time a small gust of wind comes through she stops until it passes. Her long brown hair blows in the wind and gets in her eyes. She does not let go of the hand ropes and instead shakes her head to clear her face.

Soon she reaches the very middle of the bridge. Sven says to Yentroc, "Little one better hurry."

"Why?" Yentroc asks.

"Because of that," Sven says as he points along the ravine. The others look, and off in the distance they see what appears to be wall of blowing snow approaching.

"Lyra!" Yentroc calls to her. "Hurry!"

Lyra looks at the approaching whiteout and tries to hurry. In her haste she slips and as the gust hits her Lyra is knocked down and falls through the ropes of the bridge. The rope around her waist is all that holds her as she dangles from the middle. Only the smaller lines that connect the two hand ropes to the rope used to walk on prevent her from being smashed against the side of the canyon.

"Lyra!" Evelena yells. "Hang on!" She turns to Sven and asks, "What are we going to do?"

Soon the whiteout makes it impossible to see Lyra any longer. Sven holds tightly onto the rope and says, "The rope has her for now. Everyone grab hold, Sven is going out to get her!"

The girls hold tightly onto the rope and pull as Sven disappears into the snow. Before long they feel the rope's tension give a little. They pull it tight again before it gives a little more.

"Keep pulling!" Evelena yells.

The girls all pull the rope but they no longer seem to be making progress. All of a sudden they fall back as the rope loses all tension. They pull frantically at it until Kel'ana is holding a frayed end. "Please, no," Kel'ana says.

"Lyra!" Rehma calls out. "Sven!"

"I am going out there," Evelena says.

"Wait, look," Yentroc says.

They look out into the blinding snow. Faintly coming into view they see their guide slowly making his way back through the wind. Clinging tightly around his neck is Lyra with her legs wrapped around his waist. Sven steps off the bridge and onto the ground.

"Thank the gods you are safe," Rehma says as the snow begins to clear.

"We thought we lost you," Evelena says.

"Sven had to cut rope," he explains. "Once Lyra was up and holding onto Sven you almost pulled her off again. The pulling was also making it hard for Sven to keep balance."

"I am sorry," Evelena replies. "I can't believe I didn't think about that."

"It is alright," Sven says as he takes Lyra away from the edge. "You could not see what was happening." He kneels down and says, "Alright, little one, we are safe now."

Ja'noa makes her way swiftly back across and Gelana follows. Lyra, still clinging to Sven, refuses to let go. "Lyra," Gelana says, "you can let go now."

With her eyes clinched shut, Lyra shakes her head no. "Lyra," Sven gasps, "Sven needs to breathe now. Sven promises he will not let you fall." Lyra slowly releases her grip. Gelana and Yentroc help her down as the others come over and check on her. She is shaking and breathing rapidly as Sven stands up and takes a deep breath.

"Thank you, Sven," Evelena says. "I don't know what we would have done without you."

Sven smiles and says, "Sven thinks that you would have been fine without him."

"Maybe," Gelana says, "but thank you anyway."

"Of course," Sven says.

Lyra walks over to Sven. Looking up at him she says, "Thank you." Her arms barley reach around him as she hugs him tight.

Sven pats her on the head and says, "You're welcome, little one. Now then let us continue on. Fortunately there are no more bridges to cross."

"Good," Lyra says as she lets out a big sigh of relief.

"You know," Sven says as the group begins to continue on their journey, "someday they will sings songs of this day. They will sing about the time that Sven of the North and the Amazons of the Silver Moon crossed Windy Pass of the Northwind Range."

"I doubt anyone will remember us," Evelena says.

Sven replies, "Well, they will remember Sven. Someday Sven will leave his mark on world."

Chapter 24
Frostbite

Later as the sun begins to set, the Amazons of the Silver Moon are beginning to have a hard time with the cold.

Sven looks around at the large rocks surrounding them and says, "We should probably make camp here. These rocks can protect us from wind."

The group stops and they take off their backpacks. Evelena opens hers and takes out a tent. She turns to Kel'ana and says, "Kel'ana, can you shape this ice to make a wall?"

"Sure," Kel'ana replies.

Evelena says, "If you can make a wall connecting these two boulders that would definitely keep the wind off of us."

"Alright," Kel'ana answers. She walks over to one of the two rocks that Evelena pointed to. She raises her hand and closes her eyes for a moment and concentrates. Then as she opens her eyes again she moves her hand. Directly in front of her ice begins to move. Slowly rising from the ground, the patch of ice moves fluidly and begins to stretch. As Kel'ana continues to concentrate, the ice begins to form a wall as tall as Sven and as thick as a large fist. It is only about a pace in width, and soon Kel'ana moves over and repeats the process. Little by little Kel'ana raises the ice to form a perfect wall between the two large rocks. The entire length of the barrier is about ten paces across. When she is done she sits down to catch her breath.

"Good work," Evelena says.

Rehma and Gelana begin to set up a tent next to Evelena's. Ja'noa also begins to set up a third tent. Sven begins to set up his tent and asks, "So can any of you start fire? I have some wood here so that we can have warm meal."

The sisters all look at each other and Kel'ana says, "I can do that in a minute."

Sven laughs and says, "So, Kel'ana can shape ice and create fire. What do you others do?"

Rehma looks up from the tent that she is helping Gelana with. She brushes back her long blonde hair and says, "Please tell me he didn't just ask that."

"Easy Rehma," Gelana says trying to calm her.

Ja'noa says, "Oh, I'll show you what I can do." She pulls back her coat and reaches for a dagger.

Kel'ana says, "Ja'noa, don't. I am sure he didn't mean anything by that."

Sven looks around at the young women who are clearly angry with him. He realizes that he has upset them and says, "Sven does not mean to offend. Sven is sure you all have talents. Mine is to cook, among other things."

"So you can cook, huh?" Yentroc asks. "That's good because I am starving."

"You just wait," Sven says. "Sven will make best hot soup you ever had." Sven looks over at Lyra who is shivering uncontrollably. "Lyra, are you alright?"

When Lyra doesn't' answer Evelena runs over to her and asks her, "Lyra? What's wrong?"

"S-so...cold," Lyra is barely able to say.

"Kel'ana!" Evelena calls out.

Kel'ana runs over and looks at Lyra. "Hold still," she says to her. Kel'ana then closes her eyes and as she casts the warmth spell on Lyra, a reddish glow flows from Kel'ana's hands to Lyra. She then says, "That should help."

Lyra stops shaking and takes a deep breath. "Oh, thank you," she says to Kel'ana.

"You're welcome," Kel'ana replies.

As Kel'ana sits back down she appears to be winded. Yentroc approaches and says with a smile, "Alright, Kel'ana, that is enough of being the hero today. You are tiring yourself out." Yentroc looks at Sven and says, "So, you wonder what I can do? I can do this." She looks back at Kel'ana who is exhausted from all her spell use and says to her, "Now take my strength." Yentroc closes her eyes and her hands glow white. Then as Yentroc touches Kel'ana's arm, the glow is absorbed by Kel'ana who smiles and no longer appears to be tired.

Gelana and Rehma walk over and join Yentroc and Kel'ana. Rehma says to Kel'ana, "Just let us know if you need our strength."

Kel'ana replies, "Thank you." Then as she looks around she thinks for a bit. She then says, "You know, now that we are no longer on the move, I can probably keep you all warm if you can keep my strength up."

Rehma says, "Ja'noa and Evelena cannot share their strength but Gelana and I should be able to give you more than enough."

"Thank you," Ja'noa says to Rehma.

"Alright then," Kel'ana says. She turns to Rehma and closes her eyes. The warm glow of the spell covers Rehma before being absorbed. Rehma then raises her hands and magically shares her energy with Kel'ana before stepping aside. Next Kel'ana turns to Evelena and does the same.

Sven watches as one by one the sisters are protected by Kel'ana's spell, and in return Rehma and Gelana give Kel'ana their strength. Finally, after Kel'ana casts the spell on Ja'noa, she walks over to Sven and says, "I can cast it on you now, Sven. I am not that tired."

Sven shakes his head and says, "No, pretty one. Do not waste your spell on Sven. Sven will be fine. If you have strength left then perhaps now you can make fire so that Sven can make dinner."

The others go back to finishing with their tents as Kel'ana waves her hand at the small pile of wood that Sven has set up. A fire engulfs the wood, and soon burns on its own. Sven goes into his backpack and gets out a large pot. He fills it with snow before placing it over the fire. Sven pulls two small pouches from his backpack and empties the contents into the pot.

While waiting for the soup to heat the group is surprised by a visitor.

Off in the cold away from the camp, a wolf emerges from the blowing snow. Sven is the first to see it. He yells, "Wolf!" As he gets to his feet, he draws his sword.

"Wait!" Kel'ana says.

"Wait?" Sven asks. "Are you crazy?"

"She is right," Evelena says. "Look, I think it is alone."

They watch the wolf as it slowly moves closer. It stops and lets out a whine and a short howl.

"Aw," Kel'ana says. "It's cute."

"Careful," Sven warns. "That *cute* animal can kill you."

Kel'ana puts her hand out and says to wolf, "Come here."

"Be careful," Ja'noa warns as she places a hand on one of the daggers on her chest.

"I will," Kel'ana replies. She calls to the animal once more, "Here wolfie."

"Here, wolfie?" Sven questions.

To everyone's surprise the wolf begins to wag its tail. It jumps around and stands before Kel'ana and sits down. Kel'ana pets the wolf and Sven says, "Well, that is strangest wolf Sven has ever seen."

The others cautiously approach and extend their hands as the wolf sniffs each of them. After petting the wild animal the girls sit around the fire. The sun is completely gone but the white snow reflects the light of stars and the crescent moon. Sven's soup is ready as he pours it into bowls and passes it out. He says, "Alright, now everyone please try this and tell Sven what you think."

The sisters look at each other unsure what to think. Then Yentroc says, "Well, I am hungry." She takes a drink from the bowl of soup as everyone else watches her closely. Then as she tastes it she says, "Mmm. That is so good."

The others then look at their bowls and begin to drink from them. "Oh, Sven," Gelana says. "That is really good."

Sven smiles and says, "Sven is glad you like it." Then he turns to the others and asks, "What do you all think of Sven's soup?"

"Very good," Ja'noa says. "Thank you."

"I have to admit," Rehma says. "I didn't think I was going to like it."

"Thank you, Sven," Evelena says. "This tastes amazing."

Then turning to Lyra, Sven asks, "And what does little Lyra think?"

Lyra drinks and drinks until the bowl is empty and asks, "Did you make enough for seconds?" They all laugh as Sven refills her bowl. Kel'ana asks, "So, what is in this soup?"

Sven explains, "Well, water, of course. Then a mix of some spices that Sven gathers personally from the Monastery on sapphire lake. Then a few vegetables and a little bit dried meat."

"Sounds like a basic soup," Yentroc says. "What spices do you use?"

Sven laughs and says, "That is secret recipe. Sven cannot say."

They laugh again and Kel'ana asks, "So what kind of meat is it?"

The question causes everyone to stop laughing and now they all listen for Sven's answer. Sven looks at them and says, "It is not important. Now, enough of Sven's recipe."

This answer does not sit well with the group as they all stop eating their soup. Ja'noa then asks again, "Sven, what meat did you use?"

Sven sighs and says, "Alright, Sven will tell you if you promise not to be mad at him."

"It may already be too late for that," Ja'noa says.

"Your words wound Sven," Sven says. "Why are you always so cruel to Sven?"

Gelana then says, "Sven, don't change the subject. We want to know what is in the soup."

"Alright...alright," Sven says. "Keep in mind that up here in mountains we do not have cattle or pigs. So we get by with animals that land offers." He then shifts his eyes to their new fury guest.

"No!" Kel'ana says sadly. "Wolf meat?"

"I am sorry, Kel'ana," he answers, "Sven did not wish to fool you. Sven was hoping no one would ask."

"I am not hungry anymore," Kel'ana says as she sets her bowl down.

"Me neither," Ja'noa says.

"I guess that just leaves more for me," Lyra says.

"Lyra!" Kel'ana yells.

"I am sorry," Lyra replies. "I am really hungry."

"Sven likes woman with good appetite," Sven says as he fills her bowl again.

"I think I have had enough too," Yentroc says. "Though it is good, Sven. I am just ready to go to bed."

Evelena says, "I assume we cannot maintain the fire. So Lyra, can you make us some light?"

"No problem," Lyra says as she gets up and pulls a lantern out of her backpack. She opens the lid and pulls out a small rock from inside the lantern. She warns, "Remember, don't look directly at the light." She holds the stone as she casts a spell. Soon the stone shines brightly and she places it back in her lantern and re-attaches the lid. The lantern lights up the entire area.

Sven says, "We will not need to have any watches, it is too cold for most things to travel at night except for the things that are attracted to light. So when we all go to sleep you will have to make sure you cover that up."

"Agreed," Evelena says.

"There is enough room for two people in each tent," Gelana says, "I'll sleep in Sven's tent."

"Oh, no," Yentroc replies, "you don't need to do that. I'll do it."

"No," Sven says. "As much as Sven would like to sleep next to any of you girls, Sven must sleep alone."

"I agree," Evelena says, "We can fit three of us into one of the tents."

Gelana and Yentroc look at each other disappointed. "Alright," Gelana says. "I'll sleep with Rehma."

"I'll sleep with Kel'ana," says Ja'noa.

"So I guess that leaves the three of us," Evelena says to Lyra and Yentroc.

"After I fall asleep I will not be able to maintain the warmth spells," Kel'ana says. "So make sure you all get comfortable and covered up soon."

They start to file into their tents and the wolf follows Kel'ana. Kel'ana looks at the wolf and says to it, "Alright, I guess I can let you come in the tent."

"Are you sure?" Ja'noa asks.

Crossroads

"No," Kel'ana replies. "But I don't want to leave it outside." She pulls back the opening to the tent and the wolf enters. It lies down on the end of the thick fur blankets. "Aw," Kel'ana says. "It looks like at least our feet will be warm."

"Just as long as it doesn't bite my feet," Ja'noa replies.

It is a cold clear night in the mountains. After sleeping for a few hours, Sven is awoken to the sound of Evelena's voice.

"Kel'ana!" She calls. "Kel'ana, hurry, it's Lyra. She needs your help."

Sven quickly throws on a shirt and puts his boots on. He wraps himself with his blanket and leaves his tent. He can see Kel'ana running over to Evelena's tent. Evelena is standing at the entrance and says to Kel'ana, "You have to warm her up! She is breathing but she won't say anything."

Kel'ana casts the warmth spell again on Lyra who is shivering uncontrollably. Sven runs over and looks inside at the shivering Lyra. He says, "Spell will help, but she is already cold. We have to get her warmer."

"I'll make a fire," Kel'ana says.

"Yes," Sven says, "I'll carry her out." He reaches for her and can see she is still wearing her fur coat. He pulls back the blanket and asks, "She has not changed her clothing?"

"No," Yentroc answers. "Why?"

Sven feels the fur beneath her and says, "All the snow has melted and it is wet. That is why she is cold. You have to get her into dry clothing, now."

"Alright," Evelena says.

"Put something light on her," Sven says.

"Why?" Yentroc asks.

"So Sven can share his body heat with her better," he answers. "I'll be back to get her when you are done." Sven exits the tent and walks over to Kel'ana who is maintaining a modest fire. "How long can you keep the fire going?"

"As long as I don't cast any more spells," Kel'ana explains, "I can keep this going as long as I want."

"Good," Sven says. He goes over to his tent and grabs another fur blanket. He brings it back over to the fire any lays it down next to it.

Evelena opens the tent and says, "We are ready."

By now the others have awakened and are up to see what is happening.

"What's going on?" Gelana asks.

Yentroc answers, "It's Lyra, she is freezing."

Sven hurries back to Lyra's tent. Lyra is standing at the entrance still shaking badly. She appears dazed so Sven asks, "Lyra, can you hear me?"

She looks up at Sven and slowly nods her head.

Sven opens his blanket as he leans down to wrap it around her. He says, "Alright, little one, Sven needs you to hold on to him tight." Lyra puts her arms around Sven's neck as he reaches around her to pick her up. He looks at Evelena and says, "Her arms are like ice." Sven carries Lyra over to the fire. When he reaches the blanket on the ground he kicks off his boots so he does not track snow onto the fur. He sits down on the fur close to the fire.

Lyra closes her eyes and curls up in Sven's arms. Her head is the only part uncovered as the rest of her is pressed against Sven's warm chest under the thick fur. Sven sticks one of his hands out from underneath the blanket and holds his palm out close to the fire.

"Is the fire helping?" Kel'ana asks.

"Yes," Sven says. "I will use the heat from fire." Soon the fire warms Sven's hand and he places it on Lyra's back.

"Oh," Lyra sighs as she begins to shiver less.

Sven places his opposite hand near the fire to warm it.

"Is she going to be alright?" Evelena asks.

"We will have to wait and see," Sven answers. "Come, my little Lyra," Sven says to her, "talk to Sven."

Lyra's eyes slowly open as she says, "You are so warm."

Sven smiles and replies, "And you are like glacier." Then he looks back at the others who are watching and says, "Lyra is going to be fine."

Later everyone is sitting around the fire. Lyra has warmed up enough that she is sitting on her own wrapped in a blanket. Sven gives them some advice. "When you return to your tents, you should all get out of your travel clothing and put on something dry. Then you should all share your blankets and sleep close to each other."

"Ja'noa and I are already sharing our blankets," Kel'ana says.

"Good," Sven says. "My only concern is whether or not Evelena and Yentroc are going to be able to keep Lyra warm enough."

"We should be able to," Evelena replies.

"I don't know," Yentroc says. "I am cold myself. I am not sure if I can keep her warm too."

Sven says, "If Lyra gets too cold again we will have to move her to my tent."

"What?" Lyra questions, looking uncomfortable with the suggestion.

Sven looks at her and says, "If they cannot keep you warm Sven will."

"I'll be fine," Lyra says as she gets up. "See, I am not even cold now."

"That is because of Kel'ana's spell," Evelena replies. "Once that wares off you will be cold again."

"I am sure I'll be fine," Lyra says confidently.

"Well, Sven can keep me warm," Gelana says with a smile.

"Gelana, you're not helping," Evelena says giving her a stern look.

Sven looks to Evelena and says, "Make sure if she gets too cold you will let Sven know."

"I will," Evelena says.

Sven takes his blanket from the ground and shakes off the snow. "Goodnight, everyone," he says as he walks back to his tent.

"You should go with him," Gelana says to Lyra.

"No," Lyra protests.

Ja'noa says, "Would you two leave her alone? She doesn't want to sleep with him."

"Well, we would," Gelana replies, "right, Yentroc?"

"Yes," Yentroc answers, "but we weren't invited to his tent." She and Gelana now stare at Lyra.

"I am not going to sleep in his tent," Lyra says angrily.

"I am sure he wouldn't try anything," Yentroc says.

"I am not worried about that," she answers.

"So what is it then?" Gelana asks.

"He is just so..." Lyra looks down at the fire, embarrassed.

"Handsome?" Gelana asks.

Lyra doesn't respond as Yentroc and Gelana laugh.

"That's enough, Gelana," Rehma says as she stand up. "Let's get back to bed."

"Agreed," Evelena says. "You two have had your fun, now let's all get some sleep."

They head back to their tents and Kel'ana ends her spell and the fire goes out.

Later after everyone has fallen back asleep, Sven hears his tent open. He looks and sees Lyra standing in the entrance. "Lyra, are you alright?" he asks.

Shivering once again, she says, "I-I am sorry to b-bother you."

"Not at all," Sven says. "Come in, little one. Take off your boots and come lay next to Sven."

Sven pulls back the top blanket to let Lyra get underneath. The sight of his bare chest surprises her. His muscular pectorals and rippled abdomen looks more like a statue than a man of flesh and blood. "Oh," she gasps as she looks away.

"Sorry," he says, "Sven knows you girls have not traveled much, but surely you have seen men before."

"Not like you," Lyra mutters under her breath.

"What?" he asks.

"Nothing," she answers as she looks back at Sven trying not to stare. She lies next to him and he covers her up.

As she snuggles close to him, Sven cringes from the cold touch of Lyra's feet against his legs. Despite the uncomfortable feeling he puts his arm around her and pulls her close. He then says to her, "There you go, my little Lyra. You just let Sven keep you warm."

With her head against his broad chest she looks up at him and says, "Thank you, Sven."

"Goodnight, Lyra," Sven says.

Chapter 25
Day 7
Good Morning

When the morning light shines into the tent the next day, Sven wakes up and finds Lyra still curled up next to him. Sven takes a moment to watch as she sleeps. He looks at the markings on her face of the leaf and small stars. Sven gets up slowly so that he does not wake her. He is wearing only drawers and begins to put on the rest of his clothing.

Lyra finally wakes as Sven is finishing getting dressed. "Good morning," she says to him.

"Good morning, my little Lyra," Sven replies. "Did you sleep well?"

"Yes," Lyra answers as Yentroc opens the tent door to check on them, "Thank you for last night." Lyra says.

Yentroc asks, "Wait! What?"

Sven laughs and Lyra says to Yentroc, "It's not what you think."

"What did you mean then?" Yentroc asks, teasing Lyra.

Sven explains, "Sven just kept Lyra warm last night."

"Oh, I'll bet you did," Yentroc laughs.

Yentroc leaves as Lyra jumps up and quickly puts her winter clothes on. Once she is dressed she chases after Yentroc. The others are sitting around a fire and eating breakfast. Sven's begins to take down his tent as Lyra catches up with Yentroc.

"Yentroc!" Lyra yells to her.

Yentroc turns to face Lyra who is clearly angry with her. "What?"

"Nothing happened last night," Lyra protests.

"I was only joking, Lyra," Yentroc explains. "There is no need to be upset."

"Well, I didn't think it was funny," Lyra says angrily.

"What is going on?" Evelena asks, as she joins Lyra and Yentroc.

"It's nothing," Yentroc explains. "I was just teasing Lyra about Sven. I didn't think it would make her this angry." She looks back at Lyra and says, "I am sorry."

Sven now walks over to them and says, "Lyra, is everything alright?"

"Everything is fine," Lyra answers as she begins to calm down. "Come on, Sven, I'll help you take down the tent."

Sven and Lyra walk back over to their tent. Evelena says to Yentroc, "Why are you teasing her?"

"It really wasn't that bad," Yentroc says as Rehma and Gelana walk over.

"Well, it made her pretty upset," Evelena replies.

"I thought she was going to hit you," Gelana laughs.

At the tent Lyra begins to help Sven pack. Sven says to her, "Yentroc was joking. I am sure she knows nothing happened."

"I know," Lyra says with a big sigh. "I don't know why I got so mad. I guess it's because I just didn't want her to think you tried to have your way with me. I know that you are not that kind of man."

Sven laughs a little and says, "Believe me, Sven *is* that kind of man, at least normally, but Sven would never try anything with you." He stops packing the tent and gently turns Lyra to face him and says, "Sven has too much respect for Lyra."

"Thanks," Lyra answers, sounding confused.

Then Sven laughs again and adds, "Even if Chance did not make Sven promise to be on best behavior, Sven would not have done anything last night."

Lyra, puzzled, thinks for a moment then asks, "So, even if Chance had *not* said anything to you in Copper Pass, you would not have tried anything? I don't know if I should be flattered or offended."

"Why?" he asks.

"Never mind," Lyra says shaking her head.

"Oh," he replies, "Sven did not mean it like that."

Before Sven has a chance to explain further Yentroc walks over and says, "Lyra, I am sorry about earlier."

"No," Lyra replies. "I am the one who should be sorry. I was just upset because Sven kept me warm all night and never once betrayed my trust, and I didn't want anyone to think of him as anything less than chivalrous."

"I understand," Yentroc says. "I didn't mean to offend either of you, and if I did, I am sorry."

"Thank you," Lyra replies.

"Alright," Sven says as he stands up with his backpack ready. "Everyone eat up. We are going to have a long day ahead of us."

Chapter 26
Over the Edge

It is morning on the deck of the *Red Dawn*. The ship is still docked in East Artos awaiting repairs. The crew have been summoned by the captain after returning from a long night on the town. Most of the men are tired and are wondering why they have been gathered. The crew is talking amongst themselves, and many are speculating what is happening.

Then from captain's lounge, Ariella emerges. She has at her side the cat o' nine tails. Now the men know why they are there. An uneasy silence falls over the crew as Ariella walks to the center mast of the ship. Everyone is there, including Allen and Marie who stand next to each other holding hands.

Ariella looks around at her men as they all nervously drop their eyes. It has been a long time since the captain has made an example of anyone in front of the entire crew. Ariella calls out to her two enforcers, "Drake, Leon!"

The two men step forward and with their heads down respond with, "Aye, Captain?"

Ariella then announces loudly to the crew, "Many of you may already be aware that yesterday afternoon Fernando Greythorn betrayed my trust." The crew mumbles a bit before Ariella continues. "Drake and Leon, the two of you were in charge of watching over Mr. Greythorn to make sure he did not escape, and yet that is exactly what he did." Ariella walks slowly around the two men then asks Leon, "I asked Drake to help with that door in the cave. What were you doing at that time?"

Leon looks straight ahead and answers, "I was going to help Drake with the door, ma'am."

Ariella then asks, "While you were *helping* Drake with the door, who then was watching Fernando?"

"No one, Captain," Leon answers.

"And what happened next?" Ariella asks, already knowing the answer.

"Fernando escaped, Captain," Leon says still looking straight ahead.

"That's correct, and whose fault is that?" Ariella asks as she looks up at the towering Leon.

"It is my fault, Captain," Leon answers. "I accept responsibility for his escape."

"Very well," Ariella says. "Now then, if you would please remove your shirt and face the mast. I assume you will not need to be restrained."

"No, ma'am," Leon answers as he removes his shirt. Leon then stands facing the center mast of the ship.

The captain walks up and says, "On your knees, if you would please, Leon." Leon kneels down and leans forward onto the mast. Ariella then says, "For allowing Mr. Greythorn to escape, you will receive five lashes."

Leon nods his head and says, "Yes, ma'am."

Ariella steps back. She readies the cat o' nine tails and lashes Leon with the first strike. Leon flinches from the pain. The captain strikes him a second

Crossroads

time as Marie grabs Allen's hand. Allen looks at her and quietly says, "Don't worry, I am used to the captain's whip." He smiles trying to reassure her, but Marie still looks frightened.

The third lash of the captain's whip causes Leon to grit his teeth and clinch his fists. The fourth causes him to let out a groan. Ariella pauses for a moment before delivering the final lash that causes the big man to cringe and let out a small cry of pain. Marie whispers to Allen, "I love you."

"I love you, too," Allen smiles and whispers back.

With large welts on his back, Leon rises and begins to put on his shirt. Ariella announces to the crew, "Now, after Mr. Greythorn escaped us, he came back here to the ship." Ariella walks over to Allen now, who tries to push Marie away from him. Ariella continues, "He came back to get something from my lounge." Now looking Allen directly in the eyes she asks, "Allen, I left you in charge of the ship and I asked one thing of you. What was that?"

Marie quietly tries to interject, "Captain, please he—"

"Marie, stop," Allen says as he turns to her. Gently placing his hands on the sides of her face he says to her, "I have to take responsibility for this." Then he quietly says to her, "I already told you, the captain can't really hurt me with that whip."

When he turns back around Ariella is right behind him. Glaring at him she asks, "So, Allen, I can't hurt you with this?"

Allen now looks down and quietly says, "Please, Captain, I just don't want her to worry about me."

"Oh, I understand, Allen," Ariella replies as her anger continues to grow. "You think you are beyond feeling the pain from my whip. You don't think I can hurt you anymore, is that it?"

"No, Captain," Allen begs, "Please, that's not what I meant."

Ariella then says to Drake, "Would you please secure Allen to the mast?"

"Captain?" Drake questions.

"You heard me, Drake," Ariella says sternly.

Allen says while removing his shirt, "That will not be necessary." He walks up to the mast and kneels down.

Drake looks at Ariella awaiting her response. Ariella says to Allen, "Oh, Allen, I am afraid it will be."

Ariella then nods to Drake who walks over to Allen and quietly says, "I am sorry, Allen."

Allen puts his arms around the mast and says, "It's not your fault." Drake begins to bind Allen's hands on the other side of the large wooden mast.

Ariella then announces to the crew, "Allen was the one who allowed Fernando to walk into my personal quarters and take something that was very dear to my heart." She then walks up to Allen and continues, "Furthermore, Allen, since Fernando's arrival on the ship you have been negligent in your duties and have questioned my orders. What's worse is that you even defied a direct order when you walked out of my quarters the other day. I told you that you were not excused and I ordered you to sit down, and what did you say to me?"

Allen now begins to look worried as he realizes that this is not just about his failure yesterday. He doesn't answer her as she grabs his hair and pulls his head back. She says loudly, "Allen told me to punish him if I must. Then he walked out." The crew now look at each other and mutter among themselves again.

Ariella whispers in Allen's ear, "What's the matter, Allen? Did you really think I forgot about that? I overlooked these transgressions for your sake, and this is how you repay me." Then she resumes speaking louder to the crew and says, "Since Mr. Greythorn arrived on this ship, I have taken it easy on all of you, but some of you have mistaken my kindness for weakness. It is high time that I remedied that."

Torgus turns to Marie and says, "Come with me, child, you should not watch this."

Marie says to him with tears welling in her eyes, "No, I can't leave him."

"Very well," Torgus says with a sigh. "If you insist."

Ariella steps back and readies the whip. The crew looks on sympathetically for Allen as Ariella lashes him across the back for the first time. Allen, who is used to this treatment, doesn't flinch at all. Leon looks at Drake and shakes his head knowing that this act of defiance will not go over well.

Ariella says, "So, Allen, you *are* used to this aren't you?" She steps back and whips him again. Allen only closes his eyes. This only makes Ariella even more angry. She takes a moment and draws back the whip and strikes him for a third time.

Allen's face barely flinches. He takes a deep breath now. Allen's fear of the punishment erodes away with every lash. He is now determined not to break for the captain. The sting of the fourth lash makes Allen grit his teeth. Allen now looks defiantly angry as Ariella pauses and waits before delivering a fifth strike. As Drake walks over to Allen to untie him, Ariella asks, "Drake, what do you think you are doing?"

Drake looks up at Ariella and replies, "I am sorry, Captain, I thought you were done."

Ariella walks up to Allen and says, "Allen has not yet learned his lesson, have you Allen?"

Allen doesn't say a word as he looks Drake in the eyes. Drake, seeing the anger within Allen's gaze, leans in and quietly asks him, "Allen, what are you doing? Just tell the Captain you're sorry."

"This isn't about me or what I have done," Allen says. "She is punishing me because she cannot punish Fernando."

"You see," Ariella explains to the crew. "Allen is not sorry. Look at the anger in Allen's eyes," she says grabbing Allen's face and looking at him directly. "These are not the eyes of a man who is regretful. These are the eyes of an insubordinate man. A man who needs to understand respect."

Allen glares at Ariella and says nothing. She releases his face as she steps back and says, "This will all end when Allen shows me that he is sorry."

"Allen!" Marie yells out. "Please, just say you are sorry!"

The words of Marie seem to break through to him, if only for a moment.

Crossroads

Allen does not want her to see him suffer. Ariella walks over to Marie and quietly says to her, "Marie, my dear, I don't think Allen wants you see him in pain. Why don't you go into my quarters and get the soothing root. This will be over soon, and he will need you."

"Captain, please stop this," Marie begs as tears run down her face.

"I can't stop this," Ariella explains softly. "Only Allen can end this now, and I think he will if you don't have to watch it. Now go, please."

Marie she can see the concern that Ariella has in her eyes. She nods and replies, "Yes, ma'am." She turns and runs off to the captain's quarters.

Allen watches her leave as Ariella takes a deep breath to gather herself then turns back and walks up to Allen. She then pulls his hair back again and whispers in his ear. "There, Allen, Marie is gone now. You don't have to keep this up any more. You know what I want from you. Now let me hear you."

Ariella steps back and readies the whip again. Allen, now unsure, struggles with what to do next. He wonders if he should just show the crew that he is in pain so that the captain can maintain her image of being someone not to be trifled with. He knows this is what Ariella wants from him, but the idea of giving in is conflicted with the frustration that his punishment seems to be intended for Fernando. His thoughts are interrupted by the sting of another lash of the whip.

Whether it is just stubbornness or something else, Allen does not make a sound. Drake whispers to him, "Allen, come on. You are just making it harder on yourself."

Ariella strikes him a seventh time. The pain is immense and Allen cringes, but nothing else. Allen resolves that he will not cry out in pain just for Ariella's benefit. If he is going to be broken, Ariella will have to do more. The eighth strike draws blood. The crew is uneasy now as the blood begins to drip down his back. The sight of this makes Ariella even more furious. She grabs his hair again and says, "Have it your way, Allen. If a whip is too gentle for you, then how about a spell?" She removes her glove and now many of the crew look away.

"Ariella," Torgus says attempting to intervene. "Is this necessary?"

Ariella glares at him, then looks around at the crew and announces, "This spell will do no real harm to Allen. It will only cause him pain. When he is ready for this to end all he has to do is show remorse." She then casts the same dark spell that she used on Fernando days before. She places her hands on Allen causing incredible pain. Allen clinches his fists and grits his teeth. Rather than cry out in pain Allen steadfastly refuses to show the true suffering he is enduring. The pain is too much for Allen and soon he passes out.

The crew becomes riled and a voice can be heard saying, "She killed him."

Drake checks Allen to see if he is still breathing as Ariella yells to the crew, "Everyone settle yourselves! Allen is not dead." She casts another spell that wakes Allen and yells, "Look! He is alive." As the crew begins to settle down Ariella leans in and whispers to Allen, "You win, Allen, I cannot break you. However, you will still give me what I want," she pauses to make sure the crew is still loud enough so that no one else can hear her. Ariella quietly continues,

"Because if you do not scream for me this time, Marie will have to suffer for you."

Not knowing whether or not she is bluffing, Allen begs, "No, please, I am sorry." Then quietly says, "I'll do it. Please, just leave Marie out of this."

Continuing to whisper in his ear Ariella says, "Then you better make this good, but don't worry, I'll make it easy for you." Ariella walks back and again speaks loudly for the crew to hear as she says, "Allen, when you joined my crew you were just a boy. Now you have become a strong willed man. I respect that, Allen, however you have not shown me the same respect. Every man has his breaking point. I am sorry, Allen, but you brought this on yourself." Ariella waves her hand in the air and suddenly it is as if her hand is on fire.

Jacob and John are still standing next to each other near the back of the gathering. John says to Jacob, "Oh no. The captain's going to burn him." Jacob puts his hand on his chest and rubs it remembering what the captain's wrath feels like.

Ariella says, "Let me hear you, Allen. Let me hear you beg for forgiveness."

She places her hand on Allen's left shoulder. Like hot iron Ariella's hand sears Allen's skin. This time he cries out in pain. "Ahhh, Please!" he screams, "I am sorry, Captain!" he begs. The crew all look down and listen to the screams of the man who had been so strong moments before. "Please, stop!" he cries. "Ahhh!"

Torgus walks up beside her and says, "Ariella, that is enough." Ariella removes her hand from Allen's shoulder and walks toward the stern of the ship. Marie runs past her towards Allen.

"Drake!" Ariella calls back. "NOW you can release him."

Drake unties Allen as the crew gather around them. Marie pushes her way through the crowd and when she finally reaches Allen she tells him, "Hold still, Allen." She then rubs a root on his wounds. This eases the pain a bit.

Ariella enters her quarters and closes the door behind her. She walks over to her desk and looks at the jewelry box that Fernando had taken her locket from. With a scream she grabs it and throws it as hard as she can against the wall. Pieces of the box fly everywhere as she falls to her knees and begins to cry.

Outside, Leon walks up to Allen and asks, "Allen, you are crazy?"

Allen tries to smile through the pain. This puts the crew a little more at ease. John then says, "I can't believe she did that to you."

"That wasn't fair to you at all," Jacob says.

The crew begins to get riled up again, and Allen says, "Look everyone, please listen to me!" The crew calms down as Allen takes a moment to gather himself. "I and I alone am the one to blame for all this."

Drake says, "Allen, the captain went too far." The comment begins to stir the crew again.

Allen replies, "I knew what I was getting myself in for. I was wrong to push the captain like that. She had no choice and you all know it." The crew doesn't say anything as Allen continues, "Maybe it was just my being stubborn.

I don't know, but either way it doesn't matter. Ariella Stormrage is still my Captain, and I do not want anyone here to think less of her. I disrespected her and I paid the price. I hope that will be the last of it."

Torgus steps forward and says, "Alright everyone, we have a long day ahead of us with repairs, and many of you still need to get some rest. So let's all be back here at noon." The crew begins to dissipate as Torgus says to Allen, "How are you doing, lad?"

"I'll be fine," Allen replies.

"Good to hear it," Torgus says. "Now if you'll excuse me, I have to go check on the captain."

"Of course," Allen replies.

Torgus makes his way to Ariella's quarters as Marie says, "Oh, Allen, are you sure you are alright?"

"Yes," he says.

"I am so sorry," she says as she starts to cry.

"For what?" he asks as he wipes the tears from her cheeks.

"If I hadn't kissed you," she says, "you would have been able to stop Fernando."

"I am not sure about that," Allen says. "Fernando may have just taken it anyway."

"Still, I am sorry I was a distraction."

"If that is what I have to go through," Allen says with a smile, "to feel your kiss, then I would do it again."

"Oh, Allen," Marie says, as she puts her arms around him.

"Ow!" Allen yells. "My back!"

"I'm sorry," she says as she quickly pulls her arms back. "I forgot."

"Allen," Torgus says as he approaches them, "the captain just asked me to tell you and Marie that she wanted to see the two of you in the lounge."

Allen looks up to the quarterdeck and Ariella is standing outside the lounge door. When Allen sees her she walks back inside but leaves the door open. Marie takes Allen's hand again. Allen says to her, "It's alright, we will be fine." Marie only nods at him as they walk up the stairs and enter the lounge.

When they enter, Ariella says to them, "Please close the door behind you."

Allen closes the door then turns to face Ariella. "You wanted to see us, Captain?" he asks.

Ariella walks over to them and says to Allen, "I am sorry I had to do that, Allen."

"No, Captain," Allen replies. "I am the one who is sorry. I failed you and for that I deserved to be punished."

"Well, turn around so I can heal it," she says. Allen turns his back to Ariella who places her hands on his back. Soon the white glow from the healing spell soothes the pain. "Why, Allen?" Ariella asks.

Allen questions, "Why what, Captain?"

"You had to have known that when you refused to show any sign of pain what would happen," Ariella explains. "Why didn't you just at least *pretend* it was hurting you?"

"I don't know, ma'am," Allen answers dropping his eyes. "I am sorry though."

"Since Fernando came on board you have changed so much," Ariella begins to say. "You went from a loyal hard worker, to defiant. If I didn't know better I would think that you were jealous of Fernando."

"I was...at first," Allen replies. Then looking at Marie he smiles and continues, "Then someone else made me realize that there was no need to be, and that what I really wanted was right there in front of me the whole time and I didn't even know it." Marie leans her head against his shoulder as she puts her arm around him.

Ariella smiles and says, "I am very happy for the two of you."

"Thank you, Captain," Marie replies.

"That is why I hope the two of you will understand what I am about to do," Ariella says.

"Captain?" Allen asks. "What is it?"

Ariella walks over to her desk and says, "I want the two of you to gather your things." She pulls out a piece of paper from a drawer and continues, "Allen, I release you from your contract with me."

"Captain," Allen begs. "Please, don't do this. It won't happen again. I promise you."

"I know, Allen," Ariella says as she returns with Allen's contract. "Torgus told me what you told the crew out there, and I have no doubt in my mind of your loyalty."

"Then why, Captain?" Marie asks.

"The two of you deserve to start a life of your own together," Ariella explains, "and a ship is no place to do that." Ariella then takes a small pouch from her belt and hands it to Allen. "Allen, this should be the amount of wages the two of you are owed for the last year of service. With a little something extra."

Allen opens the pouch and his eyes widen. He hands the pouch to Marie and asks, "Captain, are you sure?"

Ariella replies, "Yes, Allen, I am sure."

As Marie looks in the pouch she gasps and says, "Thank you Captain." She throws her arms around Ariella and hugs her tight.

Ariella is taken off guard by the hug but smiles, embraces her back, and says, "You are both worth it."

"Allen," Marie turns to him and says, "there is more than enough to buy a farm in South Haven just like you always wanted."

"You may want to wait a bit on that plan," Ariella warns. "Until the orcnea threat has been dealt with, I would suggest you stay far away from the east."

"I don't know how to thank you enough, Captain," Allen says, trying to hold back tears.

"Come here," Ariella says as she gives her former cabin boy a hug. "You already have, Allen," she says while holding back tears of her own. Ariella takes a deep breath and steps back and says to them, "If anyone asks, however, just tell them you were paid fairly. I don't want anyone else to get any ideas."

"Of course, Captain," Allen replies with a little laugh.

"Now go gather your things," Ariella orders.

Marie and Allen leave to gather their belongings. They walk pass Torgus on their way out as Torgus enters the cabin and says to Ariella, "That was a good thing you did."

Ariella sighs and says, "I know." She thinks for a moment then smiles and says, "You know, if it was not for Fernando, I would still have Allen and Marie. I cannot wait to find him, Torgus. I am going to make Fernando Greythorn sorry he ever heard the name Ariella Stormrage."

A short time later, the crew is hard at work on repairs. Ariella is out on deck as Marie and Allen approach her. "Permission to disembark, Captain," Allen says.

"Permission granted, Mr. Allen," Ariella replies. "Be careful out there. When the war is over I will make sure to stop by South Haven to visit."

Marie smiles and says, "We would be honored, Captain."

"I have one more thing for you, Marie," Ariella says as she holds out a small bag.

"Oh, Captain," Marie replies, "You really have given us more than enough."

"I insist," Ariella says as she hands her the bag.

Marie looks inside and starts to laugh. "What is it?" Allen asks.

"It is just something for Marie," Ariella answers. "To keep you in line, Allen."

Marie hands the bag to Allen and as he looks he finds a cat o' nine tails inside. Allen's face turns a little red. Marie laughs and says, "So you better listen to me, Allen, or else."

"Yes, ma'am," Allen says with a smile.

Allen and Marie say goodbye to the rest of the crew before disembarking. Jacob and John are standing next to Ariella when Jacob asks, "Captain, what was Allen's last name?"

John says, "Wait, I thought Allen *was* his last name."

The two of them look at the captain who thinks for a moment. She replies, "I never really thought to ask. I had always assumed that he didn't have a last name, but now that I think about it, I do remember him telling me when we first met that I could call him Allen, or Mr. Allen if I preferred." Ariella takes out Allen's contract and looks at the last page. She smiles and says, "He signed his contract Allen Allen."

"So it was both," John states.

"So it would seem," Ariella replies. "So it would seem."

Chapter 27
Day 8
Burning Bridges

    The next day along the eastern coast, King Arioch has gathered troops together about two miles south of the Northwind. Inside a large tent Arioch is meeting with his two generals as well as the captain of Northwind's guard, Levin Graves. Joining them are the same three representatives from the Amazons of the Silver Moon who were at Sheathelm a few days earlier. Chance is also there along with Resheck, the goblin representative.

    They are standing around a table with a map spread across it. Arioch speaks to the group, "At this time, my friends, we do not have enough forces to take Northwind back. Levin, I am promoting you the rank of general and I will be assigning more troops to the ones you have already brought from Northwind."

    "Thank you, Your Majesty," Levin says with a bow. "I will not let you down."

    Arioch turns to the goblin and says, "Resheck, you have more information. Would you please share it with us?"

    Resheck stands on his chair so that the others can see him better over the table. He says, "We goblins are sending our air ships, however, many of them are far across the seas. It will be many days before most of them can reach us. Right now we only have three, but that should be enough to keep their ground forces at bay."

    A'ranah speaks up and says, "Our scouts have told us that the orcneas have ten drakes with them. No doubt to help them control the skies."

*****

    "The orcneas have dragons?" Josh asks.

    "Well, kind of," Kelik explains. "To many a drake and a dragon are the same thing. In fact, they are related, but there are a couple key differences that set them apart. Both drakes and dragons have a breath attack. This can be fire, ice, or some other form of attack depending on the type of drake or dragon. The difference between a dragon and drake is size and intelligence. Drakes usually grow no larger than the smallest of adult dragons. Dragons possess intelligence as high, and often higher, than most humans, while a drake never seem to become more than a well-trained beast."

    "Can you ride them?" Laura asks.

    "They are big enough to ride," Kel'ana explains, "I even road one—uh—I mean read about one...in another story."

    Kelik looks at Kel'ana and smiles at her slip up. He then says, "While they can be ridden, most orcnea beast masters use spells to see through the drake's eyes and control them that way."

    "Are they faster than eagles?" Josh asks.

Crossroads

Kelik laughs and replies. "Well, why don't we continue the story and you may find out."

*****

Arioch looks out of his tent and up at the three air ships above. "Then we will keep the air ships back and make sure they are low enough that our archers and casters can protect them," Arioch says. "We may not be able to use them to attack the orcnea's ground troops, but as long as the bridge remains out we may not have to worry about them attacking in the first place. They are not likely to cross the river without a bridge. Do we know how many troops they have?"

Finna looks at the other two amazons and then answers, "From what we could estimate their numbers exceed twenty thousand."

Arioch hangs his head and replies, "Then they out number us four to one."

A'ranah says, "I know that the elves of Elonfar have sent word to all the other elves and will begin to send help as soon as they can."

"Until help arrives," Chances says, "I suggest we hold here. Assaulting the walls of Northwind while we are outnumbered would do nothing for us. If we buy some time and prevent them from advancing until reinforcements arrive then we will have a better odds."

Arioch adds, "We will still have an edge in the open. I am almost certain we have more ranged fighters than they do. Even with their shamans we should be able to severely hurt them if they try to advance."

One of the generals, Dale Rains, has served Arioch since the King's reign first began. He is a seasoned veteran forty eight years of age. His silvered brown hair is pulled back tightly into a tail. His goatee is of the same silvered brown mix. He turns to Arioch and asks, "Sire, shall I order my men to begin to dig a trench and place spikes?"

"Yes," Arioch replies. Then turning to his other two generals he orders, "General Burton and general Graves, you will assist him."

"Yes, Your Majesty," answers General Ramon Burton, a veteran from the Second Orcnea War.

"Of course," replies Levin.

The three generals leave as Finna says, "My sisters and I could set up traps beyond the trench. We could cast enchantments into holes and with Chance's help we could hide his fireballs."

Serena La'harn adds, "While I normally would not care for such tactics, I think we have little choice if we want to hold them off."

Arioch nods his head and says, "Very well. Chance, will you please help your sister, Finna?"

"Of course, Your Majesty," Chance replies.

"Oh, and Chance," Arioch adds, "I know you are only doing it to set a good example to the others, but for the record, I have never liked it when you address me with titles."

Chance smiles and replies, "I know, my friend, but we are at war, and order in the chain of command is important." Chance and Finna exit the tent to find other members of the Dri'el.

A'ranah says to Arioch, "If what Chance told us earlier is true, Evelena and the others should cross over into the orcnea territory in the next few days. He said there did not seem to be much activity over the mountains. If that is so, they should have no problem causing a disruption in their supplies."

Arioch replies, "Let's just hope that the orcneas don't overrun us in the meantime."

Later outside, a long line of men stretch for miles as they dig trenches and set up spikes from east to west. Amazons from the house of Dri'el are scattered about in groups of three. They are setting magical traps in the field. Chance is with Finna and another amazon named Leanara. Finna uses earth magic to create a shallow hole. Leanara casts a spell into the hole that allows Chance to place a fireball inside without setting it off. They cover the holes with some of the long grass that lies all around them. Each group creates similar traps. Casting this many spells is exhausting and they can only make a couple before having to take a few minutes to rest.

While they are resting General Graves approaches while carefully watching his step. When he gets close enough he calls out to Chance, "Sir! King Arioch wishes to see you at once, one of the goblin ships has spotted something."

The three of them stand up and return to camp. When they finally reach the King's tent they are greeted by three goblins, including Resheck, along with King Arioch. "Good," Arioch says, "you are here. The captain of the *Dark Cloud* informs me that the orcneas are close to completing a bridge across the Northwind River."

"Well, that certainly didn't take them long," Chance says. "I assume you want me to destroy it?"

"Yes," Arioch says. "I know it is dangerous but we have an idea to keep you safe."

Resheck explains, "Someone will cast an invisibility spell on you and maintain it the entire time you are away. Just in case you do come across a shaman who can see you we will also have a deflection spell that will keep you safe from any spells that he may throw at you."

"You would have to work fast," Finna says. "Those spells are hard to maintain, although those of us who can lend our strength should allow the casters to maintain the protections long enough for you to complete your task."

"Just be careful to stay away from any wolves," Arioch warns. "They usually can sense your presence even when invisible."

Chance asks, "When do we begin?"

"The sooner the better," Resheck explains. "They are on the final section right now. Nothing will keep them from crossing once it is complete."

Arioch adds, "If it only took them this long to make the current bridge, destroying it may only buy us another day, but we need all the time we can get."

A'ranah enters the tent and says, "We are ready to cast the spells."

They leave the tent and outside are several Amazons of the Silver Moon. A'ranah says, "I will cast the deflect spell. Leanara will be able to cast the

Crossroads

invisibility spell. The others will assist us in maintaining the spells so that you have enough time."

Finna also says, "I will be able to communicate with you, even in your eagle form." She places her hand on Chance's forehead. Then in his head he can hear her ask, *"Chance can you hear me?"*

"Yes," Chance thinks, trying to communicate back, *"Can you hear me?"*

"Very good," Finna says mentally. *"I can hear you well."*

Chance transforms into an eagle and A'ranah casts the deflection spell, then Leanara makes Chance invisible. Arioch says, "Good luck, my friend, and be safe." A moment later Finna laughs and Arioch asks, "What is so funny?"

Finna replies, "Chance wants me to tell you that he will be as safe as he can considering he is about to go try to burn a bridge full of orcneas."

Arioch smiles and says, "Well, that is definitely Chance for you."

Chance flies unnoticed to the bridge, and he can see that the orcneas have it almost completed. The Northwind River is wide and spans about fifty paces across. It is shallow and the currents are strong. Many years ago a stone bridge was built. When Damian evacuated Northwind he made sure that the bridge was destroyed to prevent the orcneas from following. The walls of Northwind are along the river's edge. Now the orcneas are using the base foundations from the destroyed stone bridge to support their new wooden one. Giant logs are tied together and anchored to the piles of stone.

Chance glides low over the bridge and spots a clearing along the side near the center. He lands hoping to stay out of the workers way as they continue to bring forth more large logs. Chance communicates with Finna in his mind. *"I have landed on the bridge and I am contemplating the best way to proceed."*

"Be careful," Finna replies. Finna relays the message to the King and the others.

Chance spots a patrol making their way through the workers. Four guards are leading two black wolves in his direction. Knowing the he doesn't have much time, he transforms into his elven form. Grasping his amulet, Chance channels the magic within. Raising his other hand he sends out a large wave of intense flames before him. In an instant the northern half of the bridge is completely engulfed in flames.

The orcneas run in a panic. Many jumping over the side of the bridge and into the water. On the other half of the bridge many of those orcneas also run. One shaman stands his ground and starts to cast a spell. Before Chance can stop him, the orcnea completes his spell. The orcnea looks right at Chance and begins pointing and yelling to the others.

"I have been spotted by a shaman," Chance relays to Finna.

"Hurry, Chance. Get out of there."

Four guards near the shaman ready their bows as the shaman starts to cast another spell.

Chance creates another wave of fire that ignites the rest of the bridge. The orcneas scatter with the exception of the shaman who stands unharmed within the fire. He finishes his next spell, and suddenly Chance's invisibility spell is disrupted. Chance begins to change back into an eagle as the shaman tries to target him with an ice spell. Fortunately for Chance the deflection spell is still intact, and the sharp icy daggers miss him.

Chance jumps from the bridge and takes flight as he relays to Finna, *"They dispelled my invisibility. I am on my way back now."*

"Fly quickly, my brother," Finna replies.

Chance starts to fly as fast as he can but he doesn't get very far before he hears the screech of a drake behind him

"Hurry, Chance," Finna says in his head. *"The drake is coming up behind you!"*

No matter how fast Chance flies, the drake is faster and begins to gain on him. At the camp Arioch begins to yell out orders. "Casters and archers to the ready!" he yells out. "We have a drake coming in fast. I want it brought down!" The men quickly ready their bows and crossbows, and wait.

By now the drake is right on Chance's tail. Chance knows that he cannot fly straight any more. He begins to dive and then sharply pull up in an attempt to lose the scaly beast. The drake uses its icy breath to attack Chance. Knowing the deflection spell will not protect him from the jets of freezing air, Chance veers to avoid it.

"Chance, it's an ice drake," Finna tells him. *"You should be able to hurt it."*

Chance replies, *"If it doesn't kill me first!"* Chance flies hard to the right dodging another attempt by the drake to freeze him. Then he turns to the left. The drake screeches and releases another stream of deadly cold air. Chance tries to dodge, but it catches his right wing. Chance loses control and begins to fall the drake flies pass him and prepares to circle back.

Nearly one hundred paces away, the camp watches as Chance makes a hard landing. Finna asks him through their link, *"Chance, are you alright?"* When Chance does not answer, Finna says to the others, "Chance isn't answering me!"

"No!" Arioch yells. Then he asks A'ranah, "Do you still have that shield up on him?"

"Yes," A'ranah answers, "But it will not protect him from the drake."

"No," Arioch replies, "but it will protect him from this. Archers, prepare to volley!" The men draw back their bows and begin to aim. "On my command!" Arioch yells.

Out on the field, Chance slowly gets to his feet. His right arm is badly frostbitten and even further injured from the landing. He looks up to see the drake flying right at him. Using his left hand, Chance channels his strength into a jetting stream of fire just as the drake lands and attacks Chance with another icy blast. The fire and ice meet each other with a violent steamy impact. As the drake continues to spray his breath at him, Chance continues to push it back with his flame jet.

Finna and the others look on as Arioch gives the command, "Fire!"

Chance looks up at the sky as the arrows appear to dim the sun. Chance watches the arrows fall while the drake's attention is focused on Chance. The icy attack of the drake begins to push Chance's flame jet back and just as the ice is about to overtake Chance, the arrows strike the drake. The drake is not badly hurt but the arrows injure it enough to make it break off the attack.

Crossroads

The drake then begins to flap its wings as it tries to take flight. Chance creates a fireball and channels more of his waning strength into it. Then just as the drake takes flight, Chance releases the spell and strikes the drake out of the air. The drake is now badly injured and cannot fly away. It lets out a long and low screech as Chance prepares another fireball. Before he finishes the drake off Chance says, "I am sorry it had to be this way." Chance shoots the fireball at the drakes head, finishing it off.

Exhausted and holding his right arm, Chance begins to walk back to camp. Many come out to greet him and when they finally reach Chance Finna says, "You had me worried."

"I am sorry," Chance replies with a smile, "but I was a little too busy to talk."

Finna laughs and says, "Hold still and let me heal you." Her glowing hands touch Chance's arm, and the injuries from the frostbite and from the fall are healed.

"Well," Arioch says. "The goblins just told me that the bridge collapsed."

Chance takes a deep breath and says, "Unfortunately, you can bet that they will be ready next time. We will not be able to use that trick again."

"You are probably right about that," A'ranah says. "Hopefully, you bought us enough time that it will not matter." They finish walking back to camp and begin to make their next plans in the King's tent.

Meanwhile in the city of Northwind, the orcneas are having a similar meeting. The shaman that spotted Chance is reporting to his superiors. The three orcnea generals are sitting in chairs in the main hall of Northwind. They are discussing what has just transpired. "General Ka," the shaman says as he bows, "you sent for me."

Lortec Ka stands and says, "Yes, I did. I am told that you believe you saw Chance Na'Moon, is that right?"

"Yes, sir," the shaman answers, "there is no mistake, General. It was him, I am sure of it."

Lortec laughs and says, "The Orcnea Slayer is here then, good."

"Good?" General Vork asks, "Why is this good?"

Lortec explains, "I have trained and waited my whole life for this day. The day that I could meet the infamous Orcnea Slayer on the battle field and make him pay for what he has done. Now my entire reason for being is only a short distance away, awaiting us. We must complete the bridge as soon as possible."

The massive Borak Cron stands up and says to one of the soldiers, "You, gather your men and help with gathering more wood."

"Yes, sir," the orcnea replies as he leaves to find his men.

Carr Vork now asks the shaman, "Did Chance Na'Moon carry with him the talisman of the fire dragon?"

"He was using something around his neck to cast the spells," the shaman answers.

"As long as he has that gift from Feonvaer, we must not underestimate him," Carr says. "We must also order the shamans to make it rain. We cannot lose another bridge."

Borak then adds, "I will inform them at once."

Lortec grins and says, "Next time we will be ready for Chance Na'Moon, the Orcnea Slayer."

Chapter 28
Heart to Heart

Later that night in King Arioch's camp many are gathered around the different fires that are spread along the newly dug trench. A'ranah, Leanara, and Finna have joined Arioch and Chance outside the King's tent. Leanara asks, "So, Chance, how are your children?"

Chance answers, "Ya'leigh is very much like her mother. She is fearless and strong, sometimes I think she is more La'harn than anything else. Ambra and Kelik, however, are most certainly Dri'el. They are both very good with alchemy and are in advanced classes at Dicean."

"So where are they at now?" Finna asks.

"Fortunately, Kelik and Ambra are attending summer classes at Dicean," Chances answers, unaware of where they really are, "Ya'leigh is accompanying princess Kianna in delivering supplies to Troven. They should be on their way back to Sheathelm right now."

Leanara turns to Arioch and asks, "How is Princess Kianna doing?"

Arioch looks over to A'ranah and smiles before answering Leanara's question. "She is incredibly smart, spirited, and absolutely beautiful, just like her mother."

A'ranah laughs and says, "Arioch Ravenguard, you haven't changed one bit."

"Other than being a little grayer and a little balder, you mean," Arioch says with a laugh.

"You humans and age," A'ranah says as she walks over to Arioch. She sits next to him and puts her arm around him and continues, "I guess that is one thing that I have always taken for granted. If I knew that I had only a finite number of days to live I might live as boldly as you."

"I think you already live pretty boldly," Arioch replies.

They all sit silently staring into the fire. Chance finds his thoughts drifting to Kristieana. Soon he finds himself creating her image in the flames. A'ranah asks, "Chance, is that Kristieana?"

Chance, realizing that once again he has raised questions by creating her image, quickly releases the spell and answers, "Yes, it was."

"When did you see her?" A'ranah asks.

Chance says, "I met her at Copper Pass while I was checking on the others."

"So she did go after all," Finna says to A'ranah.

"Yes, it would appear so," A'ranah replies.

"Wait," Chance interjects, "you didn't know she was there?"

"No," Finna explains, "In fact, she was told *not* to go."

"She has defied me again," A'ranah says.

Chance says, "I guess she couldn't help but worry about them. I am sure she was only looking out for them much like what you asked me to do."

A'ranah pauses then says, "You do make an excellent point, Chance, however we only asked you after we learned about how serious the orcnea threat was. She left without knowing her sisters would be in any real danger."

Finna says. "Kristina has a special bond to this group. She is as close to them as anyone. I for one am glad she is with them."

"I suppose you are right," A'ranah says. "Even though she did go against our wishes, Evelena and the others are better off with her there. I assume the group does not know she is following them?"

"I do not believe so," Chance replies.

Finna asks, "They didn't see you, did they?"

Chance sighs and replies, "Unfortunately, I was revealed after having to help take down an ogre."

"I see," A'ranah replies, "so they recognized you?"

"No," Chance replies, "but a friend of mine, Sven, was there and he made my presence known."

Leanara asks, "What did you say to them?"

"I told them I was scouting the other side of the mountain for orcneas," he replies.

"Chance," A'ranah asks. "May I ask you something else?"

"Of course," Chance answers nervously, afraid of what she may ask.

"You do not have to tell me if you do not wish," A'ranah says, "but, how well did you get to know Kristieana?"

"A'ranah!" Finna interjects before Chance can answer. "What kind of a question is that?"

"I am only asking because it's Kristieana," A'ranah replies.

Chance's eyes stare into the fire, unable to look at A'ranah. He hesitates before nervously answering, "Nothing happened between us, my lady, if that is what you are asking."

"Chance," A'ranah says, "I think you misunderstand. If something did happen, I would not be offended." Chance now looks up at her as she continues, "My daughter has been gone for a long time, Chance. No one would ever expect you to live the rest of your life alone. Sha'al would not want that for you either."

"Thank you, my lady," he replies, still uncomfortable with the subject. Chance stands up and adds, "Now if you will all excuse me, I think I will turn in for the night. May your dreams guide you all safely to the new day."

"I'll walk you back to your tent," Finna says as she stands up.

Finna and Chance walk off as A'ranah turns to Arioch and says, "Is it my imagination, or does Chance always seem nervous around me?"

"No, he is definitely uncomfortable around you," Arioch answers.

"Why do you think that is?" A'ranah asks.

"It's simple," Arioch explains, "he still blames himself for your daughter's death."

"He has to know that it is not his fault," A'ranah replies.

"That may be so," Arioch says, "but to this day he strongly believes that he failed you by not keeping your daughter safe. When it comes right down to it, Chance feels that Sha'al Ree died because of him, and he has always felt ashamed to be around you."

"That is so sad," Leanara says.

"Yes, it is," A'ranah adds, "I will have to talk with him soon."

"Are you going to warn him about Kristieana?" Leanara asks with a smile.

Arioch asks, "What about her?"

A'ranah laughs and says, "Arioch, you remember Sha'al and how much spirit she had."

"Oh yes," Arioch replies. "Chance had his hands full with her."

"Well, you see," A'ranah explains, "Kristieana is very much like Sha'al. Very strong willed and not at all intimidated by anyone. If she wants something, she will not hesitate to go after it. I wasn't asking Chance about her to make him feel uncomfortable. I was mostly curious as to how they got along."

"Well," Leanara says, "he certainly was thinking about her."

"Exactly," A'ranah replies. "So, I can only assume their encounter was more than what Chance is letting on."

Walking back to Chance's tent Finna finally asks, "So, you like Kristieana?"

Chance laughs and says, "I don't know what you are talking about."

"Come on, little brother," Finna says, "you don't make images of people if you don't have some feelings for them. By the way, you are very good at shaping fire. That looked just like her."

"Thanks," Chance answers, "and to be honest, I don't really know what I feel." They continue to walk a bit further then he smiles and adds, "She is quite something, though."

"Yes, she is," Finna replies as they reach his tent. "So, were you telling the truth when you said nothing happened?"

"Yes," Chance says defensively. "Don't you believe me?"

"If you say so," Finna says with a laugh. "I'll take your word for it."

"It's not like I wasn't tempted though," Chance says.

"So what did happen?" Finna asks.

Chance, looking up into the night sky at the stars, smiles and says, "Nothing."

Finna laughs and says, "I only ask because I care about you. We have the same mother, you are my brother. I just don't want to see you get hurt."

"That is nice of you," Chance says, "but I'll be alright."

"You know that a lot of sisters from the house of Ree have their eyes on you," Finna says with a smile.

"Really," Chances replies, "Why?"

"Well," Finna explains, "There are not too many males out there that have the blood from two houses. Those who are looking to have a child would like nothing more than to have their children be a part of all three houses. Never mind the fact that you are a hero from two wars. You are quite the prize, little brother."

"Well," Chance says, "I don't know about being a hero."

"And modest, too," Finna says with a laugh. "I am sure by the end of this war more than one sister from the house of Ree will try to claim you."

Chance grins and says, "Well, that's a little awkward."

"You don't have to tell me about awkward," Finna replies. "How do you think it makes me feel when I have friends asking me if my brother is ready to mate? *That* is awkward."

"Well," Chance says with a laugh, "you know that I am not the kind of person who is only interested in making a child. I would rather build a life."

Finna says. "Kristieana is lot like Sha'al but as far as I know, she is not interested in leaving the sisterhood. That is why I want you to be careful. I don't want to see you get hurt."

Chance looks down and slowly draws in a deep breath. "Thank you," he says finally, "but I cannot help for whom my heart beats. No matter how much it may conflict with my mind, the heart alone makes that decision." He puts his arms around his sister and says, "May your dreams guide you safely."

"May your dreams guide you as well, brother," Finna replies.

Chapter 29
Mani Dreki

Sven and the Seven Sisters of the Silver Moon have been making their way through the mountains for the last three days. As the end of the third day approaches Sven says, "We should set up camp soon. The next good place we find we will stop."

Soon the path leads them to a small plateau along the side of the mountain overlooking a valley. There is a small fire pit made up of small stones in the center of what appears to be an old encampment. "This looks good," Gelana says.

"That might even be better," Sven says as he points to a cave at the far edge of the plateau along the mountain's steep face.

The wolf lets out a growl as it digs in the ground. Kel'ana looks down to where the wolf is digging. "I don't think so," she says, pointing to the ground, "look."

Almost unnoticeable due to the freshly fallen snow are large pools of blood frozen into the icy ground. They investigate further and see that the blood is everywhere. Evelena says, "I don't think this is a good place to stop."

"Sven agrees," Sven says.

Ja'noa then asks, "Kel'ana, what do you think happened here?"

Kel'ana looks carefully at the ground. "There were orcneas here," she says as she walks around a small circle of rocks that was once a fire pit.

"So another camp that Chance got to?" Rehma asks.

"I don't think so," Kel'ana answers as she makes her way to the other side of the clearing.

"Why not?" Gelana asks.

Kel'ana kneels to the ground and then looks over to the cave and says, "Because this is not an eagle track."

As the group walks over to Kel'ana they look at the ground and see a giant print in the snow and ice. "A dragon print," Sven says as he reaches for his sword on his back.

They all look at the cave as Evelena says, "Let's get out of here."

Suddenly, a voice from behind them asks, "Are you lost?"

Surprised, they all turn and see an old man with long silver hair and a long silver beard. He is wearing a long white robe with a silver embroidery on the chest of a ringed crescent moon. The old man says, "I am sorry, I did not mean to startle you."

"Where did you come from?" Sven asks.

Before the mysterious old man can answer, Evelena steps forward. She gets down on one knee, and with her head lowered she says, "I am sorry if we are trespassing. If you wish us to leave we will do so at once."

The other sisters look at each other, perplexed. "What is going on?" Gelana whispers.

"That is not a man," Lyra quietly explains. "It is a dragon." Lyra then also kneels down before the old man.

"You are very perceptive," the silver haired man says. "Now please rise, young Sisters of the Silver Moon." Evelena and Lyra both stand as the others stare in silence. "What are your names?" The man asks.

The girls are stunned. They look at each other, not sure what to do. Finally Evelena steps forward and says, "My name is Evelena Ree, Your Majesty."

"A pleasure to meet you, Evelena," he says. "Though your respect is appreciated, there is no need to address me as your king. Please, call me Lunarus."

"Of course, sir," Evelena replies.

"Well," Lunarus laughs, "I suppose sir is better than Your Majesty." Lunarus looks to Gelana and asks, "What is your name?"

Gelana steps forward and bows her head and states, "My name is Gelana La'harn."

Lunarus looks at Yentroc, who introduces herself, followed by Ja'noa, Kel'ana, and then Rehma. The man then turns to Lyra and asks, "And what is your name, child?"

Lyra nervously steps forward and says, "My name Lyra Dri'el, sir."

Lunarus turns to Sven, who says, "I am Sven Liteburg, sir."

"From the north I assume," Lunarus replies.

"Yes, sir," Sven answers, "from tundra along northern coast."

"It is a pleasure to meet you all," Lunarus says. He looks at the wolf and says, "I think there is one more of you whose name I have yet to hear."

The sisters look at each other confused as the man says to the wolf. "Reveal yourself, child."

Everyone turns their attention to the wolf as it begins to transform. Its front paws grow to become hands. Its fur is soon replaced with a fur coat. The figure stands upright as its nose shortens. Its ears become pointed as long red hair flows down around them. Soon the girls recognize their friend and sister.

"Kristieana!" Gelana says as her face lights up with joy.

"I can't believe it," Kel'ana says, sounding disappointed, "I thought I tamed a real wolf."

Rehma, feeling both joy and frustration, says, "How are we supposed to go out on our own if no one trusts in us?" She walks over to Kristieana and then adds, "Still, I am glad to see you." She then gives Kristieana a hug.

"I am sorry, everyone," Kristieana says, "I did not wish to deceive you, but I also did not think you would want me coming along."

Lunarus walks up to the group and says, "So you are Kristieana." Then as he looks at her face he adds, "From the markings I would say you are from the house of Ree."

"Yes, sir," Kristieana replies as she bows her head.

"So," Lunarus asks. "What brings the Amazons of the Silver Moon to the Northwind Range?"

Evelena explains, "We are on our way to the northern territory. The orcneas have returned and we wish to contribute to the war by hampering their supplies."

"The orcneas, yes," Lunarus says. "I have come across several encampments lately."

"We were first told to scout the old orcnea territory," Evelena explains, "but now we have to do more than just scout."

"Well," Lunarus says, "it is getting late and you must all be cold and hungry. If you would like, you may stay with me tonight as my guests." He starts to walk towards the cave and adds, "You will have to excuse the conditions, I am not used to hosting company."

Everyone looks at each other in amazement. "We are going to be the guest of a dragon," Kel'ana says excitedly.

Lunarus turns back and says, "Unless of course, you would rather make your camp out here."

*****

In the apartment Kel'ana is the one now telling the story to the three children. She says, "They all laugh and follow Lunarus into the cave."

Kelik smiles and adds, "After they entered the cave...the Amazons of the Silver Moon were never seen again. The End." He smiles and laughs.

"No!" Haley says. "That's not what happens."

"Oh, how do you know?" Kelik asks playfully.

"Because," Haley answers, "Danielle told us other stories about them, so I know."

Josh asks, "Why did they act like the dragon was their king?"

"Respect," Kel'ana explains. "You see, the elves and the dragons have always been allies. Of course not all dragons are peaceful, but if you ever come across one it is always best to show respect."

"But what if it tries to eat you?" Haley asks.

"Most of the time if a dragon wants you dead," Kelik answers, "there isn't much you can do about it. They can be defeated but it isn't easy."

"I just want to know if the Captain ever kills Fernando," Laura says.

"I will tell you as much as I can before I have to go," Kelik says.

"What ever happened to Chance's kids?" Josh asks.

"Yeah!" Haley exclaims. "What about the princess!"

"Well," Kelik explains, "until now in the story, the Princess and her friends haven't had much to do, but that is about to change." Just then Kyle's cell phone buzzes. He looks down and checks it and says to Danielle, "Why don't you continue this part Danielle, I think you know it better than me anyway. I'll be back in a moment to tell them what the Princess and Chance's kids have been up to."

Kelik excuses himself and steps out into the hall as Kel'ana continues the story from where they left off.

*****

Lunarus leads the group into the cave. With a spell lighting the way, they reach a large cavern inside. Once there, he says something in dragon and the cave suddenly becomes brightly lit. It is surprisingly furnished with a large decorative rug that covers the floor. Along both side of the chamber entrance are two large fire pits with fires warming the chamber inside. Around the edge of the cave are treasure chests and piles of gold and silver. At the far end there is a large desk and a chair.

It is surprisingly warm inside and Lunarus says to them, "Please make yourselves at home."

"Thank you," Evelena replies as she takes off her fur coat. The others begin to take off their backpacks and heavy clothing.

Sven leans down and whispers to Lyra, "What kind of dragon is he?"

"Yes, Lyra," Lunarus says before she can answer Sven's question, "what type of dragon do you believe me to be?"

Lyra and Sven are surprised that Lunarus had heard them. The others all look at Lyra as she nervously answers, "From your robe and from your name I would guess you are a Mani Dreki."

"You are truly wise beyond your years, young one," Lunarus says.

"Thank you, sir," Lyra says as she begins to blush.

Yentroc asks, "So, you are a moon dragon?"

"Yes," he replies as he walks to the center of the room. "Out of all the names for the moon, Luna is one of my favorites. It is from an old human language. My given name would be too hard for you to pronounce. So I go by the name of Lunarus." Standing in the center of the room he says, "Now, stand back and I will show you my true form."

Sven and the others get to the edge of the cave, the old man Lunarus stands at the center of the rug. He closes his eyes, and soon his body glows brightly. Then before their very eyes this average size man begins to grow. Wings grow from his back and his neck grows longer. Lunarus's hands become claws as he grows a long thin tale behind him. The large dragon has silvery white scales and almost fills the large room.

"So beautiful," Lyra says.

"Incredible," Gelana says.

They look in amazement at the moon dragon. Lunarus says in his naturally deeper and louder voice, "Do not be afraid." Lunarus now lies down and with his long neck he brings his head around to them and asks, "Is this the first time any of you have ever seen a dragon up close?"

They all nod their heads yes. Lunarus, with a laugh that echoes throughout the cave says, "Well then, I am sure you are all afraid to ask, so I will ask you. Would you like to feel the scales?"

They all look at each other with excitement. Lyra is the first to approach Lunarus. Reaching her arm out she feels the silvery scales on his neck and says, "I never thought I would ever be able to touch a dragon."

Lunarus laughs again and says, "Very few ever get the chance. I don't usually travel outside the mountain range, and up here I don't get many visitors."

"May Sven ask something?" Sven says as he hesitantly touches Lunarus's tail.

"Yes, Sven," Lunarus replies. "What is it?"

"Did you fight in Dragon War?" he asks.

The question captures everyone's attention as they all pause and listen. "Yes," Lunarus finally answers. "I was there at the end when the ancient city was raised from the ground, and I was there when King Arioch and his men brought it down. It was a sad day for all of us dragons. Brother fighting brother in one of the few wars between our own kind."

"Sven is sorry," Sven says.

"That is alright, Sven," Lunarus says as he carefully gets to his feet. "Now then, I am going change back to a human form so that we can talk more easily." Lunarus transforms back into the old man with the long silver hair as the others watch, still amazed at the transformation.

Once he is back in human from, Lunarus says, "I have something for all of you."

"For us?" Evelena asks.

"Yes," Lunarus answers. "After all, I am a moon dragon and you are Amazons of the Silver Moon. That makes you like my children."

"Really?" Yentroc asks.

"Don't be silly, child," Lunarus replies, "of course not. I was only joking."

Gelana holds back laughter as Yentroc, embarrassed, replies, "Oh."

Lunarus walks over to one of the chests along the wall and says, "Forgive me, Yentroc. My attempt at humor apparently fell short."

"I thought it was funny," Gelana says with a laugh.

"However, I was not joking about having something for all of you," he adds as he opens the chest.

"Your Majesty," Evelena begins to say.

"Now, what did I say about calling me that?" Lunarus asks.

"I am sorry," Evelena replies. "You really do not need to give us anything."

"It would be rude to refuse a gift from a dragon," Gelana says with a smile.

"Indeed it would," Lunarus says grin. "You are traveling north into an unknown threat of orcneas. I have no use for these items, but they should serve you all very well." Then turning to Gelana he says, "For you, Gelana La'harn, I give to you Infragilis." He hands her a ring with a diamond on it and says, "Place this on your left hand and concentrate on the name Infragilis."

Gelana places the ring on her ring finger and then while holding her hand out she concentrates. Suddenly, white light emanates from the ring. The light takes on the shape of a shield on her left arm. Gelana gasps with amazement and says, "I don't believe it."

"Infragilis means unbreakable," Lunarus explains. "That shield will protect you well, and more importantly it will not weigh you down."

Gelana moves her arm around and says, "It's so light it feels like it's not even there."

"Under your will it is as light as air," he explains. "If struck, however, it will not yield. You can dispel it the same way that you summoned it."

She puts her arm down then concentrates. The shield of light is absorbed back into the ring. Then looking up at Lunarus she says, "Thank you so much." She gives the old man a hug as the others watch, stunned. Then Gelana seems to become embarrassed herself and backs up quickly and says, "I am sorry I didn't mean to..."

"It is quite all right," Lunarus says with a smile. "I do not mind at all."

"Well in that case," Gelana says. She hugs him again and says, "Thank you, Lunarus."

"You're welcome," He answers. "Now then," he says as he looks into the chest. "Kel'ana, I have something for you."

Kel'ana looks at her friend Ja'noa before stepping forward. She nervously approaches Lunarus as he pulls from the chest a bow. Lunarus says, "Many years ago another group of amazons paid me a visit. At the time I granted one of them a bow named Incendia." Lunarus hands her the bow and says, "This bow is its twin named Glacies. Draw the bowstring back if you would please." Kel'ana pulls back the string of the bow and magically an arrow appears ready to be fired. The arrow has and icy blue color to it. Lunarus explains, "This bow releases arrows of ice, while Incendia releases arrows of fire."

Kel'ana slowly relaxes the bowstring and the arrow disappears. She asks, "I don't need to load it?"

"No," Lunarus replies. "Just draw the bowstring back and you are ready to fire."

Kel'ana then puts her arms around the old man and says, "Thank you, I love it."

"You are welcome," Lunarus replies. As Kel'ana steps back, Lunarus says, "Rehma, I have just the thing for you."

Rehma slowly walks up to Lunarus as he turns around with two curved swords. He says to her, "For someone who uses two swords in battle, defending yourself from your enemy is sometimes difficult. So for you I have two swords that should serve you well. They are called Vallo swords, and while they are not unique, they are very formidable. You will find that parrying your enemy's attacks will be much easier when you use these."

Rehma draws one of the swords and says, "They are beautiful, thank you."

"Of course, you are welcome," he replies. Then turning to Sven he says, "While we are on the subject of weapons, I have something for you, Sven."

"For Sven?" Sven questions as he steps forward. "Sven is honored."

Somehow out of this average size chest, Lunarus pulls out a very long battle ax that appears to be far too large to fit inside. He turns to Sven and says, "I present to you Hellfire."

Sven takes the large two handed ax from Lunarus. When he does the ax appears to catch on fire. Sven does not flinch and is unharmed. He looks at Lunarus and says, "Sven thought Hellfire was only legend."

Lunarus replies, "Most legends start from very real beginnings."

"What does it do?" Lyra asks as she looks up at Sven who has a big smile on his face.

"Aside from being a very powerful weapon on its own," Lunarus explains. "The wielder can use it to send forth a destructive wave of fire that will burn anything in its path. Be warned, however, that the spell may only be used a maximum of three times without being recharged."

Sven carefully swings Hellfire to test its balance and asks, "How long does it take to recharge?"

Lunarus answers, "It takes a full day to regain each use of the spell. So if you use it three times in the same day you will have to wait a full day before you can use it again, or three days if you want to completely restore all three uses."

"Sven understands," he replies. "How does Sven use spell?"

"You must strike the ground before you while concentrating on the fire," Lunarus explains.

"Thank you," Sven says, almost in a daze as he stares at Hellfire.

Lunarus laughs and says, "You're welcome." Then he looks at Yentroc and says, "Now for you, Yentroc."

Yentroc smiles and steps forward as Lunarus holds out his closed fist. He says to her, "While I cannot help you with your darker spells, I can give you this." Yentroc holds out her hand as the old man hands her a necklace. In the center of the star shaped silver pendant is a round white crystal. "This will help you with your healing spells. As you already know, when you need to heal someone more than once, it becomes more difficult each time. This will make healing spells less difficult to cast."

Yentroc looks at Lyra with a smile and says, "I really could have used this the other day."

Lyra laughs and says, "That is for sure."

Yentroc embraces the old man and says, "Thank you."

"Of course, child," Lunarus replies, then turning to Lyra he says, "Now for you, my young, wise friend."

Lyra smiles and approaches Lunarus as he pulls out a large leather bound book. She gasps as he says, "This is called Infinitus Libellus."

"Infinite book?" Lyra asks excitedly.

Lunarus smiles and says, "Yes, that is what it means, but let me explain how this works." He opens the book and instead of pages there is a hollow space inside. He closes the book and says, "Now, I think of the book that I wish to read." He opens it again and inside the hollow space is an actual book. The cover of the book is white with no markings. He takes out the book and hands it to Lyra.

"Is this a real book?" she asks.

"Yes," Lunarus answers. He closes Infinitus Libellus and opens it again. Inside, just as before, there is another book.

Lyra asks. "Is it creating the books?"

"No," Lunarus explains. "It is merely a magic vessel to store real books." With the second book still inside he closes the cover once again. "When you no longer wish to read the book just place it back inside the hollow space and Infinitus Libellus will keep it safe." He opens the cover and it is once again empty. Lunarus continues, "Anytime you want to take a book out simply think of the book you wish to read and if it is inside Infinitus Libellus will give it to you. If it is not then a random book will appear instead. It will hold an entire library inside if you wish. It is quite remarkable, really."

"Yes, it is," Lyra replies. "I cannot thank you enough."

"Oh, but I am not finished yet," Lunarus says. "The book you are now holding, Lyra, is for all of you to use." As Lyra opens the white book that Lunarus handed her earlier he continues, "It is a spell book."

All the sisters gather around and look at the book with Lyra. Lyra stops at a page and says, "This is a spell that will let me read any language!"

Lunarus smiles and says, "You will have to do a lot of studying to learn that spell. There are several spells that you will need to learn first before you are able to learn that one, but once you have mastered the spell that allows you to read any language Lyra, then you will be able to read this." Lunarus hands her another book.

It is thick and has a black leathery cover. Lyra looks at the cover she says, "It looks like this is written in Dragon."

"It is," Lunarus replies.

"That's amazing," Evelena interjects. "What is it about?"

"Ancient history," Lunarus answers. "From before the fall of the great empires."

Lyra gives Lunarus a hug. Lunarus says, "Lyra, when you learn to read this, please come visit me again."

Lyra cannot hold back the biggest smile as she excitedly answers, "I will, I promise." She then turns back to her friends as they look at the book for a moment. Then Lyra gathers the two books and the Infinitus Libellus and walks to the back of the group.

Lunarus says, "Next, I have something for you, Kristieana." Kristieana approaches the old man as he hands her a staff with two large blue crystals embedded inside, one at each end. "This, my dear, is the Staff of Storms."

Kristieana takes the staff, nods her head and says, "Thank you." She looks closely at the intricate carvings of lightning that extend along the entire length of dark oak surface.

"It serves two purposes," Lunarus explains. "The first is a close range attack that will give your foe quite a shock."

Kristieana concentrates as the staff glows with a blue electrical energy. She then carefully walks over and touches a large rock with it. It makes a loud crack as the powerful charge is expelled. Kristieana smiles and says, "I like that."

"The second," Lunarus continues to explain, "Is just as the name would imply. You can create an electrical storm that you can be at the center of, or if you prefer, the edge. The staff will keep you protected from the storm. I would not cast it in here, however. You will want to cast it when your friends are at a safe distance."

Ja'noa looks at the staff and says, "Those two power stones on the ends look pretty large. Can they be used for lighting spells only?"

"Yes, my sweet Ja'noa," Lunarus answers. "You certainly know your lightning spells. While the staff may have served you as well, I have something I believe you will appreciate even more." Lunarus hands her a thick wool cloth

Crossroads

with something wrapped inside. Ja'noa unwraps the cloth to reveal two large daggers. The finely crafted daggers are brilliantly polished. Stars are engraved on the base.

"They are amazing," Ja'noa says, as she flips one around testing the balance of the blade.

"Now that they have bonded to you," Lunarus says, as he takes one from her, "watch this." He then tosses the dagger onto the ground."

"You dropped something," Kel'ana says under her breath.

Gelana hears her then elbows her in the side and whispers, "Did you really just say that to a dragon?"

"I am sorry," Kel'ana answers with a whisper. "I couldn't help it."

If Lunarus can hear Kel'ana and Gelana, he doesn't show it. He says to Ja'noa, "Now child, open your hand and call it with your mind."

Ja'noa opens her hand the dagger flies right into it. She gasps and says, "A returning dagger!"

"These are no ordinary returning daggers," Lunarus explains. "These my dear were crafted in the Mana Forge and are made of Star Steel."

"Really?" Sven questions. "So, those are Star Steel Daggers?"

"Yes," Lunarus replies. "They are loyal to you now, Ja'noa Dri'el. When you throw them they will return to you. Furthermore, they can pierce a steel breast plate as if it were only soft leather. They are very powerful."

"They are beautiful," Ja'noa says in amazement as she sniffles, trying not to cry.

"Are you crying?" Kel'ana asks.

"No," Ja'noa whines as she rubs her eyes. "Thank you so much." She says to Lunarus as she hugs the old man.

"You are welcome," Lunarus replies. Then turning to Evelena he says, "I believe that just leaves you, Evelena Ree." Evelena, still humbled by Lunarus's presence, steps forward nervously with her head held low. "For you I have something very special indeed." He pulls from the chest a gold and ivory horn. It has with it a leather case to wear on a belt. He explains, "On its own this may not be as useful as a weapon or a shield. This horn, however, may save your life someday. In times of your greatest need blow this horn and help shall come."

Evelena reads, "Horn of the Fallen?" She looks at Lunarus confused.

"I hope that you will never find yourselves in a situation that you will need it," Lunarus explains. "You may blow into it if you wish. It will not do anything out of the ordinary unless it is truly needed."

"What will it do if it *is* needed?" Evelena asks.

"It calls for help from a long lost guardian," answers Lunarus.

"Thank you, Lunarus," Evelena says. "Your gifts are too generous. I do not know how we can ever repay you."

"You do not need to do anything," Lunarus replies. "I am sure you will put them to good use. Now then, I have some matters to attend to, so I will leave you all to yourselves so that you may get some rest. I trust my treasures are safe?"

"Sven, likes treasure," Sven says, "but not enough to steal from dragons."

The others laugh including Lunarus.

"I'll see you all in the morning then," Lunarus says as he walks to the exit of the cave. "Goodnight."

They all say goodnight as Lunarus leaves. Then they prepare for bed. Kel'ana looks at her bow closely as Ja'noa asks her, "Is something wrong?"

"No," Kel'ana replies, "I was just thinking about what he said about my bow. He said that there was a twin bow somewhere out there. I was just wondering where it was."

Chapter 30
Sanctuary

Kel'ana looks at her new bow Glacies while not very far away the twin bow Incendia is carried by Ya'leigh Na'Moon. Ya'leigh, along with Princess Kianna and the rest of their party, have been walking all day around the large Sapphire Lake. It is getting very dark as they approach the Monastery on the lake. They see light from the windows inside.

"Looks like someone is home," Isen observes. "You all stay here and I'll go check on it."

"I really don't think that is necessary," Kianna replies.

Garrin adds, "These are monks, not orcneas."

"But the orcneas could have taken them over," Isen says as they get closer.

"It doesn't look like they were attacked," Ya'leigh says. "This place looks familiar though."

"Come on," Kianna says. "Let's go and knock."

"If you insist, Princess," Isen relents. "Just don't blame me if we are attacked."

Ambra and Kelik look at each other and laugh, but then get close behind Isen as they begin to walk up the stone path to the front door. Isen walks up to the big heavy doors and knocks.

The doors open as four Monks in their robes greet them. "Greetings, I am Brother Edward," Edward says.

"Pleased to meet you Brother Edward," Kianna replies. "I am Princess Kianna Ravenguard of Sheathelm."

"Welcome, Princess Kianna," Edward says as he bows his head. "Please, come in."

"Thank you," Kianna says as she enters the hall. The rest of the group follows as Isen looks around carefully.

"Forgive me, Princess," Edward says, "but we were not expecting you. You are of course welcome but we would have prepared a proper reception had we had known you were coming."

"No need to apologize," Kianna says. "We are grateful for your hospitality."

"We shall prepare rooms for you at once," Edward says as he motions to one of the other monks. The bald robed man leaves down a hall as Edward continues, "We were just sitting down to dinner, please join us."

Isen's face lights up and he says, "Oh, good, I am starving."

"You are always hungry," Gena says. "At least I don't have to create food for you this time."

The monks set a place for them at a long table in the main hall. Ya'leigh looks around at the large tapestries on the wall and says, "That looks like the Dragon Wars."

"That is because it is," Edward replies. "You are Ya'leigh Na'Moon, are you not?"

"Yes," Ya'leigh replies, "How did you know?"

"Your father used to bring you here with Princess Kianna when you were very young," Edward explains.

"That's why this place seems so familiar," Ya'leigh replies. "I can barely remember."

Looking at Ambra and Kelik, Edward asks, "You two must be Ambra and Kelik. I know you would be too young to remember being here. The last time you were here was just before your mother was taken from us."

No one responds as Ambra, Kelik, and Ya'leigh just look at each other sadly.

The awkward silence is broken as Garrin and Isen begin to eat. "This is so much better than rations," Garrin says as he takes a bite of some cheese.

"Mmmm," Isen moans with a mouth full of fresh fruit. "Not that I don't like your food, Gena, but this is delicious."

"Well, maybe they will let you bring some then," Gena says, sounding annoyed.

"Do you need supplies?" Edward asks.

"If it isn't too much trouble," Kianna says. "Isen here has eaten all his rations and forgot to buy more in Troven."

"It is no trouble at all," Edward replies. "We can even send some fruit with you that will not spoil."

"Sponge fruit?" Ambra asks.

"Yes," Edward answers. "We have a tree out in our garden."

"Are they good?" Isen asks.

"Oh, they are," Ambra answers. "Sponge fruit are like blueberries but are as big as apples. Instead of going bad they just dry out. You can add water to them and they will taste almost fresh."

"I like blueberries," Isen says.

"Is there a food you don't like?" Ambra teases.

"Yes," Isen answers, "those berries you let me eat the other day."

Edward says, "We can give you as many as you wish. We have many of them already dried out. Now, if you will forgive my inquisitiveness, Chance was already here to warn us of the orcneas, so what brings you here?"

Kianna looks at Ya'leigh before answering, "We are heading across the range to the old orcnea territory."

"Why would you go there?" Edward asks.

"The orcneas are invading Northwind," Kianna replies. "We are hoping to find the orcnea lands undefended. We may not be able to do much, but we just might cause them enough trouble to make a difference."

Edward looks at Ya'leigh and asks, "Your father didn't say anything about it. Does he know what you are up to?"

Ya'leigh looks down and says, "We saw him to a few days ago. He knew we were bringing supplies to Troven, but we were supposed to go back after that."

Then Edward turns to Kianna and asks, "Princess Kianna, does King Arioch know?"

"No," Kianna replies. "I am taking responsibility for this decision. With Isen, Garrin, and Gena, Ya'leigh and I are safe. We didn't know that Ambra and Kelik were hiding in the wagon until we got to Troven."

"Forgive me, Your Highness," Edward says, "but are you certain about this?"

"Yes," Kianna replies. "Besides we have the gate stone to take us back to the palace if anything should happen that we cannot handle."

"Well then," Edward says, "If I cannot change your minds then perhaps I should tell you that three days ago a small group of Amazons of the Silver Moon came through here. They were on a scouting mission to the northern territory. Of course we did not know at that time the extent of the orcnea's return. Perhaps you can catch up to them and join their party."

"Three days is a lot of time to catch up," Kianna says, "but if we go through the old dwarven city of Coldrock, we just may be able to."

"Assuming it still goes all the way through the mountain," Garrin says.

"Coldrock?" Edward says. "Last I knew the way was still clear, but without a guide or a map through the caves you would more than likely get lost."

"We are hoping to find a guide in Copper Pass," Kianna says.

"I suppose you could find someone with the knowledge," Edward says. "The question is what will be their price."

"We will just tell them the Princess orders them to go," Isen says.

"We can't do that," Kianna says. "Even if I wanted to, Sheathelm's control stops at the mountain's edge."

"Also," Edward warns, "it may not be a good idea to tell people she is the princess. You never know when someone might get the idea of kidnapping her for a ransom."

"Yes, Isen," Gena says. "So this time keep your mouth shut."

The others laugh at Isen as he says, "I'll try to be more careful this time."

Ambra and Kelik are now over at the tapestry and are studying it. "Look," Ambra says, pointing at one of the humanoid figures in the tapestry. "That must be Head Master Drakesbane."

"Where?" Kelik asks as he looks closer.

"Right there," Ambra says as she points again. "The one with the blue aura around him."

"Oh yes," Kelik says as he spots where Ambra is pointing.

Ya'leigh, Gena, and Kianna all get up from the table and walk over and look. Gena says, "I didn't know he fought in the Dragon War."

Kianna replies, "That is how he got his blessing of the ice magic."

"Correct," Edward explains. "He along with Chance, King Arioch, Damian, and Tharidin were able to help bring an end to the war by bringing down the giant air ship."

"I thought it was a floating city," Isen says.

"For its size," Edward continues, "is was more like a fortress or city, but it was mobile and used by an ancient race to travel to and conqueror other realms. It crashed when it came to this realm through a giant gate."

"Then," Kianna says continuing the story, "about twenty years ago, the

Dragon Slayers discovered it and begin to use the power of the dragon crystals to give it power to rise again."

"Correct," Edward replies.

"So what did this have to do with Master Drakesbane getting his power?" Gena asks.

Edward asks, "Well, do you know how the dragon crystals were created?"

"Yes," Gena answers, "the Dragon Slayers would capture a dragon and use magic to trap its soul, or life force, into a large crystal."

"Yes," Edward nods, "every dragon crystal contained the soul of a dragon. When Arioch and the others came across them they would break them and free the spirit inside."

"I thought Master Drakesbane got his ice powers from a staff," Gena says.

"From what I read," Kianna begins, "Master Drakesbane had the ice staff called Deep Frost. He used it to help defeat the Dragon Slayers. It wasn't until after the war that they learned that Deep Frost was powered by a dragon crystal. When they freed it, the ice dragon spirit that was inside granted Master Drakesbane part of his power. He has blue markings on his arms and chest that are from the blessing. He usually keeps them covered, though."

"I have always wondered about something," Gena asks, "I have always heard it called the Dragon Wars, but weren't the enemies the Dragon Slayers?"

Edward explains, "Yes, the enemies were the Dragon Slayers. By the end however, it was discovered that a dragon was behind it all. A dark dragon named Zetamat, along with a few other dragons, manipulated the Dragon Slayers into doing their bidding. The Dragon Slayers would trap dozens of dragons and capture their souls for Zetamat. Then they would use the captured crystals to raise the ancient air ship. Fortunately, King Arioch and his men would stop them by joining forces with the Amazons of the Silver Moon and the other dragons that Zetamat had set out to destroy. In the final battle, dragons fought against other dragons. Chance and Tharidin were able to destroy the crystals that were keeping the ship in the air. They escaped before it crashed back to the ground. With the ship destroyed, the fire dragon, Feonvaer, was able to defeat Zetamat and force him out of this realm."

Gena says, "So it was more of a dragon civil war."

"Indeed," Edward replies. He looks at Ya'leigh and says, "The amulet that your father carries with him, is a gift that Feonvaer granted him after the war. It too is a dragon crystal of sorts."

Ya'leigh replies, "I knew it was a gift but he never told me it was a dragon crystal."

Edward replies. "One day, Feonvaer was captured by the Dragon Slayers. Chance happened to come across them just as they began to trap his soul with a relic containing an empty dragon crystal. Chance interrupted the spell and freed Feonvaer, but not before some of his spirit had been taken. The fire dragon took the staff containing the crystal, but rather than breaking it, Feonvaer kept it. He would later cast another spell on it and return it to Chance as a gift after the Dragon War was over. That amulet contains part of Feonvaer's spirit."

"No wonder it is so powerful," Kianna says.

Crossroads

"I never knew that," Ya'leigh says.

Gena thinks for a moment then asks, "I know what became of King Arioch, Chance, and Master Drakesbane, but what ever happened to the other two?"

"Tharidin was my father's best friend," Ya'leigh answers. "He disappeared right before the Second Orcnea War."

Kianna then adds, "Damian is the lord of Northwind now. My father told me how the five of them had gone on many adventurers together."

"Now it is we who are adventuring," Ya'leigh laughs.

Later one of the monks enters the room from a hallway and nods to Edward. "I believe your rooms are ready," Edward says to them.

"Thank you again," Kianna says as they get up and gather their gear.

"You are always welcome here, Princess Kianna," Edward replies. "Now if you will follow Brother Michael, he will lead you to your rooms."

Before leaving the table, Isen grabs a couple more slices of bread to take with him. They follow Michael down the hall and to their rooms. Edward turns to one of the other monks and says, "Please go and tell Namos that I wish to see him as soon as possible in my room." The monk nods and leaves the main hall.

A short time later a young man knocks at Brother Edward's room door. He is almost twenty and is in fit condition. He wears a robe like the others but instead of a shaved head he has dark wavy hair. "Master Edward," Namos says, "you wished to see me?"

"Yes, Namos," Edward replies. Edward seals a letter and asks, "How would you like to go for a little run?"

"Of course, Master," Namos replies with a big smile. "How far?"

Edward stands and holds out the letter. "I need you to take this to King Arioch, he should be just south of Northwind."

Taking the letter from Edward, Namos thinks for a moment, "Master, that is all the way to the coast. It could take a week!"

"Yes," Edward answers. "I have a few items for you that will help make the journey much faster." Edward hands him a wineskin and says, "First you have the bottomless wineskin so that you will not run out of clean water." Edward lays a wool cloth on the desk and unfolds it. Inside there are several small vials. Edward says, "Though you probably won't need them, I am sending a few healing potions with you. I am also giving you several Potions of Rest as well as potions that will give you all the nutrients your body will need." Edward carefully folds the wool cloth and hands it to Namos. He then hands him a small pouch and says, "Here is some silver so that you can rest in the towns along the way. You must travel light so we will not send you with any tents or blankets. All you need can fit in this small backpack." He hands a backpack to Namos and says, "There is a map inside if you need it. I have one other item for you." He walks over to a shelf and pulls down a pair of sandals.

"Master?" Namos questions. "The Sandals of Celeritas, are you sure?"

"Yes," Edward replies, "You are our fastest runner. Even without the Sandals of Celeritas you could make the journey in several days. I need you to make this journey in three days."

Namos, holding the magical sandals in his hands, smiles brightly and says, "I will make the journey in two."

"Do not push yourself too hard," Edward warns. "Make sure you take breaks and pace yourself, and make sure that you deliver that message personally to either King Arioch or Chance Na'Moon."

"Yes, Master," Namos says. "I will leave at once."

"You can wait until morning," Edward says with a smile.

"I could, Master," Namos replies, "but I enjoy running in the night air. Besides, I am too excited to sleep now anyway."

"Very well," Edward says. "Before you go I have something else I would like to say."

Namos looks at Edward curiously and asks, "What is it, Master?"

"Namos," Edward begins to say, "you have been like a son to us here at the monastery. When we took you in all those years ago we knew that someday the time would come when you may leave us. Just like the young Sisters of the Silver Moon that came through a few days ago, you too need to go out into the world and make your own path."

Namos looking down asks, "So, when I am done delivering the message...?"

"You may decide what you do next," Edward says. "Travel wherever your heart leads you. Someday, if you feel so inclined, you may return here if you wish. You will always be welcome here, Namos."

Namos, looking sad, replies, "Thank you, Master. I will make you proud."

"I already am, Namos," Edward says as he opens his arms and hugs his young apprentice.

Namos takes the bag and looks inside at the map for a moment. He places everything back inside then eagerly puts on the sandals. Without another word they walk to the front door. Namos only nods before he turns to run down the path to Sapphire Lake.

Brother Edward watches Namos as he reaches the lake and begins to run down the shore line. The calm waters on the lake reflect the stars in the night sky as well as the ringed silver crescent moon that hangs low over the other horizon.

Far away on the deck of the *Red Dawn*, Ariella looks upon the same moon. "Why Fernando?" she quietly asks herself, "Why?"

At that very same moment Fernando Greythorn lies under the open sky also staring at the moon. He has been traveling with a caravan in-root to Sheathelm. With a sad smile he says to himself, "Oh, Ariella, I hope you will be able to forgive me." A shooting star streaks across the sky to the north and Fernando smiles and closes his eyes to make a wish.

Farther north on the front lines, Chance watches the same shooting star. He smiles and also closes his eyes. He thinks of Kristieana and the seven sisters. He whispers to himself, "May the gods and goddesses watch over you, Kristieana, and may you keep our sisters safe." He opens his eyes and then his thoughts drift away as he stares off into a nearby campfire.

Not very far way, in Lunarus's mountain cave, Kristieana is also staring into a fire. She is remembering her kiss with Chance. Suddenly her daydream is interrupted by Kel'ana's voice. "What are you thinking about?" Kel'ana asks her.

Kristieana looks up and asks, "I am sorry, what did you say?"

"I asked what you were thinking about," Kel'ana repeats, "You seemed to be far away."

"Yeah," she replies, "I was."

Out at the cave's entrance Sven is looking out over the valley. The crescent moon sits over the mountain tops as the silhouette of Lunarus appears to be gliding across the moon's silver rings.

It is that same moon that shines down over Namos as he continues his run. He cannot help but think about what he wants to do after he delivers the message. Memories of his youth come back to him.

He is five years old and asks Brother Edward, "Master, what happened to my parents?"

"When you were just an infant," Edward explains, "a terrible disease swept through the town of Ofarin. By the time the brothers and I had arrived to help, many had already perished. We saved as many people as we could but Ofarin was left devastated. Your parents were among those who lost their lives. You were staying with your grandmother. She asked us to care for you because she had grown too weak to do so herself. We gladly took you in, Namos. We are your family now."

Namos memories skip to lessons with the brothers. Mediation, planting fruits and vegetables in the garden, and then later magic. One day he asks Brother Edward, "Master, when will I learn how to cure a disease?"

"In due time, Namos," he replies.

"I want to learn, Master," Namos says, "so that someday I can help the sick. Then no child will have to lose their parents."

Namos's memories fade, and as he runs through the night he thinks to himself that the time has finally come for him to make a difference in the world, and that he will do everything he can to help with the sick and injured. He thinks to himself that there is no better place to help than on the front lines of war.

Chapter 31
Off Limits

Sven walks into the cavern after watching Lunarus patrol the mountain side. The others are laying down their furs near one of the two fire pits. Sven lays out his fur next to the other fire. On the far side of the cave Kristieana is sitting at Lunarus's desk and is reading the letter from Chance again.

Evelena says to the girls, "We should make sure that we dry all of our cloths. We are only half way across the mountains, and we may not come across a better shelter for the night."

Rehma sits down on her blanket and says, "This is certainly better than sleeping in the tents."

"I never knew the journey would be this cold," Gelana says.

"I don't think any of us did," Evelena replies as she sits down on her fur.

Ja'noa warms herself by the fire. She says, "Kel'ana, would you braid my hair?"

"Sure," Kel'ana answers, "but you have to braid mine in return."

"Deal," Ja'noa says as she sits down on her blanket.

Kel'ana begins to braid Ja'noa's dark wavy hair. "How does my face paint look?" Kel'ana asks, referring to the star that is stained around her eye.

"It looks fine," Rehma answers.

"The pigments are too cold to paint with," Evelena says. "We may have to wait until we get down of the mountains to re-apply our markings."

Ja'noa says, "Should only be a few more days until we are down out of the cold."

"I am not so sure it is a good idea to go anymore," Kel'ana says as she continues to tie Ja'noa's hair into braids.

"Why?" Yentroc asks.

"What if there are more orcneas on the other side than we can deal with?" Kel'ana asks.

The girls look at each other while pondering the question. Ja'noa breaks the silence and says, "Chance would have come back and warned us if there were."

"What if he couldn't?" Rehma says.

"What do you mean?" Yentroc asks.

"I mean," Rehma replies, "what if something happened to Chance."

"Not likely," says Evelena.

"Why not?" Rehma asks. "I was able to fight him without any trouble."

"That was different," Evelena explains, "you caught him off guard. I doubt he would scout with his guard down."

"All I am saying is that he is not immortal," Rehma replies.

"We will proceed with caution," Evelena says. "Perhaps Kristieana can scout ahead for us. She can turn into an eagle like Chance."

"Speaking of Kristieana," Gelana says, "what is she doing over there at that desk?"

Crossroads

"I don't know," Yentroc answers, "but it looks like our guide, Sven, is saying hello to her." Lyra looks up from her book and can see Sven at the other side of the cave talking to Kristieana.

Gelana says, "I wonder what that conversation is about."

"I don't know," Yentroc replies, "but I think Lyra better go over there and claim her territory."

Gelana and Yentroc laugh. Evelena says, "Yentroc, let's not start with that again."

"Lyra knows I am only joking," she replies, "right, Lyra?"

When there is no response from Lyra, Gelana turns and says, "Lyra?"

They all look around but cannot find her. Evelena says, "She probably went outside. I'll go and look." Evelena gets up and heads out of the cave in search for Lyra.

Across the cave, with her invisibility spell active, Lyra slowly approaches Sven and Kristieana. She stops behind Sven and listens quietly.

"So," Sven says with a smile, "would you like Sven to keep you extra warm tonight?"

Kristieana folds the letter and looks up at Sven and asks, "Does that really work with other women?"

"Yes," Sven replies, "it usually does. So how about it? Sven is sleeping over there tonight." He points at his fur blankets near the fire opposite of the women. "You can join Sven if you wish."

Kristieana can't help but laugh and say, "I cannot believe it. You introduce yourself and immediately ask me to sleep with you? I think you already have someone to keep warm at night. And I am only going to warn you once: If you ever try to do anything other than keep her warm..."

"Lyra?" Sven questions. "She is just little girl. You though, are real woman." Kristieana stands up and Sven walks up next to her. She looks up at the taller man as he says, "Sven can tell that woman like you must have hard time finding man capable of satisfying her. Chance made Sven promise not to touch others, but he did not say anything about you."

Kristieana clutches her letter from Chance a little tighter and replies, "Thank you for your offer, Sven, but I have already found someone."

Sven grins and nods his head as he steps back from her. "Very well then," he says. "If you change mind, you know where to find Sven."

Sven begins to walk away as Lyra puts out her staff and trips him. He falls to the ground as Lyra runs off. Sven looks back at Kristieana who is laughing and says, "It wasn't me."

Sven, confused, stands up and says, "Must have been rug."

Lyra runs to the entrance of the cavern, and as she steps around the corner out of the view from the others she drops her invisibility spell. She takes a moment to gather herself before walking back into the open cavern.

Sven starts to walk back over to the other side of the cave as Gelana runs over to Kristieana and asks, "Have you seen Lyra?"

"Yes," she answers, pointing to the entrance as Lyra walks back in, "she is right there."

Lyra, who is visibly upset, walks past Sven without looking at him. Sven stops and asks, "Lyra, are you alright?"

She just ignores him and keeps walking back to where she has laid out her blanket to sleep. She lies down and faces away from the others. Evelena comes back and sees her and says, "There you are, I was just looking for you. Where did you go?"

"I had to get some fresh air," Lyra answers as a tear falls onto her fur blanket.

Evelena is puzzled as she looks at the cave entrance wondering how she missed Lyra. She decides not to question it any further.

At the other side of the cave Kel'ana joins Kristieana and Gelana. "It looks like we found her." Kel'ana says. She then sees the letter in Kristieana's hand and asks, "What is that?"

Kristieana looks down at the letter in her hand and says, "This is nothing."

Before she can put it away, Gelana quickly snatches it from her grasp and says, "I don't believe you."

"Give it back," Kristieana orders.

"Relax," Gelana replies, as she unfolds it and looks at the letter. "I'll give it back." She then starts to read the letter out loud. "*Dear Kristieana,*" she begins, "*I am sorry for leaving you without saying goodbye.*"

"Stop it right now," Kristieana says as she looks across the cave to the others who do not seem to notice what is happening.

"Who is it from?" Kel'ana asks.

Gelana looks down at the bottom of the letter and pauses. She says, "You are not going to believe this, Kel'ana. It's from Chance."

"Is it really?" Kel'ana asks. "What else does it say?"

"None of your concern," Kristieana says as she grabs the letter back.

"Wait a minute," Kel'ana says with a smile. "You were there the other night at that Inn. Chance said he met you at Elonfar, but that wasn't the truth was it?"

Kristieana sighs and quietly says to the two of them, "You have to promise not to say anything to the others, especially Rehma."

"Alright," Gelana says, "as long as you tell us everything."

Kristieana again looks to the other side of the cave to make sure no one else is coming. She then begins to tell Gelana and Kel'ana what happened that night at the Inn.

A short time later Sven begins to get ready for bed. He stands up and takes off his furs and chain-mail underneath. Kel'ana and Gelana are back over with the others as Yentroc nudges Gelana and points over to Sven who is now only in his trousers. Yentroc and Gelana stare at Sven's chiseled physique.

Yentroc says, "I can't believe you got to sleep next to him the last two nights, Lyra. He can keep me warm anytime."

"You and me both," Gelana says.

Lyra, continuing to look away, says, "I am sure he would be more than happy to."

Yentroc laughs and says, "I don't think so. Remember, Chance made him promise to keep us off limits."

Crossroads

Evelena says, "Gelana and Yentroc, you two need to start focusing on why we are out here and not worry so much about Sven."

"I agree," Rehma says, "you two are acting foolish. It's embarrassing."

"You have to admit," Gelana says, "he's not bad for a human."

Sven looks up at the girls and can feel the weight of Yentroc and Gelana's stares. He climbs under his fur blanket and says to himself, "You owe Sven, Chance. You *really* owe Sven."

Chapter 32
Day 9
Eternal Night

The next morning Princess Kianna and the others head out to Copper Pass. It takes them a few hours to make the trip up the winding path. Despite being smaller and younger, Ambra and Kelik seem to be having less trouble with the climb then their older sister Ya'leigh. They are ahead of everyone.

"Wait up!" Ya'leigh yells to them.

Ambra and Kelik wait at the top of a hill. "And I thought they were the adventurers," Ambra says to her brother.

When the rest of the group makes it to the top of the steep incline they find that they are at the gates of Copper Pass. Isen walks up to the gate and knocks loudly. A few moments later a small window in the gate opens and a man peers through it. He doesn't say a word before closing the window and opening the door.

"Welcome," the man says without hesitation.

"Thank you," Isen says. "Do you know where would we be able to find a meal?"

"Are you hungry already?" Ya'leigh asks.

"I am starving," Isen replies.

The man at the door points and says, "The Pick Ax is right over there."

"Thank you," Isen says.

They make their way to the Pick Ax and enter. It is noon and the place is empty. Only the dwarven innkeeper and one human patron are there. They sit down at the counter as the dwarf asks, "What can I get for you?"

"Yes," Garrin replies, not hearing him correctly, "The sky is blue today."

The dwarf shakes his head and repeats himself a little louder, "What can I get for you!"

"I'll have an ale," Garrin replies.

Kianna then asks the dwarf, "I am looking for some information."

As the innkeeper pours the ale for Garrin he asks, "And what sort of information are you looking for?"

"We are looking for a guide through the mines," Kianna says.

"Well, there are plenty miners around," he replies as he hands Garrin his drink. "Any particular place you wish to be guided to?"

"As a matter of fact there is," Kianna says. "We would like to go through to the other side, through Coldrock."

"Coldrock?" he questions. "Well, now that may be a bit harder to find a guide for. Although there is a goblin who claims he has a map."

"Where might we find this goblin?" Kianna asks.

"His name is Kreeshaw," the dwarf answers. "He is usually here around lunch time." No sooner than he says that, the front door opens and a goblin dressed in winter cloths enters. "You are in luck," the innkeeper says. "Here he is now."

Crossroads

The goblin named Kreeshaw makes his way over to the counter and climbs up on a stool. He says to the dwarf, "The usual, please."

As the dwarf prepares a drink for the goblin, Princess Kianna asks him, "Are you Kreeshaw?"

The goblin, surprised to hear his name, looks up at her and replies, "Yes, I am Kreeshaw. What can I do for you?"

Before Kianna can answer, Isen steps in and takes over the conversation, "We are looking for a way through Coldrock to get to the other side of the mountains. We heard you might be able to help."

The innkeeper places Kreeshaw's drink in front of him. Kreeshaw picks it up and says, "Well then, I suppose I could guide you through the mountain, if you can help me retrieve something that belongs to me."

Kianna pushes Isen aside and asks, "What is it you need us to retrieve?"

"Well," Kreeshaw explains, "There are a couple large bags with some ore in them, but they are deep down in the mines. We could get them on our way."

"How would you get them back after we reached the other side?" Kianna asks.

"I have a special bag that will help me carry all of the ore at once," Kreeshaw answers.

"Then why do you need us?" Isen asks.

"Isen," Kianna snaps, "will you please let me handle this."

"Sure, Your—" Isen begins to say Highness as Kianna elbows him. "Ow!"

"My friend has a good point," Kianna interjects. "Why do you need us?"

Kreeshaw takes a drink from his mug then answers, "The problem is that they are being guarded by a giant cave spider."

"Maybe we should just go over the mountains," Garrin says nervously.

"Are you afraid of spiders?" Ambra asks.

"Scared? No." Garrin replies. After hesitating he adds, "I might have a mild fear of them."

Ya'leigh smiles and says, "Don't worry, Kianna and I will keep you safe."

"It's just a bug," Isen says. "That should be no problem."

"For you it probably won't be," Kreeshaw replies, "but I certainly can't do it alone."

"Any reason you haven't asked for help from the other miners?" Garrin asks.

"Well," Kreeshaw answers, "First of all, not many people are willing to go that far down into the mine. Secondly, I don't really want to share the ore."

"How valuable is it?" Isen asks.

"It's worth me taking you through the mountain," Kreeshaw replies.

"So if we take care of the cave spider, you will take us through the mountain?" Kianna asks.

"How do we know we can trust you?" Isen asks.

"Are you always this distrusting?" Kreeshaw asks.

Ya'leigh laughs and says, "Yes, he usually is."

"Look, there are seven of you," Kreeshaw explains. "What do you expect me to do?"

"I am sorry. Please pay no attention to Isen," Kianna says as she pushes her big guard back. "He is just looking out for us."

"Well, I can appreciate that," Kreeshaw says. "So do we have a deal?"

"Yes," Kianna replies. "We have a deal."

"Well then," Kreeshaw says as he slams his mug down, "Let's get going."

"Now?" Isen asks. "I haven't eaten yet."

"You can eat later," Gena says. "I'll make you something if you will stop with your whining."

Later the group arrives at a mine entrance just outside of town. There are a few people working outside sorting rocks into piles as they are brought out to the surface. Kreeshaw asks one of them, "Have there been any orcneas today?"

The man shakes his head and says, "No, nothing."

"Orcneas?" Ambra says, sounding nervous.

"Don't worry," Kreeshaw replies. "So far none have come up through the mines. I figured that is why you wanted to go this way, to avoid them."

"We will be fine," Isen says to Ambra. "They will have to go through me to get to you."

Ambra looks up at Isen and replies, "If you say so."

Kianna opens her backpack and pulls out a brightly glowing stone. "Everyone, get out your light stones," she says.

The group begins their descent into the mine. They make their way down further and further, until it levels off and it begins to look more like a cave. Kreeshaw says, "This is where most of the others stop and don't go any further." They enter a large cavern. The light from their magical stones is bright, but the cave is so large that they can barely see the walls.

Kelik catches a gimps of something in the darkness. "Wait a minute!" Kelik says as he carefully walks over to the left side of the cave. He shines his light on a small patch of mushrooms. "Ambra, are these Glacier Mushrooms?"

Ambra and Gena make their way over as the others follow them behind. "Yeah, I think so," Ambra replies.

"Can you eat them?" Isen asks.

"Sure," Ambra replies, "if you want to die."

"They are very poisonous," Gena explains.

"Oh," Isen says as he steps back from them. "Then why are we bothering with them?"

"Not everything has to be edible to be useful," Kianna says.

Ya'leigh asks her sister, "Ambra, do you know any potions that use them?"

"Yes," Ambra answers, "But I don't have an alchemy lab or the other ingredients."

"Are they valuable?" Isen asks.

"Very," Kelik replies.

"Well then, let's grab them and go," Isen says.

Gena warns, "We have to be careful, and we also only want to take one or two."

"Why?" Isen asks.

"Because they take a very long time to grow," Gena explains, "And if we take too many we would endanger them."

Ambra takes out a small jar from her backpack. She carefully places it behind one of the mushrooms and uses the lid to push it in. "Alright," She says, "I got one. Let's go."

The group continues on their way as Kreeshaw leads. Finally he stops and points to a place ahead where a separate tunnel branches off. "This is the place," Kreeshaw says. "My friends and I were storing our ore here when we were attacked by the spider. I was the only one who made it out alive. Take the path to the left."

Isen starts to walk down the rocky corridor and says, "Let's get this over with." He draws his morning star out and flames magically emanate from it. The fiery weapon lights his way.

Ya'leigh pulls out her bow, Incendia, and draws the bowstring. The fiery arrow that appears lights up the cave a little more. Kelik pulls a crossbow out his backpack. "No," Ya'leigh says, pushing her brother back, "You and Ambra stay here."

"But I want to help," Kelik protests.

"Stay here!" Ya'leigh repeats sternly.

Kelik sighs and says, "Fine."

Kianna begins to cast the ice dagger spell. Within the faint blue glow emanating from her hands, three icicles form. With the sharp ends facing in front of her, she channels more energy into it making them larger. She then proceeds to carefully advance as she carries the spell with her. Gena charges a lightning bolt in her hands and follows Kianna.

Garrin readies his shield and says, "I'll stay here with the children and make sure they are alright."

Kreeshaw stays back with Kelik, Ambra, and Garrin. Ya'leigh, Gena, and Kianna make their way to the split where Isen is already waiting. He looks into the next chamber, but his light does not shine brightly enough to make anything out. He turns back to Ya'leigh and says, "Can you shoot one of your fire arrows up there?"

"Sure," Ya'leigh replies. "But I don't know if it will stay up there."

"Well, I can't see a thing," Isen says.

Ya'leigh steps up and peers into the larger cavern opening. She aims her bow at the roof of the cave and releases the bowstring. The flaming arrow flies up about the height of a two level building before hitting rock. The arrow gets caught in some webbing and as the web catches fire, the arrow falls to the ground at the center of the cave. The webbing above burns only a few moments longer, but it is long enough for Isen to see movement. Isen looks closer and can see the glow of the fire reflecting off the beady eyes of the giant arachnid.

"I see it," Isen says. "Shoot another arrow."

He carefully steps into the cavern and waits, staring up at the roof. Ya'leigh draws back for another shot and the spider turns and scurries into the darkness. Ya'leigh releases the arrow, and the room lights up a little more. Now there is just enough light for the others to see the shadowy figure. With its long legs the spider nearly spans twice the length of a human. Kianna peers in and gasps at its enormous size. She nervously tries to hit it with her ice daggers but only manages to graze it. Kianna steps back and begins to cast again.

"Come on everyone," Isen says. "Get it down so I can kill it."

"We are trying!" Ya'leigh yells as she shoots again. This time she hits her target and the spider jumps down to the ground along the far back wall.

It is about forty paces away, and Isen starts to charge at it. He gets to the center of the cavern when his legs become entangled in something. "What the!" Isen exclaims as he looks down. His legs are now covered with webbing.

Gena fires her lightning bolt striking the spider. It screeches in pain. Ya'leigh aims again at the dark fuzzy creature when she feels a sting on her leg. She looks down and can see that her legs are crawling with a dozen spiders the size of her fists. In a panic she fires her bow blindly and misses the spider. She yells out, "They are on me!" She takes her bow and starts to swat them off her.

Isen can see a swarm of these smaller spiders coming at him. He swings at the ground with his flaming weapon, keeping them away. The giant spider begins to close in on Isen. Kianna fires another ice dagger at the huge beast but only hits one of its legs. Isen, busy keeping the smaller pests from overwhelming him, doesn't notice the big one is about to strike him with its fangs.

"Look out!" Kianna warns Isen.

Isen looks up at the fangs coming at him when suddenly something hits the spider in one of its eyes. The spider recoils and backs off. Ya'leigh turns to see who attacked it only to find her brother, Kelik, holding his crossbow.

Kelik raises his right hand and magically summons a blaze in front of Ya'leigh that makes most of the smaller spiders retreat. Ya'leigh stands close to the fire nearly putting herself within the flames as the spiders jump from her and flee. Kianna uses her shield to smash any spider that comes close to her while Gena user her staff to swat them away.

Isen, who is now aware of the closeness of the giant arachnid, ignores the smaller spiders even as they begin to bite him. He swings his morning star at the giant spider, striking it on the head. The cracking sound of the steel meeting the exoskeleton and the hissing sound the spider makes tells Isen that it was a solid hit. He pulls back the flaming weapon only to strike it again. The spider stops moving as Isen hits it one more time to be absolutely sure it is no longer a threat. Then he makes haste to the fire that Kelik had set moments earlier and the flames force the smaller spiders off of his legs. Ya'leigh rapidly shoots arrow after arrow into the cavern burning away the webbing and creating more light.

Garrin, Ambra, and Kreeshaw join the others.

Ya'leigh says, "My legs are really stinging."

"Hold still," Gena says, "I can cleanse the venom." Ya'leigh sits down as Gena begins to cast a spell. Her hands glow green, and as she passes them over Ya'leigh's legs she says, "That should help."

Ya'leigh takes a deep breath and says, "That is better. Thanks."

Isen then asks, "They bit me too, can you cast that on me?"

"Sure," Gena replies. Isen sits down and she casts the spell again.

"Oh, yes," Isen says with a heavy sigh of relief. "That's better."

"You're welcome," says Gena.

"Thank you," Isen says with a smile.

Kreeshaw looks in and shudders when he sees the giant arachnid in the middle of the cave. "Good work, everyone." With several flaming arrows still lighting the room, Kreeshaw walks in and finds two large sacks along the wall. He kneels down a pulls out a small bag and begins to put some of the ore inside.

"Is that really going to hold all that ore?" Isen asks.

"Absolutely," Kreeshaw answers. "It holds a lot more than it looks."

"A bottomless bag?" Kianna asks.

"Sort of," Kreeshaw says as he starts to empty the second bag, "It's limited to rocks and minerals."

"A bottomless miner's sack," Garrin says.

"Very good," Kreeshaw says as he finishes loading the ore to his new bag.

Ya'leigh walks up to Kelik and says, "I thought I told you to stay back." Kelik, surprised by his sister's reaction, stands there with a confused look. Before he can replay, Ya'leigh adds, "Thanks for not listening." She smiles at her brother and he laughs.

"I think I got it all," Kreeshaw says. "Now that you have completed your end of the bargain, it's time for me to complete mine. We have a long way to go, so we best not waste any time."

"How long is it going to take us?" Kianna asks.

"We should reach Coldrock sometime tomorrow," Kreeshaw says, "That will put us about half way to the other side."

"Hey, Ambra," Isen says. "Can you use the spider venom for anything?"

"Only if you want to poison your weapons," Ambra replies. "It is really dangerous. Most of the time you don't even know you have been poisoned until it's too late. It will just hit you suddenly about an hour after."

"Oh, then never mind," Isen says.

The group continues on their way through a world that is forever dark. They will spend three more days in this eternal night.

Chapter 33
Not a Little Girl

In contrast to the darkness of the caves below, the bright snow of the mountain top is almost blinding to the Amazons of the Silver Moon as they continue with their journey. Sven leads the way through the ice and snow. The sun is shining and as they walk through a valley the temperatures are mild.

Sven stops and says, "This will be good place to eat." Suddenly a snowball hits him in the shoulder. He is surprised and looks to see who threw it only to find Lyra standing there holding another snowball in her hands. She is glaring at Sven and doesn't say a word. Sven laughs and asks, "Why you do that?" Instead of an answer, Lyra just angrily throws the other snowball at him. He manages to put his arm up just in time to block it before it hits him in the face.

The others back up a bit and take off their backpacks as they watch Lyra pelt Sven again and again with more snowballs. She snaps at him, "I am NOT a little girl!"

The others look confused except for Kristieana, who can't help but grin as she continues to watch the situation unfold.

"What are you talking about?" Sven asks as he continues to put his hands up to prevent the snow from hitting him in the face.

Lyra stops throwing the snowballs and walks up to Sven. Looking up at the man who towers over her, she yells, "I heard what you said to Kristieana last night, and I am not a little girl!"

Sven closes his eyes with he realizes of what she is talking about. Looking down at the furious Lyra he says, "Lyra, Sven is sorry, Sven..."

She doesn't let him finish however she strikes his broad chest with her fist and says, "I know I may not look like it, but with the exception of Kristieana, I am as old as all of them!"

"Sven did not mean it," Sven tries to explain. "Sven was just..." Sven pauses and looks around at the others. He can see that they all are listening closely.

"You were just trying to sleep with her," Lyra says, finishing the words he couldn't say.

"Yes," he quietly answers. His eyes now drop to the ground, too embarrassed to look at her.

"So, it's as simple as that?" Lyra asks. "You insulted me just so you could sleep with someone?"

Sven looks up from the ground at her now as a tear falls down her cheek. "Please, Lyra, Sven didn't mean it. You have to believe Sven," he says he tries to wipe the tear from her face.

She swats his hand away and yells, "Yes, you did!" She turns to others and continues to speak, "All my life I have been called names. Not by any of you here now, but by others. I have been called a runt, halfling, and dwarf. I am always reminded how small I am by the others." She turns back to Sven and says, "I am tired of being talked down to as if I am a child. Even a few of the elders said I couldn't come on this Rite of Passage. They actually forgot how old I am. You want to know why I have so many of these black beads?" She asks holding out her necklace. "It is not because I failed. It is because I used to run away. I hated my studies with the others so much that I would steal magic books and run off to study on my own. I taught myself the light school spells. Now, when I want to be alone, all I have to do is become invisible."

Sven looks down and says, "Lyra, Sven is very sorry. Sven never meant to hurt you."

Lyra, wiping away her tears, replies, "I just want to be seen for who I truly am on the inside, and not be defined by what people see on the outside."

Sven smiles and says, "Sven promises not to call you little Lyra anymore."

Gelana puts her hand on Lyra's shoulder. The others stand around her as well without saying a word. Feeling a little better, Lyra sniffs and wipes her cheek again and says, "It's alright, Sven, if someone is going to call me little, it may as well come from someone more than twice my size."

"Sven knows what is like to be small," he says as he stands next to her.

"What do you know about being small?" Lyra asks with a doubtful grin.

Sven just laughs and says, "More than you know. So, can Lyra forgive Sven?"

Lyra replies, "As long as you promise not to call me a little girl ever again."

"You have Sven's word," he says putting his hand up. Then he says, "Now, Sven has something for you."

Lyra smiles and say, "For me? What is it?"

Sven turns his back to her and bends over for a moment. He stands up and turns back around and says, "Here, catch." In his hands is a giant chunk of snow. He tosses it at the unsuspecting Lyra who is knocked to the ground. She looks up, surprised, and the others laugh.

Lyra says with a big smile, "Oh, you are going to pay for that." She climbs up out of the snow that covers her and begins to make more snowballs before throwing them at Sven.

Gelana calls out, "Kel'ana!" Just as Kel'ana turns around to see what Gelana wanted, she too is met with snow in the face.

Yentroc says, "I think Kel'ana is the last one I would want to have a snow fight with." A snow ball pelts Yentroc, and she turns to see Rehma getting ready to throw another one at her.

Kel'ana now begins to cast a spell. At her feet the snow forms a large column and as she raises her left hand the small tower of snow also rises. With a flicking motion of her right hand, Kel'ana begins to fling snow from the top of the rising pile. Bits of snow are hurled faster and faster towards Gelana who is hiding behind her new shield, Infragilis. The snow is coming at her so fast that it is as if ten people were throwing snowballs at her.

The more serious Evelena gets herself involved as she begins to throw snowballs along with Kristieana. Chaos in the snow ensues as Kel'ana now begins to target her close friend Ja'noa. However, Ja'noa easily dodges and ducks every snow ball hurled her way. She rolls behind Evelena who now begins to get hit by Kel'ana's snowy attacks. From behind Evelena's cover, Ja'noa quickly packs together a small snow ball. She then jumps into the air and throws her snow ball at Kel'ana with uncanny precision. It happens so fast that Kel'ana doesn't have time to dodge, and is hit directly in the face.

"I am going to get you for that," Kel'ana says, as she wipes the snow from her face. Motioning with both hands she now concentrates and lifts a huge mass of snow from the ground. She sends it at Ja'noa like a wave. Unable to escape, Ja'noa closes her eyes before the wall of snow hits her.

"That is why," Sven says with a laugh, "you should never have snow fight with ice mage." Suddenly Sven is hit in the back. "Ow! Alright," Sven says as he begins to turn to see who hit him, "who's throwing the ice?"

When Sven turns to look behind him, the others see an arrow sticking out the back of his left shoulder. An orcnea, just ahead of them on the path begins to notch another arrow in his bow. Three more orcneas step out from hiding and begin to aim their bows. Before Sven and the others have any time to react, the arrows are launched.

The first arrow strikes Kel'ana in her left arm. The second is aimed at Gelana. Fortunately for her it is deflected by Infragilis. The third comes right at Lyra. Just before it strikes her Sven puts himself right in the line of fire as he turns his back to the incoming arrow. The arrow strikes Sven in the right shoulder.

"Orcneas!" Evelena yells.

Ja'noa is the first to react, and before the orcnea that fired the first arrow can finish drawing back his bow for a second attack, she throws both of her Star Steel daggers into its chest. The orcnea falls back into the snow as the daggers begin to return to her.

Sven tries to reach for the ax, Hellfire, but the arrow in his shoulder prevents him from doing so. He winces in pain as he tries again.

Kel'ana grabs her bow but her injured arm prevents her from being able to use it. Everyone else prepares their weapons and shields, as the three remaining orcnea archers fire three more arrows at Sven's back. Evelena steps in the way and intercepts the arrows with her shield. After the arrows are harmlessly deflected, Evelena lifts her shield and releases a small stone missile with her right hand. The magical attack strikes one of the three orcneas, knocking it unconscious.

With only two orcneas remaining, Gelana takes aim with her spear. She hurls the spear at one of the orcneas and injures it as Ja'noa catches her returning star steel daggers and throws them again finishing the orcnea off.

Sven turns to see the last orcnea. He fights through the pain and draws Hellfire, but before he can use it, a dark bolt is thrown by Yentroc. The orcnea is hit and falls to his knees. Rehma charges in with both swords drawn but before she can reach the wounded orcnea a bright beam of light strikes it. The bright attack sears the orcnea like a thousand suns. The orcnea lets out a scream as the light burns him. Rehma stops suddenly, and looks to see where the attack came from.

Sven also turns to see who had cast such a spell, only to see Lyra standing there. Sven asks her, "Did you cast that?"

"Yes," Lyra responds, as the others look at her with amazement. "I told you I taught myself the light school spells."

"You were not joking," Sven says. As he takes a breath, a sharp pain shoots through him and the giant of a man winces again.

"You are hurt," Lyra says, looking up at him.

"I am fine," Sven replies, "go help Kel'ana."

"I have Kel'ana," Kristieana says as she looks at Kel'ana's arm.

"Then I guess that means I'll heal you," Yentroc says as she walks over to Sven and Lyra. "Now lie down so we can get these arrows out."

"How about Sven just gets on knees," he says as he drops down.

"I guess that will work," Yentroc says. "Lyra, can you pull the arrows out while I cast the heal spell?"

"Wait," Sven says, "These aren't practice arrows. You cannot just pull them out."

"They aren't in that far," Yentroc says as she examines one of the wounds. "Your fur cloak helped protect you. It will hurt, but I should be able to heal it completely once it is out. Lyra, make sure you pull it out straight."

"I can do that," Lyra answers. She braces herself and grabs one of the arrows. "Just tell me when."

"Now," Yentroc says. Lyra pulls one of the arrows out as Sven grits his teeth. Yentroc places her glowing hands on the hole in his fur cloak. She says, "Good, that one went well. One more, just like before." Lyra puts her hands around the other arrow and waits. "Now," Yentroc says again. Just as before, Lyra pulls the arrow out as Sven winces in pain. Yentroc's hands quickly heals the wound.

Ja'noa walks over to the four orcneas. She holds out her hands as the two star steel daggers return. She wipes the blood from them on her sleeve before sheathing them. She pulls a few of the arrows from the orcnea's quivers and smells the tips. Rehma now joins her and she asks, "What is it?"

Ja'noa replies, "I was just making sure the arrows weren't poisoned."

"Good idea," Rehma replies. She kneels down and searches the bodies for bit then says, "Looks like they have nothing worth taking."

Ja'noa laughs and says, "They usually don't."

Chapter 34
A Matter of Trust

On the *Red Dawn,* Ariella is up in the lounge writing in her log. There is knock at the door. "Enter," Ariella says as she closes her journal.

Torgus enters and says, "The weather is in our favor, Captain, we will reach Bastion in two days."

"Good," she replies. "Any luck tracing my amulet or Mr. Greythorn?"

"No, Captain," Torgus replies, "I am sorry. I try every couple hours."

Ariella nods her head. She stands up and as she walks over to a chair at the center table she says, "It's hard to believe that so much has happened in the last few days. Just over a week ago we first heard of my father's treasure. Now, I have lost that treasure to a man, who until a few days ago, I had never met. I have to replace two of my crew because of him, and on top of that Fernando stole something very personal of mine. Why? What is so important about my locket that he had to steal it?"

"Maybe he just wanted something to remember you by," Torgus says.

"No," Ariella replies. "There is a reason he took that locket, Torgus. I just know it, and I am sure it has to do with that treasure."

"Captain," Torgus says, "I will keep trying to find him, of course. Sooner or later we'll get him. Right now you need to get some rest. You have been under a lot of stress lately and I am worried about you."

"Do you suppose the gods are punishing me for something, Torgus?"

Ariella sits at the table and Torgus sits next to her. "Now, what would the gods be angry with you for?" He asks.

"I don't know," Ariella says, shaking her head. "Maybe I am not on the right path. Maybe I should have tried to see Chance again years ago."

"So this is about Chance then?" he asks.

"I don't know Torgus," Ariella says sounding exasperated. "I just don't know. Seeing Chance for the first time in nearly twenty years was harder than I ever imagined. Why did he come back into my life at a time when he couldn't stay? Even if he could, I don't even know if he would want to anymore."

"I don't have those answers, my dear," Torgus says.

"Why did we stop coming to Sheathelm years ago?" Ariella asks.

"What do you mean?" Torgus asks. "We came, but your father just never docked."

"For a while, yes," Ariella replies, "but one day, we set sail to the south and didn't return until the day Chance took his vows. Was that planned?"

"Ariella," Torgus says as he stands up and heads to the door, "we stayed away from Sheathelm once Chance had mastered the eagle transformation spell."

"Father couldn't have known what Chance was doing unless..." Ariella stops and looks at Torgus. "You," she says as she holds back tears. "You told him didn't you?"

"Ariella, we—"

"Get out," Ariella snaps.

"Not before you hear the rest," Torgus says as he walks back over to her. "We had no idea that Chance had met anyone during the Dragon War. Shortly after the war your father decided that he was wrong about Chance. That is why we returned to Sheathelm. The fact that Chance was taking his vows was only a coincidence."

"A coincidence, or a cruel twist of fate," Ariella ponders. "Torgus, I have to ask you something else."

"What is it, Captain?" he asks.

"Is there something you are not telling me?" she asks. "Do you know something about this treasure that I don't?"

"Ariella," Torgus replies, "I have told you all that I can."

"You have told me everything that you can?" Ariella questions. "So, there is more, but it's something you can't tell me, is that it?"

Torgus looks Ariella in the eyes and says, "I can tell you that I don't know anything about Fernando Greythorn. I can also tell you that your father never told me what he put in that treasure chest of his, or what your locket has to do with it. To answer your question though, yes, there are things that your father never wanted you to know. We were pirates, Ariella, we did things that we were not proud of, but I can promise you this, I am not keeping your father's treasure from you. Your father and I have always tried to do what we felt was best for you."

"Like keeping Chance's letters from me?" she asks.

Torgus sighs and looks down. "I suppose I deserve that. I am sorry, my dear. I promise you that we will get Fernando Greythorn and we will find your father's treasure. Perhaps then, all of your questions will be answered."

"Until then, Torgus," Ariella says as she now opens the door for him, "Look me in the eyes and tell me that I can trust you."

Torgus looks Ariella in the eyes and says, "Ariella, I swear to you on your father's watery grave you can trust me."

Ariella, feeling a sense of relief, replies, "Thank you, Torgus."

"I'll let you know if I find Fernando or your locket," Torgus says.

Ariella nods to Torgus as he leaves. She then closes the door and walks back over to her journal. As she sits down at the desk she opens the book and takes out her quill and begins another entry.

Chapter 35
Encampment

In the cold snowy mountains of the Northwind Range, the Amazons of the Silver Moon, along with Sven, are looking upon a small orcnea encampment. Peering over the edge of a cliff Lyra watches while invisible. The orcneas are no more than twenty paces out. They are also just as far down, and everyone is hidden from the orcnea's view by the edge of the cliff. There is a very large tent with smoke coming out from a hole in the middle. Outside the tent several orcneas are skinning a mountain goat.

"There are five of them," Lyra says quietly to the others behind her. "Plus whatever is in the large tent."

"Five? This will be easy then," Rehma says, "let's just rush them."

"No," Evelena replies. "We can take them from right here without anyone risking getting hurt."

"What will *I* do?" Rehma asks, "I don't have a ranged weapon."

"You can use my old bow," Kel'ana says. "You can still shoot a bow can't you?"

Rehma sneers at Kel'ana and says, "Yes, Kel'ana, I can still shoot a bow." Kel'ana takes her old bow and hands it to Rehma, along with the cornucopia of arrows.

Sven says, "Sven will guard pass in case any come up." Staying low he moves over to the right of the group to a small ledge that leads down to the orcnea camp below. The winding ledge is about fifty paces in length and is only wide enough for one person to stand on it.

"I'll stay back and be ready to heal anyone who needs it," Kristieana says.

"Alright," Evelena says, "get ready." Yentroc, Ja'noa, Evelena, and Lyra cast their spells and wait just back from the edge for Evelena to give the word. Gelana has her spear ready while Rehma draws back an arrow. Kel'ana draws back the bowstring of Glacies and an icy arrow magically appears. All of them are watching Evelena for the signal. She nods her head they all take two steps forward and form a line along the cliff edge.

Kel'ana is the first to release her attack. The ice cold arrow finds its mark right into the skull of an unsuspecting orcnea. Ja'noa's lightning and Yentroc's dark bolt strike the same orcnea simultaneously killing it before it can even move. The three remaining orcneas look up, and one is immediately struck down with the searing light of Lyra's spell. Another orcnea is severely wounded as Evelena hurls a magically summoned stone into its chest.

Gelana throws her spear at the last of the three orcneas, but it only hits the orcnea in the leg. Rehma now releases her arrow but it misses the orcnea. "Ugh, I hate bows!" she says frustratedly.

The orcnea with Gelana's spear in his leg grabs for his shield and calls out something in orcneish that the girls cannot understand. Soon five more orcneas emerge from the large fur tent. Four of them have bows and one carries with him a long tribal staff with antlers on the end. The wounded orcnea with the shield points up to the cliff and says something else. The orcneas all look up and the archers draw their arrows back. Two more orcneas with swords and shields run out from the side of the tent and start to run towards the path leading up to where Sven is waiting.

Ja'noa quickly draws out her star steel daggers and throws them at the orcnea with the staff. The orcnea shaman puts up his hand, and with a simple gesture deflects the two incoming projectiles. Ja'noa holds out her hand and waits as the two daggers begin to fly back to her.

Kel'ana attacks again with another arrow. She shoots at one of the four archers but the orcnea easily steps to the side to avoid being hit. This does distract the orcnea, and forces him to lose his aim.

With the orcneas now aware of the attack, they are able to defend themselves. Yentroc and Evelena cast more spells but the orcneas are able to dodge them. Two orcneas manage to fire their arrows back at the group. Kel'ana has to duck along with Lyra, as the arrows fly harmlessly over their heads.

Rehma shoots the bow once again at the injured orcnea, but it is blocked, and the arrow sticks into the shield. Rehma looks over to the pathway and can see the two orcneas running up to them. She tosses the bow to the side and draws out her two Vallo swords. "Good, finally something I can hit," she says as she begins to run over to the pass."

The others continue to try to hit the orcneas below as Rehma prepares to engage in melee combat. Rehma stands ready as the two orcneas make it to the top of the pass. Just as they arrive, however, Sven charges into one of them. He lowers his shoulder and slams into the orcnea from the side. The hit sends the orcnea flying into the other and both orcneas fall over the edge of the cliff. Rehma watches as they fall to the rocks below.

"What did you do that for?" Rehma yells at Sven.

Sven turns to her with a puzzled look on his face and answers, "To kill them, of course."

Rehma moves close to Sven's face and says, "Next time leave one for me."

Sven smiles and says, "Alright, next one that comes is yours." Just as those words are spoken, a large ogre emerges from the tent. It is holding a giant club that looks like a small tree. It looks up at everyone and lets out a loud howling yell and begins to run up the path. Rehma looks as Sven, who just smiles and says, "If you need Sven's help just say."

Rehma glares at the big man and doesn't reply. Instead, as the ogre makes its way up the passage, Rehma grips her two swords and charges towards it.

Evelena yells, "Rehma! Get back here!" Rehma doesn't show any sign that she can hear Evelena's orders as she continues down the path towards the much larger enemy.

Kel'ana lands another shot on one of the archers killing it. Lyra burns another with her searing light. Ja'noa catches her daggers as they return to her, and as one of the orcnea's attention is focused on Kel'ana, Ja'noa throws her star steel daggers again. The two daggers stick into the side of the orcnea and it falls.

This gets the attention of the last orcnea archer who fires an arrow at

Ja'noa. She quickly draws a regular dagger from the leather sash across her chest. Just as the arrow reaches her she is able to parry it out of the air. Yentroc fires another dark bolt at the remaining archer. This time, with its attention elsewhere, Yentroc's spell strikes the orcnea down.

During this time the shaman has been building up a large lightning bolt. Instead of attacking the young women directly, he takes aim at the cliff edge below them. The bolt hits with a violent force that cracks the ice and snow beneath Kel'ana and Yentroc. "Get back!" Gelana warns. Her warning is too late and the cliff gives way. Yentroc turns and grabs the ledge, and Gelana dives to grab her wrist. She says, "Hold on, I have you!"

Kel'ana begins to fall as well. Grabbing for the edge she loses her bow as it falls to the ground. She is not able to maintain her grip as more snow and ice give way. Kel'ana falls to the ground below. Though the landing is softened by the snow from the cliff, the impact knocks the wind out of her, and she feels a sharp pain in her leg and back.

"Kel'ana!" Ja'noa yells. She runs over to the ledge and looks down at Kel'ana. She calls out, "Are you alright?"

Kel'ana, wincing in pain, looks up at her friend and manages to wave back. She tries to move but the pain is too much.

Evelena yells, "Lyra! Hit that shaman!"

"Alright," Lyra replies. Evelena casts another stone missile spell while Lyra begins to cast another beam of light.

Before they can attack, however, the shaman fires another bolt of lightning. This time it is at Yentroc, and because she is hanging from Gelana's hand, she is an easy target. The bolt hits her and the shock renders Yentroc unconscious. The shock also shoots up Gelana's arm stunning her. Gelana losses her grip on Yentroc and as Yentroc begins to fall Sven suddenly grabs her arm. He quickly pulls her up.

"She is not moving!" Sven yells as he carries Yentroc over to Kristieana and lies her down on the ground. Kristieana leans down and checks Yentroc's breathing.

Still fighting, Lyra's light spell misses the shaman but it causes a distraction that allows Evelena to attack the shaman without its full attention on her. Evelena releases her spell, striking the shaman in the head. The orcnea falls to the ground motionless.

Ja'noa takes aim with a lightning bolt at the orcnea still hiding behind the shield. The orcnea's shield does not fully protect him from the shock, and he, too, falls to the ground.

Rehma now has reached the ogre and stands in its path. She is waiting for an opening to attack. The ogre swings its club and when it does, Rehma is ready and steps back out of the way. Just as soon as the club goes by her, she steps in and swings her swords at the beast. Both swords hit and cut the ogre's chest, but it does little to slow it down.

Sven is now back at the end of the path looking down as Rehma steps back again to avoid the massive club of the ogre. This time, Rehma impales it with one of her swords. The ogre flinches but continues to press the attack. Rehma steps back again and waits for another opening, but the ogre waits to swing. It instead tries to close in on her as Rehma backs up further and further up the cliff face. Rehma reaches the top of the pass when the ogre takes a big step forward and swings at Rehma's left side. Rehma has little choice but to try to parry the much larger weapon. With her left sword she tries to defend, but the massive strike is too much for even her Vallo swords. Rehma's left sword is knocked from her hand. The momentum of the massive club continues forward as the attack strikes Rehma's arm with a crushing blow. Rehma is knocked to the ground.

Sven grips Hellfire tightly and takes a step towards the ogre as a bolt of light from Lyra strikes the beast. Though she is growing tired, and her bolts of light are not as powerful, the ogre lets out a roar.

Just as Sven prepares to step in front of Rehma to shield her, a bolt of lightning from Ja'noa hits the ogre and stuns it for a moment. Rehma quickly gets to her feet forcing Sven to stay back as she is now in the way. The ogre recovers from the lightning just as Evelena hits it with a stone missile. The ogre swings wildly now and the club hits the ground in front of Rehma. Before the ogre can draw back his weapon again, Rehma steps on the end of the club and swings her remaining sword at the ogre's arm. The beast drops his club as Rehma steps in and impales her sword into the ogre's chest. The ogre lets out a loud cry and stands there without moving for a moment before it finally falls to the ground.

Kristieana has revived Yentroc, and as she begins to check on Rehma, Evelena says, "Kristieana, Yentroc, we need to help Kel'ana. Hurry!" Evelena starts to run down the path to the encampment below as the others all quickly follow.

They reach Kel'ana who still has not moved from where she has landed. Kristieana asks, "Can you move?"

Kel'ana, wincing in pain, shakes her head. "No," she groans, "I think my leg is broken and my back hurts." She closes her eyes tightly and grits her teeth.

Kristieana places her hand on Kel'ana's leg and asks, "Can you feel this?"

Kel'ana replies, "Yes."

"Good," Kristieana replies. "You still have feeling, then. Alright hold on to someone. I am going to try to set it."

Kel'ana holds onto Gelana's hand, and Kristieana begins to set her leg. Kristieana quickly puts it into place and Kel'ana screams again in pain. Kristieana then touches her with her glowing hands and soon Kel'ana starts to calm down.

"Look," Yentroc says as she points to the ground under Kel'ana's back. The snow beneath Kel'ana is red with blood.

"We have to be very careful," Kristieana says. She starts to dig at the snow under Kel'ana's right side where the blood seems to be coming from. She finally stops and says, "I see it, we are going to have to lift her straight up. Sven and Gelana, can you two get on either side of her and lift her?"

"Of course," Sven says.

The two of them position themselves, and Kristieana says, "I am going to count, and on three I want you two to lift her up and move her over to the tent and lay her on her stomach."

Sven and Gelana both nod. Kristieana counts, "One, two, and lift." Sven and Gelana lift Kel'ana up and she cries out in agony again. They quickly take her over to the orcnea tent and lie her down on the ground with her back facing up.

"Look at that," Ja'noa says pointing at the ground where Kel'ana had landed. A large jagged rock covered with blood remains where Kel'ana was just lying.

Kel'ana now falls unconscious as Kristieana casts another healing spell. She lifts Kel'ana's clothing, and the wound is still there. "I don't think it worked," Kristieana says now, sounding a bit nervous. "Yentroc, you have to try."

Yentroc kneels down next to Kel'ana and grasps her white crystal she received from Lunarus. Her hands glow white and this time the wound is affected. It begins to close right before their eyes. It is mostly healed not but a scar remains.

Kristieana puts her ear up against Kel'ana's back and listens for a heartbeat. She says, "She is still alive, but we are going to have to keep her warm now that her spell is down."

"The tent is clear," Ja'noa says looking inside, "and there is a fire inside."

"Good, let's get her inside," Evelena says. "Is everyone else alright?"

"My arm is hurt," Rehma says.

"You are just lucky you didn't get killed," Evelena says angrily.

"I had it under control," Rehma replies.

Evelena says, "I understand that you want to prove yourself in battle, but let me remind you that all the honor in world will not help you if you are dead." Evelena hands her a red bead and adds, "The next time you rush off alone after I tell you to stop, you will be receiving a black bead instead."

Rehma looks down and says with a disgruntled tone, "I understand."

Kristieana walks over to Rehma and with glowing hands she touches her arm. She says, "There that should do it."

"Thanks," Rehma replies. She shrugs her shoulder and moves her arm.

Kristieana then turns to Sven and shoves him with both hands. She yells, "If I EVER see you standing around and doing nothing when one of us is in trouble, I will kill you myself! Do you understand me?"

Gelana starts to pull Kristieana back as Sven replies, "Sven was ready to help."

"You stood by while she ran after that thing alone," Kristieana says as Gelana stands between her and Sven.

Sven explains, "There was no room on the ledge for—"

"I don't want to hear your excuses," Kristieana snaps. "You should have never let her face that by herself."

"Don't worry," Sven says as he looks over to Rehma who drops her eyes, "Sven will make sure it does not happen again."

"Good," Kristieana says, "see that it doesn't."

"It is getting dark," Evelena says. "It looks like this tent is big enough for all of us and they have plenty of supplies. For a bunch of orcneas, they sure made a good shelter."

"What if more orcneas come?" Ja'noa asks.

Evelena says, "Kristieana, can you scout the area out far enough to make sure nothing will reach us in the middle of the night?"

"Sure," she replies still somewhat angry. "It should be easy enough."

"Let's make sure these orcneas are truly dead and check them for anything useful," Evelena says.

Kristieana transforms into a giant eagle and flies off to scout the surroundings, as Ja'noa picks up Kel'ana's bow, Glacies, and then proceeds to make sure the orcneas are all dead.

Rehma and Sven return to the ridge to gather the supplies left behind. Rehma says to him, "I am sorry Kristieana yelled at you. I know you only were only doing as I asked."

Sven laughs and says, "It's alright. Sven is used to women yelling at him. Kristieana does not like Sven anyway."

Rehma picks up the last backpack and asks, "You weren't going to just stand there and watch the ogre hit me were you?"

"No," he replies, "Sven would have protected you if needed, but you did good."

Rehma thinks for a bit and says, "It *was* really close. If the others had not helped..."

"Then Sven would have," he finishes.

"Thanks," Rehma says with a smile, "and I am sorry I yelled at you, too. You can help me any time."

Sven laughs and says, "That's good, because Sven is thinking if he does not, Kristieana will hurt him."

Inside the large tent, Kel'ana is lying on a fur still unconscious. Yentroc is sitting next to her. The tent has more than enough places to sleep with thick furs all around the central fire. There is plenty of wood along the sides, along with a few crates with some food.

"It's almost like an outpost," Evelena says.

"Yes," Lyra replies. "It looks like this place has been here a while. I guess Chance didn't get this far out."

"Well, the fur on the top is white and it does have some snow covering it as well," Ja'noa says. "It is possible that from the air it is hard to see."

"True," Evelena replies. "Whatever the reason, I am glad it is here."

Gelana enters the tent and says, "Look what I found." Gelana holds out a silver pennant with a sapphire set in the middle. It is on a long leather string. She hands the necklace to Lyra.

Lyra takes it from Gelana and can feel magic emanating from the pennant. "It's magical," Lyra says as she looks closer at it. "That is easy to tell. It even has the Goblin Trade Company engraved on it. I wonder what it does."

Rehma and Sven walk in and Sven asks, "What are you talking about?"

Lyra stands up and walks over to Sven and says, "Gelana found this. It is from the Goblin Trade Company and it is magical." She hands him the necklace.

"I found it on the shaman," Gelana says. "We were wondering what it does."

Sven looks at it for a minute then says, "There is one way to find out." He begins to put it around his neck.

"Don't!" Lyra yells, but before she can stop him, Sven puts it on.

Sven stands there for a second waiting as the others watch nervously. He then says, "Sven thinks he knows what it is." He walks outside and stands in the cold. He takes off his fur cloak and removes his chest armor. He stands there for a few seconds and then takes the necklace off. He says, "Yes, Sven knows what it does. It protects you from the cold just like Kel'ana's spell." Sven grabs his armor and cloak and comes back inside the tent.

Just then Kristieana enters the tent as well. She says, "Well, I didn't see anything for miles. I would say that we are safe for the night."

"Good," Evelena replies. She walks over to Kel'ana, and looking at her she adds, "Let's just hope we don't have to stay here for long."

Kel'ana moves, and as she does, she groans. Yentroc says, "Kel'ana, can you hear me?"

She slowly opens her eyes. Still very weak, Kel'ana quietly says, "Yes...I can hear you."

Everyone smiles and gathers around her. Ja'noa says, "Kel'ana, guess what?"

Kel'ana takes a deep breath then looks at her and replies, "What?"

Ja'noa smiles and says, "This time *you* dropped something." She lays down Glacies next to Kel'ana.

"Not fair," Kel'ana replies with a smile.

They all laugh for a bit and Sven says, "Alright, I am going to make us something to eat."

"Good," Lyra says, "I am starving."

Sven says to Lyra, "Here, you should take this." He hands her the necklace and adds, "Now, Sven will not have to keep you warm at night."

The others all stop and look at Lyra who takes the necklace. She looks at it for a moment then looks at Sven, and with a hint of sadness, says, "I am sorry, I didn't know I was burden to you."

He replies, "No, Sven did not mean it like that."

Lyra turns to the others and says, "If you all will excuse me, I need to go outside for a minute. I'll be back."

Lyra leaves the tent as Kristieana, Yentroc and Gelana stare at Sven. He looks back at them confused and asks, "What is wrong? Why you all look at Sven like that?"

"Because you are an idiot," says Gelana.

Yentroc smiles and says, "Most men are."

"This is why the Amazons of the Silver Moon stay away from men," Kristieana says.

The girls laugh and Evelena says, "Alright, let's not be so hard on Sven.

After all he did save you from falling, Yentroc, and let's not forget about the bridge."

"We probably wouldn't have made it this far without him," Ja'noa adds.

The smiles disappear from Gelana and Yentroc's faces as they begin to feel guilt for having fun at their guide's expense. Kristieana says, "I'll give him credit for being a good guide, but when it comes to women, Sven, you are still an idiot."

Sven smiles as they laugh again. He begins to take food out of his backpack. The others gather around Kel'ana to talk as Yentroc walks over to Sven who is now putting some spices into a pot. She hands him a long thin leaf and says, "Put some of this into Kel'ana's food. It will help her with the pain."

Sven takes the leaf and says, "Sven will make sure he puts it in her bowl."

Yentroc stands there and watches him for a moment. "Thank you, Sven. I didn't know that you saved me from falling."

Sven stands up and replies, "It is not big deal. Sven is going to get some snow for stew."

He starts towards the tent door and Yentroc follows him and says, "Are you serious? You saw what that fall did to Kel'ana." She follows Sven outside as he packs snow into the pot. "I could have been seriously hurt," she says as Sven turns to go back into the tent, "or even worse."

Sven enters the tent and walks over to the fire. He places the pot next to the fire and says, "Don't worry about it. You healed Sven's shoulder when he was hurt. It is what good group does for each other."

"Well, thanks anyways," she says. Yentroc looks over at the others who are still gathered around Kel'ana. "Would you like some advice?" she asks quietly.

"If this is about Lyra," he replies, "Sven is not an idiot. It's just that..." Sven stops as Lyra enters the tent. Instead of sadness in her eyes she now seems angry. He turns to her and says, "Lyra, Sven is sorry if he made you feel like you were a burden."

Lyra walks up to Sven and says, "Thank you for the necklace, Sven, because right now I would rather freeze to death then sleep next to you another night." She then storms away and joins the others leaving Sven standing there.

Sven turns to Yentroc and says, "Sven is going to see if goat, orcneas were skinning is fresh."

Yentroc sighs and shakes her head. She leaves Sven to his cooking and returns to the others.

Chapter 36
Day 10
Downpour

On the front lines, King Arioch's army waits under pouring rain. It has been raining heavily all night. It is morning, and Arioch receives word that a messenger has arrived from the Monastery on Sapphire Lake. Hoping that it is good news he meets with him. The young Namos has been running for a day and half a nonstop. The potions and magical sandals have allowed him to complete this extraordinary feat.

Arioch approaches the young man and asks, "You have a message for me?"

"Yes, Sire," Namos says as he bows his head and holds out the letter from Brother Edward.

"Thank you," Arioch says taking the letter. Namos steps back and waits for Arioch to read the message. Arioch reads the letter and becomes visibly angry. When he is done he clutches the letter crushing it and asks Namos, "How long ago was this sent?"

"I left a day and half ago, Sire," Namos answers.

Arioch thinks for a moment. As he begins to calm himself he asks, "What is your name?"

"Namos," he answers.

"Thank you, Namos," Arioch replies "you may go."

Namos nervously states, "Sire, if I may be of some use to you, I would like to stay."

Arioch looks at him and asks, "What did you have in mind?"

Namos says confidently, "I am a good healer, Sire."

Arioch smiles and says, "Very well." He points to a large white tent off in the distance and says, "That is the tent where you will want to go. Report there and they will tell you what to do."

Namos smiles and replies, "Thank you, Sire." Then he turns and runs off to the healing tent.

Arioch enters his tent were A'ranah meditates. Two sisters of the Dri'el are at her sides. Arioch asks, "How are they doing?"

A'ranah opens her eyes and says, "They are almost done."

"Good," Arioch says. "The sooner Chance gets back the better."

Upriver from Northwind, Chance and a small group have worked throughout the night. They are gathered at the base of the rolling hills that lead into the mountains. There are deep canyon walls and valleys that the Northwind River runs through before passing the City of Northwind where the river then meets the eastern sea. Even further up river is a marshland and a small lake within the hills. This is the main source of water for the river.

Chance along with three crossbowmen are watching out for orcneas as Finna and four other Amazons of the Silver Moon are concentrating on a spell. The five women form a circle and together have combined their magic to hold back most of the river's flow. With the torrential downpour ongoing the river still flows enough to keep the orcneas from crossing.

The Amazons have built up a massive wall of water, and have nearly filled a narrow valley throughout the night.

Chance says to Finna, "I think this should be enough."

"I hope so," Finna replies. "I don't think the canyon can hold any more. If this doesn't take out the new bridge I don't know what we will do."

Suddenly, an arrow strikes Finna in the leg. She lets out a cry and falls to the ground. "Finna!" Chance yells. He looks up and sees four orcnea archers. They are standing on the river bank. The guards take aim at the orcneas as Chance casts a fireball. He throws it at one of the orcneas as the orcnea dives for cover. The orcneas hide behind trees. "We have company!" Chance yells to the women.

The crossbowmen take positions and try to hit the orcneas. The orcneas and the men continue to shoot at each other as Chance helps Finna get to cover. The other Amazons take cover as they struggle to hold back the water.

"Finna," Chance says. "Are you alright?"

Finna, gritting her teeth in pain, says, "I think so, can you get the arrow out?"

Chance says, "Yes, I can get it." He holds Finna's leg down and pulls the arrow straight out. He then casts a healing spell and repairs her wound. "There we are, as good as new."

Two of the orcneas are hit by the crossbowmen's bolts, while one of the orcneas manages to hit one of the men in the arm with an arrow.

Chance and Finna can hear a large group of orcneas approaching. Chance calls out, "Everyone gather around!" The men fall back and the amazons join him as well. Chance says, "Finna, tell A'ranah to open a gate." Then he turns to the others and says, "Get through the gate as soon as it opens."

There is a crackle in the air and directly in front of them it appears as though a painting of the inside of Arioch's tent is standing before them as a magic gateway opens. Finna and the other Amazons stop holding back the water and instead they send it surging down the river before entering the porthole and appearing inside the Kings tent. The crossbowmen then go through the magic gate. Chance is the last one through and when he appears on the other side he says to A'ranah, "We are all through! Close it." With that, the gate disappears.

Chance rushes outside and takes flight in eagle form. He is careful not to approach Northwind too closely. He only flies high enough to watch the massive wall of water as it rushes down the river bed. The orcnea patrol that was closing in is washed away. The water crashes into the nearly complete bridge. Even though much of the water has disbursed, it is still proves to be too much for the wood structure. Like many of the orcneas, it, too, is washed away. Chance lands to relay the good news. Everyone cheers loudly with excitement. Perhaps they can hold the massive orcnea army at bay after all. Even outnumbered four to one the troops are now more confident than ever.

The people continue to celebrate in the rain as Arioch approaches Chance and Finna. "Chance," Arioch says as he reaches them, "I have something important to tell you."

"Yes, Your Majesty," Chance replies, "one moment please." Chance turns to Finna and says, "Why don't you go get some rest. You and the others were up all night with that spell."

"What about you?" Finna asks.

"I am used to not getting sleep," he replies

"If you say so. Come here, little brother," She says as she gives Chance a hug. "Thank you for healing me."

"You're welcome," Chance says. "I'll talk to you later." Finna walks off to her tent as Chance turns to Arioch and asks, "What is it you need to tell me?"

"It is about our children," Arioch answers. "I have just received word from the Monastery that they are on their way to cross into the Northern territory."

"What?" Chance questions angrily. "I told them to come back after delivering the supplies to Troven."

"They are probably half way over the mountains by now," Arioch says.

"Perhaps this is not as bad as it may seem," A'ranah says.

"What are you saying?" Chance asks. "When we first found out that they were in the scouting party you were just as upset as I was. What has changed?"

"Yes, Chance, I was," A'ranah replies, "but listen, you did say that it looked relatively empty on the other side of the mountains. They may be safer there then at Sheathelm."

"There is more," Arioch says.

Chance sighs and asks, "What is it?"

"It is more than just Kianna and Ya'leigh," Arioch says hesitantly, "Kelik and Ambra are with them."

Chance shakes his head. "What are they thinking! I have to go."

"Wait, Chance," Arioch says, "listen to me first. If they are going through the mines and caves to get to the other side you won't be able to just fly over and find them."

Chance, now pacing quickly, still looks frustrated as A'ranah says, "Chance, I am worried as well, but you need to calm yourself. I can use the amulet that Kianna wears to check on them. I am sure they are fine. The other Sisters of the Silver Moon are a few days in front of them. As long as they are close by I am sure Kianna and the others will not run into trouble."

"You can see what they are doing?" Chance asks.

"Of course," A'ranah says. "Come, we will do it now." She leads Chance into her tent. In the middle of the tent, perched on a pedestal, is a large saucer of water. A'ranah takes off a silver and emerald amulet and places it in the center of the saucer. She then closes her eyes and slowly runs her fingers across the surface of the water. The ripples begin to settle as an image starts to come through the reflection.

It is of Kianna at first, then, as A'ranah moves her hand around, the image changes. Soon Chance can see the entire group in the watery image. A'ranah and the others listen as Kelik says, "I wish father could have seen that fire."

Ya'leigh replies, "I am sure he would have been proud."

"I am just glad you shot that spider," Isen says. "It would have bitten me for sure."

"Just make sure that if we come across orcneas you and Ambra stay by Isen or Garrin and let us handle it," Ya'leigh says.

Kianna adds, "The only thing you two need to worry about is activating the gate stone if we need to get out."

"I have it right here," Ambra says as she holds up the small sandstone medallion. "I won't use it unless one of you tell me to."

Watching them through magic, A'ranah says to Chance, "Well, it certainly sounds like they have their escape plan ready."

"Thank you," Chance says as he begins to calm down.

"Isen is with them," A'ranah says, "and I helped Arioch choose him to be Kianna's personal guard. He would give his life to protect them."

"I know," Chance replies, "and Garrin would, too."

A'ranah drags her finger across the water again creating more ripples, and as they clear this time an image of Evelena appears. Just as before, A'ranah moves her hand to change the angle. The group walks by, and each of the sisters come into view including Kristieana. A'ranah glances up at Chance who cannot help but to smile at the sight of her. She says to him, "It is good to see you smile, Chance. You should do it more often." Chance looks up at her embarrassed. He doesn't say anything as A'ranah reaches in and removes the amulet form the water.

"Chance," A'ranah says, as she puts the necklace back on, "there is something I need to talk to you about."

Before either of them can say another word, Arioch bursts into the tent and says, "Come quickly both of you!" They come out of the tent as Arioch says, "Quickly, to the medical tent."

They run to the medical tent and as they go inside they see a man writhing in pain on one of the beds. "I am not sure what is wrong with him," a crossbowmen at his side says. "He was fine a moment ago, then he just collapsed. We brought him here."

Namos enters the tent and approaches the man lying on the bed. The man, in his leather armor, appears to be very weak and struggling to breath. "Let me take a look," Namos says as he starts to examine him. He looks down and can see dark veins all over his abdomen. Namos closes his eyes and soon his hands glow with a green aura. He moves them over the man's body and the dark veins begin to fade and the man begins to breathe easier. "That should do it," Namos says.

Chance makes his way over to the bed. He recognizes the man as the guard who was shot with the arrow earlier. The guard looks up at Chance and says. "It was the arrow."

A sinking feeling fills Chances chest as he turns and says, "Finna..."

"What's happening?" A'ranah asks.

Chance runs from the tent yelling, "Finna!"

Fear comes over A'ranah's face. She turns to Namos and says, "You, follow me. We have to hurry!"

They leave the tent and follow Chance. By the time A'ranah and Namos reaches Finna's tent Chance is already there, holding Finna's motionless body in his arms. Dark veins from the poison cover half of her body. Chance looks up at A'ranah with tears running down his face. "She's gone..." He says.

A'ranah lets out a cry and Leanara embraces her. Other Amazons soon enter the tent and as the look upon their fallen sister many of them burst into tears as well. As strong as these women are, their bond to one another is even stronger. They are family, and when they lose one of their own the loss is very hard. Leanara is the first to step forward. She casts a spell on Finna, removing the poison from her, and the dark veins disappear.

Serena La'harn wipes away her tears and says, "I say we try to resurrect her."

A'ranah looks up at the other Amazons of the Silver Moon who all nod their approval. She then says. "Leanara, prepare a location far away from camp. I'll go and gather the others who can cast the spell."

Chance approaches A'ranah and says, "I may not be able to cast the spell, but I am willing to lend whatever energy I can."

A'ranah puts her hand on his shoulder and says, "I appreciate the offer Chance but we will need to make sure we are not interrupted. If the orcneas should find some way to strike at us we will need you to fight. We can only attempt this once."

"I understand," Chance answers. A'ranah gathers her sisters together as Chance walks to the front line. He stares at the wall of Northwind far off in the distance. He walks past the trenches and spikes, and stands all alone in the pouring rain glaring at the horizon.

At the far end of the open field the orcneas are having another meeting. Lortec Ka stares out over the wall and surveys the damage from the flood. "It looks like they have bought themselves more time." He says to the other two generals.

"I say we let the drakes loose and make them pay for this." Borak Cron says.

"No, Borak," Lortec replies. "Even if we manage to kill some of them, we will need the drakes to defend against those goblin air ships."

"Lortec is right," Vork says as he sharpens his blade. "They would eventually bring down our drakes, and then we would have no defense from the air attacks."

"We must make them suffer soon," Borak says. "They are growing too confident, and we have suffered two losses of our bridge."

"They will pay, Borak," Lortec says. "In time they will all pay."

Chapter 37
Warmth of the Light

Just outside Arioch's camp it is still raining as the Sisters of the Silver Moon are exiting the tent they had set up to cast the ritual spell to resurrect Finna. With their heads held low they walk back to the camp. A'ranah makes her way over to the King. Arioch is watching Chance who is still standing out in the field staring out over the horizon. A'ranah asks Arioch, "How long has he been out there like that?"

"The entire time," Arioch answers. "So how did it go? Did you save her?" A'ranah looks down and shakes her head. "I am so sorry," he says as he puts his hand on her shoulder. "I'll go and tell Chance."

"No," A'ranah replies as she looks up. She wipes the rain and the tears from her face. "I need to do this," she adds. She walks slowly out beyond the spikes through the rain. Chance continues to stare across the field at the distant city. Her boots are now covered with mud from the ground as she approaches him.

Arioch watches from afar as she puts her hand on Chance's shoulder. Chance turns to face her as she says something to him and shakes her head. Chance falls to the ground as A'ranah kneels next to him. He leans against her as she holds his head on her shoulder. Arioch can no longer watch his friend suffer, and he turns to walk back to his tent.

"It's my fault," Chance says to A'ranah.

"How is it your fault?" A'ranah asks.

"I didn't think to check the arrow," Chance says. "Then I told her to go rest." Chance puts his hand over his eyes and says, "She could have been saved had someone seen her fall."

"You cannot blame yourself for this, Chance," she says as he pulls away. She places one hand on each shoulder and continues, "It was not anyone's fault."

Chance shakes his head and says, "I should have known better. Why does it feel like I always fail those who need me?"

A'ranah stands up and as she helps Chance to his feet she says, "Chance, there was something I wanted to tell you earlier. Now I think it is more important than ever that you hear what I have to say."

"What is it?" Chance asks, unable to look her in the eyes.

"First of all," she says, "Finna's death is not your fault. You were not the only one there. No one thought to check the arrows, not just you, and the fact that you asked her to get some rest did not cause her death either." Chance tries to look her in the eyes but can't. "Secondly, Chance, Arioch tells me that you still blame yourself for Sha'al."

Chance looks away, searching for the right words, "I should have been there for her," he finally says with a quivering voice.

"There is no possible way that you could have known the orcneas were going to attack," She replies. "Sha'al did not need you to follow her everywhere she went." She takes Chance by the chin and lifts his head to look him in the eyes. "Chance, no one blames you for her death. Some of the sisters were upset at the time, but I don't know a single Amazon of the Silver Moon who blames you for anyone's death."

Chances takes a deep breath then says, "Rehma La'harn does."

A'ranah sighs and asks, "Did she say something to you?"

"It was not so much what she *said*," Chance says as he looks away again. "Her actions spoke clearly enough."

"Did she attack you?"

"Yes," Chance answers, "and if not for the others, she very well may have killed me."

"I am sorry," A'ranah replies. "I didn't know she still harbored such feelings for you."

"Well, she does," Chance says. "When the others pulled her off of me she yelled out to everyone within the inn that I was responsible for her mother's death."

"Oh, Chance," A'ranah begins to explain, "Rehma is young still. She will understand in time."

"What is there to understand?" Chance asks. "My carelessness in battle cost Teresa La'harn her life."

Frustrated, A'ranah says, "Chance, we have been over Teresa La'harn's sacrifice many times. You have to stop this! You cannot be responsible for everyone's fate. You are killing yourself with guilt." Now firmly grasping his face she continues, "If you want to blame someone, Chance, right over there is the enemy!" She points across the field to the city of Northwind. "The orcneas are the ones to blame, Chance, not you!"

Chance looks back over to the walled city and says, "I understand. I am going to make them pay for what they have done."

He looks back at her and she says, "Chance, I still see a spark in your eyes. While war has defined who you are to everyone else, I know there is more to you than that, but you need to let go of the guilt before you can move on. You are not the man that my daughter fell in love with years ago." Chance tries to hold back tears again as she continues, "It has been a long time, Chance, and you need to find a way to forgive yourself."

Chance looks down again and doesn't know what to say. He looks over at the city again as the rain begins to stop. "I don't know how," Chance finally says.

A'ranah sighs deeply, then says, "Come on, let's get back to camp."

Chance and A'ranah make their way to the tent where the Amazons attempted to bring back Finna. As he enters Chance can see Finna still lying on the round table. Leanara is at her side. She looks up at Chance and sadly says, "I am so sorry, I failed." A tear rolls down her cheek as she begins to cry.

Chance walks over to her and puts his arms around her. "It's not your fault," he says as he looks back at A'ranah standing at the entrance.

Leanara replies sadly, "I was the one in charge of the spell. It didn't work. I failed her."

Chance looks down and reflects on his thoughts. He looks up and says,

"Her spirit may simply have chosen to enter the light rather than return to us."

Leanara replies, "I can't believe that she would want to leave us now."

"I know," Chance replies. "It doesn't make sense to me either, but it is not your fault. The only ones to blame for this are the orcneas, and not anyone else." Chance glances back over his shoulder at A'ranah as she nods to him before leaving.

Chance then says to Leanara, "Wherever Finna is now, I am certain it is a beautiful place. Someday we will all join her, but I don't plan for that day to come anytime soon." Chance then steps next to Finna. He leans down and kisses her forehead. He closes his eyes and takes in a deep breath. He slowly exhales as he opens his eyes and whispers, "Goodbye, my sister. May the warmth of the light embrace you."

Chance and Leanara leave the tent as the sun begins to shine through the breaking clouds. Chance looks up at clearing sky and as the sun begins to warm his face he feels as if a great weight has been lifted from him. He closes his eyes and smiles.

Chapter 38
The Wait

In the Captain's quarters on the *Red Dawn*, Ariella sits reading Fernando's letter again. There is a knock at her door that startles her a bit, "Come in!" she calls.

Torgus enters and says, "Captain, we are still on track to make it to Bastion by tomorrow."

"Excellent," Ariella replies. "I want to get rid of that orcnea as soon as possible."

"Yes, ma'am," Torgus says sounding concerned.

"What is it, Torgus?" Ariella asks as she stands up and walks over to him.

"It's just that I have always known you to despise the idea of slavery," Torgus says, "and yet here we are about to sell an orcnea just like a common slave."

"I understand, Torgus," she says with a heavy sigh, "but this orcnea was part of an attack on our ship. We are at war, Torgus, and I do not plan to keep him as a prisoner, and if he is to die, I'd rather sell him than kill him myself."

"As you wish, Captain," Torgus replies.

"I assume you still have had no luck with locating either Fernando or my locket?" Ariella asks as they walk out onto the deck.

"No, ma'am," Torgus replies. "I am still trying every few hours. Sooner or later he will take the locket out of that bottomless bag. When he does I will find him. As for Fernando, I am sure he is still wearing an amulet that hides him from my searches. He is bound to take that off as well. Until then, Captain, we just have to wait."

"I hate waiting, Torgus," Ariella replies, "and every day that Fernando makes we wait, the more severe the punishment will be when I find him.

To the north, the caravan that Fernando has been traveling with arrives at gates of Sheathelm. As they enter the capital city, Fernando breaks away from the group and makes his way to an inn called the King's Shield. Just inside the entrance is a statue of King Arioch. There is a small stage at the far end of the main hall with a smaller version of Arioch's throne in the middle. There are tables throughout the room.

Fernando looks around for someone. Looking disappointed he sits at an empty table in the corner and says to himself, "I hate waiting."

"You have a lot of nerve showing your face in here, Fernando," a woman's voice says from across the room.

"Trisha?" Fernando says as he stands back up.

A short curvy woman with long black hair angrily makes her way over to Fernando. "Don't you Trisha me!" she snaps.

"Please, my lady," Fernando begins to say, but he is interrupted by a slap across the face.

"That is for sleeping with my best friend!" Trisha yells.

"Lo siento, I am sorry," Fernando replies as he rubs his stinging cheek. "I did not know she was your friend."

She slaps him hard again and says, "The fact that she was my friend isn't the point! You were with me the night before!"

"Please do not be mad at me," Fernando says as he brushes her hair back with his fingers. "Even though you are most beautiful with that fire in your eyes."

"You!" another woman's voice says angrily.

"Of course," Fernando sighs, "she is here too."

"Look who came to say hello, Lee," Trisha says to an attractive blonde who joins them.

Lee draws back her hand as Fernando closes his eyes and braces to be hit again. Just as he expected, the young woman wastes no time in slapping Fernando as well. "How dare you show up here!" Lee yells at him.

"Ladies, please," Fernando begs. "It is such a tragedy to see such beauty with so much anger on your faces."

The women look at each other in disbelief. Lee says, "Don't you try to use your lines on us."

"Yes," Trisha adds. "We know what kind of man you are."

"Oh, and what kind of man is that?" he asks with a smile.

Again Fernando's calm demeanor throws them off, and they are at a loss for words. "You are a liar!" Trisha finally says.

"Yes," Lee adds, "and a cheat."

Fernando smiles and as he calmly steps between the two women. He places an arm around each of them and asks Trisha, "When did I lie to you?"

"You were with her the very next night," she answers.

"Yes," Fernando answers, "but did I ever tell you that you were the only one?"

Now the women look stunned. Trisha answers, "Well, no, but..."

Fernando turns to Lee and asks, "Did I ever tell you there was no one else?"

"No," she angrily relents.

"Did you ever think to ask me if there were other women?" He asks Lee.

Lee lets out an angry sigh and answers, "No."

"It is not possible to be a cheat," Fernando says as the two women remove his arms from around their shoulders, "if there was never any promise of commitment."

They stand in front of Fernando, and Trisha says, "I suppose technically you are right."

"Well then," Fernando says. "My beautiful darlings, I am truly sorry if my actions hurt the two of you, but I am only a man, and when I am in your presence I am very weak. I cannot help myself when I am near such beauty. Surely, you do not blame me falling for the two of you."

Lee and Trisha both look at Fernando and shake their heads. Fernando seems to have calmed them, but they are not being fooled by his charm. Trisha asks, "What are you doing here anyway?"

"I am meeting someone," Fernando explains.

"A woman?" Lee asks.

"No," Fernando replies as he looks around again, "it is not. So why are you two here?"

"We work here now," Lee replies.

"The pay is not as good as our last job," Trisha explains, "but it is not as dangerous."

"What did you do before?" Fernando asks.

"We worked on a ship," Trisha answers.

"Really? The two of you worked on a ship?" he asks. "Did the men give you a hard time?"

"There were no men on our ship," Lee replies. "Even the captain was a woman."

"A ship full of women," Fernando says with a laugh. "That sounds like my kind of ship."

"Well, you never met Captain McMurphy," Trisha says.

"Was she as beautiful as the two of you?" Fernando asks with a smile.

Trisha laughs and says, "Yes, but there is no way you would ever have a chance with her."

"Captain McMurphy despises most men," Lee says, "and she can read minds."

"A woman who could read my mind would most certainly be a challenge," Fernando says, "but it does not matter. Right now my heart is just not up for a chase."

"Why?" Trisha asks. "Did you finally meet a woman worth committing to?"

"Perhaps," Fernando replies, "as long as she does not kill me the next time we meet."

Chapter 39
Coldrock

Kreeshaw has been leading Princess Kianna and her companions through the caves for the last day and a half. Without the sun and stars, however, they have lost track of time, and can only guess how long they have been underground.

Ahead of them they begin to see a set of enormous doors. The towering wood doors hang off their hinges and are heavily damaged. What was once a beautifully carved doorway is now cracked and crumbling.

"Well, this is the half-way point," Kreeshaw says. "Welcome to Coldrock."

They enter through the collapsed doors, and the room before them opens up to heights beyond the range of their light. Beneath their feet is a cobble stone street that spans almost sixty paces wide. Along the sides of the cave are the buildings that make up the city. Doorways and stairs are carved right into the stone walls. Windows of the buildings overlook the street that was once lit with hundreds of magic lanterns. Now, only broken posts remain where the street lights once stood. Scattered along what was once the main walkway are large boulders and debris from the battle that took place here nearly a half century before.

They are in awe of the immense size of it all. Their light only allows them to see well for about ten paces before fading away over the next forty paces. They step over debris of stone and wood. Occasionally they see a dust covered skeleton warrior, usually with a gash through what armor he was wearing.

"That is scary," Ambra says as they pass by a skeleton with an arrow embedded in its skull.

"Should we smash them?" Isen asks.

"Why would we do that?" Ya'leigh asks.

"In case they try to kill us," Isen answers.

Kianna says, "I am sure if they were undead they wouldn't be covered with all this dust."

"I don't really think it is a good idea to disturb the dead," Garrin says.

"Alright," Isen replies. "Don't blame me when they all try to kill us."

Kelik and Ambra look at each other terrified and move closer to Isen. They follow him closely as they proceed further in. Soon they reach what appears to be a crossroad. They can continue straight down the current path, or turn left or right.

"Which way do we go to get out of here?" Kianna asks.

"We are on the main path right now," Kreeshaw answers. "Another half mile and we will exit the city at the north end."

"Aren't we going to look around?" Isen asks. "There has to be some valuable treasure around here somewhere."

"I am not so sure about that," Garrin replies, "After all this time I am sure anything valuable is already gone. It's not like this place is a secret."

"True," Kreeshaw says, "but it wouldn't hurt to check the place out, just in case."

Kianna thinks for a bit then says, "Alright, we can look around for a little while, but we are not splitting up."

"Of course not," Isen says. "When those skeletons come back to life, I don't want anyone to be alone."

"Stop it, Isen," Ya'leigh says angrily. "You are scaring Ambra and Kelik."

Isen laughs and says to the young ones, "I am just joking."

"I am not scared," Kelik replies.

Ambra laughs and says, "Then why are you standing so close to me?"

Kelik looks around and realizes that he is right next to his sister. They all laugh as Kelik takes a step back away from Ambra.

"So what does the map say?" Gena asks.

Kreeshaw looks at the map and says, well if we go to the left we can check inside the royal vault."

"Sounds like a plan to me," Garrin says.

They slowly make their way down the corridor to the left. The same tall carved walls continue throughout the entire length of the section. Finally they reach another doorway. The doors look to have been burned down. They walk through the tall archway and enter a circular room over one hundred paces across. The room has some light coming from a few remaining magic stones that hang down from the ceiling. To the left they see a small doorway. The entire room has a gradual slope that forms a mound in the very center. On the top is a large stone throne with two stone statues almost three times the height of a normal man behind it. They are statues of two dwarven paladins, each with a large shield and mace.

Isen quickly makes his way up the inclined floor to the throne. "Be careful," Kianna warns. Isen reaches the top then sits down on the throne. Kianna asks Ya'leigh, "Do those statues look magical to you?"

"Yes, they do," Ya'leigh answers.

"Isen!" Kianna calls as they hurry to catch up to him. "Watch out for those statues."

Isen looks at the two statues behind him and spots a large ruby the size of his fist at the center of one of the shields. "I'll bet this is worth a fortune," he says, as he studies it closely.

"Don't touch it," Kianna warns as they reach the top of the mound.

"Why?" Isen asks.

Gena looks around and explains, "Well, you see how this statue on the left has that gem and the one over here doesn't?"

"Yes," Isen replies. "So someone took that one."

Ya'leigh says as she points at the ground in front of the statue on the right, "It looks like this guy did."

At Ya'leigh's feet are the dried remains of someone. The helmet on the skull is crushed and in the left hand is another gem. "Then we can just take this one," Isen says as he takes a step towards the corpse on the ground.

Gena, Ya'leigh, and Kianna all yell, "No!"

"It is still magical," Ya'leigh says. "More than likely it will activate the statue if you try to take it."

"Well then we can just smash the statue first," Isen says as he draws his morning star out.

"Would you just wait a minute?" Kianna yells.

"Yes, ma'am," Isen says as he puts away his weapon.

"Now," Kianna says, "why don't we look into the vaults? I really don't wish to be crushed by a giant statue."

Kreeshaw points to their left to a small door and says, "The map says that the vault is in that room over there." He leads the way as the group follows him through a doorway. Isen stays by the throne as the others enter the room.

Once inside, the others can see a counter top, and behind it is a massive iron door leading into the vault itself. The door is open and has come off its hinges.

"It looks like this is it," Kreeshaw says as he shines his light into the vault.

The vault is only three paces wide, but almost thirty paces deep. Along the walls, holes no bigger than a man's head, are carved into the stone. Dozens of these holes are arranged in a honeycomb pattern. The holes are round and each have a small iron door attached to it. Almost all of them are open. Garrin says, "It looks like they have all been emptied."

"Not all of them," Gena says pointing to one that is still shut.

Garrin looks closely at it and tries to open it, but it is locked. He turns to the others and says, "I don't suppose anyone can open that without just smashing it."

"Not without a key," Kreeshaw replies.

"At least this will give Isen something to hit," Kianna says.

"Where is Isen?" Ya'leigh asks. Just then the ground shakes a little.

Kianna and Ya'leigh both look at each other and say, "Oh no."

The group exits the vault in search of Isen. They are now back inside the room with the counter top. Kianna heads towards the doorway leading back to the throne room, when Isen run in. A loud thumping outside sounds like a giant is running. "What did you do, Isen?" Kianna demands.

"Nothing," Isen says as he tries to hide the fist sized ruby behind his back.

Suddenly the doorway behind him is hit with the large mace of the statue. Dust and stone fly everywhere as the giant stone paladin tries to smash his way in. Part of the doorway gives and crumbles.

"Is there a way out?" Isen asks.

"Yes," Kianna says. "The way we came! You know, just past the giant stone paladin that you woke up."

"Well, at least we know for sure now," Isen says with a smile.

"Put the gem down," Gena says. "Maybe that will work."

Isen looks at the enormous ruby and asks, "Do I have to?"

"Throw that ruby out there now!" Kianna yells. "That is on order."

"Alright," Isen says as he tosses the gem out the door way. The ruby lands out on the floor behind the statue. The statue swings its mace again making a bigger hole in the wall around the door.

"Well, that didn't work," Garrin says.

"Ya'leigh! Increase my speed," Isen says. "I'll keep it busy!"

Ya'leigh moves her hands and chants as she casts a spell on Isen. To Isen, it's as if the rest of the world slows down, as Ya'leigh's spell makes Isen move faster. To everyone else, it's as if Isen is now moving twice as fast as he was before. Isen draws out his morning star that begins to emit flames as soon as he readies it. He runs out the door just as the mace comes down again with a thunderous smash.

Isen rolls out of the way and stands up. He grabs the ruby off the ground and yells, "Hey, over here!" The statue turns its attention to Isen. With every large step the statue takes towards Isen, the ground trembles. Isen begins to lead the stone giant around the large circular room as the others come out into the open.

"How long will that spell last?" Kelik asks.

"Only a minute," Ya'leigh answers.

"We have no choice," Kianna says. "It will just follow us, and you can't keep that spell on Isen long enough for us to escape."

"Well, let's see if we can bring this thing down," Garrin says.

Ya'leigh says to her brother and sister, "You two wait inside the vault and be ready to use the gate stone if this doesn't work."

Ambra nods and grabs Kelik's arm and they go back into the vault. Kreeshaw joins them.

Kianna creates a large ice sphere in her hands and channels as much of her strength into it as she can. Using both hands she starts to aim. Ya'leigh draws Incendia and a fiery arrow appears while Gena readies a lightning bolt. Garrin readies his shield and draws out a dark ax called Onyx.

"Here he comes," Kianna says.

Though the stone golem appears to be moving slowly, it is not far behind Isen. Isen stops about ten paces away from the others and turns to face it. "I'll try to keep its attention." Isen says.

The towering paladin reaches Isen and swings its massive mace. Isen dives out of the way as it hits the ground, shaking the area. The others take the opportunity to attack. Gena's lightning bolt hits, but sends only small bits of stone flying. Ya'leigh's flaming arrow also hits, but does little damage as well. Kianna releases her large ice ball and it connects with a loud crack. Though the stone is harder than the ice, the impact damages the magical defender as large pieces of the statue crumble off of it.

The paladin looks at Kianna and starts to come at her. Garrin steps forward and swings his ax at one of its massive legs. The magical properties of Onyx damages its leg and the stone guardian stops and swings his large mace, sweeping the area in front of it. Garrin cannot get out of the way, and instead tries his best to block with his shield. The blow sends Garrin flying and he lands on his back.

With the paladin's attention now on Garrin, Isen moves in. He swings his morning star at the giant's arm holding its shield. The strong attack damages the arm but does not completely destroy it. The paladin swings its massive stone shield at Isen who is also sent flying back.

Ya'leigh fires an arrow at the damaged leg. This seems to be much more effective, as larger pieces on stone fall to the ground. "Hit the damaged leg!" Ya'leigh calls out to her friends.

Kianna, who has been holding another ice sphere, and Gena, who has another lightning bolt, both aim at the leg carefully before releasing their spells. Both attacks find their mark as the damaged leg crumbles. The tall golem falls to its hands and remaining knee. Now it is much less of a threat, and Isen stumbles to his feet and charges the paladin.

The girls continue to attack with spells as Isen jumps on the stone giant's back. Standing over its head he brings down his morning star ferociously. Garrin has also made it back to his feet and swings Onyx at its neck. This all but decapitates it as Isen finishes it off with one final blow to the crumbling stone head. The animated statue falls to the ground and doesn't move.

"You did it," Kelik says peering out the damaged door.

Kianna walks up to Isen and asks, "Are you alright?"

"I think I have a broken rib," He says holding his side.

"Then maybe next time you will listen to me," She says angrily.

Garrin is holding his right arm. "I think it broke my arm when I blocked it."

"Come here," Kianna says. "Sit down and I will heal you." Garrin sits down and Kianna places her glowing white hands on his arm.

"That is much better," Garrin says with a sigh of relief. "Thank you."

"You're welcome," Kianna replies.

"Can you heal me now?" Isen asks.

"Are you going to listen the next time I tell you to leave something alone?" Kianna replies.

"Come on," Isen says with a smile. "Would I do something like that?"

The princess can't help but smile and laugh. "Fine," she says as she casts the healing spell again.

"Thank you," Isen says.

Kreeshaw comes out and asks Isen, "Well, then, are you up to seeing what is inside a mini vault?"

"Sure," Isen says. "Where is it?"

A few moments later they are standing in front the small sealed hole in the wall. Isen takes a big swing with his morning star. This smashes the small iron door off its hinges. Inside the hole, they see a small pile of gold and silver.

"Gold!" Kelik yells.

"Not bad," Kianna says calmly.

"Not bad?" Kreeshaw questions. "That is a small fortune."

Isen laughs and says, "She is used to money. After all, she *is* a princess."

"She is a what?" Kreeshaw asks.

The others shake their heads as Isen says, "I am sorry, I forgot I wasn't supposed to say anything about that."

"Well, I can't say as I am surprised," Kreeshaw says. "She did seem to be the one in charge. I wondered if there was more to her then just being an adventurer. Where are you from?"

"Sheathelm," Kianna replies, "and I am sorry if you feel we deceived you."

"Not at all, Your Highness," Kreeshaw says. "You are right not to tell people who you really are, and I promise you I am no threat. There are those out there who would gladly try to take you hostage for a hefty ransom, though."

"Thank you for understanding," Kianna says.

"Just make sure that this one keeps his mouth shut," he says looking at Isen.

Isen looks down and says, "I know, I know."

They finish gathering the precious metals and begin to leave. Isen says, "We can always get the other gem from the other statue. It wasn't that hard."

"No!" they all yell at Isen.

"Alright," Isen says. He tosses the large ruby that caused the guardian to attack in the air and catches it. "I can't wait to see how much it is worth."

They head back down the corridor to the four way split. Once they reach the center they hear a loud screech down the opposite corridor. Kreeshaw says, "We might want to get out of here now."

"I agree," Kianna says, "Which way to we go?"

Kreeshaw looks at the map and points to the left and says, "That is the way out."

Now they hear several screeches. "Let's move quickly," Kianna says.

"What is it?" Isen asks.

"I don't know," Kreeshaw replies, "but I don't want to stay and find out."

The group begins to run down the main street of Coldrock towards what they hope is the north exit. Behind them the screeching is getting louder as whatever is in pursuit is gaining on them.

Isen says, "Keep going I will cover the back." With his flaming morning star out, he continues to look over his shoulder behind them. At the very edge of his light he can make out shadowy movement. The dark creature seems to be drifting across the ground. It also appears to be following them. "How much further until we are out of here?" he asks.

"The exit should be just ahead," Kreeshaw says.

Isen looks again behind them and now can see four of these dark creatures following them. They are dark ethereal creatures and seem to glide above the ground. "Hurry, there are more of them! They look like living shadows."

"I see the door," Ya'leigh says, as she leads the way. Soon they can all see a large doorway before them. Fortunately for the group, just like the southern entrance through which they came, the northern entrance to Coldrock is also damaged and open.

"We are going to have to make our stand just on the other side!" Kianna yells. "Everyone be ready."

"I'll be ready to use the gate stone," Ambra says to Ya'leigh.

"Isen and I will try to hold them at the gate," Garrin says.

Ya'leigh, Ambra and Kelik are the first through the exit. Ambra takes off the sandstone necklace and nervously holds it in her shaking hands.

"Look!" Kelik says as he points to the ground at the doorway.

Crossroads

Kianna and Gena run through the door as Ambra and Ya'leigh see runic symbols written across the base of the door.

. Isen and Garrin come through the doorway and turn to ready themselves. Isen prepares to swing his flaming morning star as the dark shadow creatures stop at the door's edge and hiss.

"It's keeping them inside!" Kelik says.

The others look down at the symbols in the dirt. "They can't cross it," Gena says. "It is just like Azeris Deep. The spirits there are also kept inside by magic."

"It's a good thing too," Garrin says. "Look."

They look up and now see many dark figures on the other side of the door. They continue to hiss and screech at the group. Ambra and Kelik hide behind Isen.

"What are they?" Isen asks.

"Shades," Gena replies.

"What do they do?" he asks as he gets closer to the doorway to look at them.

"Stay back," Gena warns. "Their touch will drain your life."

"Oh," Isen says as he slowly takes a few steps back.

"Well, I say we shouldn't stay here any longer," Ya'leigh says.

"I agree," Kelik says.

"So where are we?" Kianna asks.

Kreeshaw explains, "Assuming the tunnel ahead hasn't collapsed anywhere, this should take us straight out and into the old orcnea lands."

Looking around the room that they see that they are on a platform and down below there is an iron track on the ground. "I'll bet this was for mining carts," Garrin says.

"If I remember correctly," Kianna says, "they used a string of mining carts to travel in and out. Coldrock started out as only a mine, but by the time the dwarves reached this far in, it was decided that it was easier to just build a city here rather than to move all the metal to another city."

They start to head down the tracks as Kreeshaw says, "From my understanding this was the most prestigious city the dwarfs had ever built on this continent. Of course, across the sea they have many large subterranean cities."

"I wonder what they are like," Kelik ponders.

"They are pretty much like Coldrock," Kreeshaw replies. "Just with dwarves instead of shades."

"I think I would like dwarves better," Ambra states.

"Me too," Kelik adds.

"So how much longer?" Isen asks.

Kreeshaw answers, "It's said that to travel from one side of the mountain to the other through Coldrock takes three days. We should reach the outside in a day and a half."

"Good," Garrin says. "I am getting tired of all this darkness."

They all laugh as they continue to walk down the track.

Chapter 40
Littlest of Giants

Meanwhile, far above the depths of the caves below, the Amazons of the Silver Moon are trudging through the blinding white snow high in the mountains. "I am so tired of all this bright snow," Yentroc complains. "My eyes are so tired."

"How much further?" Evelena asks Sven.

"We are getting close now," Sven says as he looks around at the landmarks. "We should be able to camp at base of mountain tomorrow night."

"Good," Kristieana says. "I am ready for anything other than mountain climbing."

Sven laughs and says, "And Sven thought we were all having good time together."

Kristieana sighs and shakes her head.

"Well, I had fun," Lyra says.

"Yes," Gelana says. "Meeting Lunarus was definitely memorable."

"It's not every day you get to meet a dragon," Kel'ana says.

"Or stay as his guest," Rehma adds.

Ja'noa draws one of her Star Steel daggers and throws it and says, "Or get such incredible items." She holds out her hand as the dagger returns to her.

"I just wonder what this does," Evelena says as she holds the golden trimmed ivory horn.

Yentroc replies, "It sounded like it only works in desperate times. Let's hope we don't have to find out."

"Still, the name, Horn of the Fallen," Evelena says. "It just sounds sort of ominous."

"He said it would call help," Lyra says, "Maybe it calls some ancient legend."

"Or a dragon," Kel'ana says.

"Who knows," Yentroc says. "Again, I just hope we don't have to find out."

Evelena looks back at Kel'ana who is walking with a slight limp. "How is your leg?" She asks.

Kel'ana smiles through the pain and replies, "I am fine. It's just a little sore."

Sven laughs and says, "You are lucky to be walking at all. You did well today, considering your leg was broken just yesterday."

"Well, I have Yentroc and Kristieana to thank for that," Kel'ana says as she sits down on a nearby rock.

Sven turns to Evelena and says, "This would be a good place to stop if you wish. We will still make it to base by the end of day tomorrow."

"Alright, ladies!" Evelena orders. "Let's make camp."

Yentroc walks over to Lyra who is taking off her backpack. "It's the last night in the cold," Yentroc says to her. "You may not get another chance for him to keep you warm."

Lyra looks up with a puzzled look on her face and asks, "What are you talking about?"

"Sven," Yentroc answers. "I know you said you would rather freeze to death..."

Lyra clasps the magical amulet that has kept her warm for the last day and replies, "I have this now, and I don't need him."

Yentroc laughs and says, "If you say so. I am just trying to help."

"Thanks," Lyra replies as she looks over at Sven as he sets up his tent, "but there is nothing going on between us that needs your help."

A short time later the group is gathered around the fire eating soup that Sven had prepared. Kel'ana says, "Sven, you didn't use any wolf meat did you?"

Sven laughs and answers, "No, Kel'ana, there is no wolf meat in stew. Sven used meat of mountain goat from yesterday."

Kel'ana looks at her bowl of soup for a moment before taking another bite. "Good," she replies. I like it better this way."

Evelena turns to Sven and asks, "Yesterday you said that knew what it was like to be small. What did you mean by that?"

Sven looks over at Lyra who stops eating to listen to his response. He then looks around at the others, only to realize that they all are waiting for him to answer. He swallows his soup and says, "You want to know about Sven?"

The others nod their heads, and Evelena says, "I am sorry. If you don't want to talk about it..."

"It's alright," Sven says. He puts down his bowl and takes a deep breath. He looks at Lyra and says, "Sven is from small town far north called Sigtuna."

"That is where the Goliaths live," Lyra says.

"Is that like a giant?" Gelana asks.

"More like half giants," Evelena answers.

Sven replies, "We are sometimes called half giants, yes."

"You are a half giant?" Evelena asks, sounding surprised.

"Yes," he answers.

"No offense," Evelena says, "but I always thought Goliaths would be bigger than you."

Sven smiles and says, "Yes, they are. Sven is smallest in family. Sven's brothers are much taller than Sven," he says as he puts his hand up over his head showing how tall they are. "Sven's sister is even taller than Sven, though not by much."

"So that is what you meant," Lyra says with a smile. "You are smallest in your family, just like I am the smallest in mine."

He smiles and replies, "Not only is Sven smallest in family, Sven is smallest of all Goliaths."

"So you are the littlest of giants," Lyra says.

"Yes," Sven says as he looks down. "That is why Sven left his village when he was old enough. If Sven could not make name for himself in home town, then maybe Sven could make name for himself among humans."

Lyra looks down now with sad eyes and says, "I am sorry, Sven."

Sven answers, "Don't worry about Sven. It has been very long journey, but among men, Sven is a giant, even if among giants, Sven is only man. Someday they will sing songs of Sven, the littlest of giants. Sven will make name for himself, and Sven's family will proud of him."

Sven picks up his bowl and wipes it out with some snow. Everyone is silent until Sven stands up and says, "Tomorrow we will be down from mountain heights and out of snow. Sven is going to bed now."

As he gets up to go to his tent, Yentroc says, "Sven, wait."

Sven stops and asks, "Yes?"

Yentroc looks at Lyra and says, "I was telling Lyra earlier about how cold I have been at night." Lyra looks at Yentroc, confused, as Yentroc smiles and continues, "She suggested that because we have the necklace now, that I could wear it."

Lyra stands up approaches Yentroc. When she reaches her she quietly asks Yentroc, "What are you doing?"

Yentroc leans over to her and whispers, "You can thank me later." She then turns to Sven and walks up to him and says, "While the eight of us Amazons are crowded into three tents, you have one all to yourself. So Lyra said she would sleep in your tent again."

Sven looks at Lyra who is glaring at Yentroc. He whispers to Yentroc, "What are you doing?"

"You can thank me later," she whispers back. Then louder she says, "Assuming, of course, that Lyra is not a burden to you."

Not wanting to upset Lyra any further, he says, "Lyra is not burden to Sven, but she did say she would rather freeze to death then let Sven keep her warm again."

Yentroc laughs and says, "She didn't really mean that. She was just upset because you made her feel like she was a bother to you."

Sven looks at Lyra who looks nervously back. He says, "Lyra, Sven is sorry if he made you feel like bother to him. He did not mean it."

Lyra looks back at Yentroc who smiles and says, "See, you were not a burden to him, but if you are still having second thoughts, I guess you could keep the necklace for yourself and I could sleep—"

"No," Lyra says cutting her off, "You can take the necklace." She takes off the enchanted necklace and hands it to Yentroc who has a big grin on her face. Lyra walks to Sven and says, "I am already getting cold, so if you are ready to go sleep now..."

"Come on then," Sven says as he walks towards his tent, "Let's get inside."

After Lyra and Sven enter his tent, Gelana says, "I cannot believe that just happened."

"What?" Yentroc says with a grin.

"You know what," Gelana replies, "you are trying to get the two of them to fall for each other."

Yentroc smiles and says, "I don't know what you are talking about. I just didn't want to be crowded next to her again, and besides, I got the warmth necklace."

Kristieana says, "I hope you know what you are doing. I still don't like or trust him."

"Lyra will be fine," Yentroc says. "Sven isn't going to do anything to hurt her."

"He better not," Kristieana replies, "or I am going hurt him."

"You won't be the only one," Gelana says.

"Alright everyone," Evelena interrupts, "we all need to get some rest, Kel'ana especially. I want this to be the last night in these mountains."

Everyone stands up and prepares to go to their tents. Kel'ana waves her hand over the fire and magically extinguishes it.

Inside Sven's tent, Lyra curls up next to Sven and puts her cold feet against his leg. He cringes a bit from the shock of it. She says, "Sorry, my feet are freezing."

"Yes," he replies, "Sven noticed."

Lyra curls up against Sven. With her back against his chest she says, "Thank you, Sven. You are much warmer than that necklace." Lyra brushes back her brown hair. Sven can see the leaf and stars painted on Lyra's cheek.

Sven smiles and looks down at the petite young woman snuggling close to him. He takes a slow deep breath and says, "Goodnight, Lyra."

Chapter 41
Day 11
Return to Bastion

    In the hot tropical jungles, at the far southern end of the continent, is the large city of Bastion. It is ruled by a warlord named Dahooras, though his official title is Makon. The Makon rules over Bastion and its people with power and fear. Bastion is outside the influence of Sheathelm's laws and operates as its own city state. A haven for pirates, Bastion is a place that many avoid. Slaves are sold openly here. Male slaves are often sent to the arena to fight. Women are often sold to the brothels where they are forced against their will to perform for the male clients. It is for this very reason that Ariella despises this place. Unfortunately for her, there is little she can do to change it. The Makon has a very powerful army that West Artos fears. It is for this reason that West Artos now hesitates to send their reinforcements to Sheathelm.
    The docks at Bastion are as large as any in the entire world of Runefell. For the brave seafaring trader who wishes to buy or sell cargo, Bastion's docks has a bustling market. It is said that if you can't find it in Bastion, it can't be found. The Goblin Trade Company operates here, and has a mutual agreement with the Makon that keeps them both satisfied.
    It is in Bastion that Ariella's father, Red Beard, became famous. After successfully defending against several attacks to take his cargo, Red Beard found the taste of battle to be most enjoyable. He would lure in pirates by masquerading as a simple merchant vessel. When they found themselves under attack, Red Beard and his men would easily turn the tables on the would be pirates, making the hunters become the hunted.
    For several months this worked well, and Red Beard gained much fame and fortune. Soon the others became aware of his reputation, and pirates became more selective of their targets. Without anyone attacking Red Beard, he soon became disinterested and would travel to the east. He tried to become a privateer, however, there were too few enemies to quench Red Beard's thirst for battle.
    Red Beard then embraced open piracy and became Red Beard the Pirate. Instead of waiting for someone to attack the *Red Dawn,* Red Beard became the aggressor and began attacking any ship that crossed their path. Despite his offensive nature, he was still known to be fair and never cruel. If a ship surrendered he would always treat them kindly and leave them with plenty of supplies to return to safety. There were those who fought back however, and Red Beard would fight them ferociously. When the time came for the other ship to surrender, Red Beard would treat his enemy with mercy.
    One of his best friends and companions, Corthag, did not particularly care for the amount of time it took to care for the enemy's wounded. Corthag and Red Beard would often argue about the best way to handle a ship that did not surrender. Their mutual friend and partner, Torgus, always sided with Red Beard, and Corthag was outnumbered.

Crossroads

It was because of Red Beard's mercy that the King of Sheathelm, prior to Arioch, would come to Red Beard for help during the first orcnea war. He gladly helped the king defeat the orcneas, and soon after became a privateer once again. When Arioch became king, Red Beard maintained his title as privateer for Sheathelm and continued to assist Arioch throughout the Dragon War and then the Second Orcnea War.

Over the last ten years, with peace throughout Sheathelm's borders, Red Beard traveled back to Bastion. He found a few challengers and would quickly make them pay. Red Beard was still the most feared captain in all of Runefell. Even though he never outright attacked a ship since the First Orcnea War, the *Red Dawn* was still looked upon by many as a ship not to be trusted.

Now, over a year since her father's death, Ariella returns to the place that made her father famous. Having already docked, Ariella and Torgus lead the way across the docks as Leon and Drake follow behind with the orcnea prisoner. Many of the people turn and stare at the daughter of Red Beard. "You certainly know how to draw attention in a crowd," Torgus says.

Ariella replies, "That is because most of these pathetic men are not used to seeing a woman who is not under the control of a man. Never mind a woman who is captain of her own ship."

One of the dock masters says, "Welcome back to Bastion, Captain Stormrage. It has been a long time since your last visit."

"Thank you," Ariella replies as she continues past him.

Soon they reach a small building with a man outside holding a large book and a quill. As the well-dressed man writes something down on his sheet of paper, his assistant, hands a small pouch of coins over to a dark haired man with a tricorne hat. In exchange for the coins the dark haired man hands the assistant a chain with a man bound to the other end. The man in chains has just been sold.

Ariella walks up to the man with the papers and says, "Are you the manager?"

"Yes," the man answers, "I am."

"How much are you paying for an orcnea?" She asks.

The manager looks surprised at the sight of the orcnea in chains. He thinks for a moment and says, "I'll give you fifty silver."

Ariella says angrily, "Is that some kind of a joke? You know how much an orcnea would fetch in the arena."

"One hundred silver then," the manager replies.

"How about fifty gold?" Ariella asks.

"Have you taken leave or your senses? Captain," he replies. "No one is worth that much."

Just then two men approach as they struggle to drag a girl in chains behind them. One of the men is well dressed in red silk. He has several gold rings on his fingers and is also wearing a thick gold necklace. The other man is taller and plain clothed. The larger man holds tightly onto the chains of the girl as the well-dressed man says to manager, "I demand my money back for this worthless wench!" The short young woman that the men have brought back pulls angrily at the chains. Her short blonde wavy hair hangs down just above her shoulders. Her tattered clothes and messy hair is not enough to hide her youthful beauty. She continues to struggle against the big man holding her.

Ariella fists clench when she hears the man talk. Torgus whispers to her, "Careful, Captain."

"What seems to be the problem?" the manager asks as he gets closer to the girl's face.

Suddenly the girl spits in the manager's face. "You see," the man in gold jewelry says, "I have tried and tried with this one, but she is too defiant for my customers. I want my money back."

"Fine," the manager relents. He hands the man a small pouch then motions for two of his men standing near the doorway to come and take the girl from them. They try to take her away as she kicks one of them in the groin.

"I like her," Ariella says to Torgus.

While the other man tries to hold her still, the man who was kicked backhands her across the face. Ariella tries to step in but Torgus grabs her wrist. The girl looks up, and as blood drips from the corner of her lip, glares at the man with a defiant grin.

"I'll buy her!" Ariella yells over the noise.

The slave manager says, "I am sorry, but she is not for sale."

"What do you mean she is not for sale?" Ariella asks. "You just bought her back, so you can sell her again."

"This one is useless," the man says calmly. "She will just have to enter the arena."

"I'll give you fifty gold," Ariella replies, "and you can have the orcnea."

"Fifty gold?" the manager asks. He looks at girl and thinks for a minute. Then he says, "I am sorry Captain I must refuse."

"You said no one was worth that much," Ariella says.

"No one is worth fifty gold for me to buy," the man says with a smirk. "But, if you are looking to buy her from me...she is worth a bit more."

Ariella takes a deep breath. She turns to the young girl and looks into her eyes. "One hundred gold," she says, "and the orcnea."

"Captain," Torgus says, "are you sure about this?"

"Yes," Ariella says to Torgus. She then leans close to the manager and whispers in his ear, "I suggest you take the offer, or so help me I will make you regret it for the rest of your short, miserable life."

The man, now intimidated, replies nervously, "Of course, my lady, your offer is more than fair."

"Good," Ariella says angrily. "Drake, please hand over the orcnea." Ariella walks up to the girl and says to her, "My name is Ariella, and I promise you that no one is going to hurt you anymore."

The girl, looking confused, replies, "Thank you, ma'am."

"You can call me captain," Ariella says. "What is your name?"

"Annalee, Captain," she replies as the other men take the orcnea away and hand Annalee's chain to Leon.

"Annalee," Ariella says, "I am going to have Leon take you back to the

Crossroads

ship now. I have some other business I must attend to." Annalee looks up at Leon nervously. "Leon, would you please escort Miss Annalee to the lounge and watch over her."

"Yes, ma'am," Leon replies.

"Don't worry, Annalee," Ariella tells her. "Leon will not harm you. Now, I want to make one thing very clear to you. Do not mistake my kindness for weakness. I have just paid a lot for you. I would appreciate it if you didn't try to escape until after we get to know each other."

"Yes, Captain," Annalee replies. "I promise I will not leave."

"Good," Ariella says with a smile. "Just to be on the safe side, Leon, I want you to leave the chains on her until I return. I hope you understand, Annalee. I have recently developed some...trust issues."

Annalee nods and replies, "I understand, Captain."

"Leon, make sure she is fed," Ariella says. "I will return to the ship shortly. Drake, you and Torgus will come with me. I have someone I would like to see."

Leon and Annalee walk back to the ship as Leon says to her, "Can I ask you something?"

Annalee replies, "If you must."

"How old are you?" he asks.

"Old enough," she replies.

Leon smiles and says, "I can see why the captain likes you."

"Why is that?" Annalee asks.

"Because you are a feisty one," Leon replies, "just like her."

Annalee grins as they walk down along the docks back to the ship.

Soon Ariella, Torgus, and Drake are sitting in a large room with marble floors and beautifully crafted pillars. Above them is a vaulted marble ceiling with stained glass windows that allow the light in. It is the palace of Bastion, and they are waiting in a large corridor. A dark skinned man with glasses comes out from two large doors and says, The Makon will see you now, Captain Stormrage. The three stand up to enter as the man adds, "I am sorry, but only lady Stormrage may enter."

Ariella says, "That's alright, Torgus. You and Drake wait here. I won't be long."

Drake and Torgus sit back down on the white marble bench as Ariella enters the other room. The two large doors close behind her.

"Welcome to my palace," the deep voice of the Makon, Dahooras says. The luxurious room is filled with large plants and has a small fountain on each side of the red carpet that leads all the way to a large marble throne. Sitting upon the throne is Dahooras. Standing as tall as Drake or Leon this dark skinned man is a hulking mass of muscle. Wearing only a loose fitting white cloth around his waist, his muscular chest is meant to show his strength. With gold necklaces and rings, his wealth is also on display. Two women stand at either side of him creating a breeze with large decorative fans.

Ariella walks up the red carpet and says, "Thank you for seeing me, Your

Majesty."

"That will be far enough," he says. Ariella stops and he continues, "I know all about your spells, daughter of Red Beard, and I prefer to keep you at a safe distance." The assistant who showed Ariella in walks up and whispers something in the Makon's ear. Dahooras looks up at her when he is done and says, "I understand you purchased yourself a young lady earlier."

Ariella forces a smile and says, "Yes, Your Majesty, as a matter of fact I did."

"Captain, I am not a king. I am only a humble public servant of the people," he says with a smile. "Please, call me Makon, or if you wish you may even call me by my name, Dahooras."

"Of course, Makon," Ariella says, wanting to stay formal. "Your manager down at the docks would have thrown that poor girl in the arena."

The Makon chuckles and says, "I also hear that you traded an orcnea for her. Thank you very much. An orcnea will be a much bigger draw to the arena than a woman."

"You are welcome," Ariella replies. "I would like to point out that I paid one hundred gold for her in addition to the orcnea."

"Really?" He asks, "So it was not just an even trade?"

"No, Makon," Ariella says. "I paid one hundred gold and an orcnea for that girl's life."

Dahooras ponders for a moment then he stands up and motions to the man in glasses. He says something to him that Ariella cannot hear. His assistant leaves and Dahooras says, "If I remember correctly, your father never much cared for slavery either. I am surprised to see you here."

"Well, I didn't have anything else I could do with an orcnea," Ariella explains. "Other than draining every last year of its life from him, but I don't want to be twelve years old again."

Makon laughs and says, "I am sure that you are not here to discuss our social practices. What may I do for you?"

Ariella says, "While I doubt you know him, I have to ask, have ever heard of Fernando Greythorn?"

"Fernando Greythorn?" he says reflectively. "As a matter of fact I have. There is quite a reward out there for him, I believe. He has caused some problems for a few of our businesses."

"What kind of problems?" Ariella asks.

The Makon replies, "Let's just say that he owes several brothels a lot of money."

"So he leaves without paying?" Ariella asks.

"You would have to ask them," Dahooras says, "but the reward is up to five hundred gold pieces."

"That certainly is a large reward," Ariella says. "I don't suppose he would show up here then."

"No," Dahooras replies. "He is not allowed within our city walls. Any guard who sees him is supposed to turn him in immediately."

"Well," Ariella says, "if you find him, I would like to contribute to the reward. I will pay another hundred gold, but I need him alive."

"Alive? Well, Captain," Dahooras says with a smile, "you may want to find him before anyone else. They just want to see him dead. If I see him you will be the first to know. May I ask why you want him?"

"It is personal," she answers.

The man with the glasses returns and shows Makon a piece of parchment. He also hands him a good size pouch. Makon says, "Here, Ariella," he tosses the pouch to her. It is heavy and full of gold coins. "There is your one hundred gold back. It appears that my manager at the dock neglected to report it on his paperwork. I appreciate you pointing this out to me, and I will make sure that I deal with him very soon."

Ariella smiles and says, "Thank you, Makon. If you would like to keep it to add to Fernando's reward..."

"No, Ariella," Dahooras says. "As a favor to you, I will put up the extra hundred gold for him and inform you at once if we see him."

"Thank you, Makon," Ariella says again.

"Oh, and one more thing." He says as he walks up to her and puts his arm over her shoulder. "Since word of your father's passing, there has been a lot more... *activity* in the waters. Be careful out there, daughter of Red Beard. I am sure there is more than one captain who would like to make a name for himself at your expense."

Ariella nods and says, "Thank you for the warning."

"Goodbye, Ariella," Dahooras says.

Ariella replies, "Goodbye, Makon." The man with glasses opens the door for her as she leaves with her gold. When she reaches Torgus and Drake she says, "We better get back to the ship."

Back in the lounge of the *Red Dawn*, Annalee is eating as if she hadn't had food in days. Leon watches over her as she devours everything in sight. Apples, cheese, breads, and some smoked fish. She stops only to drink water before eating more. Outside, John and Jacob peer through the porthole.

"Who is that?" John asks.

"I don't know," Jacob replies.

"How old do you think she is?" John wonders.

"Can't tell," Jacob says trying to get a better look at her. "She is so small. I think she is just a child."

John squints his eyes and says, "I ain't so sure about that. Sure, she's short and has a cute face, but her body is far from a child's."

"See anything interesting gentlemen?" Ariella asks. Her voice startles them and they jump.

"Sorry, ma'am," Jacob says as he hangs his head low and turns to face the captain. "We was just curious."

Ariella smiles and says, "That young lady is our guest." Then she moves in really close to the men, and staring them down she adds, "I trust that I do not need to remind you two how to treat a lady."

The men nervously shake their heads and John replies, "No, ma'am."

"Good," she says as she steps back to give them room to leave. "Now, go find something to do."

The men quickly leave and Ariella enters the lounge. "You may remove the chains, Leon," she says as she walks over and sits next to Annalee. Leon begins to unlock the shackles as Ariella continues, "It seems that due to a paperwork error you only cost me an orcnea. So I will leave this decision up to you. You may go if you please, or if wish to stay on board the *Red Dawn* as my personal assistant, I would be happy to have you as a member of our crew."

Annalee looks up from her now empty plate with a look of shock. She hesitates before finally asking, "Are you saying I am free?"

"Yes, darling," Ariella replies. "I don't know how much that orcnea was really worth anyway, and the thought of having someone working for me against their will has always been a line I did not wish to cross."

For almost as long as she can remember, this young woman has been treated like property. For the first time she is able to choose her own fate. She is both relieved and terrified at the same time. "I don't know what to do," she says sounding distressed.

"Well, you don't have to make a decision right away," Ariella tells her. "I doubt you would want to start a new life for yourself here anyway."

Annalee laughs and says, "You are right about that, ma'am."

"You are so pretty when you smile," Ariella says. "Can I ask how long have been a slave?"

The question brings back unfortunate memories. Sadness eclipses her smiling face and she answers, "The ship that I was on with my family was attacked when I was nine. I have spent half my life as a slave. Being traded from one person to the next. Being forced to..." she stops unable to say what Ariella already knows. Tears begin to run down her cheeks.

"It's alright," Ariella says as she places her hand on her shoulder. "You don't have to talk about if you don't want to."

Taking a deep breath, and slowly letting it out, Annalee continues, "Then a year ago I was traded to a ship named the *Misty Water*. The Captain on that ship treated me well. It was a trading ship and I was actually happy there."

"So how did you end up for sale in Bastion?" Ariella asks.

"About a week ago we were traveling around Bastion," Annalee explains. "We thought we were far enough away to avoid pirates, but we still came under attack. They took me and sank the ship. After I punched the captain who attacked us in the face they sold me in Bastion. A brothel owner bought me but I refused to let the men...you know. He was returning me when you showed up." She looks down again and as tears start to roll down her cheeks she says with a cracking voice, "I don't know what I would have done if you hadn't..."

"Shh," Ariella says as she embraces her. Annalee lays her head on Ariella's shoulder unable to hold back her emotions any longer. "No one is going to hurt you now," Ariella says comforting her. After Annalee regains her composer Ariella says, "Now let's get you cleaned up." Holding up a small package she adds, "I picked up something for you to wear."

"Thank you, Captain," Annalee says with a sniffle as she wipes her face.

"You're welcome," Ariella says with a smile. "I like my assistants to look their best."

Chapter 42
A Little Pick Me Up

Sven and the Amazons have finally made it far enough down the mountain that the temperatures are no longer below freezing. Evelena says, "This looks like a good place to rest for bit."

Everyone finds a place to sit down including Sven who is visibly tired. Yentroc walks over to him and says. "Sven, are you alright? You look exhausted."

He replies "Sven did not get good sleep last night."

Yentroc smiles and says, "Really? So did Lyra keep you up all night?"

Sven sighs and says, "Not like that."

"What do you mean?" Yentroc inquires.

Sven looks around to see that they are alone before answering, "Do you have any idea how hard it is for Sven to lay next to a woman all night and have to try to fall asleep?"

"So you like her then?" Yentroc asks.

"It would be the same for you or any of your sisters," Sven answers.

"Admit it," She says with a smile. "You have feelings for her."

Sven dolefully replies, "Whether Sven has feelings for Lyra or not is not important."

Yentroc laughs and says, "Yes, it is. Why don't you tell her? Is this still about Chance's warning?"

Sven looks over at Lyra who is reading a book. He looks back at Yentroc and says intensely, "This is not just about Chance and that you are his sisters, or that Kristieana threatened Sven not to touch her as well. It is only about one thing. Sven is not good for Lyra."

"What do you mean?" she asks.

"I mean that Sven is not good for any woman," he says. "Sven would only hurt her, and Sven would rather hurt self than Lyra."

"I don't understand," Yentroc replies.

Sven sighs and says, "It is not important. Just promise Sven that you will not say anything to Lyra."

Yentroc looks over to Lyra who is still reading, and says "Alright, I promise."

"Good," Sven replies. "Now, I have a favor to ask."

"What is it?" Yentroc asks.

"You are healer of group, so maybe you can help Sven," he says. "Do you have any spells that you can help keep Sven awake?"

Lyra's voice makes them both jump when she asks, "Why do you need something to keep you awake?"

Sven, startled, laughs and says, "Sven is very tired, and wants to stay alert in case of orcneas."

"Why are you tired?" Lyra asks. "Did you not sleep well?"

"Sven is used to warm soft beds at night," He explains. "Sven was asking

Crossroads

Yentroc for something that can help keep him awake. Sven will make sure he puts bed in good place tonight."

Ja'noa overhears them and says, "I have something that can keep you alert." She opens her backpack and digs through it for a moment. She pulls out a small pouch and says, "I have some Tofeen leaves. Just chew on one when you are tired, but don't swallow it."

"Thank you," Sven says as he takes the small leather pouch from Ja'noa.

"You're welcome," she replies.

"Alright," Evelena says, "A couple more hours, and we will make camp for the night."

Everyone rises and continues down the pathway. Yentroc and Lyra walk next to each other, and Lyra asks, "Did Sven say anything else to you?"

"No, why?" Yentroc asks.

"I was just wondering," Lyra says.

"Oh," Yentroc replies as they follow behind the rest of the group. "He was just describing the rock that was in his back all night." She looks at Lyra and adds, "So how did you sleep last night?"

Lyra smiles and answers, "I slept great. Sven is so warm, and I can't really describe it but I feel safe when I am with him."

"Well, he did pull you up from the bridge," Yentroc says, "and took an arrow for you. Not to mention keeping you warm at night."

"I guess that is probably it," Lyra says with laugh and a smile.

Yentroc thinks for a moment and says, "He is also big and strong as well as handsome."

"Yes," Lyra says with a smile while looking ahead at Sven.

Yentroc notices the smile on her face and says, "I knew it."

As if from out of a daze Lyra looks at Yentroc and questions, "What?"

"You like him, don't you?"

"No," Lyra replies quietly as she stops walking. "I don't know...maybe. It doesn't really matter though."

"Why?" Yentroc asks.

"Because," she answers, "I am not going to leave the sisterhood."

Yentroc asks, "What if Sven has feelings for you?"

Lyra's smile disappears and she says, "It wouldn't change anything. I would just end up hurting him. I am not worried about that though. Sven has been with enough women that I doubt I am anything special." She looks down and adds, "He won't say it, but I am sure he still just sees me as a little girl."

"You never know," Yentroc says as they continue walking.

Chapter 43
Midnight Run

In the modern day apartment, Kel'ana continues to tell the story to Josh, Haley, and Laura. She says, "Now as night falls over Bruen, The Seven Sisters of the Silver Moon finally make camp on ground that isn't frozen. Princess Kianna and her group finally make it out of the caves, and the two groups are unaware of each other even though they are only separated by two miles."

Kelik then continues where she leaves off and says, "On the front lines of the war, it was an uneventful day as Arioch and Chance planned what to do next. Still anchored at Bastion, Ariella prepares to leave under the cover of night."

"What about Fernando?" Josh asks.

"Well," Kelik explains. "When Fernando showed up at the tavern on this day to meet with whomever he was waiting for, the inn keeper gave him a message telling him to be there the next night."

"Who is he trying to meet?" Haley asks.

Kelik smiles and says, "Well, you will just have to listen and find out what he does, but first..."

*****

The sun sets over the sea to the south, and Ariella walks out onto the deck of her ship. "Are we ready to depart, Chris?" she asks.

"Yes, Captain," Chris answers. "We can go at any time."

"Good," Ariella says as she takes out her looking glass and looks at the horizon. "There are two ships out there and I want to avoid any conflicts if possible. I just got the *Red Dawn* repaired, I don't need holes in her hull already."

"Yes, ma'am," Chris replies.

Ariella then opens the door to her cabin and says to Annalee, "Come, my dear, let's introduce you to the rest of the crew."

Annalee comes out from the cabin in her new clothes. She has blue leggings and a mid-length blue and white skirt. Her white silk blouse shows her feminine curves. The blouse is highlighted with a dark blue vest. Her sandy blonde hair has not been brushed, and is a chaotic contrast to the new clothing.

John elbows Jacob as they watch from below and says, "That defiantly ain't no child."

"Now then!" Ariella announces. "This is Annalee, she is currently our guest, and with any luck she will join us as my new assistant. If I ever hear that one of you touches her without her permission, you will have to explain to my father in the afterlife why exactly you are there. Do I make myself clear?"

The crew all answer with a collective, "Yes, Captain!"

"Excellent," Ariella says. "Now who would like to be a gentleman and show Miss Annalee around the ship?" All of the thirty men currently on deck raise their hands enthusiastically. Ariella laughs as she leans over to Annalee who looks embarrassed and quietly says, "I figured there would be no shortage of volunteers."

"Alright," Ariella says loudly, "John and Jacob, you two show her around. As for everyone else, make sure the ship is ready to go at a moment's notice. We plan on making a midnight run out of here."

The other men get to work as John and Jacob quickly run up the stairs. They stand before the captain and Annalee with their hats off. John nervously says, "My name is John, ma'am and I will be showing you around the ship."

Jacob adds, "I am showing you around the ship too...oh, and my name is Jacob."

Annalee, who is not used to being tended to, smiles and says, "Thank you."

Jacob and John lead the way as Annalee follows them for a tour of the ship. Torgus says to Ariella, "Are you expecting trouble, Captain?"

"The Makon warned me that there have been more attacks in the waters lately," Ariella explains. "I don't need some overzealous captain to try to become famous at our expense."

"You know that most pirates wouldn't stand a chance against us," Torgus says.

"I know," she replies. "I just don't want to have to make repairs again so soon. We haven't made much gold lately, Torgus, and since Mr. Greythorn betrayed us, I am not sure what out next step will be. Although, if we find him before some bounty hunter does, he is at least worth five hundred gold."

"Well, he certainly made some enemies other than us," Torgus says as he leans on the railing.

"Apparently so," Ariella says, "but until we find him, what should we do?"

"We could always attack the orcnea ships," Torgus suggests.

"I am not so sure we would fair very well against them," Ariella says. "Those weapons they had were like nothing I have ever seen."

Torgus thinks for a moment then says, "You know, only the one ship had them. The other just had the shamans."

"Either way," Ariella replies, "I am just not sure how long we would last out there against them. We are short on spell casters."

Torgus nods his head and says, "Aye, Captain, that we are."

Below deck John and Jacob are showing Annalee the crew's quarters. There are several other men following them. A man named Steven leans on a hammock and says, "Hey, sweetheart, this is where I sleep, so any time you are lonely you come and see me, alright?"

The other men laugh. Annalee doesn't seem to be phased by the comment. John says, "You all heard what the captain said."

"That I did," Steven replies. "And I ain't touching her."

"Well," Annalee says as she slowly walks up to the man. "She said you can't touch me without my permission. How about I let you touch me once, and I get to touch you back."

Now the crew is in an uproar as Steven laughs. He leans down to Annalee and says, "Sweetheart, you have yourself a deal."

Annalee smiles and replies, "Alright then, you go first."

The men now quiet down as the man takes a deep breath. He seems to be thinking about what to do as he looks Annalee over. Annalee just stands there with a smirk. Finally he reaches his hands around and grabs her on the rear. He holds her for a moment looking her in the eyes as she just smiles back. The men are now cheering it on.

John and Jacob look at each other confused. After a few moments Annalee backs up and asks, "Did you enjoy that?"

"You bet I did," Steven laughs.

"So now it is my turn to touch you," Annalee says with a smile.

"Oh yes, sweetheart," the man replies. "Touch me."

Annalee just looks up at Steven and says, "One touch deserves another." She clinches her fist and before the men realize it, she lands a hay maker right into his nose.

The punch knocks Steven to the ground, and the men start to laugh at him as he holds his hands over his face. He gets to his knees and blood is dripping down through his hands and onto his shirt. He yells, "What the hell did you hit me with?"

John looks at her hand and doesn't see anything in her fist. She replies, "Just my fist." She then walks up to Steven and because he is on his knees she looks down at him and says, "Would you like to touch me again?"

"Maybe later," Steven says with a bloody grin. "Welcome aboard Miss."

Later that evening Ariella tells her crew to get under way. Annalee has finished her tour and John and Jacob bring her back to the captain. "Well then, did you have a nice time?" Ariella asks.

"Yes," Annalee says with a smile.

"Any problems?" she asks John.

"Nothing she couldn't handle, Captain," he replies.

"Very well then," Ariella says. "Now if you gentlemen would return to your posts, we need to be ready. Then she calls out, "All lights out!" The men cover or blow out any lanterns and candles.

"The wind is favorable, Captain," Chris says. "We should be able to get out and around the peninsula quickly."

"Then set sail back to East Artos," Ariella orders.

"Aye, Captain," Chris replies.

Ariella turns to Annalee and says, "Alright, my dear, let me show you were you will be sleeping." Ariella leads Annalee through the officers' quarters and opens the door to Ariella's quarters and they go inside. "This is my room and over here is the way to your room and to the lounge upstairs." It is dark and the Captain pulls a small glowing stone from her pocket. It gives off enough light that they can make their way through Ariella's room. After they reach the far left corner of the room Ariella opens a door. They enter a much smaller room that contains another door to their left and a stairway leading up. "That is the stairs to the lounge," Ariella explains, "and this is your room over here." Ariella opens the other door, and on the other side there is a long narrow room. There is a porthole above a small dresser. On the other side, built into the wall, there is a bed. "It isn't much," Ariella says, "but it is all yours as long as you wish."

"Thank you, Captain," Annalee says as she walks into the room and looks around. "I love the porthole. It makes me feel less..."

"Like a prisoner?" Ariella asks.

"Yes," she says with a smile. "Thank you."

"Here, take this," Ariella says as she hands her the small glowing stone. "We are trying not to be noticed right now, so only use it if you have to."

"Yes, Captain," Annalee replies. "If it is alright with you, I would like to turn in now. I haven't slept in a bed in a long time."

"Of course," Ariella says as she turns to leave, "Sleep well, Annalee."

"Thank you, Captain,"

Chapter 44
Day 12
Reputation

The morning's light shines down on the waters of the south sea as the *Red Dawn* sails to East Artos. Trailing behind them is a ship with unknown intentions. Ariella looks closely at the ship with her looking glass. "How long has that ship been following us?" Ariella asks Chris.

"The crow's nest spotted it about an hour ago," he replies. "I think it is gaining on us."

Annalee is also next to the Captain and she asks, "May I see it, Captain?" Ariella hands her the looking glass and as she looks through it she says, "Captain, that is the same ship that attacked the *Misty Water* a week ago."

An intense feeling of rage comes over Ariella. "Are you sure?" she asks.

"Positive, Captain," she replies as she hands back the looking glass.

"Well then," Ariella says as she walks down the two flights of stairs and to the main mast, "they must have been following us all night from Bastion." She yells down the stairs to Drake, "Get everyone topside now!"

"Aye, Captain," the seasoned veteran replies.

"What are we going to do?" Annalee asks as she follows the captain back up the stairs.

Ariella says with a sly grin, "We are going to do what my men do best."

From below deck the crew quickly emerges up the stairs. Soon they fill the deck and await word from the captain. Drake comes up from below and he nods to Ariella. With a bold and confident tone in her in voice she announces, "Gentlemen, behind us is a ship what wishes to test us!" Her words resonate with the crew as they begin to look at each other with smiles. "It has been a year since my father was killed, and now we have returned to where he once ruled the sea." The crew listens closely to the captain, hanging on her every word. "The captain of that ship hopes to make a name for himself at our expense!" Now the crew becomes riled as they clinch their weapons in their hands and shake their heads no. "They believe that without my father the *Red Dawn* in now weak!" A dull roar of the crew can be heard as she asks, "Are we weak?"

With a collective yell the crew answers, "No!"

"You're damn right we aren't," Ariella replies. "Just because we tried to avoid conflict last night does not mean we are afraid of a fight. The *Red Dawn* does not run from anyone!" The crew cheers loudly as Ariella smiles and yells, "Bring us about, and let's show them why the *Red Dawn* is still the most feared force on the seas! Men, prepare for Sleeping Serpent!"

The men roar and all scatter in an organized fashion. Some of the men lift up small hatches on the deck and enter them. Others enter the officer's quarters beneath the quarterdeck. Within twenty seconds the deck is completely empty. Ariella turns to Annalee and says, "I want you to go into your room and wait. This won't take long."

"But, Captain," Annalee says.

"Now, Annalee!" Ariella snaps.

"Yes, ma'am," she replies as she quickly runs off.

"Torgus, are you ready?" Ariella asks.

"Of course, Captain," Torgus replies.

Now the ships are heading right for each other. Only Torgus and Ariella remain up top at the helm. The ships come closer as the enemy ship furls their sails and raises a black flag making their hostile intentions known. "Well then," Ariella says to the old dwarf, "it begins." The other ship fires arrows into the air. The arrows arc and fall onto the deck of the *Red Dawn* as Ariella and Torgus look at each other with a smile. The arrows fall harmlessly all around them as Torgus has cast a spell to protect himself and Ariella.

"How pathetic," Ariella says. "I believe they have no spell casters at all. Torgus, please show them what a real volley looks like."

Torgus summons a large stone and hurls it into the deck of the oncoming ship that is now off their port bow. Ariella casts a bolt of lightning that shreds the mast of the other ship. The men on the other ship scatter away from where the spells impact their ship. Then they gather themselves and use grappling hooks to tie the ships together.

They begin to board the *Red Dawn* and stop and look around at the empty deck, confused. A tall thin man yells out, "Captain Stormrage, you will surrender your ship to me at once!"

Ariella laughs and says, "If you want my ship, then come and take it!" Just then the sound of a horn blasts out from the crow's nest above, and the crew of the *Red Dawn* springs into action. Trap doors in the deck open downward and the men standing on the planks fall down into netting and are surrounded by the men waiting below. The rest of the crew of the *Red Dawn* rush out from hiding and take the enemy crew by surprise. The captain of the other ship jumps over the rail to the *Red Dawn*. Ariella quickly approaches him as Torgus follows right behind her. He summons smaller stones in each hand and hurls them those who would try to attack Ariella.

"I have you now, Captain," The tall man with dark hair says as he draws his sword.

"I would love to duel with you," Ariella says as her hand starts to glow with dark mystical energy. "But I don't have time to play today."

"Do you have enough time to die?" The man asks as lunges forward and thrusts his sword at Ariella. She spins around avoiding the blade and steps next to him. Side by side, she places her hand on the man's arm before stepping back. The other ship's captain looks at Ariella, confused for a moment, before he suddenly drops his sword. Then as the pain of her spell over takes him, he drops to his knees and lets out an agonizing cry. The fighting immediately stops as the other ship's men watch their captain lying helpless on the ground at Ariella's feet.

"Surrender now and I will let you live!" Ariella yells out over the ship.

The tall, thin captain continues to scream in pain. He begs, "Please! Make it stop!" His men drop their weapons, and as quickly as the battle started it is over. Drake and Leon pick up the enemy captain before Ariella discontinues her spell.

A short time later the crew of the enemy ship is lined up along the port railing of the *Red Dawn*. Their hands are tied behind their backs as Drake and Leon watch over them with large crossbows. Ariella's men are bringing crates over from the other ship as Annalee comes out onto the deck from the officer's quarters.

"What is your name, Captain?" Ariella asks the captain of the other ship.

"His name is Captain Rinehart," Annalee says answering the question.

"Annalee," Captain Rinehart says. "It is good to see you again." Some of his men laugh at the comment.

"I see you already know the latest member of my crew," Ariella says.

Annalee walks up to Captain Rinehart, and as she stares at him angrily, he asks her, "What are you looking at, girl?"

Ariella watches as her new, short companion makes a fist. She punches Rinehart in the face, and Ariella notices something peculiar about Annalee's hand as she hits him. The man falls to his knees with a broken nose. "Captain, are you going to let her treat me like that?" He says as blood flows down his face.

Ignoring his question, Ariella looks at Torgus and quietly asks, "Did you see that?"

Torgus nods and says, "I believe I did."

"Captain, this is no way to treat a prisoner," Rinehart protests.

"Shut up!" Ariella snaps back at him. "Leon, would you please bring Captain Rinehart here?" Leon steps forward and takes Rinehart's arm. He leads him over to the captain as Annalee follows. Ariella then says, "On your knees, Rinehart."

He gets down on his knees and asks, "What is the meaning of this, Captain?"

Ariella continues to ignore Captain Rinehart and says, "Annalee, would you please shut this man up?"

"Yes, ma'am," Annalee replies. She smiles sadistically before slamming her fist again into Rinehart's face. Ariella watches closely as Annalee's fist appears to become metallic for a split second as she punches him. The blow knocks Rinehart unconscious. Ariella looks at Torgus who nods and says, "That is definitely magic, Captain."

"My hand, ma'am?" Annalee questions, "yes, it is. At least that is what someone told me once. I don't even know how I do it. I never studied magic."

Ariella eyes light up as she says, "Did you hear that, Torgus? She has never been taught magic and yet she is already casting a spell." She then turns to Annalee and says, "Annalee, I would like very much to take you on as my apprentice."

Annalee smiles and replies, "I would be honored, Captain."

Ariella puts her arm around Annalee's shoulder and says, "Now then, are there any other men here that you have a score to settle with?" The captives all look down to avoid eye contact. Annalee slowly walks in front of them. She stops at one and says, "This one."

Ariella nods to Leon, and he walks up to the man Annalee identified. Leon pulls him forward as he begins to plea, "Please, Annalee! I am sorry."

Annalee kicks the back of his knee so that he falls to the ground. She then walks over to the main mast and picks up some rope. The man begs again, "I didn't mean to hurt you."

She wraps the rope around his neck, leans down, and says, "Let's see how YOU like to be choked." Annalee pulls back on the rope, and the man's face turns red as he struggles to breath. The other prisoners all look frightened except for one young man. The man, in his early twenties, tries to hide his smile, as Annalee continues to pull on the rope wrapped around his shipmate's neck.

Annalee finally releases the rope, and as the man gasps for air she punches him with the same steel like fist. Blood now covers her hand as she steps back and looks at the line of men again.

Annalee looks down the row as the men all look away. When she sees the man who was smiling she looks into his deep blue eyes for a brief moment before he looks down at the deck. Annalee smiles and Ariella asks her, "Is he another one?" Annalee walks over to Ariella and whispers something to her. Ariella approaches the blue eyed man and commands him, "You, step forward!"

The tall muscular man steps forward, looking confused. Ariella looks back at Annalee who nods. She then says, "Come over here with me for a moment." Ariella walks over to the center mast with Annalee as the man follows behind her.

"Captain," John calls out from the other ship, "I think we got everything!"

"Excellent," Ariella replies. "Get everyone back on board. We will release them soon and be on our way."

"Aye, Captain!" John answers.

Ariella turns her attention back to the handsome young man. "What is your name?"

"Seth, Captain," he answers.

"Do you know why I wanted to talk with you?" Ariella asks.

"No, ma'am," Seth answers, sounding nervous.

"Annalee, here, told me that out of all the men on that ship of yours, you were the only one who treated her well," Ariella explains.

Seth looks at Annalee as she looks away. "Yes, ma'am," Seth replies. "I am not like them, ma'am. I didn't like the way they treated her."

Ariella thinks for a moment and then asks, "Why do you serve Captain Rinehart?"

The young man with sandy blonde hair answers, "I did not know when I signed on that he took prisoners for slavery. I just needed the work and didn't ask questions." He then looks at Annalee and says, "I am sorry."

Ariella sighs and asks, "How would you like to work for me?"

"Aboard the *Red Dawn*?" he asks, sounding excited. "I would like that very much, Captain."

Ariella says, "Let me untie you and you can go gather your things, but first

I want you to look me in the eyes and swear to me that you will serve me loyally."

Seth looks her in the eyes and without hesitation he says, "I swear to you, Captain, I will serve you loyally."

"Excellent," Ariella replies as she finishes untying the ropes from Seth. "Now hurry and gather you things."

"Aye, Captain," Seth says as he runs off.

Captain Rinehart regains consciousness, as Leon picks him up and stands him back in line. Ariella now addresses her captives and says, "Gentlemen, I am now going to have to ask you to return to your ship. It has been a pleasure having you all here. Before you go, however, I would like to make one thing perfectly clear." Ariella walks up to the still bleeding Captain Rinehart and says, "Do not mistake my kindness for weakness. If I ever come across your ship again, Captain, I will give you one chance to allow us to board you peacefully. If you resist us, I will send you all to the bottom of the sea. Is that clear?"

"Of course, Captain," Rinehart replies. "But why would you be boarding us?"

"When I board you," Ariella explains, "I will be looking for one thing and one thing only. If I find that you have taken anyone as a slave, you will wish you were at the bottom of the sea. Now, is *that* clear, Captain?"

Rinehart's anger is only outweighed by his fear as he answers, "Yes, Captain."

"Excellent," Ariella says with a smile. "Now back to your ship."

Seth returns with a small bag as the others all return to their ship. The lines are cut, and soon the *Red Dawn* is on its way once more.

Seth stands next to Annalee and Ariella asks, "Now then, Seth, there is just one other thing."

"Yes, Captain?" Seth asks.

"If this young lady here asks you to do something," Ariella says looking at Annalee, "you will do as she says."

"Yes, ma'am," Seth replies.

"I don't care if she asks you to bring her a glass of water," Ariella continues, "or cut her food. Unless I tell you otherwise, her orders are as good as mine. Unless, of course, those orders are munitions."

"Of course, Captain," Seth replies.

"Annalee," Ariella says with a grin. "This handsome young man is all yours."

"What?" Annalee asks.

"You have had to serve others most of your life," Ariella says. "Now it is time for someone to serve you."

"Thank you, Captain," Annalee replies, "but I don't want someone to give orders to."

"I understand," says Ariella, "but he is not a slave. If you don't have any need of him at this time, then I'll have John show him to his hammock."

Annalee nods then the captain calls out, "John!"

"Yes, Captain," John replies as he runs over.

"This is Seth," Ariella says introducing the two. "Seth, this is John."

"Pleasure to meet you, sir," Seth says offering his hand.

He shakes his hand and replies, "Just call me John."

Ariella says, "John, show him below deck. He can take Allen's hammock."

"Yes, Captain," John replies.

Ariella then laughs and adds, "It's fitting really."

"What is, ma'am?" Annalee asks.

"I lost two of my crew recently," Ariella explains. "A young man and a young woman. It seems that fate has found a way to replace them for me. Come, let's go up to the lounge and discuss your talent for magic."

Chapter 45
Who's Following Who?

Walking down the streets of Sheathelm, Fernando Greythorn is biding his time until he meets with his contact at the King's Shield. It has been a long couple days for him as he nervously checks around almost every corner for any of Ariella's men.

He makes his way through the market district when he notices someone wearing a cloak seems to be following him. Fernando turns to see the person's face beneath the hood but the hooded figure looks the other way. Unsure if he is being followed, Fernando decides to try to lose him in the crowd. He pulls up the hood of his own cloak and begins to walk briskly through the crowded street.

Checking behind him Fernando can tell that he is still being followed. Just as he comes out of the crowd Fernando runs down a side street before ducking into an ally. He waits as the hooded one makes his way around the corner, Fernando grabs the cloaked person and slams him against the wall. As he does the unmistakable sound of a woman's groan come from under the cloak.

He grabs the hood and pulls it down only to reveal a familiar face. "Marie?" Fernando says. "What are you doing here?"

Then Fernando can feel the point of a sword at his back as he hears Allen's voice reply, "We should ask you the same question. Now give me one good reason, Mr. Greythorn, why I shouldn't run this sword right through you."

Fernando slowly raises his hands over his head and turns. "Allen, is Ariella here?" he asks.

"Thanks to you," Marie says angrily, "Allen and I were kicked off the ship."

"I am so sorry, Allen," Fernando say regretfully.

"I bet you are," Allen says, sounding unconvinced.

"Really, I am," He says, trying to explain. "I did not mean to cause you any problems."

"So, where is it?" Allen asks.

"Allen," Fernando says as he lowers his hands, "you don't understand."

"Then why don't you explain it to us," Allen says pointing his sword at him. "Why don't you tell us why you lied to us for almost a week and then left without any explanation?"

"I will tell you everything that I know," Fernando replies. "Let's go find a place that we can sit and talk."

"Sure," Allen says, "but first hand over the locket."

"I have hidden it somewhere safe, I promise," he replies.

Allen then looks at the gold medallion around Fernando's neck and says, "Alright then, give me the medallion."

"Allen, please," Fernando begs.

"Why do you want that, Allen?" Marie asks.

"Because, unless I am wrong, that medallion is preventing Torgus from tracking him," Allen answers.

Crossroads

Fernando puts his hand on the round piece of gold around his neck and says, "Fine, I will give you this, but you have to hear me out."

"No, you are going to give that to me, then you are going to give me the captain's amulet," Allen replies.

Fernando takes a deep breath and sighs. "Have it your way," he says, removing the necklace. "Here you go." He tosses it to Allen and as Allen tries to catch it, Fernando quickly draws his sword. Before Allen has any time to react, Fernando disarms him. Fernando steps back so that Marie does not get behind him. "Now, listen to me," Fernando says as he kicks Allen's sword to the side, "I know you have no reason to trust me, and I am truly sorry that my actions have affected the two of you, but you have to understand that everything I have done was not of my own choice."

"What are you talking about?" Allen asks.

Fernando takes the medallion from Allen and steps back and places it back around his neck. "Come," he says, "follow me and I shall tell you." Fernando is careful to keep his distance from Allen and Marie as he walks around them and into the street where he sheaths his sword. Allen then picks up his sword and also sheaths it before he and Marie follow him down the street.

Far to the north there is another group being watched. Kristieana has been scouting the area in eagle form. She lands with the others and transforms. She says, "We are definitely being followed."

"By who?" Evelena asks.

"I don't know," she replies, "but I am pretty sure they aren't orcneas. I am going to go back and try to get a closer look. Do any of you have a looking glass?"

"I do," Ja'noa replies as she sets down her pack and looks through it.

"Sven," Kristieana asks, "do you have a crossbow?"

"Yes," he replies.

"I need it," Kristieana says.

"You are not going to shoot them, are you?" Gelana asks.

Ja'noa hands her a small looking glass and Sven hands her a crossbow as she replies, "Not if I don't have to." She slings the weapon over her shoulder and puts the looking glass in her belt and transforms again and takes flight.

Evelena looks around at the large rocks and says, "Maybe we should set up here just in case."

"Agreed," Sven says.

The group starts to take positions in the nearby rocks.

About one mile back over the rolling hills is the group in question. Princess Kianna and others have been following the same path that the Amazons of the Silver Moon have been on.

"Well," Kreeshaw says. "I think it is safe to say that I have fulfilled my end of the bargain. I am going to go back now to Copper Pass."

"Oh," Kianna says, "Alright then. Thank you very much for your help. How are you going to get back?"

"I can teleport," he replies. "It only works for myself though. Thanks for your help with the spider, and good luck."

They all say goodbye as he disappears as the air around him pops.

"Someday I am going to learn how to do that," Kelik says.

"Well, you aren't going to learn it," Ya'leigh says, "if you keep skipping summer classes."

High above in the sky, Kristieana looks down on the Princess and her group. Isen says to the others, "Look, there it is again. That giant eagle."

"Could it be Father?" Ambra asks.

"I don't think so," Ya'leigh replies.

Kianna looks up as the eagle starts to land about one hundred paces ahead of them. She says, "Isen, flank around behind it and stay out of its view. The rest of us will keep walking."

Up ahead, Kristieana lands behind a large boulder. She transforms back and pulls out the looking glass. She slowly gets down on the ground and crawls around to the edge of the giant rock and looks through looking glass. She can see them all clearly now. "I thought there were seven of them," she says to herself as she looks around for the missing Isen. Suddenly, she hears a noise behind her.

Isen, who has run up behind another large boulder, slowly peeks around the corner to where he had just seen Kristieana. He can see the large boulder that she was hiding behind. He looks further and further around the edge trying to spot her when he realizes she is no longer there.

Just then, he hears her voice behind him. "Don't move," Kristieana warns. "I have a crossbow pointed right at your head."

Isen slowly turns around and doesn't see anyone there. "Why are you following us?" he asks.

"I am not following you," she explains. "You are following me."

Isen stands there with his hands up and asks, "How could I follow someone who can fly?"

Frustrated by the questioning she asks, "Who are you?"

"Isen," he answers.

Kristieana is now more frustrated and asks, "And why are you here?"

"Why are you pointing a crossbow at me?" he asks as he now puts his arms down. "How do I know if you really have a crossbow?"

Kristieana continues to aim the crossbow at Isen with her right hand while she pulls back the hood of her cloak with her left hand. As the cloak is removed she becomes visible once more. She asks, "Now, do believe me?"

Isen puts his hands back up and says, "Yes, I do. Thank you."

Suddenly Kristieana hears a voice behind her say. "Drop the crossbow now!" It is Kianna and standing next to her is Ya'leigh with Incendia drawn. Kianna has her sword drawn as Ya'leigh aims her bow.

Kristieana slowly lowers the crossbow and turns to Kianna and Ya'leigh. As soon as they can see the markings on her face they lower their weapons. "You are an Amazon of the Silver Moon." Kianna says.

"Yes," she replies. "My name is Kristieana."

"I am Kianna Ravenguard of Sheathelm," she says.

"I have heard about you," Kristieana replies. "I am fifth generation Ree, so I believe that makes you my great, great aunt."

"Really?" Isen asks.

"Elves have more complex family trees," Ya'leigh explains. "My name is Ya'leigh Na'Moon, and that is Isen."

"Na'Moon?" she asks looking at Ya'leigh. "Chance's daughter?"

"Yes," Ya'leigh answers, sounding confused. "Do you know my father?"

Looking away nervously she answers, "I have only heard of him."

"So are you alone?" Kianna asks.

"No," Kristieana replies as she puts her crossbow away. "My sisters are up ahead. They are on their Rite of Passage, and I am accompanying them. Originally it was supposed to be a scouting mission. Now that we know the orcneas have declared war again, we are going to see if we can do more than just scout."

Garrin and the others now come around the rock. Kianna says, "That is what we were going to do. Perhaps we should join forces."

"That sounds like a good idea," Kristieana replies. "We are about a mile ahead of you now, I am sure we can catch up to them if we go fast."

Gena sighs and says, "I don't know how well I will be able to keep up but I'll try."

Kristieana looks at Isen and says, "You know you are lucky I fell for that. I could have just shot you to prove that I had a crossbow."

Isen laughs and replies, "I wasn't trying to trick you. I really didn't think you had one."

"Then you are fool, Isen," Kristieana replies.

"And you are lucky she wasn't the enemy," Ya'leigh adds. They all laugh as they begin to follow Kristieana to the others.

Back in Sheathelm, Allen, Marie, and Fernando are inside another tavern. They are sitting at a table, and their drinks have just been brought to them. "So tell me," Allen starts, "what do you mean that your actions are not of your own accord?"

Fernando looks around and then leans in over the table and quietly begins to explain to them his side of the story. "I was approached a couple weeks ago by two goblins. They said they had my father's sword. They told me all that I had to do to get it back was to obtain Ariella's locket. They had a plan all laid out, and all I had to do was to gain her trust so that I could steal the locket. They had a few different plans for escape, however when no opportunity presented itself to take the locket, I had to lead her to that cave. Inside the cave there was a lock pick and this medallion. After I went in first, I grabbed the lock pick and when they were all busy with the door inside, I had the perfect opportunity to escape and lock them inside. That gave me enough time to come back to the ship and take the locket."

"Why didn't you take it the other night?" Marie asks. "You were looking in the jewelry box. You could have taken it then."

"It was too soon," Fernando explains. "Had the captain checked on it the next morning I would not have been able to hide it. I had to get a bag of holding in town to hide it from Torgus. The goblins told me where to get one from. The plan worked perfectly except for one detail."

"What is that?" Marie asks.

"Whether you believe me or not," Fernando explains, "I grew to care for Ariella."

Allen thinks about what Fernando has just said. Then he asks, "So that explains how you did it, but who are these goblins and why do they want her locket?"

"I do not have those answers, Allen," he replies. "Tonight I am going to turn it over in exchange for my father's sword. I am sorry, but I have to do this. Believe me if there is any way that I can get my father's sword and keep the locket, I will, but these goblins knew a lot. They knew about me and Ariella. I don't know who exactly we are dealing with, but in my experience those who know this much usually are prepared for anything."

"We can come with you," Allen suggests. "We can go before you and sit somewhere else. When they give you your father's sword I will come over and we can make sure we get some answers."

Fernando thinks and says, "I am not confident that it will work, but I am willing to try."

Chapter 46
Crossroads

The Amazons of the Silver Moon are introducing themselves to Princess Kianna and her group. Now the two groups together are fifteen members strong.

"Sven!" Garrin yells, "How are you?"

Sven replies, "Garrin! Sven is doing well. How are you? Sven has not seen you in years."

"I am alright," Garrin answers.

Gelana rubs the top of Kelik's head and says, "I love his curly hair. Hey, Kel'ana, you can tell the two of you are related."

Kel'ana laughs and says "It must be in the Ree bloodline."

Garrin, Isen, and Sven move off to the side talking amongst themselves. "Great," Garrin says, sounding disgruntled, "More women to take care of."

Isen laughs and says, "I'll take good care of them."

Sven says, "Sven is going to have to say no. Chance warned Sven not to touch them, and if Sven cannot do anything, then you will not either. As far as taking care of them, they do not need us. Sven has fought at their side more than once, and they are very impressive."

"So, Chance said not to touch them?" Isen questions, sounding disappointed.

"Yes, except for her," Sven says, motioning to Kristieana. "Sven thinks she is older sister who is looking out for them. Be careful, she is not as friendly as others. She told Sven that she has man in her life, but Sven is not so sure. She does not like Sven."

Isen laughs and says, "Yes, well, she had a crossbow pointed at my head earlier. So I am not so sure about her."

Yentroc walks over to the men and says to Isen, "Hello, my name in Yentroc. What is yours?"

"Forget it," Sven says to her. "Sven already told him what Chance told me."

"Why?" she questions. "After everything I have done for you."

"What are you talking about?" Sven asks.

Yentroc pulls Sven aside and says quietly, "You know, to help with Lyra."

Sven sighs and says, "Lyra and Sven are just friends."

"If you say so," Yentroc says, sounding disappointed as she turns and walks away.

Kel'ana walks over to Ya'leigh and says, "Your bow looks like mine." She holds out Glacies.

"Yeah, it does," Ya'leigh says as she takes Incendia off her back. "It's called..."

"Incendia?" Kel'ana asks.

"Yes," she replies. "How did you know?"

"I have its twin, Glacies," Kel'ana says as she draws back the bowstring of Glacies, showing an icy arrow.

Ya'leigh smiles and draws back the bowstring of Incendia, and a fiery arrow appears. "I never knew it had a twin."

"That is amazing," Kel'ana says as she slowly releases her grip. "I never expect to ever see it."

Evelena walks up to Kianna and says, "So you are the Amazon Princess. I am Evelena Ree I think that makes you my great great aunt or something like that."

They both laugh, and Kianna replies, "Please call me Kianna."

Rehma is off to the side sitting down. Yentroc sits next to her and asks, "Don't you want to meet your cousin's children?"

Rehma looks at her with an angry smile and says, "I guess they seem alright to me. Even if they are Chance's."

"It looks like you and Ya'leigh have the same swords too." Yentroc says looking at the two Vallo swords on Ya'leigh's back.

Rehma looks over and says, "Hmm. So she is a dual wielder as well." She then smiles and adds, "Maybe she and I will get along after all."

Evelena says loudly to everyone, "We should probably eat now before we get moving."

Sven says, "Sven will cook."

"Good," Isen says. "I am starving."

A short time later as the group begins to eat, Kianna says, "I think it is incredible that we found each other out here."

"It is almost like fate," Evelena replies.

Gelana nudges Kel'ana and says, "It's like our different paths have met at the crossroads of life."

Kel'ana and Gelana both laugh as Kristieana glares at them both. Kristieana stands up and walks over to them and says quietly, "I need to talk with the two of you, right now." Kristieana walks away from the group as Kel'ana and Gelana look at each other nervously before following her.

When Kristieana gets far enough away that no one will hear them she waits. When Kel'ana and Gelana reach her she angrily asks, "When did you read my letter from Chance?"

"What are you talking about?" Gelana asks.

"'The crossroads of life'?" Kristieana questions. "Chance wrote those words to me. When did you read my letter?"

Gelana looks down and answers, "Yesterday."

Kristieana asks, "Did you tell anyone else about it?"

"No," Gelana replies.

"What about you?" Kristieana asks Kel'ana.

"I haven't said anything," Kel'ana answers.

"Only the two of you know anything about this," Kristieana says, "and I want it to stay that way."

"Alright," Gelana replies, "I was only joking."

Kristieana takes a deep breath and says, "I know, but those are his children over there. They cannot know about it."

"What is the problem?" Kel'ana asks. "Nothing happened between you and Chance anyway."

"That's right," Kristieana replies, "*Nothing* happened, but I already made the mistake of telling Ya'leigh that I have never met him."

"Why?" Gelana asks.

"What was I supposed to say," Kristieana asks, frustratedly, "'I met your father just the other day and then I almost slept with him'?"

"I see your point," Gelana says.

"It is important," Kristieana says, "that no one else finds out about the letter, or that I ever met him. They wouldn't understand. Now promise me."

"I promise," Gelana replies.

Kristieana looks at Kel'ana who says, "I promise, too."

"Good," Kristieana replies before turning and walking back to the camp.

Chapter 47
Rain of Fire

On the front lines of war, King Arioch's troops scramble into position. The nine remaining drakes have been spotted taking flight. They have split off into three groups each containing three drakes. One group circles above Northwind while the other two split off in opposite directions and come around to flanking positions. They stay far out of reach of Arioch's archers and wait just above the horizon.

Arioch commands, "All ranged-fighters, be ready to take those drakes down!"

Suddenly a goblin appears as he teleports down from one of the air ships above. He says to the King, "King Arioch! They are crossing the river!"

Chance says, "I can try to destroy the bridge again."

"No," Arioch replies. "I am sure they are ready for you this time. This is it. We need to protect the air ships. If we can protect them, they will be able to drop spells down on the orcnea ground troops. Chance, I need you to help protect them."

Chance looks to his left and then to his right at both groups of drakes and says, "I will do everything I can."

"You will not be alone, brother," Leanara says as she approaches with several sisters of the Dri'el. "I am going to fly with you. Yarwin will be protecting you from arrows, and Jadelyn will keep a spell on you that will protect you from the ice attacks. I assume you can protect yourself from fire?"

"Yes," he replies with a laugh. "I have the fire covered."

"Good," Leanara replies. "I won't have protection from arrows, so I will have to stay up on the ships and out of their archer's range, but I will be protected from ice and fire."

Chance smiles and says, "Excellent, I'll cover the left if you can cover the right. Just watch out for the drake's claws."

Jadelyn suggests, "We should get back behind these tents so that we can maintain the spells without interruption."

"Great idea," Leanara replies. They all walk back around the corner of a tent and wait as they watch the drakes hover over the horizon.

A mile across the field of war, the orcneas cross the Northwind River. First hundreds, then thousands of orcneas take position on the other side and begin to advance. The three generals Lortec Ka, Borak Cron, and Carr Vork are among them. "This is the day," Lortec says. "The day that Chance Na'Moon will die!"

"We must take down those airships," Borak says.

"Now that we advanced our troops," Carr says, as he points his staff at the orcnea army, "they will have to come out to us, away from the cover fire of their archers."

"Just make sure the beast masters don't make any foolish mistakes," Lortec says to Carr. "I am going now to the front line."

Crossroads

"Good hunting to you," Carr says with a deep laugh.

The orcnea armies start their march. Chance anxiously paces back and forth watching as they begin to cross the large field. He turns to the others and says, "Yarwin and Jadelyn, cast your spells now. I am not going to wait any longer. Maybe I can keep those three drakes out of the battle altogether." Yarwin and Jadelyn cast their protections on Chance as he casts his own protection from fire. Then, he transforms into the giant eagle and takes flight.

Higher and higher Chance flies until he is looking down on the entire battlefield. He is high enough in the sky that he even looks down upon the drakes. The orcneas are now about one half a mile out, and the three goblin air ships begin to move out over the battlefield to intercept them. Chance begins to dive down as the groups of drakes along the sides begin to move in.

Leanara transforms to an eagle as well and flies to the airship on the right. She takes position on top of the balloon portion and transforms back into her elven form. She watches the three drakes from the right flank approach as she stands ready. Chance gains more and more speed as he continues to dive towards the trio drakes to the left. The drakes fly directly under him as he turns and matches their speed. Chance glides over one of the drakes in the rear unnoticed. In mid-air, he transforms back into his elven form, and as he falls he draws one of his swords. He lands on the long neck of the flying beast. With both hands holding the sword over his head Chance drives it down into the back of the neck, just at the base of the skull.

The drake dies instantly and as it begins to fall, Chance quickly puts his sword back into its hilt and jumps free. Chance falls as he changes back into an eagle and dives to gain more speed. One of the other drakes begins to dive after him.

Chance tries to lose the drake that is right behind him. He flies low and fast as the drake gives chase. The icy cold breath attack of the drake hits Chance but does not affect him thanks to the spell Jadelyn has cast. Chance flies with great speed along the front line. The king's archers fire their arrows at the beast doing it some harm. Chance veers hard to his right and flies through a narrow gap in the spikes along the ditch. The large injured drake is not able to maneuver through the same space and finds itself impaled upon the wooden defenses.

Meanwhile, Leanara has her hands full as the three winged drakes from the right are coming in fast. She summons a massive ice dagger and releases it at the center drake. The large drake is not able to turn fast enough out of the way, and the ice impales it. The badly wounded drake falls to its death.

With three of the nine drakes down, General Carr commands the final three drakes that have been circling the city to move in. Chance flies up and lands on top of the airship to the left, and watches as the other three drakes begin to close in.

The airships, while more intended for bombarding ground troops, are not defenseless on their own. The goblins are ready with harpoons that are fired from ballistas. On the ship protected by Leanara, the two remaining drakes close in and attack with their fire breath. The goblins shoot their harpoons at the lower one while Leanara shoots another ice dagger at the other.

It is enough to take out the two drakes, but not before they ignite the balloon on fire with their fiery breath. As the drakes fall to the ground, Leanara tries to put out the fire with a water jet spell. As she tries to contain the fire, the captain of the air ship orders, "Prepare to rain fire!" The goblin crew begins to scramble.

Chance waits for the remaining drake from the left group to make an attack. The scaly creature flies above the goblin's arc of fire. It has made one pass already, but with only an ice attack. The drake now makes its second pass, and Chance hurls a fireball at it. The drake rolls to the side and the fireball misses. Before he can cast another spell, the ice drake flies by with another ice attack. Though it doesn't hurt Chance, his vision is hindered. The ice drake flies by as it strikes Chance's left arm with its tail. This leaves a gash in his armor right above the elbow and slices into him.

Chance is knocked back and begins to slide down the side of the balloon. The drake makes a wide turn to prepare for another pass. Chance knows that if he transforms, his injured arm will affect his wing as well. Fortunately, he is sliding down a crease where a rope is tied around the balloon. He grabs the rope with both hands and stops himself just as he is about to go completely over the edge.

The pain is excruciating as the drake begins to charge once again. Chance has no choice but to try to grab a healing potion from his belt with his injured arm. With his right hand griping the rope, his left arm continues to bleed. Chance fumbles for the vile containing the healing potion. He winces in pain as he brings it to his mouth and removes the top. He drinks the potion just as the drake begins to drag his tail along the side of the balloon, creating a gash as it continues right for him. Chance lets go of the rope and kicks away from the balloon just as the drake flies by.

Chance free falls as the potion takes effect. Before he reaches the ground he transforms again and pulls up as the orcneas below try to shoot him with arrows. With Yarwin's protection he is still safe from their attacks. The drake that had injured him now dives as well. Chance turns toward the final three drakes and flies low. The ice drake that follows him tries to hit him with its icy breath, only to hit the orcneas close by.

With two of the airships damaged and now starting to fall, the goblins begin to throw jars containing bright orange potions over the edge of the rail. The alchemy bombs hit the ground and explode violently. Many of the orcneas below are taken out from the bombardment. Because of the sheer numbers of the enemy, many more orcneas make it through and now charge the last two hundred yards to the spiked trench along the front line.

The orcneas run right through the magical minefield laid by Chance and the Amazons days earlier. More are slain by the explosive effect of the hidden spells. They continue to push forward and once in range, Arioch yells, "Fire!" The archers and spell casters attack relentlessly. The orcneas charge and while many of them fall, some still manage to reach the front line. Now the real test begins for Arioch and his men.

Crossroads

Out over the battlefield, Chance is still leading the ice drake head on into the last three drakes. Two of the three drakes continue directly toward the third airship, ignoring Chance. The third comes straight for him. With the ice drake getting closer to Chance from the rear, he continues to fly straight at the oncoming enemy. They continue to close in on one another until the last moment when Chance pulls up as hard as he can. The two less maneuverable drakes collide and fall to the ground.

Chance turns back and tries to catch up with the last two drakes. By the time the drakes reach the ship, Leanara is already there. One of the drakes flies over the top of the large balloon as she shoots an ice dagger at it. Leanara's attack injures the drake and it tries to land on the top of the balloon. The claws of the beast rip the canvas as it lands. Leanara casts another ice dagger and hits the injured creature, knocking it back off the edge of the balloon. The drake is killed as it crashes to the ground below, crushing several orcneas that are not able to move out of its way.

The third airship is heavily damaged now and the final Drake strafes the balloon with fire. Leanara dodges the claws and transforms before making her retreat. The drake turns to follow her but as it does Chance streaks by and uses his claws from his eagle form to get the drake's attention. The drake follows Chance now but instead of using its breath attack it tries to bite him. Chance dives one last time and the drake follows him blindly to the front line where King Arioch has been fighting the orcneas in close combat. Chance approaches with the drake right behind him, Arioch smiles as he switches his grip on his spear and prepares the throw it. Chance flies over head as the King steps forward throwing the spear directly through the drake's heart. The beast crashes down behind the lines.

Back at Northwind, an orcnea rushes up to general Vork and says, "Sir! They have just killed all of our drakes."

Vork grins and says, "Yes, but it is too late. Look." Carr Vork points above the battlefield where the three goblin airships are now descending to the ground.

Inside the healing tent, Namos has been very busy. Rushing from one injured man to another he is pushing the limits of his abilities. He is fatigued and is now only able to heal minor wounds. An orcnea that has made its way through the front line barges into the tent. With its sword it slashes down one of the other healers.

Namos looks around and finds a staff laying on the ground. He picks it up and charges the orcnea intruder. The orcnea swings his sword at Namos who parries it to the side. Namos uses the long rod to sweep the feet out from under the orcnea. The enemy falls on its back as Namos swings the staff at its skull. The orcnea is knocked unconscious as Namos checks on the man it had attacked. Namos checks for breathing but the man is dead.

At the front lines, A'ranah fights side by side with King Arioch. They fend off the orcneas that make it through the spears. During a brief reprieve in the action, Arioch looks out and also watches the three airships continue to fall. He turns and can see Resheck laughing. "What is so funny?" Arioch yells.

Resheck replies, "We have one final surprise for the orcneas, Sire, and in a few moments you will see it."

On board the airships the goblins are evacuating through magic gates. One of the crew members says to the goblin captain, "That's all of us, Captain. We must go now!" The captain unlocks a panel on the wall of the quarterdeck. Inside is a lever that he pulls down before walking through the gate. Inside the bottom of the ship, gears are set into motion. A small jar containing a flame is lowered into the cargo hold below and hangs above an open barrel of black power. The entire length of the cargo hold is filled with more barrels waiting to be set off.

On the front lines, Arioch continues to fight the orcneas, when suddenly, smashing through the spikes, is General Lortec. Lortec yells, "Give me the 'Orcnea Slayer,' give me Chance Na'Moon!"

One of Arioch's soldiers runs up to attack Lortec, only to be slashed down. Man after man charges only to be easily killed by the orcnea general. A'ranah is busy defending against orcneas coming from behind them as Arioch charges Lortec. Both are armed with a shield and sword. They clash together as others engage in combat all around them.

Lortec says, "King Arioch, since Chance is not here you will have to do."

Arioch swings his sword only to have it parried. Arioch replies, "Chance may be the one with the title of 'Orcnea Slayer', but you will find that I am as good as anyone in combat."

"Good," Lortec says with a laugh. "I'll enjoy the challenge and put an end to this war at the same time." He tries to strike the king, but Arioch quickly parries. Arioch follows through with a counter attack that almost hits the general. Lortec pushes Arioch back with his shield before swinging his sword low at his feet. The King jumps over the attack and as Lortec tries to knock the ruler of Sheathelm off his feet with a second shield strike, Arioch angles his shield to safely deflect the blow and maintains his balance.

The King then uses his shied for offense and swings it at the orcnea. The much larger and stronger Lortec, easily blocks Arioch's attack with his own shield. Back and forth they battle, neither able to get an advantage until finally Arioch is able to catch the big reddish-orange foe off guard for a moment. It is just enough to get through his defenses and cut his arm.

The sight of his own blood enrages Lortec who uses all his might to hit Arioch with his shied. Arioch is knocked off his feet. Both of their shields are now damaged. Lortec approaches the downed King, who is stunned.

Lortec draws back his sword and prepares to strike. Suddenly he hears Chance's voice from behind him call out to his king, "Arioch!"

Lortec stops and turns to face Chance, "I have been waiting for you, Chance Na'Moon."

"I am sorry to have kept you waiting," Chance replies.

Lortec starts towards the enemy he truly wants to face. Chance casts an explosive fireball and releases it at him. With what little remains of his shield, Lortec blocks the explosive attack. The shield is destroyed and Lortec charges at the Orcnea Slayer. Chance ducks and rolls to the side and, before Lortec can turn around, Chance blasts him with a flame jet from each hand. Lortec is engulfed in flames. To everyone's surprise, the orcnea general slowly turns to face Chance and begins to walk towards him.

Chance pushes more of his strength into his fiery attack, but soon Lortec is standing before him, unaffected by the fire. Lortec lets out a loud battle cry as he uses his gauntlet to strike Chance with a powerful back swing that sends Chance to the ground. Standing over him Lortec says, "You disappoint me, Orcnea Slayer, I expected more of a fight from you."

Lortec draws back his sword as Chance looks up at him and says, "I suppose it is only fair, considering I expected less of a fight from you." Chance quick draws his sword just in time to stop the blade that was coming straight for him. He then gets to his knees and draws a second sword and swings at Lortec forcing him back. Chance stands up and says, "So, you are protected from fire."

Lortec laughs and says, "That is right, Orcnea Slayer, you will find that I will not be an easy kill." He steps in and swings his sword as Chance uses both swords to stop the bigger blade. Lortec uses his strength to push Chance back enough so that he can kick him in the chest. Chance is knocked down once again.

Chance catches his breath as the first of the goblin airships lands on the ground. Orcneas swarm all over the fallen air ship. Chance gets to his feet as the other two ship land and become overtaken by the enemy. Just as Chance is about to attack Lortec, the first ship explodes in a massive fireball. Wood from the ship flies out violently like shrapnel. The thunderous explosion stuns everyone including Lortec. The orcnea army begin to flee.

Lortec yells at his men, "No! Where are you going?"

Carr Vork magically appears out of nowhere next to Lortec and says, "We have to go! Our forces are fleeing."

Lortec turns to Chance and says, "This isn't over, Chance Na'Moon."

Chance holding his attack replies, "Well, you know where find me."

Carr places his hand on Lortec's shoulder and they teleport away with a pop.

Chance walks over to King Arioch who is with A'ranah and asks, "Are you alright?"

"I am fine," Arioch replies, "but we are also going to have to leave. They still outnumber us three to one, and without any air support we will not have the advantage we did this time."

"I can fly ahead and start the evacuation of Dury," Chance says.

"Yes," Arioch says, "We will gather our things quickly and begin to fall back. As soon as you get word to Dury, come back to us. I have a feeling they are not going to make this easy."

"Yes, Your Majesty," Chance replies.

"Chance," A'ranah asks, "Did you know that orcnea?"

Chance looks out over the battlefield full of fire and replies, "No, I do not."

"Well, he knows who you are," Arioch says, "and he seems intent on killing you."

Chance looks out at the retreating orcneas and says, "Yes, he does."

Chapter 48
Mysterious One

It is evening in Sheathelm and waiting inside the King's Shield Inn is Fernando. Off in the opposite corner across a full room Marie and Allen are watching over him. It is so busy that Allen almost doesn't see the two short goblins that walk up to Fernando's table.

"Mr. Greythorn?" one of the goblins asks.

He looks up from the table and answers, "Yes, I am Fernando."

"The boss sent us to get you," the goblin says.

Allen and Marie start to walk over as Fernando asks, "Do you have my father's sword?"

"First things first," the goblin replies, "Did you bring Captain Stormrage's locket?"

Fernando pulls out the small box containing the locket. He opens it and holds it up and says, "Ariella's locket, and you can have it after I get my sword."

Allen, now standing behind the goblin, asks, "Why do you want the captain's locket?"

The goblin turns and replies, "I don't know who you are, boy, but that is none of your concern."

"Ariella was my captain," Allen says, leaning down into the face of the much shorter goblin. "Fernando stole it from her on my watch. So it *is* my concern."

The goblin turns back to Fernando and says, "Mr. Greythorn, if this is some kind of trick?"

"Not at all," Fernando answers. "I was hoping to be able to talk with your boss about possibly retaining the locket when he was done with it."

The goblin sighs and says, "You'll just have to ask him yourself. Now if you will just follow us, I will take you to him." Then looking at Allen and Marie who is still standing behind him he adds, "Your friends can come too."

"Thank you," Fernando says as he stands up. The goblins turn and start to make their way through the crowd as Fernando takes off the medallion from around his neck. Allen looks at him puzzled, and Fernando says quietly to him, "Just in case things don't go well, Torgus will be able to at least find my body."

At that very moment out at sea, Torgus has been sitting and meditating in his quarters. Suddenly from out of the trance he opens his eyes, smiles, and says to himself, "I found you, Mr. Greythorn." He immediately gets up and leaves to inform the captain.

In the Captain's quarters Ariella is explaining to Annalee about Fernando. Ariella says, "And that, my dear, is why Fernando Greythorn will pay dearly when I find him." The smile fades from her face as she says, "To be completely honest though, I don't know if I'll have it in me to stay mad at him. There is just something about him."

Annalee grins and says, "Don't worry, Captain, I'll make sure he pays for what he has done, and I don't care how charming he is. That will not work on me."

"I am sure it won't," Ariella replies. "Very well, if you want to do the dirty work, he is all yours."

Just then, Torgus barges through the door and says, "Captain, I have found him!"

"Fernando?" She asks. "Where?"

"Unfortunately," Torgus explains, "as near as I can tell he is back in Sheathelm."

"Sheathelm?" Ariella contemplates. "Damn him. We can't go there with all the orcnea ships."

Drake knocks at the door and says, "Captain, you have a visitor."

Ariella looks confused and as she stands up and walks to the door she asks, "A visitor? Who is it?" Ariella exits her quarters and begins to walk through the officer's quarters.

Drake answers, "I believe it is the female elf from the *Silver Tide*."

Ariella follows Drake out to the main deck as she sees the familiar female elf standing right outside the door.

"Captain Stormrage," Eveoh greets.

"I remember you," Ariella replies. "You were the elf that helped us fight the orcnea ship."

"Yes, Captain," she says. "My name is Eveoh."

"What can I do for you, Eveoh?" Ariella asks.

"We are on our way to Sheathelm to help the humans against the orcneas," Eveoh explains.

"Who is *we*?" Ariella asks.

Eveoh walks the starboard railing. She holds her right hand up over her head and a bright light emanates from her palm. The cloudy sky has made for an exceptionally dark night. A few moments later a light from off in the distance appears. Then another followed by a few more.

"Captain! They're ships off the port and starboard bow!" the man calls down from the crow's nest.

Ariella looks off the port bow as more and more lights appear. Soon the sea looks as if the stars themselves have descended upon it as dozens of lights from ships alongside of them appear.

Eveoh says, "We were hoping you would join us, Captain."

Ariella looks at Torgus with a smile. He smiles back and Ariella says to Eveoh, "It would be a pleasure."

"I will tell Resif immediately," Eveoh replies. "Thank you, Captain." Eveoh closes her eyes and disappears with a popping sound as she teleports away.

Ariella says with a smile, "Well, this is a cause to celebrate. Come, Torgus, Drake, and you too, Annalee." Ariella walks up the stairs to the top of the quarterdeck as the others follow her. Ariella enters the lounge and stops suddenly.

Sitting at Ariella's desk with a black cavalier's hat with the left side cropped up is a woman. Instead of the typical feather usually placed on hats, there is a dark violet daisy. She is wearing a long black coat over her white blouse and has matching black trousers. Her leather boots extend almost to her knees and her feet are up on the desk as she leans back in the chair and is reading Ariella's journal. The brown haired woman turns to them and says with a mild Irish accent, "You know, Ariella, you really need to run a tighter ship. I feel like I just walked in here without anyone stopping me."

"Captain Fidelma McMurphy," Ariella grumbles. "What are *you* doing here?"

The woman, who is a few years younger than Ariella, laughs and replies, "Now, Ariella, is that any way to welcome me?"

Drake steps towards her as Ariella holds him back and says, "It's alright, Drake." Ariella looks over and sees Leon standing at the wall, staring straight ahead. "Leon?" she says. "Leon, what are you doing?"

Leon does not respond to Ariella. "Oh, I am sorry," Fidelma says, "allow me." She then turns to Leon and says, "Leon, you may leave now."

"Yes, ma'am," Leon says. He turns and walks with a blank expression pass the others towards the door.

Ariella says to Drake, "Take Leon down below and make sure he is alright."

"He is fine," Fidelma says as Leon walks out of the lounge followed by Drake.

"Mind control, Fidelma?" Ariella asks, "That is against the laws on every continent, including Bruen."

"Please, Ariella," Fidelma says as she stands up, "it is no more illegal than, let's say, draining someone's youth." She closes Ariella's journal and tosses it onto the table.

Ariella glares at the intruder. She grabs the journal and angrily says, "Enough of this! Why the hell are you here?"

Fidelma smiles and looks at Annalee. She says, "You would think that she would be nicer to her sister, wouldn't you?"

Annalee looks at Ariella. "She is *not* my sister," Ariella says as she walks over to her desk. She places the journal inside a drawer before closing and locking it.

"Not by blood," Fidelma replies, "but you were very much like a sister to me." She looks at Annalee and says, "She taught me my first spell."

"That was a long time ago," Ariella says.

"Yes," Fidelma replies, "it was."

"Are you going to tell me what you want or not?" Ariella asks, sounding angry.

Fidelma laughs. "Why are you so angry?" she asks. "After all, I am the one who should be angry with you."

Ariella sighs heavily and says, "That also was a long time ago."

"Captain, if you don't mind..." Torgus says.

"You may go, Torgus," Ariella replies.

"Thank you, Captain," Torgus says as he exits, leaving the three ladies alone.

"So who is this young lady?" Fidelma asks as she looks at Annalee.

Ariella replies, "Fidelma, this is Annalee. Annalee, this is Fidelma McMurphy."

"A pleasure to meet you," Fidelma says.

"Likewise," Annalee replies.

"Now then," Ariella says, "I assume you haven't tracked me down just to pay me a visit."

"Right you are," Fidelma replies. "I am here to make you a deal."

"What kind of deal?" Ariella asks as she stands face to face with Fidelma.

"I heard you were looking for someone," Fidelma replies. "Someone by the name of Fernando Greythorn?"

Ariella grabs Fidelma's coat by the collar with both hands and yells, "I swear to the gods, that if you have something to do with him—"

"Relax," Fidelma says calmly. "I have never met the man."

"Then how did you know I was looking for him?" Ariella asks, still gripping her coat.

"The Makon told me," Fidelma answers. "I was there looking for work and he told me that you had just added more gold to his reward." Fidelma places a wanted poster on the table. It has a portrait of Fernando on it and says 'Wanted alive 600 Gold or dead 500 Gold.'

"You are a bounty hunter?" asks Annalee.

"Yes," Fidelma replies. "The best in all of Runefell. Fernando Greythorn's bounty will be enough to pay off my new ship."

"And you want me to help you?" Ariella asks.

"You don't need to," Fidelma laughs. "I already know where he is. I am here to help you."

"Really?" Ariella questions.

Fidelma smiles and says, "You seem surprised. Is it because you don't believe I know where he is? Or is it because you know I still have every reason to resent you."

"Both," Ariella answers.

Fidelma laughs and says, "Well, I can tell you that he is in Sheathelm, but I think you already knew that. As for our past..." Fidelma looks at Annalee with a smile. She looks back at Ariella and says, "Can I tell her? I do love to tell a good story."

Ariella pulls out a chair and sits down and replies with a sigh, "If you must."

Fidelma turns back to Annalee who doesn't know quite what to make of all this. Fidelma says, "When I was a young girl, my father worked for hers. Ariella would sneak me aboard and I would hide in her cabin. I had the ability to cast magic, and I wanted to go to Dicean, but my parents did not make enough money to send me. So Ariella would teach me about magic. Over the years we became best friends. I was even there for her the day that Chance Na'Moon broke her heart. After that, how do you think Ariella repaid me?"

Annalee doesn't respond. She looks over at Ariella who says, "You make it sound as if I did it intentionally."

"Intentional or not," Fidelma replies, "it doesn't really matter." She looks back at Annalee and says, "The night before I was to take my vows with the love of my life, Ariella slept with my fiancé."

"Do you feel better now?" Ariella asks. "That is not the whole story and you know it." Ariella looks at Annalee who looks uncomfortable and says, "I had just arrived the night before to attend the ceremony when I met a man at the local inn. I had no idea who it was." Ariella looks at Fidelma and says, "Besides, at least you got to know what kind of man he was *before* you married him."

Fidelma glares at Ariella. Angry, she closes her eyes and takes a deep breath. She exhales slowly as a smile returns to her face. She says, "Either way, it was a long time ago. I am here to find out what it is you need Fernando Greythorn for. The Makon did not know why you were looking for him."

"Why should I tell you?" Ariella asks.

Fidelma shrugs her shoulders and replies, "You don't have to tell me anything, but let me assure you that I can capture Fernando far before you ever reach Sheathelm. Not only do I know where he is staying in Sheathelm, but I have two of my former crew keeping a close watch on him as we speak. The Makon told me that only you wanted him alive. Five hundred gold is far more than I need for my ship. I don't care if I take him in dead or alive. In fact it is usually much easier if they are dead. So if you don't want to tell me..."

"Fine," Ariella says as she stands up. "He has some information that I need."

"I see," Fidelma says with a grin. "How about this then. I will help you obtain that information. In exchange, once you have it, I get Fernando for his reward. In addition to that I'll let you keep your gold, and you let me use Corthag's book."

"Corthag's book?" Ariella asks. "What do you want with that?"

Fidelma laughs and says, "Well, it's obvious isn't it? I want it for the same reason you do. I want to add a few years to my life. Look at you now. You look almost as young as me. All I want is the same opportunity."

Ariella asks, "And just who will you take these years from?"

Fidelma grins and answers, "My dear Ariella, I am a bounty hunter. Many of the people I catch are going to be executed anyway. I find many people who are unworthy of the years they have. Finding someone would be easy."

Ariella looks down in deep thought. She looks up and says, "So, you will help me get my answers in exchange for use of the book?"

"And," Fidelma adds, "Fernando to turn in for the reward. I will even give you part of it."

"I am not concerned with his reward," Ariella says, "or what happens to Fernando once I get my answers. You can do whatever you like with him."

A smile comes across Fidelma's face. "So we have a deal then?" she asks as she holds out her hand.

"We have a deal," Ariella answers. The two shake hands. "How did you get in here anyway?"

Crossroads

Fidelma walks to the back door surrounded by the stained glass windows that leads out to a balcony at the stern of the ship. "You really should keep this door locked," she says as she opens it. She walks out onto the balcony and whistles. Ariella joins her on the balcony as a rope falls from above. Fidelma says, "We will leave tomorrow morning on my ship, you can bring one other person."

Fidelma grabs the rope and whistles again. Ariella looks up, and from out of the darkness of the night sky the wooden keel of a small ship suddenly appears high above them in the air. "A flying ship?" Ariella asks in amazement.

"Yes, Captain," Fidelma replies. "It's the *Sea Griffin*."

Drake suddenly bursts though the door of the lounge and says, "Captain! A ship just appeared above us out of nowhere!"

"Sorry to have startled your crew, Ariella," Fidelma says as the rope begins to lift her upward to the ship. "We needed to stay invisible and out of sight. We had no idea how you would have greeted us."

Ariella watches as Fidelma is lifted up. She says, "I'll see you in the morning, McMurphy."

"Goodnight, Ariella," Fidelma replies as she reaches the side of her ship.

On the docks of Sheathelm, Fernando, Allen, and Marie are led by the goblins to a nearby building. The goblins enter and the others follow them inside. Once in they can see many goblins working as they carry crates around the large room.

"Come this way," says the goblin who has been doing all the talking thus far. He leads them to a dimly lit room. Behind a desk a short figure sits wearing the hood of his cloak over his head. A goblin is sitting next to him.

"Greetings, Mr. Greythorn," the goblin sitting down says. "My name is Riktog. Please sit down."

The goblin who brought them leaves as Fernando, Allen, and Marie find a few chairs against the wall and sit. "Thank you," Fernando says.

The one in the cloak leans over and whispers something to Riktog. "The boss would like to know why you did not come alone." Riktog says.

"Well," Fernando replies with a smile, "one can never be too careful, wouldn't you agree?"

"Indeed," Riktog replies. "Do you have Captain Stormrage's locket?"

"Yes," Fernando answers.

Marie nervously clings to Allen's arm. Riktog says impatiently, "Well, where is it?"

Fernando slowly pulls out the small bag containing the locket and places it on the table. Riktog picks up the bag and pulls out the locket. He studies it for a moment before handing it to the one in the cloak.

"Now that I have completed my end of the deal," Fernando says, sounding a little nervous, "I believe you have something for me."

The hooded figure does not respond. Instead he reaches down and picks up a small wooden chest at his feet and places it on the table in front of him. Then he opens Ariella's locket and looks very closely inside. Fernando watches as he then does something to the front of the chest that he and the others cannot see. Allen looks at Fernando urgently but Fernando motions for him to remain calm. Finally the chest opens and the dark hooded one reaches inside and pulls out a sheathed sword.

He hands it to Riktog, and Fernando notices that the hands of the one in the cloak are not green like the goblins. "You're not a goblin," he says. "Who are you?"

The goblin holds out the sword to Fernando and says, "That is not important to you. Here is your sword. Now take it and leave."

Fernando stands up and takes the sword as Allen also stands up and asks Fernando, "What about the captain's treasure? What about her locket?"

Before Fernando can answer, the hooded one slams his fists on the table. With a thick dwarven accent he snaps, "Boy, you are still alive because I allow you to be, but do not mistake my kindness for weakness!"

Fernando, Marie and Allen all look at each other confused. "I only know one other person who says that," Fernando says, "and that person is Ariella Stormrage. Tell me, just how do you know Ariella?"

"Know her?" The man replies as he stands up. "I more than just know her, Fernando, I am her father." He pulls back his hood and standing before them is a dwarf with the unmistakable red beard and hair of the former pirate and captain of the *Red Dawn,* Red Beard.

*****

The cell phone of Kelik rings, bringing Josh, Haley, and Laura back to reality in their apartment. The surprise of it actually makes them jump. Kelik stops and reads the message as the others laugh at each other. "I am sorry," Kelik says. "I have to get going."

"Aw," Haley whines. "I want to know what happens next."

"Me too," Josh adds. "Red Beard is alive?"

Laura laughs and says, "I hate to admit it but I am really hooked on this story too."

"Well, it is late anyway," Kel'ana says, "and you all should be going to bed."

"If you want to hear more about the story," Kelik says as he reaches into his pocket, "go down to the library and visit your Aunt Nica. Tell her you want to read about the Third Orcnea War in the Runefell Chronicles." He pulls out a business card. Kelik writes something on the back as he says, Kelik hands the card to Laura and adds, "Give her this."

"Wait!" Laura says as she takes the card from Kelik, "You mean these stories that you have been telling us for years are from books? Why didn't you tell us?"

"Not all the stories we told you are in the books," Kel'ana answers.

Kelik adds, "You also were too young for the books. I have been modifying the story a bit so it was more appropriate for you."

Laura looks at the business card. On the front it simply reads, Kyle Silsby, and has a phone number below the name. She reads the writing on the back aloud and says, "'Nica, call me if you have any questions, Kyle'." She looks at Kelik and asks, "Just give her this?"

"Yes," he replies. "Nica should be able to help you."

"Alright everyone," Kel'ana says. "Off to bed." She looks at Kelik and says, "I'll be right back."

The kids go down the halls and to their rooms as Kelik reads the text again.

Kel'ana turns off the lights in Josh's room and says, "Goodnight."

"Goodnight, Aunt Danielle," Josh replies.

Kel'ana turns off the light in Haley's room as Haley says, "Danielle?"

"What is it?" she asks as she walks into Haley's room. Haley doesn't answer and as Kel'ana sits on the edge of her bed she sits up and brushes Kel'ana's hair back. "What are you doing?" Kel'ana asks.

"Just checking," Haley says with a smile.

"Checking for what?" She asks.

"I was just checking your ears," Haley answers with a smile. "To see if you are an elf."

Kel'ana laughs and as she stands up she says, "May your dreams guide you safely to the new day."

"May your dreams guide you safely, too," Haley says with a yawn.

Kel'ana then walks by Laura's room and says, "Goodnight."

"Goodnight," Laura replies as she looks again at the back of the card. "Danielle, there is something else written on the back of this card."

"There is?" Kel'ana questions as she comes into Laura's room.

"I didn't notice it at first," Laura replies, as she hands Kel'ana the card, "but now it looks like glow in the dark ink, but it's in some other language and I can't read it. Do you know what it says?"

Underneath the message to Nica, Kel'ana reads a secret message written in magic. Only a person with an innate magical ability is able to see it. The message is written in elven so even though Laura can see it, she cannot read it. Kel'ana reads it to herself and it reads, *"Lyra, We need to talk soon, Kelik."*

"I think it is just a watermark of the printing company," Kel'ana says as she hands back the card. "I am sure it is nothing. I'll ask Kyle though if he knows. Goodnight."

"Goodnight," Laura replies as Danielle turns off her light.

Kel'ana walks out to the living room and Kelik is putting on his coat. "I'll walk you out," she says to him.

"Good," Kelik replies, "because I still have to talk with you about something."

Kelik and Kel'ana walk out of the apartment and into the hall. She looks around and says, "I am sorry about all that, I know you came to tell me something important."

"It's not a big deal," Kelik replies. "It is good to see the kids are doing well."

"Well, I know you didn't come all this way to tell stories," Kel'ana says.

"What's going on?"

"I got a message from Yentroc," Kelik explains. "She wasn't sure, but she says she has found something that we will want to see firsthand."

"Do you think she found a way back to Runefell?" Kel'ana asks quietly.

"Possibly," he answers, "I am leaving in the morning to find out what it is."

"She didn't tell you what it was?" Kel'ana asks.

"No," he says as he looks around. "You know we can't text or talk about anything to do with gates or magic over the phone."

"Right," Kel'ana replies. "So, is she still down in the Bermuda Triangle?"

"Yes," Kelik answers, "on the company ship."

"I want to go!" Kel'ana says excitedly.

"I was just going to go myself," Kelik replies, "but if you want to go, I suppose I could activate the gate at The Daily Scoop."

"Thank you," Kel'ana says as she jumps with excitement. "What time do you want to leave?"

"We would have to leave by 10:30 in the morning," Kelik says.

"I'll be there," Kel'ana replies. "I can't believe that all this time a gate has been out in the open like that in plain sight," she says with a laugh.

Kelik laughs and says, "Well, it is not like someone can accidentally open a gate. Only a magic user who knows what they are doing can use it. You are right though, it is funny that an old brick archway in the wall of some ice cream shop is really a magic portal."

"Oh!" Kel'ana says standing in the doorway. "I almost forgot to tell you, Laura saw the magic writing on the back of the card. She couldn't read it, but she could see it."

"She did?" Kelik asks, sounding amazed.

"Yes, and you know that that means?" Kel'ana says happily. "Laura has the ability to use magic."

"That is incredible," Kelik says. "I thought it was lost from their bloodline two generations ago."

"Apparently not," Kel'ana says. "I don't know about Josh or Haley though."

"We have to tell the others," Kelik says.

Kel'ana, still standing in the doorway asks, "When do we tell the kids the truth?"

Kelik looks down and gives the question some thought. "I suppose if Yentroc has found a clue as to how to return to Runefell, then we will have to tell them sooner then we planned."

"Yes," Kel'ana replies. "Well, can't wait until tomorrow. I miss the warm weather. May your dreams guide you safely, Kelik."

"And may your dreams guide you safely, Kel'ana," Kelik says with a smile.

Kel'ana closes the door as a flash of lightning lights up the hallway. Then in the blink of an eye, Kelik disappears as the pop of his teleportation spell is masked by the echoing thunder.

###

Crossroads

Thank you for taking the time to read this book. I hope you found it as enjoyable to read as I did to write. If so, I hope you will take a moment to review it at your favorite retailer.

Thanks!
Shawn Sodman

About the Author

As long as I can remember I have always been a daydreamer. In fourth grade it became more of a distraction than normal. My grades were marginal, and at the end of the year I was informed that if I were to continue on to the fifth grade I may find it too difficult. Ultimately, my parents and the school left the choice up to me. While it was a hard decision, it was not one that I regret. I repeated the fourth grade with my best friend at the time who was also struggling. One silver lining was that I was going to be able to hear my teacher, Mr. Sheathelm, read from *The Chronicles of Narnia*, by C.S. Lewis for a second time. Out of all of books that he read *The Voyage of the Dawn Treader* was my favorite. Despite having to repeat the grade, Mr. Sheathelm became my favorite teacher.

My short attention span and daydreaming didn't end there. To this day, I often find myself thinking of places within my imagination. I have even wondered if I spend more time daydreaming than thinking about reality.

The Birth Of Runefell

I have struggled with exactly what to share in this part. Too much information could ruin the experience for some. Then there is the privacy issue of those who many of my characters are based on. I will start at the beginning and share with you the original story that would mark the birth of Runefell.

Over twenty years ago, I was introduced to role-playing. Not the live action type, but the pen and paper type. The very first character I ever created was named Chance. I would participate as a player for a few sessions of "gaming" before I would become the GM (Game Master) I would then be the one in charge of creating the storyline for our gaming sessions.

One of my friends played a bard named Arioch. I asked if he would mind if I created a back story for him that even the character himself wouldn't know. He said he was alright with it, so I soon came up with the idea that he was of royalty and was the proper heir to Sheathelm. The group helped him ascend to the throne. One of them was my character, Chance. Another friend of ours played an ice mage named Kyle Drakesbane. A third friend played as a fast drawing, knife wielding man named Damion. Two of these three are in the book. A fourth friend created a character named Tharidin who only got mentioned.

Runefell

These were the four main characters who I did the most role-playing with. Later we would play the heroes in the story of the Dragon Wars. As GM, I came up with a foe named Red Beard, and the group faced him more than once. As time went on, the man who played Arioch moved out of the state, and life didn't allow much time for role-playing. All of our stories would be put on hold. To this day we have not seen each other all at the same time.

In the years that followed, I did GM for a different group. The only original member was my nephew who played Damion. We were all playing different characters but I tried to tie it all in with the same original world. We would play for quite a while before that group separated as well.

Then, almost twelve years after the original game, my daughter, who was sixteen at the time, wanted to start up a role-playing game like the ones I used to originally play with my friends when she was little. A couple of her friends were interested as well, and so was the father of one of her friends. He was someone I rode the bus to school with years ago.

I decided to dust off my old books and create characters for them, and soon the game was revived. I adjusted the time-line so that my daughter could play my original character's daughter. That way Chance would have a reason to show up from time to time. Her friends created other characters, including Kianna and Gena. I tied Kianna into the old storyline as well and said that she was the daughter of Arioch. The group decided that their characters had met Gena at the magic school of Dicean. Since I was tying everything together I said that Chance's friend, Kyle Drakesbane, was now the head master of Dicean. I was delighted to tie the old stories in with the new. The father/daughter duo played Garrin and Aria, but soon the girl who played Aria would stop joining us for the gaming sessions, although her father continued to play. That is why Aria is only referred to in the book. She was not part of the story that this book is centered around.

My nephew who played as Damion years before, made a new character named Isen. We decided that he was assigned to be Kianna's personal bodyguard. Kelik and Ambra are based on my other two children. They started to join us for gaming just about the time that I began to write.

The book did not start out as the story of my children's adventurers, however. I would the place story in the same world as my other adventures but I had a different plan at first. By the time I started to write, I had decided to make Red Beard less of a foe and more of a neutral ally. I would give him an adopted daughter, named Ariella.

Ariella is one of the few characters in the book that was not ever role-played by anyone. I drew inspiration for her from a few different sources. Fernando was a character that I had played in other adventures when I was not playing as the GM. He is a bit of a cliché character, but I always had fun role-playing as him. I set out to make a romantic story involving these two. Soon I just couldn't resist putting Chance in the middle.

Everything fell into place quite well, but now I needed to have an overall story going on in the background that was bigger than just Ariella's search for her father's treasure. An obvious solution was already staring me in the face.

The time lines matched up to place this story alongside the adventure that my daughter's group was on, and thus the title of "Crossroads" was born. Chance would act as a proverbial crossroad and be the point where multiple story-arcs would come together.

I then tied those stories to one more. I had frequently used the Amazons of the Silver Moon in the adventures that I was the GM, but they were mostly in the background. Once my oldest daughter begin to play with her friends, I moved the Amazons to the forefront of the stories. They were nothing new to Runefell.

The seven sisters in the book, however, were somewhat new. To summarize, they were a part of another gaming group. Each of them had a part in the creation of their own character. Namos and Annalee were also based on real life people. (No, she cannot turn her fist into steel.)

As far as Sven goes, he was another one of my characters from past gaming sessions. A typical, rugged, manly man. During the role-playing session involving the seven sisters, I had put Sven into the story to be a guide over the mountains, while the goblin, Kreeshaw, was there to give them an option to go under the mountains. The group chose to go with Sven.

Most of the main characters in the book are based on real life people. I have received permission from everyone who I have based a character on to write this book. It is my dream that the books do well enough that I can buy them each a new car, but for now, I'll settle for selling enough to carry me over until the next book is released. At the time of my writing this, I am over sixty pages into the first draft of Book two: Castles and Oceans.

It has taken a lot longer than I had anticipated. The editing has taken the longest. I would be remiss if I didn't thank my editor who had the patience to help point me in the right direction. While this book may not appeal to everyone, it would have been far less impressive without her.

Stay Connected with Runefell

Thank you again for reading this book. I invite you to like the Facebook page. If you do not have Facebook you can still visit the page and learn more about the next book.

https://www.facebook.com/Runefell
https://www.facebook.com/AriellaStormrage

Made in the USA
Monee, IL
27 September 2020